THE
LEGACY

Previous novels by the author

The Prosecution
The Defense
The Judgment

THE
LEGACY

D. W. BUFFA

WARNER BOOKS

An AOL Time Warner Company

The events and characters in this book are fictitious. Certain real locations and public figures are mentioned, but all other characters and events described in the book are totally imaginary.

Library of Congress Cataloging-in-Publication Data
Buffa, Dudley W.
    The legacy / D. W. Buffa.
        p. cm.
    ISBN 0-446-52738-6
    1. Legislators—Crimes against—Fiction. 2. African American students—Fiction. 3. San Francisco (Calif.)—Fiction. 4. Medical students—Fiction. 5. Trials (Murder)—Fiction. I. Title.

PS 3552.U3739 L44 2002
813'.54—dc21   2002016814

For My Mother
Beverly Johnson Buffa

Acknowledgments

Wendy Sherman, my agent, once again gave me the irreplaceable benefit of her experience and judgment. Rob McMahon, my editor, worked diligently to help me make this book what I wanted it to be.

"That City of Gold to which adventurers congregated out of all the winds of heaven."

—Robert Louis Stevenson
on San Francisco

One

When they finally divorced, my mother told me that she had married my father only because she had been pregnant with me. My mother made this remark as if it were something she was sure I knew already. She seemed to have assumed that I must have understood—from the beginning, as it were—that she had never loved him and had lived with him all those years only so that I could be raised in the proper way. I was not nearly so intelligent, and nothing as insightful, as she wanted to imagine. It had never occurred to me that there was anything wrong, anything unusual in the way we lived. If my mother and I went away every summer, it was only because my father was a doctor who had to stay close to his patients.

Every year, a few days after the school year ended, he would see us off at the station when we started the overnight train trip to The City. That is what my mother always called it, the place where she had been born and raised, the place where she had met my father when he was still a student. The City. Everyone who ever lived there, everyone who lives there now, calls it that and looks at you like there is something a little wrong with you if you do not immediately understand they are talking about San Francisco.

We went there every summer. We stayed with my aunt—my mother's sister, made a widow by the war—and, without anyplace to play outside, I spent most of my time indoors. The only fun I had was when my cousin Bobby, three years older, took pity on me and let me go somewhere with him. Sometimes, after my mother, all dressed up, tucked me in and said good night and then went somewhere with my aunt, Bobby and I would sneak down the back stairs and wander around the streets, watching through windows at what went on in the neighborhood bars. Once we followed two sailors and the two women they had picked up to their car and waited until the windows started to steam up. That's when we were supposed to bang on the car door and then run as fast as we could. We crouched down, just below the passenger-side window. Bobby raised his head just enough to see inside. He turned away, an angry, frightened look on his face, grabbed me by the shoulder, and, pulling me behind him, ran up the street. He never told me what he had seen, and he thought I was still too young to guess.

We kept going there, to the city, my mother and I, summer after summer, and sometimes Christmas as well, until I started high school. My mother still visited her sister, but for only a few weeks at a time, whether because she missed me or was afraid of what other people might think, I'm not sure even she could have said. Not truthfully, anyway. My mother was never one to flaunt convention, not when she was so good at deception. It is one of the things I inherited from her, this talent for appearances, this need to believe that all my transgressions are forgivable because they are somehow always the fault of someone else.

She had done what she had to and had done it as long as she could. I was finished with school and had become a lawyer. She would have preferred that I had become a doctor, but if I could not do that for her, at least I could have joined a Wall Street firm. Night school lawyers became sole practitioners willing to take any criminal case they could get, but not graduates of Harvard Law School.

She was telling me all this while she packed her things, getting ready to leave for the last time, measuring her martyrdom by the almost willful defiance with which I had disappointed her expectations. Without the advantages of a Harvard education, she reminded me with no little irritation, my cousin had become a junior partner in one of the most prestigious firms in San Francisco. It was the last thing I wanted to talk about and the only thing she had on her mind. Everything was Bobby, and how well he had done, and how she had always known I could do even better. It was only because of the example of my father, she insisted, that I had never developed the right kind of ambition.

She was talking out loud, and I was standing right there in front of her, but she was really talking to herself, and the more she did, the more worked up she became. She had told me without any apparent regret she had married my father because she was pregnant with me; now, wondering why she had done it at all, she told me she should have waited until my real father was divorced and married him instead.

It seems strange when I think about it now, but at the moment she said it, I did not care if it was true or not; I only cared that my father, the only father I had ever known, did not know. When she said that she had not told him and never would, I was almost grateful that she had chosen to tell me instead.

We never spoke again about what had been said the day she left. If she made some passing reference to my father in the years that followed, I never detected even a hint of irony in the way she used the word. It would have been like her to have forgotten that she had ever said anything to me about my own illegitimacy. She had a remarkable capacity for putting out of mind things she found unpleasant.

If she had any purpose in what she said to me the day she left, I suppose it might have been to convince me that my lack of ambition was not an inherited trait beyond my power to change. It was astonishing how little she knew me: I had more ambition than she imagined, though not for the kind of things she prized. I certainly had no desire to end up like my cousin, a lawyer who made his living advising the wealthy how to take advantage of every legal loophole in the tax code, a lawyer who had never tried a case and never would. Yet I could not blame her for thinking what she did. When we were growing up, he was everything I thought I wanted to be and was afraid I could never become. Bobby was an all-league running back on one of the best high school football teams in California; I was last string on the freshman team at a high school no one outside Portland had ever heard of. The year he became an All-American at the University of California, I finally made the high school varsity. Bobby was always surrounded by people who wanted to be his friend and girls who wanted to go out with him; I was uncomfortable around people I did not know very well and even at that age far too intense, and far too secretive, to devote any time to making any friends of my own.

We seldom saw each other after my mother stopped taking me to San Francisco for the summer, but from a distance I followed at least the major events of his life. He invited me to his wedding when he got married his senior year at Cal, but I was still a freshman at the University of Michigan and it was much too far to go. I had not seen him for almost twenty years when his wife died of cancer and I flew down for the funeral. A few weeks later, he sent me a handwritten note thanking me for coming and expressing the hope that we would see each other more often. A year later we had dinner together in San Francisco while I was in the city trying a case in federal district court. That was nearly two years ago. I did not hear from him again until he called and asked me if I might be willing to talk to his partner about taking a case. It was a case that every defense attorney in the country would have given anything to get.

Since the night it happened, the murder of Jeremy Fullerton in a parked car on a San Francisco street had been the only case anyone could talk about. The murder of a United States senator was bound to be news, but Fullerton had also been the Democratic candidate for governor of California. What made it even more interesting, Fullerton, according to all the stories now being written, had only been running for governor because he thought it was his best chance to become president.

Bobby explained to me that the police had made an arrest but that his partner, Albert Craven, seemed convinced they must have made a mistake. Even if they were not mistaken, Craven had known the mother of the suspect for a long time. He had promised to do everything he could to find a lawyer who could help.

"That shouldn't be difficult," I remarked. "This is the kind of case that can make a career. It's once-in-a-lifetime. Lawyers will be lining up to take this case, begging to take it."

"Nobody in the city will touch it," replied Bobby.

It made no sense. Whoever took this case would be famous. Something was not right.

"Albert promised her he'd get her son one of the best."

I remembered the way I had looked up to him when we were kids, and how I had wanted to be just like him. I wondered if he had thought about that when he called and if he knew that just by saying he thought I was one of the best I would like him even more. I listened to him tell me that there were probably half a dozen lawyers in the city who could do it but that they were all afraid of the possible repercussions.

"Repercussions?" I asked automatically when he paused. It did not matter to me what they might be.

The following Monday morning I watched out the window as the plane from Portland began its descent into San Francisco. They were right to call it The City. It had always drawn everything toward it. Before the bridges were built, before the Golden Gate connected the north shore and the Bay Bridge connected the east, millions of people were ferried back and forth every year. After the bridges were built, millions more came by car and by bus and by train. Everyone wanted to be here, but the city, rising up at the end of the narrow peninsula that jutted out between the ocean and the bay, could never become larger than it was. The great light-blocking buildings of Manhattan could never be built where at any moment a slight shift in the fault that ran miles below the surface could lay the whole city in ruins, the way it had once before. That earthquake, the one that happened in 1906, the one that seemed to destroy everything, had saved it from a more permanent form of destruction.

Other cities kept growing, outward, upward, each new monotonous glass building crushing out everything that was individual and unique in a relentless march toward an amorphous gray efficiency. San Francisco, no matter how long you had been away, no matter how much you might have changed, was still the place you had always dreamed about, still the place that was just the way it had been the last time you were here, even if you had never been here before in your life. But the city, at least the part you saw with your eyes, had begun to change. With the same unstoppable ingenuity that threw bridges over miles of open, treacherous water, skyscrapers were brought to the city, built on enormous steel coils to absorb the shocks that would otherwise bring them down. When the next big earthquake hit, the skyscrapers swayed from side to side, but the buildings that were destroyed were the old ones built of wood and cement. Searching the skyline, down the hillside to the water's edge, buried behind blocks of glass and steel, I caught a glimpse of the clock tower on the Ferry Building. It did not seem that long ago that it was the tallest building in town.

Bobby was there when I landed, an eager smile stretched across his mouth as he waited off to the side of the crowd. There was something about the way he held himself, the way his shoulders hunched slightly forward, the way he kept his feet spread apart, the way his blue eyes were in constant movement, seeing everything around him, alert, ready for whatever came next, that made him seem like he was already in motion before he had taken a step. It was only when he was in motion that he did not seem to be moving at all.

He insisted on carrying my bag. When we stepped outside the terminal into the balmy California air, he raised his head, looked around for a moment, then waved his hand. I thought he was signaling for a cab; instead, a limousine, which had been waiting a half block away, pulled up to the curb.

I settled into the back seat, across from Bobby. He looked different now, older, with the first touch of gray in his hair and the first telltale lines at the corners of his eyes. The smile still flashed, quick and alert, but it was a little dimmer, like a light that almost imperceptibly had begun to fade.

"It was good of you to come," he remarked as he turned away from the driver, to whom he had just given instructions. "I know it's an imposition, and I appreciate it."

His voice was as clear as ever, but he spoke a little more slowly than the way I had remembered.

"It's not an imposition at all," I told him. "Whether or not I take the case, I'm glad you thought of me."

He shook his head emphatically, as if it were for some reason important that I understand I was wrong about that.

"No, this wasn't my idea. Albert Craven asked me to call you. He's done a lot for me, and he never asks me for anything. That's the only reason I did it: because I couldn't think of a decent way to say no. But I made it clear to him that while I was willing to ask you to talk to him, I wouldn't ask you to take the case. It's up to you whether you do it or not. And if you decide not to, that's all right. You don't owe Albert anything; and you don't me anything, either. Okay?"

Suddenly it was right there in front of us, gleaming in the golden light, sweeping down across the hills toward the bay. The City.

Bobby saw the look in my eye. "Ever think about living here?"

I shook my head. "I think I'd miss the rain," I said with a lying smile.

Leaving the freeway, the limousine began to crawl through the city streets.

"You said something on the phone about repercussions. You said none of the lawyers here were willing to take the case. And now you've just finished telling me in no uncertain terms that you're not asking me to take the case. What's the reason no one wants to be involved in this? Is it because Fullerton was a United States senator who wanted to be president, and, from what I hear, had a pretty good chance of doing it?"

It was not the reaction I expected. Bobby laughed, and then he sighed.

"It doesn't have anything to do with Fullerton—not directly, anyway. You won't find many people—people who actually knew him—who are all that upset that he's dead."

We pulled up in front of a dark gray stone facade in the heart of the financial district, where the firm of Craven, Morris and Hall had established their offices long before any of the new skyscrapers had been built. The firm had grown with the city. Many of the small banks and businesses that had retained its services in the beginning had become major financial institutions and international corporations. Fees, which had been barely large enough to cover the monthly overhead, had gradually become enormous, and the original three partners, nearly destitute when they first started, had become wealthier than they had ever dared dream.

Morris and Hall had largely withdrawn from the active practice of law and only dropped by the office to provide occasional, and seldom more than cursory, supervision over the dozens of junior partners who all worked like slaves in the hope of one day becoming as rich and leisured as their masters. It was the way of the world, or at least that part of it made up of lawyers who started out wanting to conquer the world and ended up settling for a place in Palm Springs.

Albert Craven was something of an exception. Palm Springs, he insisted, was too hot and golf too boring. It did not matter that he actually believed both these things to be true; he would have said them had he thought they were false. It was the kind of facile remark he liked to make, especially when it gave him a way to avoid a direct response to the question of why he kept working as hard as he did. After all these years, he was still the first in the office in the morning and the last to leave at night. He dismissed any suggestion that for a man his age this was rather singular behavior with the observation that he had to make up for the two- and sometimes three-hour lunches he regularly took with some one or the other of his socially prominent friends.

He would have done nothing differently had he had no friends. After four miserable marriages, the practice of law was one of the few remaining things for which he permitted himself any serious enthusiasm. Carrying a caseload that would have exhausted the energies and taxed the talents of a lawyer half his age, Albert Craven worked relentlessly. Others might use a standard form or, if they were a bit more creative, devise a form of their own and then use it over and over again; Craven still drafted from scratch every document he needed. In a none-too-veiled allusion to the slipshod habits rampant in the profession, he claimed he owed it to his clients to think the whole thing through from beginning to end. Craven practiced what in the trade was called office law. In his entire career he had appeared in court only twice, and on both occasions had become physically ill. Bobby was sure I would like him; I was not at all certain that I would.

I stepped out of the cushioned silence of the limousine into the shrill, heart-pounding sounds of the city. Pedestrians crowded the sidewalks; cars honked their horns; somewhere around the corner a cable car clanked its bell. All the noise, all that raucous music of daily life shut behind us the moment we entered the thick-carpeted third-floor chambers of the firm. The receptionist greeted Bobby, or rather Mr. Medlin, as she called him, in the same hushed whisper with which I had just heard her answer the telephone. A bud vase on the counter held a single red rose, new that morning and, I was sure, every morning.

There were dozens of people who worked there, but it could not have been quieter had you found yourself completely alone. We walked down a long hallway, every door we passed closed, until we came to the private office at the end. The door opened before we could knock, and Albert Craven, his oval pink face beaming, extended a small soft hand. He introduced himself, thanked me for coming, and, slipping aside, invited us into a room more elaborately furnished than all but a handful of homes I had ever been inside.

On one side of the long rectangular cream-colored room, above the mantel of a gray marble fireplace that looked as if it were fully serviceable, hung an oil painting of San Francisco in flames, the immediate aftermath of the earthquake of 1906. On either side of the fireplace, other paintings, depicting in their immense variety other scenes from the city's past, filled up the wall. At the far end of the room, below a window in the corner farthest from the fireplace, was Craven's desk, an enormous reddish black Victorian creation quite unlike anything I had ever seen. Four thick bulging bow legs supported a tabletop with intricate filigree around the sides and an inlaid chocolate brown writing surface in the middle. It was incredibly ugly, so ugly that any question about it—where it had come from or how long he had had it—would have seemed utterly tactless. It was like dealing with the unfortunate disfigurement of a relative: There was just not too much you could think to say. All you could do was try not to notice too much.

Craven was dressed in a dark blue suit, light blue silk shirt, and pale yellow silk tie. Sitting behind his massive desk in an overstuffed pearl-gray chair, he looked at me over a pair of small rimless glasses perched at the end of his pudgy nose. He was about to say something when Bobby, who was directly to my left in one of two matching beige brocaded chairs, asked, "Isn't this the ugliest piece of furniture you've ever seen in your life?"

Resting his smooth, perfectly manicured fingers just below his chest, Craven allowed a subtle smile to edge its way across his cherubic face.

"I admit it isn't terribly attractive, but I'm not sure I would go quite so far as that." The smile grew broader. "What Robert really wants me to do is tell you how I happen to have it. For some reason the story seems to amuse him, though I really can't think why. It's more a tragedy than a comedy. You see, Mr. Antonelli—"

"Joseph," I insisted.

"You see, Joseph," he went on, acknowledging with a slight nod the abandonment of strict formality, "Agatha, my second wife . . ." He hesitated, a perplexed expression clouding his brow. "Or was she my third?" he asked, glancing toward Bobby. "Well," he said with a shrug, "she was one of them, and she bought it for me. It was a gift; more than that," he added, frowning, "it was a wedding gift."

He caught my reaction before I was conscious that I had one.

"Yes, yes, I know," he said, rolling his eyes at the ceiling. "It was doomed from the start. But, you have to understand, Agatha thought it was a treasure. Not because of the way it looked," he quickly added. "She didn't care anything about that! No, she had to have it as soon as she discovered it had originally been owned by J. Pierpont Morgan. She bought it at an auction at Sotheby's in New York, made arrangements to have it shipped here, and had it installed while we were away on our honeymoon." Bright with mischief, Craven's eyes bounced from one side of the ceiling to the other. "You can imagine my surprise when I found it here," he said with a grin. "I hadn't thought the honeymoon had gone that badly!"

"That explains how you got it," said Bobby. "It doesn't explain why you still have it."

Dropping his eyes, Craven folded his arms and retreated into his chair. His mouth pulled back into a grimace, his nostrils flared, and he slowly shook his head. Then he lifted his gaze and explained, "She insisted upon it as part of the divorce."

He sprang forward and sat up straight, resting his elbows on the solid surface of the article neither party to their divorce wanted to have.

"It isn't what you think," he went on, a sparkle in his eye. "It wasn't because she hated me. It wasn't that at all. Agatha thought I would be devastated and thought that leaving me this was the least she could do to alleviate the pain."

With his bare knuckles he rapped the hard finish twice. "What could I say? That the only pain I felt was the prospect of having to look at this damn thing every day?"

The smile lingered on his mouth, but his eyes grew serious. He raised his chin and sniffed and the smile faded away.

"You didn't come all this way to hear the history of my furniture. You of course know about the murder of Senator Fullerton. A young man has been charged with the crime. I want to retain you to represent him."

"*You* want to retain me?" I asked.

"The young man they have accused," he replied without hesitation, "doesn't have any money, and neither does his mother. I've known her for years, and while I've never met her son, I can't imagine he could have had anything to do with this. Though I have to admit, it doesn't look very good," he added with a sigh. "In any event, I want him to have the best defense attorney available, and that's why I'm asking you to do it."

It did not feel right, and I still could not believe that there was not someone here he could get to do it.

"There are a lot of attorneys in San Francisco," I replied. "I can even recommend one or two."

"No," said Craven quite firmly. "Only someone from the outside can do this. I've spent my whole life in San Francisco. It isn't like other places. Everybody here knows everybody else, and Jeremy Fullerton knew something about all of them: the people who run this city, the people who own it. None of them are all that eager to have what he knew spread across the front pages of the morning paper. And by the way," he added almost as an aside, "I wouldn't be the least bit surprised if one of them was behind his murder."

Two

The first, frenzied news reports had told everyone all they needed to know about who had murdered Jeremy Fullerton and why. A United States senator had been shot to death by a black teenage boy who had stolen his wallet. It was every white person's nightmare: the black kid without a conscience; the drug-crazed gangster with the dead eyes, the defiant grin, and the rapid-fire, mind-numbing speech stringing together one obscenity after another; the mindless predator with the smooth, tight-muscled, coal-colored skin, armed to the teeth with every conceivable weapon of destruction, ready to blow you away for no other reason than because he felt like it.

Jamaal Washington did not look like that at all. His hair was cut close and clean. He had no scars, no tattoos, none of the markings that serve as a badge of honor among the grown-up children for whom death has become the only meaning of life. He was sound asleep in the starched white sheets of a white-lacquered hospital bed, his light brown hand resting across his abdomen, an I.V. connected to his arm. A metal tray was suspended partway over the narrow bed. A straw dangled out of a half-pint juice container, and a white plastic spoon was stuck in a half-eaten Jell-O cup. The curtain was pulled back and the early afternoon light streamed through the iron-barred window.

There was one chair in the room and I moved it close to the side of the bed. I started to wake him up but then changed my mind. There was no hurry, and I wanted a chance to think. My cousin, whom I had seen less than half a dozen times since the summers we used to spend together as kids, had a partner who wanted me to defend the son of someone he said he had known for years in a case that every lawyer should have wanted to have and none of them wanted to take. Each time I asked Albert Craven the reason he wanted me, an outsider, to take the case, he deflected the question with vague allusions to future discussions that would explain all I needed to know about the way things worked in San Francisco. He was no more specific about why he was willing to pay for the defense of someone all of the prominent attorneys in town were apparently afraid to defend. He shrugged it off as if it were something anyone would do for someone who had been a longtime friend. He sat behind that monstrosity of a desk he had been too kindhearted to get rid of and let you believe that he was someone of whom others had often taken advantage but, because he had gotten used to it, had learned somehow not to mind. Craven was charming and urbane, but whether there was anything beneath that engaging manner was a question I could not yet answer.

I liked Albert Craven. Bobby had been right about that. Craven was too outrageous, too flamboyant, not to like; but there was something a little too staged about it to make me think I could simply take him at his word. He was too caught up in his need to be thought worldly and sophisticated, too interested in saying something at dinner that would be remembered the next day at lunch, to worry about whether he should have said it at all. I had let him go on, telling me the reasons he wanted me to do this, reasons that would have made anyone with a more conventional sense of shame blush with embarrassment. And then, when he was finished, a satisfied look on his round face, certain of my response, I told him there were two conditions that had to be met before I would even consider taking the case. He nodded affably, as if it were only to be expected, when I told him I had first to talk with the defendant. He looked at me with a blank expression, as if he did not immediately comprehend my meaning, and then nodded seriously and said a check could be cut by the end of the business day tomorrow when I told him the size of my fee.

I had made a great deal of money as a criminal defense lawyer, but I had never asked anyone for anything close to the amount I asked of him. I suppose I did it in part to see how someone would react, someone who could afford it, someone like Albert Craven, who, if you looked at him just the right way, would think that you were used to getting it. The rich will put up with almost anything rather than admit there is something they cannot afford. I should have asked for twice as much.

With a low moaning sound, Jamaal Washington started to turn over, bumped against the metal tray suspended across the bed, and opened his eyes. It took him a moment to realize he was staring at a stranger.

"I'm Joseph Antonelli," I said. "I'm a lawyer," I added, to explain why I was there.

He gave me an appraising glance and I was struck by how quickly he had become fully alert. There was about him a clarity of expression, an intelligence that, perhaps because of the circumstances in which I found him, surprised me.

"My mother said she'd find a lawyer. She told me when she was here this morning that she thought someone would be coming by. How did she happen to find you?" he asked in a quiet, civil voice.

"Albert Craven—a friend of your mother's—found me."

"Why?" he asked, looking at me with candid eyes. There was no edge to his voice, nothing in his manner to suggest doubt, much less suspicion, about the motives of someone who wanted to help. There was certainly no resentment. It was just a question, something he was curious to know. I was not able to give him much of an answer.

"He said because he's known your mother for years."

There was no reaction, no change of expression, just that same interested look.

"What's he like—Mr. Craven?"

Evading his question, which I was scarcely in a position to answer, I asked one of my own: "What has your mother told you about what he's like?"

"Nothing," he said with a brief shrug. "She never talks about her work."

"I don't think she works for him."

As soon as I said it, I realized that, for all I knew of Albert Craven, she might. The only thing he had told me about her was that he had known her for years.

"What kind of work does your mother do?"

"She works as a maid. She cleans other people's houses," he said with what I thought was a trace of bitterness.

He started to say something else, but suddenly he winced with pain and sank back down against the pillows.

"What are they giving you?" I asked.

"Morphine," he replied with an effort.

"Want me to get the nurse?"

"I'm okay," he said with a feeble smile as I got to my feet.

"You need to rest. Why don't I come back tomorrow? We can talk then."

He grabbed my wrist. It seemed to take all his strength to hold on to it.

"Don't go. I want to tell you what had happened. I didn't do anything," he said in a faltering voice.

Pausing frequently to rest, Jamaal Washington described what had happened the night a man he had never met was murdered on a San Francisco street he just happened to pass.

He began by telling me that he had just gotten off work, a little after midnight, and was on his way home.

"You work at the Fairmont Hotel?" I asked, just to be sure I had heard him right.

"Yes—three nights on weekends. I work in the kitchen, washing dishes, cleanup, you know," he said, dismissing what he did in a fashion similar to the way in which he described what his mother did for a living. "Then, after the event," he added, explaining why he worked so late into the night, "I'm on the crew that tears everything down and sets up for the next one."

Small, disconnected pieces of information started to come together in my mind.

"You were working there a week ago Saturday night—the night Senator Fullerton spoke at that dinner?"

I could see it, all the well-dressed people sitting in the shadows of a convention ballroom, their attention concentrated on the man who wanted to be governor and maybe something more besides. Just a few yards away, in the sweat and steam and shouted confusion of a vast commercial kitchen, Jamaal Washington labored over an endless line of pots and pans and heard nothing of the great dreams someone else had for his country.

Long after the last limousines had pulled away from the ornate Nob Hill entrance to the hotel, Jamaal Washington, bundled up against the chill night air, left by a side door and began making his way down one of the steep streets that led to the Civic Center. He had just enough time to make the last bus. The fog had rolled in, thick and heavy, from the ocean, and the farther down the hill he went, the thicker it became, until he could barely see a foot in front.

"I was playing a game with myself: sticking my hand in front, watching it disappear. I've been walking that route every weekend night for a year. I could do it blindfolded, and that night I almost was. I've never seen the fog that thick."

Then, suddenly, from somewhere that seemed right in front of him, he heard what he thought had to have been a gunshot. With a candor that made me willing to believe he was telling the truth, he admitted that his first instinct was to get away, run as fast as he could, just vanish into the night. Then he heard a car door close and the sound of footsteps—quick, hurried footsteps—fading into the distance. He stood still, trying to decide what he should do. He wanted to get away, but he thought that someone might be hurt, might need help. Finally, after what was probably less than a second, but a second that must have seemed to him like an eternity, he took a deep breath, crouched low, and forced himself to move forward until he was right next to the car. The fog, swirling all around, cleared just a little. He peered through the passenger-side window and saw someone in the driver's seat, his face twisted up against the glass. Blood was oozing out the side of his head.

A moment before, he could not decide whether to stay or run away; now, gazing at that awful scene, he did not hesitate: He opened the door and slid inside. He pressed his fingers against the man's right wrist, searching for a pulse. There was nothing. He moved his hand up to the man's throat to be sure. The man was dead. There was a phone in the car, on the console between the seats. Jamaal started to reach for it, to call for help, but then, on the floor below him, he saw a gun. More than the dead body next to him, the gun made him feel vulnerable and afraid. He picked up the phone and started to dial, but he thought of something he believed might be important, something the authorities would want to know. Reaching inside the dead man's jacket, he found his wallet and fumbled through it, looking for a driver's license, some form of identification, something that would give him a name he could give the police. A light pierced through the fog and lit up the inside of the car. Instinctively, he dropped down below the dashboard, the gun that had already killed one man just inches from his face.

Every fear Jamaal Washington had ever felt raced through his mind, each one building on the other. Imagining only the worst, Jamaal was certain the killer was coming back, perhaps to get the gun he had left behind. Too scared to think, he bolted out the door and ran for his life.

He remembered that: He remembered how he flung open the door, how he bent his head down, how he pumped his arms and raised his knees; he remembered that the only thought he had, the thought on which he concentrated like he had never concentrated before, was that if he could just get three or four fast steps into the fog, he would become invisible and whoever was out there would never find him.

"You didn't see anyone?" I asked. "You didn't hear anything?"

His gaze turned inward as he tried to take himself back to that night more than a week before. "No," he said presently. "All I remember is I was running, and then everything went black. I woke up here—in the hospital. They told me I'd been shot," he explained with a puzzled expression on his face, as if he could not quite believe that it had really happened.

"What about the gun?" I asked.

"What gun?" he asked blankly.

"The one you had in your hand when the police shot you."

"I didn't have a gun," he insisted.

I watched his eyes, trying to see if he was telling the truth. The police claimed that instead of stopping as he was ordered, Jamaal had turned toward the officer in pursuit and raised his weapon. The officer had no choice but to fire.

"What about the gun in the car?" I asked. "The one on the floor, the one you said was right in front of you when you tried to hide. You didn't pick it up—grab it when you jumped out of the car?"

His eyes were growing heavy with fatigue, his voice little more than a trembling breath.

"What would I do with a gun?"

It seemed a strange thing to lie about. The police said he'd had one and that if he had not been shot in the attempt he would have used it to kill or at least wound a police officer. Moreover, the gun, the one that had almost certainly been used to murder Jeremy Fullerton, had been found on the sidewalk where—again according to the published reports—it had fallen from the hand of Jamaal Washington when a bullet from a police officer's revolver had ripped into his body and nearly taken his life.

He lay on the hospital bed, exhausted, looking at me, someone he had never seen before, wondering whether I believed him. I had seen that look before. It was more somber, and in a way more terrifying, than fear. It was the look of someone cast out, made a permanent exile; someone who knows that nothing will ever make anyone change their mind about what they think he is. I had seen that look in the eyes of men I knew were guilty and on the faces of men I thought were innocent: the knowledge that the world now thought of them as criminals who should be imprisoned and as liars no one should ever trust. The difference was that when you were innocent it was a little like being buried alive.

I got up to go, but I had one more question.

"The footsteps you heard—the footsteps running away from the car. Could you tell if it was a man or a woman?"

"No, I don't know," he said, surprised. "I guess I didn't really think about it."

I tried to prod his memory. "High heels sound different, especially if someone is running away."

His brown eyes narrowed as he concentrated on what he might have heard.

"No," he said finally, "I don't know. I'm sorry."

I put my hand on his shoulder and tried to give him some sense of assurance. "Don't be sorry. You've done very well. Last thing: Do you remember what you were wearing?"

"Just my jacket and a pair of dark gray pants. I had a wool hat on my head."

"What kind of shoes?"

"Running shoes. They were almost new."

"Then you wouldn't have made any noise coming down the street?"

"You mean like the footsteps I heard? No. No one would have heard me coming. Or seen me, either. The fog was really thick."

"Were you wearing gloves?"

"Yes. It was cold out."

I nodded and told him to get some rest, then turned toward the door. Before I had taken the first step, I remembered something he had said.

"You said you worked at the hotel three nights and weekends," I reminded him as I turned around. "What do you do the rest of the time?"

"I go to school."

He looked nineteen or twenty, too old for high school. "Where?" I asked, expecting him to name a local community college or perhaps a trade school of some sort.

"Cal," he replied without any sign that he thought this in any way remarkable.

He told me that he was a sophomore at Berkeley. I asked him what he was majoring in. A faint, ironic smile crossed his mouth.

"I'm premed," he explained.

When I left the hospital I knew I was going to take the case. I might have made the same decision even without the money Albert Craven was willing to pay; but the money, I have to confess, had become almost irresistible. It was like that glow, that sense of well-being, you get when you do something other people admire and perhaps even envy; that feeling that you are the center of attention and that everyone wants to know you and get close to you because they know everyone else wants to as well. It is the feeling that while it lasts defines who you are, or who you think you are: It is what the rich love about money and what the addict loves about his drug. It was stupid, and I knew it, and I could not help myself.

I would like to think that I would have taken the case if Jamaal Washington's mother had asked me herself and offered me nothing more than however little she could afford. Her son was too intelligent and too well educated, with far too much to lose, suddenly to assault someone in his car and murder him for whatever money he might find in his wallet. He was innocent, I was sure of it; which made all the more intriguing how quickly everyone in this city—the city so willing to tolerate anyone and everything—assumed he must be guilty. No one would ever admit it was because he was black, and no one had to. Not yet anyway. The case was open-and-shut. Jamaal Washington was shot fleeing the scene, shot threatening the life of a police officer with the same gun he had just used to execute a member of the United States Senate.

I took a cab down the noisy narrow crowded streets to Union Square and got off in front of the awning-covered entrance to the St. Francis Hotel, the place I stayed nearly every time I came to the city. Someone from Albert Craven's office had already brought my bag and checked me in. It was a little past four, and instead of going up to the room, I decided to have a drink in the bar.

Some bars in San Francisco have a regular clientele where everyone knows everyone else; others, like the tourist traps in North Beach, lure wide-eyed, sweaty-palmed visitors to the dull perversions of live sex shows. Whatever intimacies were discussed in the bar just off the marble-columned lobby of the St. Francis remained the private affairs of its patrons. Well-heeled strangers, in the city for business or pleasure or both, used it as a meeting ground; those who spent their life in the city came here to have a drink in the anonymous quiet of a place that never changed.

In the superfluous habit of a lifetime, the bartender wiped down the already gleaming hard-varnished surface of the bar directly in front of me. Thin, of medium height, with a taut, lined face and wavy silver hair, he was a few years either side of seventy. He was always here, behind the bar, as permanent a fixture as the statue of victory high atop the column across the street in the middle of Union Square that celebrated Admiral Dewey's triumph in the Philippines.

"Welcome back," he remarked as he brought me a scotch

and soda. With a different towel he began to wipe the glasses that were standing upside down next to a small stainless steel sink just back of the bar.

"Do you remember everyone who comes in here?" I asked after I had taken a sip.

"You've been coming here a long time," he replied as he finished drying one glass and picked up another. "Two or three times a year. You always come in late afternoon; you always come in alone; you always take that seat; and you always order a scotch and soda." He put down the glass he had been working on and proceeded to the next, wiping first the inside, then the outside. "And you never have more than one," he added.

"You live in the city?" I asked as I took another sip.

"My whole life," he said, suggesting by the tone of his voice that he would not have wanted it any other way.

"Tell me something. Do you ever get out of the city—go anywhere else?"

His wiry gray-black eyebrows lifted up; his mouth curled down at the corners.

"I have a sister over in Marin. I visit her once in a while," he said vaguely.

Perhaps because I had such a hard time imagining him anywhere other than behind that bar, or perhaps because I thought I saw a slight hint of amusement in his eyes over what he had just said, I asked him, "How long ago? When was the last time?"

Holding the glass up in front of his eyes, he examined it closely. "Five years ago this summer." He made it sound like last weekend.

"Why is it that people who are born here, raised here, never want to leave?"

"Why would anyone ever want to leave San Francisco?" he replied with a shrug.

"But the city has changed. It isn't the way it used to be."

He stopped what he was doing and leaned across the bar.

"If you had lived here as long as I have, you'd know that nothing has changed at all." He knitted his brow and for a moment stared down at my glass. "I've been married to the same woman for fifty years," he said, lifting his gaze. "She doesn't look the same way she did when I married her, but she hasn't changed: She's still a mystery. You see what I mean," he said as he turned away. A woman sitting alone at the end of the bar needed another drink. She did not know it yet, but he did.

Three

We drove across the Bay Bridge, away from the city, down on the lower deck where the only view from between the steel girders was of Berkeley to the left and Oakland—the there that Gertrude Stein claimed had no there—to the right. When you drove toward it on the upper deck, you could see the city stretching out from the Golden Gate on the right, running over the hills and down to the bay, beckoning to you like the end of every rainbow you had ever seen and every dancing dream you had ever had. It was another of the great vanities about San Francisco: the belief that after you left there was nothing else worth seeing and nothing else worth remembering.

Halfway across the blue-gray bridge, we passed through the tunnel that cut through the top of Yerba Buena Island and came out the other side, still high above the gray waters of the bay.

"You remember Grandpa?" Bobby asked, his right wrist draped casually over the top of the steering wheel.

I was watching out the window at the way the sunlight glanced off the silver surface of the water far below.

"A little," I replied, thinking back to when I had been a very small boy. "I remember the chair he used to sit in, and I remember his knees, and I remember his hand when he would reach down and pat me on the head or give me a shiny half dollar."

I turned and looked across at my cousin. "I don't have any memory at all of what he looked like, no memory of my own, nothing except the photographs I've seen."

"He told me a story once when we were crossing the bridge," said Bobby with a faraway look in his eye. "Two friends of his, guys he had known since they were kids together, died—right about here," he said, gesturing with his hand toward the bridge. "It was back in 1937, four years before the war. They were pouring cement into the piers that anchor the bridge. It was the longest bridge ever built—did you know that? Everyone who needed a job wanted to work on it. You did what you were told and you never complained, not if you wanted to keep working. They were pouring cement and something happened: The planks they were standing on gave way, or one of them slipped and the other one tried to grab him and fell with him—no one knows, or if they knew they didn't talk about it. They fell in— and this was the part I never forgot—everyone else kept working, kept pouring cement. Two men are falling, buried under an avalanche of wet concrete stone, and no one even tried to stop it. There was no reason to stop it. They were dead as soon as they fell. When Grandpa told me that, I kept trying to imagine what those two men he had grown up with must have felt, knowing that nothing could save them, that they had maybe two or three seconds left to live, two or three breaths left to take."

Bobby looked across at me, a rueful smile on his mouth. "I remember the look on Grandpa's face when he told me. There wasn't any sadness, there wasn't any regret; there sure as hell wasn't any fear—not on his face! I don't think he was afraid of anything. No, it was more like he was proud of them, not because they died, but because they knew the risk, knew that one misstep meant death, and they were tough enough to do it anyway."

He paused, his gaze fixed straight ahead, as we left the bridge and began to navigate a maze of interlocking freeways. Slowly, he shook his head and emitted a low, reluctant laugh. He glanced at me, a boyish grin on his face.

"Can you imagine if that happened today? It would be all over the television news, front-page story in the morning paper. There'd be an investigation, lawsuits: The thing would go on for years. But back then—just keep pouring the cement. There was a bridge to be built. I'm not sure it wasn't a better way to live."

Threading his way through one interchange and then another, Bobby reached the Caldecott Tunnel and then, on the other side, got off at the Orinda exit. Cutting back under the freeway, he followed a narrow two-lane road through a three-block village. Circling past the country club, the road crossed in front of a small reservoir, disappeared around a corner, and then climbed into the oak-covered hills. About a mile later, the road dipped suddenly, careened off to the left, banked abruptly back to the right, and then, just beyond an intersection, banked back again. Bobby turned across the road through a pair of open gates and down the driveway. He parked in a garage connected by a tile-roofed breezeway to the house.

I stepped out of the car and onto the driveway. The air was fresh with the scent of the eucalyptus trees that ran along the edge of the road just beyond the adobe walls that circled the grounds. The house was a rambling two-story Spanish-style structure with white stucco walls covered with ivy that must have been growing there for years. It had been tied back and trained to grow around the windows, which were covered with an elaborate black iron grillwork of their own.

"You should have seen this place. Nobody had lived in it for years. It was a crumbling wreck, half the roof gone, cracks in the walls large enough to swallow your hand. I told my wife it looked like a Tijuana jail. I wouldn't have bought it on a bet," he said as he led me toward the door. "But she loved it right from the start. She did everything to it. She had a talent for that kind of thing."

While Bobby changed, I waited in the living room. Hand-knotted rugs were scattered over the Mexican paver-tile floor. Along the wall that faced across the room toward the windows, bookshelves, crammed to capacity, rose toward the dark wood-beamed ceiling.

"You have quite a collection," I observed when Bobby, now dressed in an oxford shirt and a pair of khaki pants, returned. "Lawrence Durrell, James Joyce, Hemingway, Fitzgerald. I even saw a copy of Virginia Woolf."

"They belonged to my wife," he explained, waving his hand toward the hundreds of volumes stacked neatly together. "I probably haven't read more than a half dozen of them—and only those because she practically begged me to."

He had put on a pair of cotton socks but no shoes. He still moved the same way he had when we were young: sort of soft, like he was gliding, up on the balls of his feet.

We went outside and sat at a round, glass-topped table under a blue umbrella next to a kidney-shaped pool. It was nearly seven in the evening, but the air had the hot smell of dry yellow straw and made you think that in this place, summer, instead of turning into fall, would go on forever. Beyond the pool, on the other side of the yard, across the narrow valley below, dark green oak trees, bent beneath the burden of the remorseless light, shielded with their shadows the tinder-dry, tan-colored hills. In a long lazy spiral, a solitary hawk, wings resting on the currents of an invisible wind, searched for prey.

Clutching a cold bottle of beer in his hand, Bobby slouched against the back of the white patio chair, stretched out his legs, and crossed one ankle over the other. His face raised toward the smoldering warmth of the blood-red sun, he closed his eyes. A cryptic smile edged across his lips.

"I liked the way you told Albert what your fee would be," he said, his eyes still shut. "It reminded me of what I've always imagined our grandfather must have been like. You had that same look, a sort of calculated indifference; that look that lets everyone know there's nothing you need, nothing you want so much you have to have it; that tells everyone you're ready to walk away from anything, that you'll do things on your terms or not at all."

His eyes snapped open and his head dropped to the side closest to me. "I have a picture of him, taken when he was about the age you are now. You look just like him. Dark hair, dark eyes— it's the eyes, mainly: detached, a little arrogant." He flashed a smile. "I suppose *confident* would be a better word."

He took a drink and then put the bottle down on the table. He stared across the close-cropped green lawn on the other side of the pool, out over the rolling hills in the distance.

"It's kind of ironic, isn't it? You become a great criminal lawyer, and he was a great criminal."

My grandfather was an old man who wore a wool cardigan sweater and a flannel shirt. He sat in a rocking chair that had a brown leather seat and wide flat arms. I had no memory of him anywhere else—not even of him standing up—only in that chair, slowly rocking back and forth, a kindly old man who would never hurt a soul.

"He was a fisherman," I said. "He had a fishing boat, didn't he?" I asked, wondering where I had first heard it and whether I had perhaps only imagined it.

"That was later, when he was much older, after he lost everything else. I don't quite know when it all started. In New Orleans, I guess. That's where he was from."

Bobby looked at me a moment. "You didn't know anything about this, did you—where he was from; why he came here; what he did; what happened to him because of it?"

I did not know anything, and only now, when he asked, did it strike me as strange that I did not. My grandfather had died when I was still a boy, and I had a vague recollection that my mother had gone to his funeral. I do not remember that she said anything about him when she came back home to Portland, except that, in the phrase so often used to give comfort to others, it had been for the best. It never occurred to me to ask why this was so, why it was best that he had died. I assumed, I suppose, that he had been suffering or that there was no chance he would ever get better; though I had not been told he was ill and, beyond a few fragmentary allusions to his heart, never knew why he had passed away. I was still a boy, or rather, still a child; I believed in the things children were taught to believe: I believed in God, and I believed in heaven. That night, the night my mother came home and told me Grandpa had died and gone to heaven, I said the same prayer I said every night in the warm comfort of my bed; the prayer that when, after all these years of forgetfulness, I think about it again, gives me a different kind of comfort: the knowledge that there was once a time when I was still an innocent boy with a pure heart and a clean body who only wanted to do good. Only that night, while I heard through the wall the muffled tones of the argument my parents had every time my mother stayed away longer than she had said she would when she left, I took a chance and instead of asking for the usual blessings asked God to say hello to Grandpa.

"Where's he buried?" I asked Bobby.

It took him by surprise. "Do you want to go out there?"

"Sometime while I'm here. I've never been there."

The sun was sinking below the western hills, burning the sky a brilliant reddish orange. The shadows on the hillside began to spread out from beneath the trees, crawling toward the coming night.

"Tell me about New Orleans and everything else you know about him."

"I don't know much about New Orleans, except that he was there and that he had to leave. All the immigrants to this country—the Irish, the Italians, all the people that came here the end of the last century—everyone thinks they all came through Ellis Island and that half of them were given new names because the names they had were too difficult to pronounce in English. But our grandfather—Leonardo Caravaggio—didn't have his name changed and so far as I know never got within a thousand miles of New York. He landed in New Orleans, a boy of five or six, with his parents, from somewhere in Sicily, in the late 1880s or the early 1890s. After slavery was abolished, white southerners had to find another source of cheap labor. That's how we happen to be born in America: because our great-grandfather, whose name we don't even know, agreed to do the work the slaves had done in exchange for free passage from Sicily and barely enough in wages to keep himself and his family alive. There wasn't much difference in the way they were treated, either. If they got out of line, did something they weren't supposed to do, there was about as much chance being found guilty of murder for lynching an Italian as for hanging a black man. That's why Grandpa left New Orleans. He did something, or he was suspected of doing something—what it was, I could never find out, but it was something serious. Somebody once told me they thought he had killed someone, but I don't know if that's true or not. All I know is that the night he found out the police were after him, he left New Orleans and never went back. He knew if he stayed, he'd be caught; and he knew if he was caught, he'd be dead."

Bobby leaned closer, mischief in his eyes. "How does it feel to find out you're the descendant of a runaway slave, chased out of New Orleans by a lynch mob?"

"Do you think he could have killed somebody?" I asked, juxtaposing in my mind the two pictures I had of him: an old man sitting in his chair and a strong, energetic young man filled with fear running for his life.

"Sure, why not?" Bobby replied with a quick, emphatic nod. "I heard a lot of stories about him growing up. He wasn't someone who would have backed down."

Bobby nodded a second time and gave me a look that seemed to signify he knew it was true about our grandfather because he knew it was true about himself. Certain of his own reaction, he assumed his instincts were inherited and had come to him from at least a generation back.

"If someone had come after him, he would have known what they were going to do before they did. Were you ever in a fight when you were a kid? One that started with an argument, and you knew—just a split second before the other kid knew—that he was going to throw a punch at you, and you hit him first, because it was the only way to defend yourself? That's what he was like, I think. Whoever came after him—I don't think they would have had a chance to do anything. He was too quick, too smart, to give anyone that chance. Yes, he could have killed somebody; but it would have been somebody who wanted to kill him first."

"I wasn't much of a fighter," I admitted.

"You were too smart," said Bobby with a distant smile. "You could see it coming in time to avoid it altogether."

"That's the kindest definition of cowardice I think I've ever heard," I said, laughing softly.

Bobby put down the bottle of beer, got to his feet, and stretched his arms.

"I don't know how he got to San Francisco, and I don't know what he did when he got here."

Bobby stared down at his socks, a pensive expression on his face. "But during Prohibition he controlled most of the liquor brought into the city and he was one of the wealthiest men in San Francisco, worth millions. Then someone tipped off the cops. These guys weren't Elliott Ness. They arrested him, all right, but they gave him a choice: He could go to prison or he could give them the money and they'd leave him alone."

Bobby picked up the bottle from the table and took a drink. "If he had gone to jail, he could have kept the money, and we all would have been rich. But he had an old-fashioned sense of honor. He thought jail would disgrace his family, make it more difficult for his children and their children to be accepted. He had a choice between poverty and dishonor."

Bobby looked at me for a moment, his light-colored eyebrows arched high. "Do you think anyone would have remembered where the money had come from or that he had gone to prison for a while because of it? It might have been interesting to have been part of one of the wealthiest families in San Francisco."

He started back toward the house, a wry grin on his face, beckoning me to follow. "Don't you ever wonder what it would be like to have your picture on the society page every other week? We might have ended up like Lawrence Goldman," he remarked as he held open the door.

I had no idea who Lawrence Goldman was, which, as I was soon to discover, meant that I understood next to nothing about the way things worked in San Francisco. There were those who believed that without Lawrence Goldman, San Francisco would not work at all.

"I wanted you to see the house," Bobby remarked as we pulled out of the driveway. It was almost dark out. The long line of eucalyptus trees, sheets of bark peeling away from their trunks, stood like cutouts against the blue-black sky. High overhead a low wind rustled through the dry brittle leaves. "I hoped you'd change your mind. Why don't you stay with me? I could use the company."

He'd invited me as soon as I told him I was going to take the case and was disappointed when I declined on the ground that, at least at the beginning, I thought I had better stay in the city. I was a little surprised, and a little touched, when he offered again. We were cousins, and we had not seen each other very often since we were boys, but I felt closer to him than to any of the uncles and aunts whose names, if pressed, I could still remember, but who were barely more to me than identifiable strangers. Bobby and I had shared secrets together, sometimes without knowing until much later in life what the secret had been.

"Thanks," I replied, watching the cars fly by me as we merged into the freeway traffic. "Maybe after I get used to what I'm doing here. But I think I better stay in the city for a little while, anyway."

We passed through the tunnel we had come through before and spiraled along the sweeping curves of the highway that led down from the hills. Straight ahead, across the churning black waters of the bay, the lights of San Francisco lit up the sky like some exotic midnight sun.

Bobby knew what I was thinking.

"I drive this every day. I've been doing it for more than twenty years, and I never get tired of it: the bay, the bridge, the city. It's never the same and it never changes. It's like staring into a fire."

He drove along, lost in his thoughts. He did not speak again until we had passed through the short white-tiled tunnel that cut through the rock summit of Yerba Buena Island halfway across the Bay Bridge.

"Remember when that was the biggest thing you saw?" he asked, gesturing toward the clock tower on top of the Ferry Building.

I don't know why I said it. Something about his question brought it all back to me, as clearly as when it had happened years ago, that summer when we were still both small boys.

"Remember the night when we sneaked out of the house and followed those two sailors and the two women they had picked up in the bar and we were going to pound on their car door and then run like hell?"

Bobby kept his eyes focused straight ahead. "When did you figure out who they were?"

"As soon as I saw the look on your face after you looked through the window."

"Did you ever say anything about it?" he asked, still staring straight ahead.

"No," I replied, "never."

He looked across at me, a sad smile on his face. "How did it make you feel?" he asked.

I started to shrug it off, make some glib, superficial remark. Then I changed my mind.

"Alone," I confessed, as I looked away. "Completely alone."

A somber, melancholy look came into Bobby's eyes. The

lines at the edges of his eyes spread out, cutting into his temples, and for the first time I noticed weblike traces at the corners of his mouth as he pressed his lips together, concentrating on some private and, as I thought, painful reflection of his own. It did not last very long, a few seconds at most; then, as he batted his lashes like someone waking up from a bad dream, his mouth stretched into a grin and he glanced across at me, eager to tell me about the restaurant he thought I was going to like.

It was a small, crowded Italian restaurant in Columbus Circle, one of those places where everyone looks familiar and the waiter sometimes knows more about some of your relatives than you do. After we had eaten a little, Bobby moved away from the table far enough to cross his legs and drape his arm over the back of his chair. For a moment, he studied me, an ambiguous smile on his mouth.

"You sure you want to take this case?"

"The money is pretty good," I replied, starting to laugh before I could quite carry off the cynical shrug with which I had hoped to impress him.

"You like that feeling, don't you?" he asked, trying to taunt out of me a confession of self-importance. "The million-dollar case. It wouldn't be the same if it were nine hundred ninety-five thousand, would it? Seven figures: That's what makes all the difference—doesn't it? I almost don't have the heart to tell you that around here serious money doesn't start before you hit eight."

He was badgering me, the way he had when we were kids, letting me know, whatever I did, not to think too much of it. He was what I always imagined an older brother was like: ready to put you in your place, and ready to beat the hell out of anyone else who tried to do the same thing.

Satisfied with what he had done, Bobby again picked up his fork. Suddenly his expression became more serious. For a moment, he hesitated, as if had not quite made up his mind about something. Then he slowly put down the fork and lifted his eyes.

"I meant what I said before: about the way you reminded me of our grandfather. I know you wouldn't take this case for the money. It might be better if you did," he said with an enigmatic look. "When Fullerton was killed, it was like everyone held their breath, waiting to see what would happen next. When the police announced they had the killer in custody and that it was some black kid who had tried to rob him, you could almost hear the sigh of relief. No one cares if the kid is guilty or not: They only care that their reputations and their secrets are still safe. You start looking around, trying to find out who was really behind his murder, the one thing you can be sure of is that no one is going to tell you the truth or anything close to it. And if you start to get too close to what really happened, then . . . well, let's just say there are some fairly ruthless people around here—and if any of them were involved . . ."

He stopped for a moment, and from the distant look in his eyes I could tell he was thinking of something else, something that made him shake his head from side to side, as an expression, first of sorrow, then of disgust, crossed over his mouth.

"Fullerton really was extraordinary. He was like that nursery rhyme we learned as children, the one about the little girl: 'When she was good, she was very, very good, but when she was bad, she was horrid.' "

Half embarrassed by the allusion to childhood things, he looked at me as if he should have been able to think of a better way to describe what he meant. He struggled to find another way to put it and then with a bashful grin gave it up.

"Nope. He was like that. I was there, the night he was killed, at the Fairmont Hotel. I'm not much interested in politics, but Craven bought a table and insisted I come along. It was one of the greatest speeches I ever heard. There must have been a thousand people there, and by the time he was finished I think every one of them would have done anything he asked them to do. Hell, they would have marched on the White House if he had told them to. The odd part, though," he added, still puzzled by what he had witnessed, "is that he was a candidate for governor but he spent most of his time attacking the president. Afterwards, I asked Albert about it. There's no such thing as a straight answer with him, at least not before he has exhausted all the possibilities for humor or exaggeration. In fact, instead of an answer, he asked me whether I remembered the line Fullerton had used—something about how the administration reminded him of a famous British government of the nineteenth century. Then, before I could answer, Albert's eyebrows shot straight up. He quoted exactly what Fullerton said: 'Not the one called the Administration of All the Talents—the one called the Organized Incompetence of the Country.'

"Albert thought that was one of the greatest things he had ever heard. Then he told me that he didn't think Fullerton could find Britain on a map and that he was certain he could not have named a single British prime minister from any century, not even Winston Churchill, much less the name given to a particular British government.

"You've met Albert," he said, rolling his eyes. "So you know how he is. We were standing there, at our table, as the dinner was breaking up, and he's just chattering away, taking me 'round and 'round in circles until I had forgotten what I had asked him in the first place. 'Do you know who wrote that speech?' he asked me out of the blue. 'Ariella Goldman, Lawrence Goldman's daughter. She works for Fullerton—writes most of his speeches. She's extremely good. Fullerton is extraordinarily lucky. He has that knack—being lucky. He gets the talent of the daughter and the considerable financial support of the father. Lawrence can raise more money than anyone in California,' he explained. 'It's really a double advantage for Fullerton. Lawrence has always been the governor's principal financial backer, so every dollar he now raised for Fullerton is also a dollar that Augustus Marshall is not going to get. Half the people here tonight were here because of Goldman, maybe more. He pretends it's only because of his daughter, but that's not the real reason at all.'

"Albert likes to do that: make you guess instead of just telling you what he knows. It's his way of letting you know that what he's about to tell you is something hardly anyone else knows, either. If no one had any secrets, I don't know what he would find to talk about. He's the biggest gossip I've ever known."

He stopped, afraid he had left me with the wrong impression.

"At the same time, if there is one person I thought I could trust with a secret, it's Albert. He would never betray a confidence, I'm certain of it. But he does love gossip," he said, talking once again with the easy assurance of someone sharing secrets of his own. "People tell him everything. And he knows so much about everyone that he can put into context, and find the meaning, of the kind of stray remark or casual observation that with anyone else would appear to have no meaning at all. When he told me the reason—the real reason—Lawrence Goldman had decided to abandon the governor—someone he had known, someone he had helped, from the beginning of his career—and do everything he could for his opponent, I knew it wasn't because Lawrence Goldman or anyone else had explained it to him. It was because Albert had put all the pieces together and figured it out on his own."

Caught up in his admiration of Albert Craven's considerable

powers of deduction, he seemed to forget that I knew nothing about the conclusions that had been reached.

"What was the real reason?" I asked.

He looked at me, a blank expression on his face. Then he blinked, and his face again became animated.

"The real reason is that Lawrence Goldman didn't care who was governor; he'd had governors. He wanted a president, and with Fullerton he had the best chance he was going to have. Albert had it all worked out.

" 'If Goldman controls the money that Fullerton needs to get there—and the money he needs to stay there; and if his daughter—the wonderfully gifted Ariella—controls what he says; then who really controls the power of the presidency?'

"Something changed in Albert's expression when he said that. It became harder, perhaps even a little bitter, as if he thought Goldman was a little too calculating for his own good. Then he tossed his head and laughed. 'It's really rather incestuous, isn't it? And, of course,' he went on, tripping over the words in his excitement, 'Lawrence, as he always does, left himself a way out if things don't work out quite the way he hoped. If Fullerton loses, then he can tell his good friend Augustus Marshall that he was only doing his duty as a father.' "

Bobby looked at me. "Albert had done it again, you see: forced me to ask the question that would let him show me how much he understood about the way things really worked. 'And Marshall will accept that?' I asked.

" 'Yes, of course,' Albert assured me. 'And to show Goldman just how happy he is that they're once again on the same side, the governor will ask him to head up a major fundraiser to help him pay off the debt he ran up during the campaign. Isn't it marvelous?' "

Turning up his hands, Bobby shrugged his shoulders.

"Maybe Albert was wrong; maybe Goldman really was doing it for his daughter. It became pretty obvious that night that his daughter's interest in the good senator went way beyond politics. What a scandal! It was one of the most embarrassing things I've ever seen."

"Something happened at the dinner?"

"No, not then—afterwards, at a private reception at Goldman's apartment; what Albert called 'an intimate gathering of two or three hundred of Lawrence's closest friends.'

"Goldman's apartment is right across the street from the Fairmont, the entire top floor of a building on the Golden Gate side of Nob Hill. He and his daughter and the senator were greeting people at the door. We had just arrived. Albert had just finished bantering with Goldman's daughter when, all of a sudden, Fullerton's wife goes up to Ariella and says, 'Tell me, what do you think is worse—a man who sleeps with a woman because it's the only way he can get to her father's money, or a woman who sleeps with a man because it's the only way she can get close to the power she so desperately needs?' "

"She really said that?" I asked, wondering whether he had not taken something that was bad enough and exaggerated it into something that was truly awful. "In front of the woman's father?"

"And in front of her own husband," Bobby replied. "And in front of about a hundred people standing close enough to hear."

"What did she do—Goldman's daughter?"

Bobby lifted his chin and narrowed his eyes. A slight shudder passed through him.

"It didn't seem to faze her. She looked at Fullerton's wife the way she might have looked at someone in the street who was asking her for money. And then she said something so unbelievably cruel, so incredibly hurtful, I had to turn away. She said,

'What's worse is a woman who won't give up a man who doesn't want her anymore.'

"There was a dead silence. I looked back in time to see Meredith Fullerton looking at her husband. He would not look at her. She just shook her head and without another word walked out the door.

"Jeremy Fullerton didn't do a damn thing. He started a conversation with the next person in the line as if nothing had happened, as if his wife's outburst had been nothing more than the ignorant comment of an ill-mannered stranger."

"Fullerton was having an affair with Goldman's daughter, and his wife found out about it?" I asked intently.

Bobby was still thinking about what Fullerton had done, or rather, what he had not done.

"He just let her go like that, let her walk away. He didn't care what she felt; all he cared about was to somehow smooth it all over, treat it as if it were some minor unpleasantness best forgotten." He paused and, with a significant look, added, "Yes, she knew he was having an affair. And if you had seen the expression on her face—the torment, the outrage—you knew she had known about it for a long time."

For a moment we just stared at each other.

"Are you thinking that Fullerton's wife could have killed him?" asked Bobby.

"He was sleeping with another woman, and he had just finished humiliating her in front of a couple hundred people. Yes, I could imagine that might be a motive for murder."

Four

Albert Craven lived in the Marina, directly across the street from a small grass-filled park and a thin strip of sandy beach. A few blocks down the shore, white-hulled boats bobbed lazily at a gray cement dock. In the other direction, a black-funneled freighter steamed under the Golden Gate, bound for somewhere the other side of the Pacific, somewhere the other side of the world, where San Francisco, like Mecca and Marrakech, was the name of other men's dreams.

I stood on the doorstep of the pale yellow stucco house, beginning to regret that I had accepted the invitation to dinner. It was a gorgeous Saturday late afternoon, the warm air crisp and clean. I would rather have spent the time wandering in the city by myself than sitting around a table with strangers engaged in the kind of meaningless small talk that passed for polite conversation and that usually made me self-conscious and tense.

The door swung open before I had rung the bell. Albert Craven's pink face was beaming.

"I was afraid you might decide not to come after all. I saw you through the window," he explained as he took me by the arm and led me inside.

I had been the last to arrive, and Craven, a smile floating on his oval mouth, introduced me to his other guests, gathered together in the living room. Robert Sanders—or Sandy, as he insisted I call him—was in his early sixties but shook hands with the firm grip of a man who had taken care of himself. As I gathered from Craven's endless commentary, Sanders was an investment banker who had grown rich through the acquisition of large holdings in small start-up companies that had gone on to become famous names in the high-tech industry. Sanders had dark, intelligent eyes, and when he spoke used the fewest words he could find to make his point. He was someone used to saving time.

His wife, Naomi, had nothing of her husband's easy precision. With large, cavernous eyes and high, sharp cheekbones, she held out her hand with a rigid, wincing smile. Certain we had not met, she thought it unlikely I was anyone she wanted to know.

"And this is my date," Craven announced as I let go of Naomi Sanders's tepid hand.

With a shrewd smile, Ruth Winthrop lifted her wrinkled red-splotched hand from the black-lacquered cane she held in front of her and fixed me with her ancient rheumy blue eyes.

"Don't let Albert fool you," she said in a voice that had more life in it than I would have expected. "I'm much too young for him."

"They say she was already here when Sir Francis Drake first sailed into the bay," Craven whispered cheerfully under his breath as he moved me from one side of the living room to the other. "Old San Francisco in every sense," he added. "She loathes the nouveau riche, which of course includes everyone who made their money after the Second World War. She positively hates Naomi Sanders." He hesitated just long enough to wink. "Which of course is the reason I invited them both."

Craven introduced me next to a couple that looked more like brother and sister than husband and wife. Charles and Dana Hendricks each had chubby friendly faces and tiny hands and feet. They ran an art gallery where Craven apparently was a frequent client. After the Hendrickses, I met Clifford Overbeck, a young associate in Craven's firm, and his wife, Nancy.

With a few well-chosen words, Craven described the essential trait or the major accomplishment of each of his guests and, with a slight change in the way he said it, introduced me as the famous lawyer who was about to conduct the most famous case in San Francisco. It was flattery, pure and simple, but Albert Craven had a gift for it. He made you feel far more important than you were and did it in a way that made you start to believe that you had perhaps seriously underestimated your own achievements. He appealed to your vanity and made you think yourself modest in the bargain.

With his hand on my arm, Craven steered me toward a large, round-shouldered man with a few strands of gray hair combed neatly over his gleaming round head. There was a curious indentation high on the upper right corner of his forehead, as if he had been dropped as a baby or cruelly beaten as a young man. He had a full face that at first gave the impression of someone slow-moving and lethargic. I say at first, because as soon as he looked at you with those piercing blue eyes you knew you were in the presence of someone with a mind as quick as anyone you were ever likely to meet.

Holding a drink in his hand, he was engaged in conversation with a woman whom he had apparently just met. She had large dark oval eyes and a rather long straight nose. Her hair, shiny black, was pulled tightly back and her head was tilted high. Her mouth seemed always on the verge of laughter. She was tall, with long elegant fingers. She stood with her weight on one foot rather than balanced on both, the posture of a ballerina at rest. She was interesting and exotic, like something out of a painting by Gauguin: one of those silky-eyed women of the South Seas, graceful, seductive, more mysterious than any product of a civilized education.

"Joseph," said Craven with a gleam in his eye, "allow me to introduce Marissa Kane. Marissa is a wonderful dinner partner. I thought you two would enjoy each other."

"Hello, Joseph Antonelli," she said as she held out her hand.

I kept looking at her, holding her hand, watching the laughter in her eyes, while Craven began to introduce me to the man next to her.

"Andrei Bogdonovitch," Craven was saying. "Andrei," he went on as I finally turned toward him, "is—or I suppose I should say was—a Russian spy."

I glanced at Craven to see if he was serious. Then I looked again at the imposing figure directly in front of me and realized without quite knowing why that what Craven had just said was probably true. Bogdonovitch denied it.

"It's not true—what Albert said. I am not a spy," he insisted in a dark, deep voice that seemed to come from all around me. He glanced at Marissa Kane. "I never was," he assured her, beaming with the amused indifference of someone for whom the truth and the lie are merely different aspects of the same thing. "I was only a lowly member of the Soviet Consulate." He turned back to me and explained, "Albert likes to exaggerate my importance."

It was time to go in to dinner. Wedged between the living room in front and its view of the bay, and the kitchen in back where the chef had been working for hours, the dining room had no windows. The absence of natural light had been remedied by hanging a crystal chandelier between mirror-covered walls. Whichever way you looked, you saw your own endless repetition, and the room, barely large enough for a table for twelve, seemed to center on a privileged few whose every gesture became a model for imitation by the crowd of admirers swirling all around them.

The table was set with Limoges china and Waterford crystal and two-hundred-year-old silverware acquired at a London auction. When everyone was seated, Craven announced with a flourish that dinner had been prepared by Angelo DelFranco, the chef at what was then the most talked-about and, it went without saying, the most expensive restaurant in the city. Patting his side pockets as if he had misplaced something, he reached inside his jacket and pulled out a small piece of paper folded neatly in half.

"Here it is," he said as he put on his glasses. "The menu." He said it like a lawyer reading the last will and testament of a wealthy man to a roomful of expectant heirs. Each item was greeted with a gasp of delight followed by a burst of embarrassed laughter.

I had been seated next to Marissa Kane. Halfway through Craven's recitation, she whispered, "Why are you smiling?"

"I was just thinking about what I had for lunch and wondering whether this would be as good," I whispered back.

When Craven finished reading, he placed the paper on the table, removed his glasses, and then motioned toward the maid who had been waiting next to the door to the kitchen. She was a young and rather pretty white woman. The maid turned and pushed open the door, letting in behind her the warm aroma of a dozen different scents. Around the table, the upturned faces of

Craven's guests were each a study in concentration as they tried to be the first to identify what each one meant.

"And just what did you have for lunch you liked so much?"

Her elbows on the table and her fingers intertwined, Marissa lifted her chin. A whimsical expression floated over her lips as she waited for my reply. For a moment I could not say anything. The longer I looked at her eyes, the larger they seemed to be, until, finally, the only thing I could see at all was a small picture of myself staring back at me.

"A hamburger and a chocolate shake," I said, drawing back.

Her eyes flared and a smile ran quickly across her wide mouth.

"And is that what you prefer, Mr. Antonelli—instead of what we're having here this evening?"

It was a simple, straightforward question, but she made it sound like a dare, an invitation to something unconventional. I tried to turn it back on her.

"And I'll bet you would, too."

There was a slight twist of her head, a brief quiver at the corner of her mouth.

"You'll have to ask," she said.

I did not think about it; it was all instinct.

"Would you like to get out of here?" I began, reaching for the napkin on my lap.

"Mr. Antonelli."

I turned and looked down the other side of the table. Andrei Bogdonovitch nodded politely.

"I'm very much interested in this case of yours. Perhaps you could tell us something about it."

Sitting next to him, Naomi Sanders threw up her hands. "Now I remember!" she exclaimed, quite pleased with herself. "You're Andrei Bogdonovitch," she announced as if she had somehow discovered that very public fact on her own. He looked at her, amused and slightly embarrassed.

"You're the one who defected," she cried, glancing all around the table. "I saw you interviewed on television. You were with the KGB, weren't you?"

Noiselessly, the maid and another, younger woman began to serve the first course.

Bogdonovitch tried to dismiss what had been said with a wave of his hand.

"I'm afraid you make me out to be far more important than I ever really was," he protested with a smile meant to disarm any further suspicion. "I did not even really defect: I simply did not go home again. When, as you say, the wall came down and the Soviet Union dissolved, I just decided to make my stay here a permanent one."

Naomi Sanders was not in the habit of being put off. "But you were given asylum here. Isn't that what happened? You gave information to the CIA about Soviet espionage, isn't that right?"

"The newspapers, the media, write and say a lot of things," Bogdonovitch replied, attempting to deflect her inquiry with a show of urbanity. "Sometimes," he said with a laugh, "they even get it right."

"He just can't talk about it," Naomi Sanders's husband interjected. "It's all secret," he explained, as he started on his salad. "Isn't that right, Mr. Bogdonovitch?"

"Please, call me Andrei. But no, there's nothing secret. Your wife is right. I did refuse to go back to Russia, and your government was kind enough to let me stay. And while I would be glad to tell you, or your government, or anyone else, everything I know, the unfortunate fact is that I don't know very much. And besides, the Soviet Union no longer exists."

The soft heavy lids that hung down over his eyes closed a little tighter. A cryptic smile crawled over his soft malleable mouth.

"History finally caught up with it," he said with a sigh. "The past no longer concerns me. I'm much more interested in the future," he added, brightening. "And, as I was saying," he went on, turning toward me, "I'm particularly fascinated by this case of yours, Mr. Antonelli."

Andrei Bogdonovitch was just a little too polished, a little too practiced in the art of saying things he did not mean for the effect he wanted to produce. I was put on my guard, or thought I was. Perhaps it was precisely by making you think you were watching him closely that Bogdonovitch could most easily manipulate you in the way he wanted. It is a measure of just how subtle, how serpentine he could be that even now I cannot be completely sure.

"Why would you be particularly interested in that?" I inquired, affecting a certain indifference.

"Despite what I just said," he began, brushing with his hand the side of his face, "I can't completely escape my past. I'm interested in this case of yours because, from what I've read in the papers, the young man you represent is accused of killing a United States senator, a man expected by many people to one day become a serious contender for the presidency. They say this happened during the course of a robbery. The case interests me, not only of course because someone of the stature of Senator Fullerton was killed, but because this is the sort of thing I was trained to believe could never happen.

"You must understand, we believed—believed absolutely— in history. Everything that happened was either in the service of history or was part of an organized attempt to delay and subvert the movement of history. Chance had no part in any of it, because, you see, if it did, then nothing was inevitable and there would be no such thing as necessity. History would be as meaningless as a lunatic's dream."

Bogdonovitch paused long enough to drink from his wineglass. He set it down and for a moment stared pensively at the gold band that ran around the edge. He lifted his gaze until our eyes met.

"When the Soviet Union was still in existence, and particularly during the time of Stalin, if someone as close to the center of power as Senator Fullerton had been murdered, it would never have occurred to anyone that it was, as the newspapers keep insisting, just a 'random act of violence.' That would not have been an acceptable suggestion," he added with a thin smile of cynicism and nostalgia. "A killing like that would have immediately been seen as part of a conspiracy aimed directly at the heart of the Soviet Union. A thorough investigation would have been made; anyone thought to be even a potential enemy of the state would have been interrogated; if there had been any doubt about their innocence, they would have been punished."

"Punished?" I asked.

Bogdonovitch smiled and stroked his chin. "Shot in the back of the head. Or perhaps," he said, relenting in the face of an audible gasp, "sent to Siberia."

"Sounds like something we should try here," Robert Sanders muttered cheerfully as he continued to eat his salad.

Ignoring him, Bogdonovitch flashed an apologetic smile. "All I meant to say, Mr. Antonelli, is that I've been struck by the differences between the way people here are so willing to believe that the murder of a prominent official like Senator Fullerton could have happened so to speak by chance and what would have happened in the Soviet Union, where it was believed that nothing—at least nothing important—could ever happen by chance."

Putting down his fork, Robert Sanders wiped his mouth with a napkin. With his lips pressed tightly together, he shook his head abruptly.

"You seem to forget that this country has had a few murders of high officials that were not, as you put it, matters of chance. Surely you don't believe that the Kennedy assassination was some 'random act of violence'? Everybody knows there was a plan, that there was a conspiracy, and everyone knows who was involved," he declared, inviting Bogdonovitch to disagree.

Bogdonovitch, a blank stare on his face, said nothing.

"Everybody knows it was the CIA and the Mafia," Sanders explained, quickly running out of patience.

His wife rolled her eyes. "I thought it was Lee Harvey Oswald," she said dryly. She closed her mouth and, adopting an attitude of bored disbelief, sucked in her cheeks until they were tight up against her teeth.

Her husband was not amused. He shot her a quick, withering glance.

"Of course it was Lee Harvey Oswald," he snapped. "Everybody knows that, and everybody knows he didn't act alone."

"Ah, but it appears that he was acting alone," said Albert Craven, leaning forward from his place at the head of the table. "Andrei may perhaps have something to add, but if I'm not mistaken, now that at least some of the Soviet archives have become available, we know that the Russians thought Oswald might actually be an American agent and that even if he wasn't, they thought he was dangerous and unstable."

I watched Bogdonovitch as Craven talked. His thick lips were parted slightly, as he clicked his front teeth together while he followed each word. The folds of skin at the outside corners of his eyelids cut across at a somewhat sharper angle than I had noticed before, giving him a slightly Asian, or to be more precise, Mongolian aspect. I had seen pictures of Lenin that conveyed that same impression.

Bogdonovitch's response was oblique.

"I used to hear from some of my old colleagues in Russia," he said, staring at his hands, which were touching the edge of the table. When he lifted his gaze, his eyes were glittering. "Do you know what they wanted to ask me about?" he inquired with an expansive gesture that took in the whole table. "They wanted to know what kind of story would bring the most money when someone—a writer, a producer—wanted them to tell what they knew about the Kennedy assassination. It's ironic, don't you think?" he remarked, as he raised his glass to his mouth. He took a drink, then looked around the room. "When we were adversaries, you wouldn't believe anything we said. And then, when we weren't, you were willing to believe almost anything!"

Stabbing the air with her arthritic finger, the ancient Ruth Winthrop suddenly announced with absolute certainty, "The Russians killed Kennedy. Oswald was working for them."

Bogdonovitch laughed heartily. "Why would we have done that? There was no reason."

"The Cuban missile crisis," Robert Sanders said alertly, apparently intrigued by the possibility that it had been the Russians and not the CIA, after all. "Kennedy forced Khrushchev to back down. They killed him in retaliation."

Bogdonovitch laughed even harder. "If we would have killed anyone over that, it would have been Castro!" he roared. "That idiot would have killed us all!" He threw up his hands. "Do you really believe we wanted to get into a nuclear war with the United States over Cuba?"

Sanders was sure of it now. "Then it was the CIA?"

Removing his handkerchief from his breast pocket, Bogdonovitch blew his nose. "The CIA!" he mumbled disparagingly. "Yes, I've seen your movies and I've read your books. It's all very entertaining."

Sanders made no response, concentrating instead on the food in front of him. The discussion had apparently reached its end, but Albert Craven, as I was beginning to learn, seldom missed a chance to stir up controversy—at least polite controversy—whenever he could.

"But Andrei," he remarked amiably, "you must have a theory. It's almost a condition of citizenship to have a theory about how and why John F. Kennedy was killed."

Andrei Bogdonovitch lifted his eyebrows and smiled. "Unfortunately," he drawled, "I'm not a citizen, and I really don't have a theory about who killed John F. Kennedy."

Turning away from Albert Craven, he looked across the table at me.

"It is odd, though, isn't it? All these people who make all these movies and write all these books: They always ask who had what to gain from Kennedy's death, but they're so fascinated by Vietnam they forget how strongly J. Edgar Hoover opposed what the Kennedys were trying to do in civil rights."

"Are you suggesting that J. Edgar Hoover had John F. Kennedy murdered?" I asked while everyone around me looked on in disbelief.

His eyes stayed on me, and I had the feeling he was studying me, trying to find out how far I was willing to go in drawing out the conclusions, no matter how controversial, that followed from what he had said.

"No, of course not," he replied. "I'm just trying to show how far-fetched these conspiracy theories can become. As I said before," he added, trying to dismiss the whole thing as a harmless dinner table diversion, "I'm sure I know less about it than anyone here."

Another course was served, and another one after that, an endless succession of dishes, each of them accompanied by a running commentary begun by one person, taken up by another, everyone trying to find something to say that none of the others knew about the food and its preparation. Things were put in categories; distinctions were drawn; conclusions were reached; propositions were advanced, only to be questioned, argued, refuted; and all of it done with the kind of intellectual effort and emotional zeal with which churchmen in the Middle Ages once debated the number of angels that could sit on the head of a pin.

I felt a hand on my sleeve and bent my head toward Marissa Kane.

"Did you know you were coming to a seminar on the metaphysics of Gorgonzola?"

I brought my eyes around until they met hers. "Head of the Jesuit Order, 1563 to 1576. Tortured as a heretic by making him listen to endless readings from the cookbook of a French abbott, St. Antoine the Glutton. Is he the one you mean?"

"I must have," she said, suppressing a grin.

After the last course had finally been served, critiqued, and eaten, coffee was poured.

"I'm afraid that we earlier became distracted by our discussion of the relative workings of history and chance," Bogdonovitch began as he stirred the silver spoon slowly around the red and gold translucent china cup. "I really am interested in your case, Mr. Antonelli. What can you tell us about it? Was the murder of Jeremy Fullerton a matter of chance, or did it perhaps have in some way something to do with history? What do you think, Mr. Antonelli?"

Behind his bluff, affable manner, there seemed to be something more at work than simple curiosity. I was almost begin-

ning to believe that he knew something about the case, or about
Fullerton, or about something I myself did not yet know.

"He can't talk about it," Robert Sanders interjected when I
did not immediately reply. He looked down the table to where
Bogdonovitch was sitting. "A lawyer can't tell you that his client
did it," he explained.

"My client didn't do it," I said, trying not to show my irritation with Sanders's smug self-assurance. "In answer to your question," I went on, pushing back from the table, "I don't know if
it had anything to do with history; it certainly had a lot to do
with chance, at least with respect to the involvement of my
client, a remarkable young man by the name of Jamaal Washington."

"He just happened to be in Fullerton's car?" Sanders asked
sarcastically.

"No, he didn't just happen to be in the car," I replied, letting
more of my annoyance show than I should have. "He happened
to be in the car because, after working late into the night, he was
walking down the street, heard what he thought was a shot,
heard a car door slam and the footsteps of someone running
away. He happened to be in the car because he thought someone
might be hurt and that he might be able to help."

"You seem to forget," said Sanders, "your client had a gun—
the gun that killed Fullerton. Not only that, he tried to shoot a
police officer with it."

I could feel myself growing angry. I waved my hand impatiently and shook my head.

"First, he didn't try to shoot anyone. Second, he picked up
the gun—if he picked it up—" I added darkly, "out of panic
when he heard what he thought might be the murderer coming
back to the car."

An investment banker, Sanders made money by understanding the way numbers worked; he had little capacity, and even less tolerance, for facts that were subject to more than a single interpretation. With a sense of triumph he reminded me of what I had obviously forgotten:

"He also had the senator's wallet."

I stared back at him. "He goes to the car to help. He checks for a pulse: The man is dead. He sees the gun on the floor. He picks up the car phone to call for help, but then decides he better find out the identity of the man who has just been killed. He takes the dead man's wallet out of his coat, and just at that moment a light shines through the window. He crouches down, still clutching the wallet in his hand. He thinks the murderer may have come back; he thinks the murderer may have heard him open the car door; he thinks the murderer may have thought he was a witness; he decides to make a run for it."

Sanders was not impressed. He lifted his eyebrows and flared his nostrils, a picture of condescension.

"Yes, well, I suppose you have to come up with some kind of theory. That's your job, isn't it?" He bent over his coffee and began to stir.

Bogdonovitch had watched closely, an amused expression on his mouth, the detached spectator who enjoys the game even when played by amateurs.

"Tell us, then, Mr. Antonelli: If your client didn't do it, who did? Was that also a matter of chance, or did it have something to do with history?"

With both thumbs under my chin, I tapped my fingers together, searching Bogdonovitch's narrow eyes. What was it about him that made me want to trust him at the same time some other, perhaps deeper, instinct kept telling me I should not? I put my hands down and shifted position until I was nearly sideways to the table.

"I don't know who killed him," I admitted. "One possibility is that it was just what the newspapers have said it was: a robbery gone bad, only instead of Jamaal Washington it was someone else."

I glanced up at Marissa Kane and felt that same strange magnetism I had felt before. I shifted my gaze to Robert Sanders, expecting to see some reaction to what I had said. He was just putting down his cup. I watched him push back his sleeve, trying surreptitiously to check the time.

"Fullerton got into his car," I went on, turning back to Bogdonovitch.

There was, I thought, a glimmer of recognition, a shared understanding, an instantaneous acknowledgment that Robert Sanders was not a very interesting man. I paused just long enough to smile.

"Fullerton gets into his car. Somebody slips in the passenger side with a gun. Fullerton resists—or refuses—or does something—and the robber shoots him. That would explain why he leaves both the gun and the wallet: panic. He has to get away. He knows someone will come, and in that fog, someone, even the police, might be just around the corner."

"If it was a robbery gone bad," said Robert Sanders, staring at the ceiling and doing his best to sound bored, "and the guy is in such a hurry to get away that he doesn't bother to take the wallet, and he's in such a panic that he manages to leave the gun behind, how does it happen that he apparently had the presence of mind to wipe the murder weapon clean of his own fingerprints?"

He knew everything he needed to know about the case: He had read it in the newspapers.

"Maybe he wore gloves," I replied with a shrug. "Jamaal Washington had them on that night. It was very cold."

"You said that was one possibility," Bogdonovitch reminded me. "There is another?"

"Yes. Suppose it was not a robbery at all. Suppose someone intended to kill Fullerton. Then what?"

"I'm not sure I follow," Bogdonovitch replied, leaning forward, his eyes still on me.

"You still have the same sequence," I explained. "Someone shoots him, doesn't take the wallet, and leaves the gun."

Bogdonovitch threw up his hands and laughed. "I still don't quite follow."

"Suppose someone killed him and tried to make it look like a robbery. What is your first question?"

He twisted his head slightly to the side. A shadow came over his eyes as he thought about it. "Why didn't he take the wallet?"

Then his face brightened and I knew he had the answer to his own question.

"Because if he had taken the wallet—if he had taken the time to take the wallet—then why would he leave the gun?"

"Yes," I agreed. "And the gun was a cheap Saturday night special—not the kind an assassin would use, but the kind of gun everyone would expect to find if some kid had tried to rob someone he didn't know."

"Isn't there another possibility?" Sanders interjected. "It happened just the way the police said it did. Your client did it and they shot him when he tried to get away."

"No, Mr. Sanders, I can assure you, that is not a possibility."

Sanders crossed his legs and extended his arm over the back corner of his chair. He raised his head until he was looking at me down the length of his nose.

"This has all been very interesting, Mr. Antonelli, and I'm sure you're a very good attorney, but I knew Jeremy Fullerton, so you'll have to forgive me if I don't have a great deal of sympathy for the young punk who killed him. You're going to lose this case, Mr. Antonelli, just as surely as our friend here lost," he said with a dismissive nod in the general direction of Andrei Bogdonovitch.

"Lost? I'm sorry," Bogdonovitch inquired, "precisely what is it I'm supposed to have lost?"

Sanders waved his hand in the air. "You, the Soviet Union, the fall of communism—that's what I meant," he explained irritably.

Quite deliberately, Naomi Sanders rolled her eyes. She opened her mouth to speak, but before she could, Andrei Bogdonovitch said something that caused an immediate sensation.

"What makes you think we lost?"

Robert Sanders stared at Bogdonovitch as if he had lost his mind.

"I'll grant you," Bogdonovitch remarked with an affable smile, "it certainly seems that the West, that capitalism, has won."

"Seems!" Sanders blustered. He planted both feet on the floor and both elbows on the table. "Seems that capitalism has won. Let me tell you something. We generate more wealth in a year in Silicon Valley alone than the entire Russian economy is likely to produce in the next decade." He shook his head with contempt. "Seems!"

"But what if this isn't the end of history at all, but just a stage? What if Marx wasn't wrong after all? What if the Soviet Union had to be destroyed before history could move beyond capitalism to communism? What does this new world market economy—the economy that has made you all so fabulously wealthy—what does it mean if not the abolition of all those national boundaries and policies which for Marx were impediments to history, vestiges of the late stages of capitalism? Whether you know it or not, you have all become Marxists."

Lowering his eyes, Bogdonovitch ran the tip of his thick middle finger around the circumference of the thin cup in front of him. A shrewd, subtle smile etched itself on the left corner of his mouth.

"The last stage before communism was not the so-called dictatorship of the proletariat; it was what Marx called the 'withering away of the state,'" he said, turning his head to take a glimpse of Robert Sanders. "Isn't that what you people really want: no government at all? Isn't that what you people really believe: that economics is the only thing that matters? Isn't that it, Mr. Sanders—politics doesn't matter, government doesn't matter, only the unrestricted access to worldwide markets? Now, Mr. Sanders, consider if you will that by doing this, by turning everything into a question of economics and worldwide markets, by producing through science everything everyone needs, have you not moved closer to the end of history the way Marx meant it: not by the victory of state socialism—which is what the Soviet Union represented—but through the victory of what for lack of a better phrase I'll simply call 'market socialism'?"

Though Sanders tried to strike a pose of unruffled urbanity, he could scarcely contain the rage that was boiling up within him. "That's very interesting, Mr. Bogdonovitch," he said in a peremptory tone. "But of course it makes no sense at all. The simple fact is that the Cold War is over and we won it."

"Yes," Bogdonovitch acknowledged, "you're perfectly correct: The Cold War is over."

He paused and seemed to consider what he was going to say or if he was going to say anything more at all. He had been speaking in a voice that enveloped the room, speaking with tremendous energy and force; but now, when he began to speak again, his voice was little more than a whisper, and instead of the large gestures he had made with his hands and the lively expression that had taken possession of his features, he shrugged his shoulders with a sort of weary indifference and folded his hands in his lap.

"But what have you won? For fifty years both sides thought they were engaged in something important. The competition between us imposed a discipline on everything we did, both of us. This of course is just my opinion, but I've lived in both countries, and I believe there is a sense in which both of them—the United States and the Soviet Union—were necessary to each other; that they were in a way mirror images of each other; that the destruction of either one had to lead to the destruction of the other. Yes, Mr. Sanders, the Cold War is over; but while it lasted, all of us were engaged in a struggle to achieve something we thought important—more important than ourselves. What do we have now? I am not being entirely ironic, Mr. Sanders, when I suggest that while we Marxists always denied that the soul existed, you Americans seem not to have noticed when you lost the soul you had."

No one knew quite what to say. Albert Craven seized the moment to announce that we were all about to have the privilege of meeting the famous chef who had done us the honor of preparing our dinner. The mood around the table changed immediately. Everyone began to talk at once, gratified they could talk about something they understood, something that was really important. The chef, a young man in his early thirties with a small mustache, a crooked smile, and a name so obviously contrived that you hesitated to think him a fraud, made his appearance and, like a visiting dignitary, took questions from the floor.

I glanced across at Bogdonovitch. He was smiling to himself—rather sadly, I thought—while he slowly drank what was left of his coffee. He caught my eye before I could look away, and for a moment we stared at each other like two strangers from the same country who find themselves on foreign ground.

"So you still have family in Russia?" I asked, wondering what it must have been like to become an exile.

"No," said Bogdonovitch quietly. "I was an only child and my parents both died when I was young. There is nobody."

At the end of the evening, while everyone said their good-byes, Marissa Kane asked me if I was staying with friends while I was in the city.

"I'm staying at the St. Francis."

She bent her head slightly to the side, a whimsical look on her face. "Do you have a car?"

"No," I replied. "Do you need a ride?"

This seemed to amuse her even more. "No, I don't need a ride. I have a car. But how did you get here?"

Finally, I understood. "I took a cab."

"I'll drop you off," she said casually, laughing at me with her eyes.

"Is it on the way?"

I thought she was going to laugh out loud. "It's not far out of the way."

She said we were going to take the scenic route, and from the way she said it I had a hunch it was going to be something unusual. We drove up a narrow street between three-story wood-frame buildings with garage doors facing the sidewalk and, jutting out above them, three-sided windows that let in the light and gave a distant, neck-craning view of the bay, glimmering in the darkness far below. The street seemed to get steeper with each block and it seemed to take all the power the engine had to keep us moving. When we reached the summit and stopped at the light, I tried not to think of how fast we would roll backward if the brakes did not hold.

"It's one of the things I love most about this place: driving up these hills," she said, glancing at me as she made the turn. We had gone less than a block when she asked, "Do you know where you are?"

"We're on Nob Hill," I replied as I looked out the window. "This isn't the first time I've been to San Francisco. When I was a kid I used to spend summers here."

We passed the front of the Fairmont Hotel. Shiny black limousines were lined up in a row, while a bell captain in a scarlet coat and gold braid waved the next one into place.

"How well do you know Albert Craven?" I asked.

She turned onto California Street and began a precipitous descent. The pavement vibrated beneath us as, two blocks below, a cable car lurched its way along the iron tracks, heading for the top.

" 'Climb halfway to the stars,' " she sang under her breath. Her eyes glittered at the way she had connected the cable car and the famous song. "Some people like Tony Bennett and 'I Left My Heart in San Francisco.' Don't misunderstand me, it's wonderful, it really is. But I prefer 'San Francisco,' maybe because I always loved Judy Garland. Which do you like?"

"Judy Garland. Or do you think I'm only saying that?"

"Would you?" she asked, giving me a quick glance with her mirthful, long-lashed eyes. "Would you tell a lie because you thought that's what I wanted to hear?"

I would have told her every lie she ever wanted to hear.

"Never," I swore, laughing. "But on a point on which I had no settled opinion, I might be tempted to yield to yours."

"And are there many things on which you have settled opinions?"

"Only about Judy Garland. Now tell me, how long have you really known Albert Craven?"

"I've known Albert for years," she replied, her voice suddenly soft and affectionate. "He did the legal work when I opened the first store."

"The first store?" I asked blankly.

"I don't know why he agreed to do it," she went on. "All I had was an idea; no experience, and next to nothing in the way of money. I went to him because I was told that Albert Craven was the best lawyer in the city for that kind of thing. I wanted the best," she added with a bright, self-deprecating grin. "It never really occurred to me that it might be expensive. When he told me what it would cost, I must have looked like I had just swallowed something awful. Poor Albert! He couldn't help himself: He felt sorry for me. He denies it, but that is exactly what happened: He felt sorry for me and he decided to help. He became my lawyer and his only fee was a small percentage of the stock."

"What kind of store was it—the first one you opened?"

"Women's apparel. I called it The Way of All Flesh," she said, her eyes sparkling. "Do you like it?"

"I liked the book; I've never seen the store. It's a wonderful name, though."

"You read Samuel Butler?"

"Long time ago. But if you've known Albert Craven that long, you must know my cousin, Craven's partner."

She looked at me with a puzzled expression. "Albert's partner?"

"Bobby—I mean Robert—Medlin."

At first she seemed not to believe it. "You're Bobby's cousin?" she asked, glancing at me and then turning back to the road. "Bobby's wife was one of my best friends."

We had taken the scenic route, all the way down to the bottom of California Street, where the cable car tracks ended, then back up Market to Powell and then the few blocks around to Union Square. She pulled up in front of the hotel.

"I was thinking of driving up to the Napa Valley in the morning," she said as I started to open the door. "Would you like to come along?"

Five

Early the next morning Marissa Kane picked me up in front of the St. Francis Hotel.

"I thought you might need this," she said, laughing quietly, as she handed me a steaming cup of black coffee.

The night before, the top had been up on her green Jaguar convertible, but this morning she had taken it down. Her hair was wrapped in a dark red silk scarf and her eyes were hidden behind a pair of dark glasses. We drove through the deserted streets of the city and out onto the Golden Gate Bridge, where for a moment we were almost blinded by the sun rising above the low-lying hills on the far side of the bay. The pale blue high-arching sky was streaked pink and scarlet and gold. The cool moving air rushed past my face, while down below the bay glistened silver-smooth, as still and shiny as glass. I turned up the collar of my jacket and slouched down until my head was resting against the top of the leather seat.

She was driving in the outside lane, next to the railing, keeping a steady pace. In the morning light, all the thousands of buildings that curled their way around the farther reaches of the bay looked like an enormous Bedouin encampment, just arrived after a long night's journey, that would be gone again when the sun slipped down below the far horizon.

"Do you know," she said when we were halfway across, "that more than a thousand people have jumped off the bridge, and not one of them ever did it from the other side?"

We were so close that our shoulders touched, but her voice, though clear and distinct, seemed to come from a distance.

"They always jump facing the city," she went on. "They want to die, and the only thing they can think about is seeing San Francisco one last time. I know it sounds strange," she said with a soft, self-deprecating laugh, "but I think there is something rather wonderful, something sad and haunting and romantic about that."

I looked up at the steel cables, strung like harp strings down each side of the bridge.

"I don't think it sounds strange at all. Would you do that?" I asked after a pause. "Jump off the bridge—if you were going to take your own life."

"No," she said, suddenly quite serious. "I'd never do it in such a public way. I'd get a prescription for something, something that wouldn't hurt at all—I'm not a great believer in pain of any kind—and then I'd get into my own bed and close my eyes and go to sleep and never wake up," she said, as her voice trailed off.

"What about you?" she asked a moment later, her face once again full of expression. "Would you—jump off the bridge?"

"I have a fear of heights," I admitted. "Besides, halfway down I'd probably change my mind."

With a look of concern, she glanced across at me. "Does it bother you—driving across like this?"

Suddenly I felt like a coward. "No," I lied, "it doesn't bother me at all."

Then, to make the lie credible, I told the truth. "I don't think I'd want to walk across it, though."

She tossed her head, darted a look back, and changed lanes as we left the bridge behind us.

"Would you do it with me?" she asked, a teasing lilt in her voice. "I wouldn't let you fall. I promise. I like high places—I like the view. I wouldn't want to jump off the bridge—that's true," she said, laughing, as she gunned the engine. "But there are days—great, glorious days—when you almost wish you could just walk right out to the edge of the world and into the setting sun."

She made it sound like it would be the simplest thing imaginable and the only thing you had ever really wanted to do, though you had never once in your life had that thought before.

We drove on, heading north, away from the bay. An hour later we were in the Napa Valley, crawling along the narrow street through St. Helena. On the other side of town, we passed under a tunnel of dark trees reaching across from each side of the road trying to touch. Off to the right, like some green-coated army, row after row of dusty grapevines swept across the valley to a temporary line of advance halfway up the surrounding hills.

Without warning, Marissa cut across the road into a large gravel parking lot already filled with tourist buses and private cars. Lost in a crowd of strangers, we wandered through a cave carved into the hillside, listening to the echoing voice of a guide explain why the wine was left to age so long in the vast oaken casks that lined the smooth cement floor. At the end of the tour, after we had seen everything there was to see, we stumbled out into the light. Marissa took hold of my sleeve to steady herself, laughing at how awkward she had for the moment become, and then let it go.

I bought us a soft drink and we sat on a stone bench behind the narrow Victorian mansion that had originally been built for the owner of the vineyard. For a number of years it had served as the office and the tasting room for the winery. Now it was a gift shop for tourists.

"When I first came out here, to San Francisco," said Marissa, remembering something now gone forever, "you could come up here on a Saturday or a Sunday and stop at any winery you liked and almost never see anyone else at all."

Two young couples came out of the gift shop together, carrying paper shopping bags with the logo of the winery fashioned on the side.

"By the end of the day, if you stopped at enough places," continued Marissa, "you could be pretty well buzzed."

Her long arms stretched straight behind her and her legs sprawled out in front of her, she turned her face, glistening in the light, up to the sun.

"It was better then, I think."

There were people all around, crunching the gravel with their steps as they moved to and from the gift shop, filling the air with the muffled sound of their many voices; but it all seemed to come from far away, somewhere outside the circle where we sat. Bending forward, I rested my elbows on my knees and scratched the dirt with a twig.

"We were younger," I reminded her.

"There weren't so many people," she said in a soft, dreamy voice.

She closed her eyes all the way and lifted her face even closer to the sun.

"And the ones there were," she whispered, moving her face slowly from side to side, savoring the warmth, "I liked better than the ones I know now."

Her eyes opened and she rolled her head to the side until she was looking at me.

"Not all the ones I know now, of course. It's strange, though."

I dragged the small stick through the final curve of a figure eight. "What's strange?"

"That you should be Bobby Medlin's cousin."

"Why is that strange?" I stared at her for a moment and then looked back down at the ground, stirring the dust until the figure eight was gone and I could start another one.

"You're not the least alike."

I could feel her eyes on me. I kept mine fixed on the point of the stick as I kept moving it around.

"Bobby is so outgoing—brash, even, full of life, always a good time. He can always make me laugh."

I started to smile, not just because she was so right about Bobby.

"Bobby is never serious, or almost never serious, and you're always serious, even when you don't mean to be." She thought of something. "Even the way you walk."

"The way I walk?" I asked, laughing self-consciously.

"Bobby walks like he doesn't care where he is going; you walk like there is always someplace you have to be."

I knew what she meant—about Bobby, at least. It was that way he had of seeming to be able to move at any moment in any direction he wanted to go.

"Bobby was an All-American," I started to explain.

She did not hear me, or if she did, she paid no attention. "When I was in college, I knew a boy like you: always so serious, so intense."

She tilted her head, gazing at me as if there were something she wanted to be sure about. "He had eyes just like yours—dark, brooding eyes. I could have fallen in love with him."

She paused and then, her eyes glittering, added, "Maybe I did and just never admitted it to myself."

I was a little confused. "You didn't want to fall in love with him?"

"I couldn't," she replied with a hushed, rueful laugh. "I knew I would, though—if I kept seeing him. So after our third date . . ." She laughed again. "Date! We went out for coffee—in the afternoon. I told him we couldn't do it anymore. And when he asked why, I said in my nineteen-year-old cleverness that I was 'anti-hurt.' Yes, I said that. Anti-hurt."

She shrugged her shoulders and, almost imperceptibly, bobbed her head from side to side, the amused and not altogether displeased spectator of her own youthful performance.

"We were walking across campus, the grass covered with the last leaves of autumn. The air was biting cold. I remember watching his breath when he started to tell me that it didn't make any sense. He wasn't the kind of boy who could ever just let anything go: He thought there were reasons for everything. I think he really thought," she said with a shrewd glance, "that if you gave him a reason for something, he could find a better reason than the one you had and talk you out of it."

She bit her lip and smiled sadly to herself. "I told him that we couldn't see each other anymore; I told him that my mother had always told me that if I ever brought home a boy who wasn't Jewish, I could never come home again."

I looked at her, not certain whether to believe it. "What did he say to that?"

"He didn't believe me, not at first. He knew there were people who didn't like Jews; he didn't know it worked the other way around as well."

She did not say anything more about it, and there was nothing I could think to ask. We began to talk about other things, and then, after a while, we left the winery and drove farther north, hugging the road that ran along the base of the western hills, past the spreading vineyards that covered the valley floor, until we reached the outskirts of Calistoga. High on a billboard, a pair of goggled eyes stared out from a face covered with an oozing brown liquid. The original Calistoga mud baths, discovered a century before, were, according to the sign, guaranteed to draw out through every pore every kind of bodily infirmity.

We parked the car and started to walk along the single street that ran the short length of the town. It was clogged with short-sleeved visitors, and when we reached the other end we ducked into the restaurant of a small two-story white stucco hotel.

There was a thirty-minute wait for a table inside. We quickly accepted the invitation to help ourselves to sit at one of the available wooden tables scattered around the deck outside. We found one next to a railing, just above a narrow, rock-filled creek. The fall rains, if they came at all, were still months away. The shallow creek bottom was dry and cracked and filled with brown, brittle reeds. Through the branches of an oak tree, the sunlight made a latticework pattern on the table. In the warm, still air, everything seemed to move with as little hurry as something seen through a twilit dust.

"Lawrence Goldman," she repeated, raising her eyes from the menu, when I asked if she had heard of him. A smile danced across her lower lip and lingered at the corners of her mouth. She put the menu down and gave the waiter her order.

"Everyone knows Lawrence. Did you think I didn't?" she asked with a look that warned me I had come close to injuring her feelings.

"No, of course not," I assured her. "I'm the one who doesn't know him; and it seems like I'm the only one who doesn't know him."

She was eager and even, I thought, a little excited to tell someone who had only just learned Lawrence Goldman's name everything she could about him.

"Everyone knows Lawrence Goldman because Lawrence has spent fifty years or more making sure they do," she began. "His name is the first one mentioned in the newspaper stories about any social event he attends; his name invariably heads the list of all the wealthy, socially prominent people who pledge contributions to any charitable cause. I don't think you can find a plaque on a building in the city that doesn't have his name on it."

She paused while the waiter brought our order.

"Thank you," she said when he had finished. "It looks wonderful."

He must have heard it a dozen times a day, but when he heard it from her, heard that magical voice, you would have thought no one had ever thanked him for anything before.

She picked up her fork, then put it down. With a quick glance first to one side, then the other, she leaned forward, playing the conspirator.

"What I never knew until Albert Craven explained it to me is how he does it all with other people's money. It's really quite an enviable talent: using other people's money to support your own reputation for generosity. And the worst part," added Marissa, her mouth curled down in a look of amused disdain, "is that there really isn't a whole lot anyone can do about it."

She noticed immediately the confusion in my eyes.

"Lawrence," she explained, "is very persuasive." Her eyes opened wide and her mouth pulled back into a whimsical smile. "A lawyer might think of it as extortion. Lawrence controls so much of the commercial real estate in the city that some people think he owns half of San Francisco. And of course Lawrence does nothing to discourage that impression. It's really quite ingenious, the way he operates. Other people have more money, and there are—at least one would like to think there are—public officials with more power; but none of those with more money have as much influence, and no one who holds public office will make as much in their lifetime as Lawrence makes in a week. Albert Craven thinks he's one of the most dishonest men he's ever known."

Her chin tilted up and then, slowly, came down again.

"A lot of people think that; not many of them would ever say it. It's not the kind of thing Lawrence would ever forget. Lawrence, you see, has managed to create a world in which everyone thinks that incurring his displeasure is the only unforgivable sin."

She stopped and for a while sipped on her Chardonnay. She had taken off the red silk scarf and each time she tossed her head, which she often did when she was caught up in something she was trying to describe, her hair flew back over her shoulder. I could not imagine her with anything other than long black hair. It was part of the slightly unconventional look that set her apart, made her different in a way that made you wonder how different she really was and how much of it was a game she played in which she was the mystery everyone wants to solve.

She put down the glass and gave me one of those wide-eyed stares that taunt you with the vague suggestion that nothing has been decided and anything might still be possible, an unspoken invitation to see what happens.

"You should have a conversation with Lawrence sometime," she suggested, her eyes bright and shiny. "It's always the same.

His voice never changes: always soft, unhurried, so quiet it forces you to concentrate on everything he says. And then, when you talk to him, he listens to what you say as if it were not only the most interesting, but also the most serious thing he has heard in a very long time. He watches you with those pale blue eyes of his, hooded like the face of some wise and benevolent monk; watches you with friendly curiosity. He bends his head forward, at just a slight angle. Like this," she said, laughing as she lowered her forehead and gave her neck a slight twist. "He bends his head like he's about to ask a question. Then, when you're at the end of what you have to say, he nods once, smiles once, and then, for just a moment, his eyes still on you, there is a complete silence, as if he wants to be sure, absolutely sure, that there's nothing more you want to say that he might inadvertently interrupt."

She took another drink and picked at her lunch. A moment later, she looked up.

"He talks to you in that same unhurried voice, explaining in the same reasonable way the same request he's been making for years now: 'I've promised to raise two million for the new wing of the hospital,' he'll say. 'And I'd like it very much if I could count on you for a hundred thousand of it.' Or two hundred thousand, or five hundred thousand—whatever he thinks you should pay. And no one ever says no, because everyone knows that they would never again be given the chance to say yes. Because, you see, only those who say yes can be sure they're still part of things, still part of the select circle permitted to do business with Lawrence Goldman, without whom there might not be any business at all."

I had no particular interest in the peculiar machinations of Lawrence Goldman, no matter how ingenious, or insidious, they may have been; but she was so easy to listen to that I had almost forgotten why I had asked her about him in the first place.

"Bobby was there, at the Goldmans' apartment, that night—"

"So was I."

"And he told me that—"

"He told you about Jeremy Fullerton's wife and what she said to Ariella? What a scandal that was. Everyone knew they were having an affair. . . . You don't think that had anything to do with his death?"

"Do you?"

A sly grin slid across her mouth as she searched my eyes. "Are you going to be a lawyer now? Are you going to cross-examine me?"

I felt the blood rush to my cheeks. "Sorry. Habit. I don't know enough to think anything. All I know is what Bobby told me. And yes, I wonder whether Fullerton's wife might have been angry enough to do something more than just exchange words with the woman her husband was sleeping with."

Marissa became serious. "If Meredith Fullerton was going to kill her husband for sleeping with other women, she would have done it a long time ago. No," she said emphatically, and rather sadly, "there's no chance in the world she could have done it. She loved him too much."

"You know her?"

"Yes, I know her," she said as she took a bite and then put down the fork. "A long time ago, when Jeremy was first running for Congress. I knew her then, not very well, but I knew her. And I liked her. I still like her. And believe me, she loved Jeremy."

Tilting her head to the side, Marissa gazed at me with what seemed like a question in her eyes.

"What?" I asked.

"Oh, nothing," she replied. "It's hard to explain to a man, and it seems stupid to say it. But every woman was in love with Jeremy."

I laughed. "Were you?"

She looked at me again, and there was still a question in her eyes; and though I did not know what it was, I knew it was somehow different from the one that had been there before.

"I think I could have been," she replied, trying to be honest. "In a certain place, at a certain time."

"Like that boy you knew in college?"

"There were things they had in common," she said after she had thought about it.

I looked at her and waited. She bit her lip and then her eyes opened wide as if she had found the exact phrase for which she had been searching.

"You thought they were poets," she said softly, "and you worried they might be frauds."

The question in her eyes—whatever it had been—vanished. She forced a smile.

"I said that every woman was in love with Jeremy Fullerton, but I'm not sure it's really true. I'm not sure that Ariella was in love with him at all. I'm not sure she's capable of being in love with anyone."

Reaching across the table, she patted my hand.

"You should have been there. If you had just seen them all there together—Lawrence, his daughter, Jeremy—you would understand everything."

She had a gift for description, and, listening to her describe what happened that night, I could almost see Ariella Goldman, wearing a long black dress with her hair pulled up, a pair of diamond earrings dangling next to the smooth white skin of her neck, standing there with cool, lucid eyes, measuring with each movement of her slender hands the few graceful words she bestowed on each of her father's guests.

"And every time someone asked about her mother, Lawrence would explain in that same unchanging, unhurried voice that 'Amanda wanted to be here, but she's down at the ranch getting everything ready, and she just couldn't get back.' "

Everyone understood. Whether it was the two-story Nob Hill apartment, or the two-hundred acre Sonoma Valley vineyard, or the three-thousand-acre ranch in the mountains above Santa Barbara with the long view of the Pacific, or the fifteen-thousand-square-foot hideaway tucked into twelve secluded acres down the Peninsula in Woodside, surrounded by what had become some of the most expensive real estate in the world, they were always moving from one house to the next, getting the next place ready almost before they had settled into the one where they had just arrived. It was a way of life that could rather easily become a convenient pretext for living apart. In the case of Lawrence and Amanda Goldman, one of them seemed always to be just one house ahead of the other.

"Odd, when you think of how they met," Marissa remarked as she pushed her plate aside.

Signaling the waiter, I ordered more wine.

"I shouldn't," protested Marissa mildly.

"It's only a second glass. Why is it odd because of the way they met? By the way, how old is he, anyway?"

She had to think about it. "Mid-seventies, I suppose," she said presently. "Hard to tell, really. Lawrence has that look men get who are well taken care of: snow-white hair and a reddish tan face. He could be seventy; he could be eighty; he could be older. When they have that look, you can only be sure of three things: They're rich, they're old, and they could live another twenty years or be dead tomorrow morning."

The waiter set new wineglasses in front of us both.

"That sounds a little like Albert Craven," I said, peering over the glass as I lifted it to my mouth.

She tossed her head and then laughed when she caught me watching the way her hair sailed back over her shoulder.

"No, that isn't Albert at all."

Still laughing, she narrowed her eyes and tried to concentrate.

"Albert isn't . . . sleek. That's it! Sleek. Old men without any lines in their faces, all very smooth, very—how shall I say?—rounded, contoured, like someone took a statue while the surface was still soft and rubbed out all the rough edges. You know what I mean: old men with faces as smooth as a baby's bottom."

Across the deck, through the windows, the animated faces of the crowd inside the restaurant lent a sort of shared solitude to our own conversation, a sense that what we had to say was private and strictly between ourselves. I wondered for a moment what someone sitting inside would have thought had they looked out and seen the way we were leaning toward each other across the table, looking for all the world as if we wanted nothing so much as to be left alone. I guessed that even the waiter, who after all had heard her voice, must have thought I was madly in love with her.

"Why are you smiling?" she asked, laughing again at me with her eyes.

"Nothing," I halfway lied. "I was just thinking about the way we think about things because of the way they look—Lawrence Goldman's face, for example. Now tell me, how did they meet and why does it make the way they live now seem so odd?"

The story of how Lawrence Goldman met his wife, and what happened when they did, was one of those astonishing tales that have been whispered so many times and in so many places that it becomes the kind of legend everyone believes even when, or perhaps especially when, they are almost certain it cannot possibly be true. It was the kind of story everyone wants to believe, because it tells everyone what they want to hear. Some thought it meant that even the powerful would do anything for love; others thought it only proved that the rich did what they wanted and never gave a damn about whom it might hurt.

They met at a party given by Lawrence Goldman and the woman to whom he was then married in honor of someone called Richard McBryde, a new vice president recently hired away from a large developer in the East. Lawrence Goldman was then forty-six years old and had been married for exactly half his life. His two sons were still in college. Richard McBryde was in his early thirties, and his wife, Amanda, was only twenty-four. From the moment he first saw her, Goldman could not take his eyes off her. There were sixteen people gathered around the perfectly decorated dining room table, but all through dinner he talked only to her. When dessert was served, he got up from his chair and with a strange, troubled look in his eyes announced he had to leave.

"I just remembered," he said as he put his napkin down on the table. "I have to go to Los Angeles for a few days." Then, for just a moment, he stared down at the table as if there were something he was trying to decide. When he raised his eyes he looked directly at Amanda McBryde. "Why don't you come with me?"

There are those who later claimed it was not even a question; that it was more like a decision he had made for both of them, a decision she had somehow authorized him to make. That was the sort of judgment that could be made after the fact. At the time, no one could do anything but watch with open-eyed amazement as Amanda McBryde rose from her chair and, without so much as a glance at her husband, left the room with a man she had met for the first time barely two hours before.

Like every story told often enough to become something of a legend, there were serious differences of opinion about where this had all happened. In some accounts, the dinner had been held in Goldman's lavishly furnished apartment in San Francisco; in other versions, it had taken place at the Tuscan-style villa that had just been constructed in the middle of his Sonoma vineyard. There were even those who claimed that Lawrence Goldman and the young wife of his most recent employee had not flown off to Los Angeles or anywhere else that night; that they had instead walked into the palm-lined darkness of the cool California night, driven away from the white stucco Santa Barbara mansion with the red tile roof and the private beach, and stopped at the first motel they found on the highway that stretched south along the Pacific shore.

Everyone thought they knew what had happened, but the only thing anyone would ever know for sure is that nine months later two divorces had been arranged with ruthless efficiency; a marriage was announced after the fact; and, with as little public notice as possible, the only child of Lawrence and Amanda Goldman drew the first breath of what was certain to be an interesting life.

Six

As soon as I agreed to represent Jamaal Washington, I waived on his behalf the requirement that he be arraigned at once on the murder indictment returned by the grand jury. Instead of in a hospital room where he was recovering from the surgery that had removed the bullet that had passed dangerously close to his spine, I wanted his first appearance to be where everyone, especially the press, would see that he did not look anything like what they imagined he did. Now, two weeks later, I was finally in court, waiting to make my first formal appearance in a case the whole country was watching.

Peering through thick tortoiseshell glasses, the district attorney, Clarence Haliburton, folded over at the corner the stapled page he had just read and began to read the next one. Without any apparent break in his concentration, he kept reading when the side door opened and the bailiff ordered everyone to rise. His eyes still on the document, Haliburton waited until James L. Thompson was halfway to the bench before he slowly pushed back his chair and raised himself just high enough above it to satisfy the technical requirement that he be on his feet when a judge entered a courtroom.

Grumbling to himself, Thompson glanced around the hushed courtroom, jammed to capacity with reporters come from all over the world to cover the trial of the first murder of a prominent political figure in the United States in more than thirty years.

"Call the case," he said, nodding toward the district attorney.

Still reading, Haliburton did not look up.

"Call the case," said the judge again, his gray eyes turning hard.

Haliburton cast aside the document he had been holding and reached for the case file.

"Can't you even remember the name of it?" hissed Thompson.

It had no effect. Haliburton picked up the file and with slow, deliberate movements got to his feet. He buttoned his suit jacket and pushed his tie down inside. He was of medium height, with square shoulders and strong hands. His nose was a little too broad, and his eyes a little too close together. It gave him a look of concentrated pugnacity, of someone who, if he did not go looking for a fight, was always secretly glad when he found himself in the middle of one.

"*People v. Jamaal Washington,*" he announced, reading the title on the case file.

Clarence Haliburton had hundreds of assistant district attorneys who prosecuted cases in the criminal courts. This was the first case he had prosecuted himself in more than three years; he tried to make it sound as if it were not any different than any of the thousands of other cases handled by his office every year.

"Thank you," said Judge Thompson with a dismissive smile. He turned to the bailiff. "Bring in the prisoner."

Thompson sank back in the high leather chair and, shaking his head, stared at the ceiling.

Dressed in the standard denim jail uniform, Jamaal Washington was brought into court in a wheelchair. In a tribute to the mindless power of prescribed procedure, his ankles were shackled together with a six-inch chain. He was put next to me at one of the two tables at which the defense and the prosecution had their places. We were at the table on the right, facing the bench, closest to the empty jury box.

I wondered what passed through the district attorney's mind when Jamaal was first brought in. This was the young man he had publicly accused of having committed one of the most depraved murders on record, and he did not look depraved at all. I thought I saw him start to stare, as if Jamaal's intelligent eyes and sensitive mouth had caught him by surprise. Perhaps it was only my imagination. And if it had been there, that little look of astonishment, what then? He was there to prosecute, to win, and it would not have taken him any time at all to remind himself that killers come in different disguises and that the most dangerous were often the ones who looked like murder was the last thing they would ever think about doing.

"Is your name Jamaal Washington?" asked Judge Thompson in a thin reedy voice that in moments of anger had been known to break.

Jamaal looked straight at him. "Yes, your honor," he replied respectfully.

Thompson peered down at him, taken, I thought, with the tone of Jamaal's response. "Mr. Washington, you are here to be arraigned on a criminal charge. That means the prosecution is required to inform you, on the record, the crime or crimes of which you have been accused. This is to give you notice so that you can defend yourself."

Thompson raised his gray wispy eyebrows and tilted his head

slightly to the side. "Is that clear to you? Do you understand all this?"

Jamaal's gaze never wavered. "Yes, your honor."

"Now, before we begin," said the judge patiently, "let me advise you that you have the right to be represented by an attorney of your choice at all stages of these proceedings. Do you understand?"

"Yes, your honor."

Thompson looked at him a moment longer. "I see you have an attorney with you." He glanced at me, nodded, and then looked down at the court file he had open in front of him. "Joseph Antonelli," he said out loud.

He looked back at Jamaal. "You wish to have Mr. Antonelli serve as your lawyer, Mr. Washington?"

As soon as Jamaal had assured him that he did, the judge turned to the prosecutor. Haliburton reached inside the case file and extracted a single-page document.

"Let the record reflect," he announced with the routine solemnity that begins every criminal prosecution, "that I am handing the attorney for the defense a certified true copy of the information charging the defendant, Jamaal Washington, with the crime of murder in the first degree."

Without bothering to glance at it, I laid it face down on the table.

"Your honor," I said, turning back to the bench, "the defendant wishes to enter a plea of not guilty."

"A plea of not guilty will be entered," replied the judge impassively as he made the requisite notation in the court file.

"Your honor, I would ask that bail be set."

When he wanted to, Haliburton could get to his feet quick enough.

"The People oppose bail in any amount," he cried with great

energy. "I don't think I need to remind the court that this is a capital crime, or that the victim was a respected—no, a distinguished—public servant. The enormity of the crime, the risk of flight—either of those things by themselves, and certainly both together," he went on, pumping his hand in the air, "make bail or any other form of pretrial release simply unacceptable!"

Thompson did not look at him once while he spoke, and he did not look at him when he finished.

"The court will determine what is and what is not unacceptable," he remarked as he directed his attention to me. "Do you wish to be heard, Mr. Antonelli?"

"Your honor, the defendant has no criminal record. He is a student at the University of California. He is a lifelong resident of the city. And as you can see," I continued, pausing just long enough to look down at Jamaal, "he is confined to a wheelchair. There will be months of therapy before he can begin to walk again." I glanced quickly across at Haliburton. "Flight would not seem to be a very serious risk, your honor."

The judge seemed sympathetic, but how much of that was because of his obvious irritation with the district attorney I could not tell. He hesitated, as if he were trying to make up his mind.

"I'll set bail," he said finally, "in the amount of five hundred thousand dollars."

"Your honor," I started to protest, "this young man has no money; no one in his family has—"

The judge held up his hand, cutting me off.

"I believe you had another matter you wanted to raise with the court, Mr. Antonelli?"

The question of bail had been decided, and I knew better than to quarrel with a decision I could not change.

"Yes, your honor. I filed a motion with the court, and—"

Haliburton was back on his feet. "May counsel approach?" he asked as he began to walk around the table.

We huddled together at the side of the bench, out of earshot of the roomful of reporters. Haliburton had something he wanted to say about my motion, but he did not want to say it in public. Thompson looked at me. When I did not object, he waved his hand, motioning for us to return to our places.

"Court will be in recess," he announced. "I'll see counsel in chambers."

I did not know what to expect. I had written twice to the district attorney asking for the personnel files of the two police officers who had discovered Jamaal Washington in Jeremy Fullerton's car and then shot him in the back when he supposedly attempted to escape. When both letters were ignored, I filed a motion to compel. If the district attorney was not going to give me an answer, he could explain to the judge why he was unwilling to give me what I needed to defend my client.

Without a word, Judge Thompson gestured toward the two wooden chairs in front of his desk. As we sat down, he opened the court file, found the motion to compel, and began to read through it.

One side of the judge's desk was shoved against the wall. A three-drawer metal file cabinet stood in the corner behind his chair. On top of it was a stainless steel coffeepot and two white mugs discolored with age and chipped around the edges. Just above it, a grimy wire-covered glass window let in a gray lusterless light.

Thompson tossed the motion onto his desk. "So what's the problem?" he asked.

I was sitting next to the wall. I began to study the corroded sprockets jutting out from the base of the coffeepot, wondering how close the next person to plug it in would come to electrocution.

Thompson glared at Haliburton. "Shall I ask again?"

"No, you don't have to ask again," replied Haliburton, a caustic edge to his voice. "Antonelli is asking us to provide personnel files on police officers."

Thompson opened his palms. "I read the motion," he said, waiting to hear something he did not already know.

Haliburton let his eyes roam around the room, and then, shrugging his shoulders, he laughed. "We're just not going to do it."

My head began to beat back and forth, as if I were keeping time to a song I had listened to a thousand times before.

"You're 'just not going to do it'?" Thompson repeated the phrase as if it were the refrain of the most frequently indulged stupidity he had ever heard. Picking up a pencil, he drummed the eraser on his desk, a tight, cramped smile on his face. "You're 'just not going to do it'?"

"No, we're not. A United States senator was murdered, but Mr. Antonelli here wants to distract everyone with a little sideshow about the police. Apparently he's decided the way to defend his client is to make everyone believe his client was the victim instead of Jeremy Fullerton. Police personnel files don't have anything to do with whether or not the defendant committed the murder, and that, I thought, was the whole reason we were here!"

Judge Thompson tossed the pencil on the desk, threw himself back against his chair, and rolled his eyes. " 'And that, I thought, was the whole reason we were here.' Listen, Clarence, we both know the reason you're here. But if you think I'm going to let you use my courtroom to start your campaign for governor, you're out of your mind!"

I stared down at my black tasseled loafers. They needed a shine. Stretching out my legs, I rubbed first one shoe, then the other, against my pant cuffs.

Thompson moved forward, resting his elbows on the desk. "Who do you think you are? First you announce you're not going to comply with a motion on which no ruling has yet been made; then you give me a lecture on relevance?"

He picked up the pencil and began to tap the eraser against his thumbnail, staring hard at the district attorney.

Haliburton stared back but then, perhaps realizing that he had gone too far, tried to laugh it off as a simple misunderstanding. "Let's not get off on the wrong foot. It didn't come out the way I meant it. What I meant to say is that the People oppose the motion because—"

Thompson threw the pencil down on the desk. "Forget the motion."

I looked up from my shoes.

"Forget it. Let's just settle this thing right here and now."

He turned to me as if we were the only two people in the room. "Why don't you plead him to second-degree murder?" he asked calmly. "Apparently he had the victim's wallet. If it was a robbery and the gun went off in the struggle, then there was no premeditation. It's a good offer."

Stroking the bridge of my nose, I tried to give the impression that I was thinking it over. Judges were not always very fond of prosecutors, or lawyers generally, but I could not remember seeing anything quite like this. They hated each other. Thompson was trying to use me to make some point at the district attorney's expense. I was not there to be fair; I was there to win. I did what he wanted.

"Take it," he urged. "You won't be able to do any better."

"Well," I replied as if I were still a little uncertain, "you may be right about that." I looked him straight in the eye. "If you think this is the best way to resolve this, then yes, I'd certainly be willing to talk it over with my client."

"A wise decision," said Thompson, a shrewd glint in his gray eyes. He turned to Haliburton. "Then we have a deal?"

The district attorney was beside himself. "No, we do not have a deal," he said between clenched teeth. "There isn't going to be a deal, not unless he pleads to first-degree murder, and even then the People are going to seek the death penalty."

Judge Thompson shut his eyes and shook his head. An instant later his eyes shot wide open and he threw up his hands.

"That's it, then. No plea bargain, no mercy, nothing! You want to have your trial—have your circus—you're going to get it!"

He sat straight up, grabbed the pencil, and jabbed it up and down.

"On the question of Mr. Antonelli's motion to compel the production of . . . let's see, here."

Leafing quickly through the document, he found the language he was looking for.

"Yes. 'All documents, papers, memoranda, and reports, including, but not limited to, the official police department personnel records, pertaining to the conduct and performance of San Francisco police officer Marcus Joyner and San Francisco police officer Gretchen O'Leary.' "

With a grim, defiant smile, he looked at Haliburton. "Sounds about right to me. Motion granted."

Haliburton started to object but realized that anything he said now would only make matters worse.

"We'll do everything we can to make sure you have everything you want, Mr. Antonelli," he said frostily, his eyes still on Thompson.

"That's what the order says," was the judge's terse response.

Thumbing through a black leather-bound calendar that sat on the corner of his desk, Thompson asked how long we thought the trial would take. Haliburton was the first to reply.

"It's going to take a couple of months."

"It's not going to take a day more than three weeks," Thompson told him.

"It can't be done," the district attorney protested. "It's going to take that long to pick a jury."

Still studying his calendar, Thompson did not look up. "No," he said simply, a stern smile on his lips, "it will not." He closed the leather-bound book and announced the trial date. "Anyone object?"

We went back to the courtroom and took our places. The two of them had done nothing to disguise their contempt for each other in private, but now that they were once again in the public eye they treated each other with elaborate courtesy.

Judge Thompson asked, "Does the prosecution have something it wishes to take up at this time?"

"Yes, your honor," Haliburton replied, flashing a candidate's smile as he turned just enough so that the reporters crushed together on the benches behind him could glimpse his profile. "After a full and thorough discussion in chambers," he announced, "the matter raised by Mr. Antonelli has been resolved. I would therefore, for the record, indicate that the People do not oppose the motion—"

I was not about to let the prosecution appear more reasonable than the defense.

"Your honor," I interrupted, "Mr. Haliburton is entirely correct, and for that reason I would ask leave of the court to withdraw the motion to compel."

Almost drowning in goodwill, Judge Thompson turned to Haliburton.

"I assume this is acceptable? With the understanding, of course, that the discovery arrangements discussed in chambers will remain binding on the parties."

"Of course, your honor," Haliburton replied.

He waited until Thompson turned away.

"That leaves only the matter of the trial date, your honor."

He said it as if the judge might have forgotten it, and then, as if he were only trying to be helpful, reminded him of the date.

Grumbling beneath his breath, Thompson turned to me. "Do you have anything you wish to add, Mr. Antonelli?"

"No, your honor. I think Mr. Haliburton has covered it all."

Thompson rose from the bench. "Court stands adjourned," he announced as he slouched away.

The courtroom began to clear. A deputy sheriff began to wheel Jamaal away from the counsel table. I barely had time to whisper a few words of encouragement and promise to see him in the next day or so.

"Don't forget," he called to me over his shoulder.

Out of the corner of my eye, I noticed Haliburton coming around behind me on his way out of the courtroom. I began to put my copy of the document charging my client with murder into my briefcase when I felt his hand on my arm.

"You handled yourself well in there," he said, nodding toward the door behind which Judge Thompson had just vanished. He bent his head toward me so none of the reporters who were crowding the aisle, waiting to ask their questions, could overhear. "You haven't tried a case here before, have you? Things work a little differently in San Francisco." He leaned closer. "Forget what I said to Thompson. I'm willing to discuss a plea."

I turned toward him, but as I did, he slipped away, smiling

at the reporters as he opened the gate in the wooden railing. Bantering with them, he made his way toward the double doors in the back. I waited until they were gone and then followed. In the hallway outside, under a glaring white light, a battery of television cameras were trained on the district attorney. Staying close to the wall, I moved to the back of the crowd and watched.

Haliburton was used to this. In an instant he made himself into someone new. The sullen, lazy look on his face was replaced with an eager, energetic expression. He could hardly wait to answer any question anyone might want to ask. He stood as straight as a soldier on parade. He looked younger, more alert; there was a sparkle to his eyes that had not been there before. His voice, dull, caustic, and at times almost inaudible—an instrument of ridicule and derision except when in open court he had to say something on the record—was now warm, vibrant, insistent. It was the voice of someone who had convinced himself that if he could only talk long enough he could convince anyone of anything.

Surrounded by the media, Haliburton became something that was more their creation even than his own. With the unerring instinct of the successful democratic politician, he moved deftly from one frantic inquiry to the next, repeating as he went all the stock phrases, all the trivial expressions that were expected of him but managing somehow to make it sound as if they had never been said by anyone else before. He had even brought with him the requisite prepared statement.

"After a complete and thorough investigation, we have assembled enough evidence . . ."

He looked up from the text to stare directly into the black lens of the nearest television camera.

"More than enough evidence to obtain a conviction in the murder of United States Senator Jeremy Fullerton."

The hand that held the written statement dropped to his side.

"There will be no plea bargain, no deal, nothing to prevent justice from being done. Jeremy Fullerton was killed in a senseless act of slaughter, murdered for nothing more than the contents of his wallet. This case will go to trial."

Folding up the single sheet of white paper, Haliburton glanced at the sea of faces in front of him.

"At the end of that trial, the defendant, Jamaal Washington, will be convicted, and the People will ask that the death penalty be imposed."

I was certain that Haliburton had meant it when he told me that despite what he had said in front of the judge, he was open to a plea agreement; and as I watched his performance in front of the cameras, I was certain that he meant it when he told the world the case would go to trial. He was not the first politician, or the first lawyer, to care more for the immediate effect of what he said than the inconvenient question of whether it was entirely consistent with what he had said before. I had to admit, however, that I had never seen anyone change position so quickly or so often. I walked outside into the warm afternoon sun, laughing silently to myself as I suddenly remembered the childhood game, pulling the petals off a clover, repeating with a gambler's reliance on fate, 'She loves me, she loves me not.' It seemed to mimic perfectly the workings of Clarence Haliburton's mind.

A block away from the courthouse, people were moving up and down the sidewalks, intent on their own affairs, caught up in their own random thoughts, some perhaps as strange as my own. I waited for the light to change at the intersection and then stepped into the crosswalk. A car came hurtling around the corner, honking at me to get out of the way. My heart racing, I jumped back on the curb. Embarrassed by the way I had almost daydreamed my way into death, I tried to appear unshaken while I struggled to catch my breath. I started to step out again, but someone's hand held me back.

"It's red. Better wait for it to change."

The voice was like the echo from the bottom of a well, and it seemed strangely familiar. I looked around and found myself staring at someone I was certain I knew.

"Andrei Bogdonovitch," he reminded me.

The light turned green. He took me by the elbow as we began to cross the street. Besides the fact that it was so utterly unexpected, I had not recognized him because of the way he was dressed. At Albert Craven's dinner party, he had worn an expensive suit and Italian shoes. Now he was wearing a rather drab, loose-fitting brown sports jacket, dark gray slacks, and a pair of dusty brown loafers. He was not wearing a tie, and his white dress shirt, which looked as if he had worn it several days in a row, was open at the collar. At Craven's he had made an immediate impression; today he blended in with the crowd, just another face no one would notice.

"I was wondering, Mr. Antonelli, whether you might be free for lunch? I've been wanting to talk to you."

He still had hold of my elbow when we reached the other side of the street. There was something a little uncomfortable about the way he held on to me, as if I were being guided somewhere without being told the destination. Something in the tone of his voice told me that our meeting had not after all been a matter of chance.

"Were you at the courthouse?" I asked as I turned toward him, disengaging my arm.

"Yes. It's quite a madhouse over there, isn't it?" He paused and nodded thoughtfully. "Yes. I followed you out of the courthouse. It was too crowded in there to talk." His eyes, sunk into his broad face, started to shine. "You move faster than I do. I couldn't catch up until you had to stop for the light. By the way," he added, a caution in his voice, "you could have been killed."

His tone seemed genuine, and I regretted that a moment before I had felt uncomfortable having his hand on my arm.

"I'd be delighted to have lunch with you," I replied apologetically to his invitation, "but I'm afraid I already have an engagement. As a matter of fact," I added, glancing up the street, "I'm on my way there now."

Bogdonovitch smiled politely, but disappointment, and perhaps something more, passed over his eyes. He took hold of my arm again, not on the elbow, but around the wrist, and with surprising strength held it tight.

"I have to talk to you, Mr. Antonelli. It's very important."

With a curt nod, he let go of my wrist and, without waiting for a reply, turned on his heel and disappeared into the crowd.

I stared after him, stunned both by his sudden insistence that he had to see me and by his abrupt and apparently angry departure. I began to walk up the street, wondering what could possibly be so important. That night at Albert Craven's he had given me such a strange look, as if there were things he wanted me to know, things he did not want to take up in front of the others. But if that was it, why had he waited for two weeks, and why had he thought it necessary to wait for me after court instead of just picking up the telephone? Andrei Bogdonovitch was one of the more interesting men I had met, but I was beginning to wonder if there was something not quite right about him.

Seven

When he had invited me, Albert Craven apologized for not having asked me sooner. It was not because he was not interested in the case and what I was doing, he insisted. He simply had not had the time to do anything except concentrate on a particularly complicated civil matter that had, he was glad to report, finally come to an end. As I headed toward the entrance to his building, he signaled from the open window of a limousine parked in front.

"I thought we might have lunch at my country club," he said amiably as I climbed in. He tapped the driver on the shoulder. "Lake Merced."

Sinking back against the corner of the plush leather seat, he started to say something, then shook his head and began to search through his pockets.

"Yes, here it is," he said as he extracted a small piece of paper from his left suit coat pocket. Fumbling for his glasses, he studied what someone else had written.

"This came in just before I left," he explained. "The district attorney called and left a message that he was serious about what he said and that if you wanted to discuss it further to please call him as soon as possible."

Craven was not sure what to make of my reaction. "It strikes you as funny?"

"We go into chambers and he tells the judge—Thompson—that there isn't going to be any plea bargain. As we're leaving court, he tells me to forget what he said to the judge. Then, two minutes later, he's out in the hallway promising the world that there's going to be a trial, but only because you have to have one before you can have an execution. And now, apparently the moment he gets back to his office, he calls to let me know I should not take seriously anything he says to anyone else."

Craven formed his small mouth into a knowing smile. " 'Haliburton the halfhearted.' He's always like that. He says things for effect, not because he means them. He wants to use this case for everything he can get out of it. That doesn't mean he wants to spend the next several months slugging it out in a trial."

I corrected him. "Three weeks."

"Three weeks for a murder trial?" He was astonished but then, a moment later, certain he knew the reason. "Haliburton said it would take more time, and Thompson told him he couldn't have it. Am I right?" he asked, eager to know.

When I told him that he was, he beamed.

"They really hate each other," he explained, without any apparent regret that they did.

I asked him why they hated each other.

He leaned toward me, a shrewd grin on his face. "They've hated each other so long they don't know why themselves. But I know why. They started out together, years ago, in the district attorney's office, both of them just out of law school. Like any other new assistant D.A.s, they started with misdemeanor cases.

After a few months, Haliburton got promoted to felony cases. Thompson had to wait more than a year."

Craven gazed out the window as the limousine maneuvered through traffic on its way out of the city. I waited for him to look back and go on with the story of why Haliburton and Thompson had such contempt for each other. But when he did finally turn around, it was only to comment on the weather.

"What happened between them?" I asked, still waiting. "Why do they hate each other so much?"

"I just told you," he said with a shrug. "Haliburton was promoted first."

"That's it?" I asked. "That's all there was?"

There was a sort of benevolence in the way he looked at me, a kind of sad resignation to the follies, the stupidities, and perhaps even the crimes of human beings.

"When you think about it, that's really quite a lot," he suggested. "Thompson and Haliburton were two ambitious young men, and at the very beginning of their careers—the beginning of their lives, really—one of them is judged better than the other."

Craven moved closer, his eyes searching mine. "How do you imagine Thompson felt—how would you have felt? Don't you think you would have resented it—thought it was unfair, and maybe even worse than that: an object lesson in favoritism? But now turn it around. How do you imagine Haliburton felt? Do you think it did anything to make him more modest, less ambitious, less certain that he was always going to be a success? You've met him. Do you think it had no effect on what he thought about Thompson or on the way he treated him? It seems to me that for anyone watching at the time it would not have been too difficult to guess that those two were going to be enemies for life."

I had thought Albert Craven pretentious and superficial, endlessly engaged in finding something clever and outrageous to say in the presence of one or the other of his hundreds of ephemeral friends. But I was beginning to discover that he had an insight into the nature of human beings that was nothing like the shallow optimism so often exuded by the character he usually played.

We arrived at Lake Merced. Craven told the driver to come back in two hours. The flag in front of the clubhouse, hanging like all the others in California at half-mast to honor the memory of Jeremy Fullerton, flapped quietly in the gentle midday wind. A few desultory voices could be heard coming from the far side of the long low one-story wooden frame building, as the members of a foursome, adding up their totals, made their way from the eighteenth hole to the locker room. The spikes on their golf shoes tapped out a leisurely cadence on the blacktop path.

Everyone knew Albert Craven. We must have stopped half a dozen times on our way across the cafeteria-sized dining room to the table that, if he did not own it outright, had always been available for him, to exchange a word or two with another old friend. It was a weekday and the restaurant was not quite half full. If there was a man there under forty, he looked older than his age. The only women were middle-aged waitresses who moved at the unhurried pace of an accustomed routine. Except for the presence of a bar, where two gray-haired men in alpaca sweaters passed a dice cup back and forth, wagering for drinks, it might have been the dining hall of a retirement home.

The table Albert Craven had occupied for more than a quarter century was in the far corner, at the juncture of the windows that ran from the floor to the ceiling. Outside, as far as the eye could see, sunlit green fairways cut through forests of fir and cypress trees. In the distance, a single golfer, his arms brought back over his shoulders, the long thin club gripped tight in his hands, watched the flight of a ball I was too far away to see.

"What do you see when you look out there?" asked Craven after he ordered us both a drink.

"You mean other than a golf course?"

"Yes, exactly. That's what everyone sees. It's rather a stupid question, isn't it? Look around this room. They've all been coming here for years, playing golf, eating lunch, drinking—some of them—more than they should, telling stories, telling lies, telling themselves what great lives they have. There isn't one person here who could tell you that just out there," he said, pointing toward where the golfer who had just hit his shot was trudging up the fairway, "is the place where, before Jeremy Fullerton was murdered, and before Bobby Kennedy was killed, the last United States senator was shot to death in California."

The waitress came with our drinks. Craven thanked her by name and watched her walk away.

"Nice woman," he said as he took a sip.

"Well," he went on, his face all lit up, "I suppose you can't really blame anyone for not remembering. It was a few years back." He had already begun to smile at what he was about to say. "A few years, and then some. Before the Civil War, actually: 1859. September thirteenth, to be precise. There wasn't a golf course here then." He said this as if it were a kind of dark secret that, should it become widely known, might reduce the value of membership. "There wasn't anything here then. Just the lake, on the border between the counties of San Francisco and San Mateo. I suppose that was the reason they chose the place: the seclusion, and perhaps some grasp of the technical difficulties in determining jurisdiction if the authorities had tried to stop it. You see, it wasn't exactly a murder; it was a duel, the last public duel with guns ever fought in California. It was a duel, believe it or not, between David S. Terry, a judge of the state supreme court, and Senator David Broderick. They were both Democrats, which, despite what my Republican friends would think, doesn't explain anything. Broderick, the senator, opposed slavery, and Terry, the judge, was part of what was then called the pro-South 'Chivalry' wing of the California Democratic Party."

Pausing long enough to take another sip, Craven's pale blue eyes widened.

"The judge seems to have been one of these people who have to keep pushing things. He could not help himself. He had to start making derogatory remarks about the anti-slavery wing; the senator, who was clearly in the right, called the judge a 'miserable wretch.' Well, that was all it took for the peculiar southern sensibilities of the judge. He challenged the senator to a duel. Later, there were allegations that the pistols were supplied by an associate of the judge and that the one given the senator had a hair trigger which caused it to fire early, but the only thing known for certain is that the judge's pistol worked perfectly. The senator was shot dead early that morning, September thirteenth, 1859, right out there, where that fellow is now trying to sink his putt."

"What happened to the judge?" I asked, staring out the window toward the red flag flying in the far distance above the green.

"To his credit—or his discredit, depending on how you look at these things—he was true to what he believed. When the war broke out, he joined the Confederate army and rose to the rank of brigadier general. What he actually did in the war, I don't know. But he survived it and eventually came back to California and retired to Stockton."

After a long pause, Craven added, "There was a peculiar twist to the whole thing. Terry must have had a more-than-usual taste for violence, or perhaps a more-than-normal hatred of the government. In 1889, exactly thirty years after he shot to death a United States senator, he tried to shoot a United States Supreme Court justice. Stephen Field, a fairly famous justice in his time, was attacked at the train station in Lathrop. The attack failed. Terry was shot and killed by Stephen Field's bodyguard."

The waitress came back to the table and patted Craven on the shoulder.

"Do you need menus?" she asked, smiling down at him with the affection of an old friend.

"Margaret," he said, patting her hand, "I want you to meet Joseph Antonelli. He's going to be with us for a while."

We exchanged a greeting and with a wink she gave me some advice. "Don't let him talk you into the bean soup."

"But I always have the bean soup," he protested, nudging his shoulder against her hip. "Well, all right," he went on with a quick glance at me. "I'll have the bean soup, but you can bring him a hamburger. Mr. Antonelli prefers that to just about anything."

A wistful look in his eye, Craven watched as the waitress ambled serenely toward the kitchen.

"Twenty years ago, when she first came to work here, men would have left their wives for the chance to spend the night with her." His eyes came back around to me. "A few of them did."

I leaned back and studied him for a moment. "You've been talking to Marissa, haven't you?"

Craven's eyebrows shot up. "Yes, Marissa. She's one of my favorite people, you know. And now I'm afraid you're about to steal her away."

Reaching quickly across the table, he took my wrist. His hand was soft, pliable, without a callus or a rough edge anywhere. "No, I'm teasing. We're very old friends, Marissa and I, and if I have a certain almost parental affection for her it's because—well, it's because she's so much more interesting than most of the other women I know."

Frowning, he thought about what he had just said.

"That's not exactly right. The rest of the women I know—and I know quite a lot of them—" he assured me, "are all very nice and all and, despite what I just said, all really quite interesting. But Marissa—and this is really quite astonishing when you consider how outlandish Marissa can be at times—is about the only one of them who isn't, underneath it all, quite fraudulent."

It was closer to what he wanted to say. Enlivened by his success, he bounced once on the edge of the chair.

"I really think she's the only woman I know—the only one over thirty-five, at any rate—who hasn't had major plastic surgery. Do you know," he went on, a droll smile on his round lips, "most of my so-called friends have a private hospital they go to? I think it even has an emergency room entrance where they go every Sunday night or Monday morning to repair the weekend damage. It's true!" His small eyes danced with irreverent delight. "Why do you think these people are always endowing hospitals? They're blackmailed into it!" he chortled.

"I like Marissa," he said, suddenly quite serious. "Maybe she's the only one I really do like. Is that true? I wonder. Yes, well, perhaps it is."

His eyes wandered around the room, as if searching for someone who could tell him for sure. He looked back at me.

"I think it must be because of the money."

"The money?" I asked blankly.

His eyes made another circuit of the dining room.

"Money is everywhere now," he said vaguely. The solemn expression that had begun to cloud his visage vanished, replaced with the same ebullience with which, just a moment earlier, he had regaled me with stories about private hospitals and overnight cosmetic surgeries.

"It's just another way that Marissa is different from most of my other female friends. Women in this city—well, let's just say they have in common a wonderful instinct for the vanity of men. Older, rich men, you understand. It's really quite shrewd, the way they put that instinct of theirs to work. They don't just attract older men, they marry them, and because the men they marry are always so much older, their husbands are always dying and leaving them vast sums of money. I can't tell you how much I admire the sheer intelligence involved in all this. Think of it. They have their social position because, of course, they still have their husband's name; and they have everything else they want because now, of course, they also have their dead husband's money. The best part is that there are always other older men to marry. Of course, when they do that," he added confidentially, "they keep their former married names as well as their new one. I mean, why give up the obvious advantages of a well-known name—especially, let's face it, a name known for money? After a while"—he snorted, leaning back against the chair as he placed both his hands in his lap—"you begin to wonder if some of them haven't somewhere along the line made a mistake and somehow managed to marry themselves!"

Craven's eyes fluttered like the flag outside. For a moment, he stroked his small, barely visible chin.

"Marissa isn't like that at all. She earned her money." A smile started at the corners of his mouth. "You didn't know she had money, did you? No, of course not. It's not something she would ever talk about. Good. Well, she does. And she certainly didn't get it from that husband of hers. After her divorce she went out on her own—no help from anyone, just her own talent. She started a clothing line, very small at first; then she opened a store, then a few more, and now of course a whole chain."

"A whole chain," I repeated dumbly. "She said something about a store. The Way of All Flesh."

Craven laughed and then told me the name, the very famous name, of the stores Marissa owned. I am not certain whether it made her more or less interesting, more or less attractive; all I knew for sure was that it made her seem different than the woman in whose company I had grown surprisingly at ease. I felt in a strange way betrayed, as if it were something she should have told me; and I wondered if the reason she had not was because she sensed that I might not like her quite so much if I knew how much she had.

The waitress brought Craven his bowl of bean soup and set a plate with a hamburger and a small mound of coleslaw in front of me. She tucked a cloth napkin into Craven's collar and spread it out over his shirt and tie. It was apparently something she always did. He kept on talking while she did it and did nothing by way of acknowledgment when she finished. He lifted the spoon, blew on the hot soup, took a first, tentative taste, and then, wincing slightly, set it down to cool a little longer.

"They haven't changed the menu since I first became a member. They haven't changed the soup, either. I think they made a huge batch ten or twenty years ago and they just keep adding a few more things, stirring it up, a little more every day." He lifted the spoon again, repeated the same ritual, but this time began to eat.

"I ran into your friend Andrei Bogdonovitch outside the courthouse today," I told Craven. "It wasn't an accident. He followed me. He said he had to see me about something. Do you have any idea what it might be about?"

Craven seemed surprised. "He followed you?"

"From the courthouse. If he wanted to talk to me, why wouldn't he just have called?"

The response was a reminder that I did not have a telephone, much less a number of my own. I was about to suggest that Bogdonovitch might have left a message the same way the district attorney had.

"You forget. He was a spy. I can't imagine he talks very much on the telephone."

"Not even to invite someone to lunch?" I replied, not at all convinced.

"Not if he didn't want anyone else to know," he suggested with a serious look.

Craven stirred his soup, then let go of the spoon. "I've known Andrei for years, since sometime in the late sixties. He was with the Soviet Consulate, but he was very adept at moving in all the right social circles. Try to imagine what he was like then: younger, but with that same Old World charm and that same rich, cultured voice. People who met him forgot he was a communist and remembered only that he was Russian. He talked about Tolstoy and Pushkin and every great writer Russia ever had; he never mentioned Marx or Lenin. And he never talked politics. Never. He was KGB. There's no doubt of it. But I was always convinced that he was still a decent and a generous man. He was on the other side, that's all. And I don't think it was necessarily the side he would have chosen for himself."

"He did choose sides, though, didn't he? He defected."

Holding his hands just below his chin, Craven tapped his fingers together and looked out the window, down the long stretch of fairway to the flag that fluttered above the green, the place where the judge had shot the senator.

"There was really only one side left," he observed dispassionately. "Did he defect? Who knows? He says he just decided to stay. One thing I can tell you about him for sure: He never lies, and he never tells the whole truth. There's something else," he said, still gazing out the window. "He never gives answers; he just asks questions that seem like answers." Craven's head turned until his eyes met mine. "That business about the Kennedy assassination, for example."

I had not forgotten what Bogdonovitch had said that night at dinner, nor the way he had said it.

"And J. Edgar Hoover."

"Yes, exactly," said Craven, nodding his head. "He didn't say anything, did he? But he certainly left the impression that he had. He does that; he's always done that. Andrei Bogdonovitch is an engaging, intelligent man, as well read as anyone I know, and he has an absolute genius for concealment. It would be interesting to know what he wants to see you about."

The conversation drifted off into a discussion of the working arrangements of my stay in San Francisco while I prepared for the trial. Craven was not only paying my fee, but covering all the expenses as well. He had only one condition, but it was a condition on which he insisted. I was to tell no one that he had any involvement in the case beyond the fact that he had helped Jamaal Washington's mother find a lawyer and that, because my cousin was his partner, I had been given the use of the office. The check for my fee would be issued from an account he had with a European bank.

"I have a lot of friends in the city," was the only explanation he offered. I did not have to ask if one of them was Lawrence Goldman.

We were standing outside, waiting for the limousine that was just pulling into the parking lot, when he told me that though he had to be discreet, he did not have to be, nor would he be, disengaged.

"I know all about your reputation. I know you know how to win. But this case is different. It involves too many people. Jeremy Fullerton affected too many lives. There aren't that many people really interested in the truth. You need to understand something about these people, and about Fullerton, if you're going to have any chance to find out what really happened that night. I can help you with some of that. I hope you don't mind," he added as we got into the back seat of the limousine, "but I already have."

"Have what?" I asked as I stretched my arm across the back of the seat and turned toward him.

"Have tried to help. I've made arrangements," he said, turning away from me to stare out the window, "for you to see Meredith Fullerton, Jeremy Fullerton's widow."

He did not say anything more about it. From the bleak look on his face as he continued to stare out the window, it was apparent that he did not want to be asked. We drove along in silence, the only sound the tires humming over the road. The soft smooth skin on Albert Craven's cheek was no longer pink and blooming but a sallow, lifeless gray. For a moment I thought he might have become ill, but then I remembered that when they were just a little tired, old men could suddenly show their age. His mouth opened, as if there were something he wanted to say, but then he closed it and a moment later shut his eyes. We kept driving, surrounded by that monotonous hum, and I wondered if he might have fallen asleep. Smiling to myself, I turned away and watched out my own window as the shop fronts and houses slipped by as we drew closer to the city.

"I've lived here all my life, and I'm still mystified by it," I heard him say, his voice again surprisingly strong and clear.

I looked over my shoulder and saw him gesturing out toward the crowded office buildings as we crossed Market Street and waited behind a cable car on Powell.

"Sometimes I'm not sure it really exists, that it isn't all a dream. Do you know," he said as if what he was about to tell me would explain what he meant, "both my grandmothers lived through the earthquake of 1906. One of them swore that when it was over, Enrico Caruso came out on the balcony of the Palace Hotel where he had spent the night and, to calm everyone, sang an aria. My other grandmother swore that he came out on the balcony and was still so scared that when he opened his mouth to sing, nothing came out."

The driver parked in front of Craven's building and held open the door. "The appointment with Mrs. Fullerton is for this evening," Craven informed me as we went inside. "Six o'clock. I'm sorry it's such short notice. It was the best I could do. She's leaving town tomorrow, and God knows when she'll be back." He hesitated and then added, "Don't believe what anybody tells you about her. In her own way, she's quite a remarkable woman. I don't know anyone else who would have put up with what she did all those years."

Eight

It was the ultimate San Francisco address. The Spreckles, the Stanfords, the Huntingtons: the men who for a while owned a large part of California, and no inconsiderable part of America, had all lived here, high above the city with a view that had once taken in nearly all the bay. The streets that led up to it were almost impossible to climb, but they never walked when they could ride, and anyone who could not afford to ride had no business being there. Later, when the new hotels—the Fairmont, the Mark Hopkins—were built on the rubble of the old stone mansions, automobiles were allowed to park perpendicular to the curb lest they slip loose and plummet straight down to the bottom. The cement sidewalks were grooved like washboards to give traction to those who, with shoulders hunched forward and heads bent low, tried to walk, and something for their fingernails to grab on to if they fell.

We used to come here, Bobby and I, on summer Saturday nights when the fog rolled in and made the sidewalks slick, just to watch tall women in high heels and tight dresses grab the front fenders of cars parked like steps in a long horizontal row and, like children hanging on to the rails of a staircase, try to lower themselves down the street. All the glamour, all the mystery of San Francisco seemed to be concentrated right here in this one place, the top of Nob Hill.

Though it was only half a dozen blocks away, I hailed a cab and watched out the window at the way the early evening light softened the hard edges of the buildings and added a kind of bittersweet luster to the faces of the people who wandered down the street. At the top of the hill, the driver pulled up in front of a dark green awning. For no reason at all, I gave him a tip that doubled his fare; and then lingered for a moment, basking in the illusion that I was still young enough to be on my way to a date with a beautiful rich woman who lived on Nob Hill. As the cab drove off, I looked down the block at Grace Cathedral. Despite its gothic spires, the architect who designed it had without apparent irony called it a "truly American cathedral." He must have meant that it was something borrowed by money.

The doorman said that Mrs. Fullerton was expecting me and that her place was on the top floor. The elevator creaked and groaned as it made its way up. I tried to think of a worse place to be in an earthquake. Each tiny jolt made me more nervous. I could see the steel-threaded cable that twisted up the coffinlike shaft begin to unravel and then tear itself apart the moment—a moment that might be just a second away—there was a slight shift of the tectonic plates on which San Francisco floated over the earth. When the door opened on the fourteenth floor, I stepped out as if I had just landed on solid ground.

Jeremy Fullerton had been famous, and his picture, which had been seen often enough while he was alive, had been everywhere after his death. But even in the photographs that were run in conjunction with the murder I could not recall having once seen a picture of his wife. Fullerton had been a few months short of his forty-sixth birthday on the date he died; because he had been married only once, and married when he was still quite young, I assumed she must be about the same age. From what I had heard about her behavior at the private party the night the senator was murdered, I imagined a graying woman filled with self-doubt, disturbed at the prospect of having grown too old to keep her husband from a younger, more beautiful woman. What I found was something completely different.

With ash-blond hair swept straight back from her forehead and light, luminous eyes, Meredith Fullerton had a face that, if not so beautiful as it must once have been, was perhaps more interesting. There was something noble about her face, something that told you that you were in the presence of a woman of exquisite sensibility and unusual intelligence. In a room full of strangers, all of them trying to meet everyone else, she would have been the one, the only one, who let everyone come to her.

"Thank you for coming, Mr. Antonelli."

She spoke those ordinary words with a kind of quiet grace. Had I not known what she must have been going through, it might have made me feel like an invited guest rather than a stranger intruding on her grief.

She led me into the living room and asked if I would care to join her in a drink.

"I was glad when I was told you wanted to see me, Mr. Antonelli," she said, handing me a glass. "I know that the boy you're representing didn't kill my husband."

She gestured toward the sofa but remained standing while I sat down.

"Jeremy thought nothing could touch him; he thought that nothing could stop him. I think that in a way he thought he would live forever." She paused, searching my eyes. "Have you ever known anyone like that, Mr. Antonelli?"

She asked the question as if she were certain I had and that this created a sort of bond between us, an acknowledgment of our own unspoken imperfections.

"Jeremy wasn't like other people," she went on.

She began to walk slowly around the room, her gaze landing on one thing and then drifting away to something else.

"Jeremy was the most intelligent man I ever knew," she said as her eyes came back to me. "That's one description of him I'm sure you haven't read, but he was. Americans distrust serious people, Mr. Antonelli. Jeremy convinced everyone that while he had a great admiration for literature and the arts, he really preferred the same kind of books and the same kind of music as everyone else."

A proud, almost defiant expression flashed across her face. Then, suddenly, she laughed.

"Do you know what he used to do? He would be giving a speech somewhere and he would quote someone famous—Lincoln or Churchill or someone like that—a quotation he had inserted himself—and then he'd look up with that bashful grin of his and say something like, 'My speechwriters like to let me know how smart they are.'

"You see what he was doing?" she went on, anxious that someone should know the truth about her husband. "He was giving the speech he wanted to give, a serious speech, and he was doing it in a way that seemed to say, 'Look, I'm no smarter than you are.' But it was more than that, you see; much more. He was also saying, 'We may not be the smartest people in the world, but we know when something has been said we should take seriously.' I think he was trying to get them to listen to themselves, to what they would say if they knew how to say what they felt deep down, in that private, lonely place where everyone really is serious."

Meredith Fullerton sat down on the facing sofa and placed her glass on the coffee table between us.

"I buried my husband, Mr. Antonelli. Everyone was there: the president, the vice president, the governor. The services were right across the street," she added, nodding toward the window. "Grace Cathedral. Jeremy would have loved that."

She picked up her glass, and while she drank, the pale reflection of nostalgia entered her eyes.

"We lived over there when we were first married," she said, nodding again toward the window as she rose from the sofa and walked toward it. From where she stood, you could see the Golden Gate and, farther on, past the steep untouched hillside that curved north along the bay, the village of Sausalito, sheltered at the water's edge.

"We lived over there because it made more sense for Jeremy's political career, but there was another reason as well."

Lingering at the window, a faint smile hovering over her mouth, she watched the place she had lived with her husband recede into the shadows while the bay still sparkled with the soft golden light of a late summer day.

"Did you ever read *The Great Gatsby*, Mr. Antonelli?" she asked, her eyes still fixed on something perhaps only she could see. "Remember the green light? This was Jeremy's green light— San Francisco. He was in love with it, the way Gatsby was in love with Daisy, the Daisy of his dream, the dream he had dreamed all those years he was trying to make his fortune and become what he thought she wanted him to be. In Gatsby's mind she had never changed, never grown older, never been married, never had a child: She was always the beautiful girl, ageless, unchanging." Jeremy Fullerton's widow went on in a slow, melodic voice that sometimes grew so faint I could barely make out the words.

She leaned against the window, her eyes pensive and dark, a furtive smile flickering like candlelight on her mouth.

"Jeremy started with nothing, and he loved the city, and he knew he had no chance to be anyone unless he became somebody else, made money, did something to be noticed. We lived there, in a small house on the hill, and every night he would sit there, watching, thinking about how it was all going to happen, how he would become the one the city loved.

"Sometimes, late at night, after the bars closed and the tourists had gone, we would wander down to the end of the main street of Sausalito and watch the lights of the city dance on the dark black waters of the bay. You should do that sometime, Mr. Antonelli—stand out there late at night, breathing the cool sweet air, and look across at San Francisco rising up from the center of the bay like Babylon rising up from the desert.

"It was everything he wanted: It was the city of his youth, the city of his dreams, the one place—the only place, I suppose— where he never felt the urge to leave or had the feeling there was someplace else he ought to be. He'd stand there next to me, and I knew he was thinking of her—the city. It was like he was watching the girl he loved dancing at her wedding to someone else, someone she had married for money and could never really love; not the way, deep down, he knew she really loved him.

"I think that is what he wanted more than anything else. The House, the Senate, even the presidency; part of the reason— maybe the only reason—he wanted any of that was so he could be the center of everyone's attention, the only one the city really loved."

Her arms folded in front of her, she kept looking out across the bay to where they had started the beginning of a journey that had now reached its end. After a while, she looked at me over her shoulder.

"He ended up like Gatsby, too," she said with a strange detachment, as if she were describing someone she had not seen for years. "Murdered, and no one really cares why. Oh, they all came to the funeral, and they all said all the right things; but they were glad he was gone. He was an outsider; he didn't belong; and he was going to take something away that belonged to them: their power, and much more than their power—their sense of their own importance, their sense of who they were. One of them killed him. I'm sure of it."

She looked out the window, then glanced back as if there were something more she wanted to say. Instead, she just shook her head.

"Is there anything else you can tell me?" I asked tentatively. "Anything your husband might have said?"

She became quite still, and very quiet.

"A few weeks before he was killed," she said presently, "Jeremy had a private meeting at the White House with the president, just the two of them, late at night. The president told Jeremy that if he beat Augustus Marshall, if he became governor, and then tried to run against him for the nomination, Jeremy would never survive. Jeremy joked that he thought the president meant that he would not survive politically, but that there had been something about the way he said it that left him a little unsure."

I was watching her as closely as I could, trying to figure out what she really knew and what she simply wanted to believe. No one wants to accept a meaningless death. No matter how famous, no one remembers the victim of a random act of violence the same way they do someone who dies for their country or is murdered because powerful people are afraid of what he might do.

"Strange, the way things happen," said Mrs. Fullerton. "No

one could beat Jeremy. That was why the president was so worried. Jeremy was so far ahead of the governor that some people—the ones who like to get quoted in the papers—were starting to say that the only way Augustus Marshall could get reelected was to do the same thing he had done the first time he won a statewide election."

I was not from California and I had no idea what she meant.

"Hope that his opponent died," she explained. "Years ago, Augustus Marshall ran for attorney general in the Republican primary. He was running against the Republican incumbent, who was enormously popular, and he was not given any chance at all. Then, a few weeks before the primary, the attorney general had a heart attack and died."

I lowered my eyes and tried to think of a decent way to excuse myself. Meredith Fullerton knew no more about the death of her husband than I did. Glancing at my watch, I got to my feet.

"It's getting late. I've taken enough of your time."

She turned toward me, a slender, sympathetic smile on her mouth.

"You're right, Mr. Antonelli. I don't know who killed my husband. I can't help you in that way. But I do know a few things you might find helpful."

For an instant, I caught in her eyes a glimpse of the lonely desperation of a woman who does not know what to do. Then it was gone, hidden behind the elegant manner of a woman for whom the worst sin was to inflict her own suffering on someone else.

"I think I need a cup of coffee," she said as she began to walk across the room. "Why don't you have one with me?"

I followed her into a long, narrow kitchen and took one of the two chairs at a small round table next to the only window.

With one hand on the corner of the stainless steel stove and one foot locked behind the other, Meredith Fullerton, lost in thoughts of her own, waited for the kettle to boil. When it began finally to steam, she carefully measured two spoonfuls of instant coffee into one of the two mugs she had taken down from a cupboard above the sink. Then, glancing over at me to make sure she was right, she put one spoonful in the other.

She sat down across from me, holding her cup in both hands. The warmth of it seemed to give her some comfort. With her eyes closed, she took several slow breaths.

"You should talk to Robert Zimmerman—Jeremy's administrative assistant," she said after she sipped tentatively on her coffee. "I'm afraid I never liked him very much, but he was devoted to Jeremy. He came to see me day before yesterday. He'd come out for the funeral, of course, but then had gone back to Washington. He called last Saturday and asked if he could come out to see me. I thought he was coming to talk about what we should do about Jeremy's Senate papers, but it wasn't that at all. He wanted to talk about the campaign."

Confused, I put down my cup. "Campaign?"

"Jeremy's campaign for governor. I hadn't thought about it at all, not since the night Jeremy was killed. Good God, that was the last thing I would have thought about!" A rueful smile started onto her lips. "But of course that's all that some people had been thinking about. In politics—and perhaps not just in politics—that's all anyone's death really means: what it does to someone else's chances."

Narrowing her eyes, she sipped some more on her coffee. "You remember that famous old phrase: 'The king is dead, long live the king'? Well, Jeremy is dead, so Augustus Marshall can still have his own dream about becoming president; the president can still dream about a second term; and someone else can dream about running for governor and—who knows?—something else as well."

With each word she seemed to become more tense. Peering intently into my eyes, she asked, "Can you guess who that is going to be, Mr. Antonelli? Can you guess who is going to take my husband's place as the candidate for governor against Augustus Marshall?"

"No, I'm sorry," I said, fumbling for an answer.

"Do you know who Lawrence Goldman is?"

"He's going to run for governor?"

"No, Mr. Antonelli," she said, a disdainful expression on her face. "He's not going to run—his daughter is."

"The one who worked for your husband?"

"That's right: the one who worked for my husband. Ariella Goldman is about to become the Democratic candidate for governor. The politicians who run the state party will make the decision this weekend, but it's just a formality: It's already done. They've been working on it from the very beginning—the day after Jeremy was murdered. Robert Zimmerman told me all about it. Ariella called him on Sunday—the day after the murder—and told him she thought they should keep the campaign together. She told him she had already talked to Toby Hart, who was running the campaign, and that Hart had agreed. She told him Jeremy would have wanted them to keep fighting for the things he stood for."

Meredith Fullerton stared out the window. Lights were beginning to flicker around the long arc of the bay as the first stars began to appear high in the darkening sky.

"Robert Zimmerman knew then that something was going on. What was she doing, asking Toby Hart to stay on? She wasn't running the campaign: She was a speechwriter."

Mrs. Fullerton looked back around at me. "But of course she

was a lot more than that, wasn't she? She was Lawrence Goldman's daughter. Robert understood: The Goldmans—father and daughter—were taking over. But even then it never occurred to him that Ariella might become the candidate or that her father might use all his influence and however much money it took to make his daughter the next governor and—who knows?—the next president."

She stared down into her cup for a moment, smiling to herself.

"You don't believe that's possible, do you, Mr. Antonelli?" she asked, as she looked up. "With enough money, you can buy almost anything."

She still had not told me anything that could prove that any of the powerful people who had had something to gain by the death of her husband had had anything to do with his murder. The eager willingness of Lawrence Goldman and his daughter to take advantage of a death was perhaps unseemly but no more damning and, from the point of view of the young man I was defending, no more helpful than the private relief both the governor and the president may have felt at the elimination of a formidable competitor.

"What happened that night?" I asked as I put down my cup. "You were with your husband at the dinner at the Fairmont and then, later, at a gathering at Lawrence Goldman's apartment, weren't you?"

She got up and went over to the stove. "Would you like another cup?" she asked as she turned on the burner.

I shook my head by way of reply. "Why weren't you with him later on—when he went to his car?"

Staring at the kettle, she tapped her fingernails against the hard metal surface of the stainless steel range. "After the dinner,

I came back here." She looked up. "I couldn't stand Lawrence Goldman," she explained.

Turning back to the kettle, she began to tap her foot on the white tile floor. The water in the kettle was still warm and did not take long to boil.

"I didn't like Lawrence Goldman," she said evenly, stirring two teaspoons of instant coffee into the cup of hot water. "Watching the way everyone fawned over him made my skin crawl. It's amazing how little self-respect some people have in the presence of someone with money."

Holding the cup just below her mouth, she sat down and blew on the scalding black liquid until it was cool enough to drink.

"I heard about what happened there that night, with Lawrence Goldman's daughter," I said as gently as I could.

She took another sip, then put down the cup and smiled.

"Yes. Strange that even now I feel compelled to lie about it. That was stupid of me. I apologize. Yes, it's true: Ariella Goldman was sleeping with my husband. Jeremy was always sleeping with someone. You must have heard that about him, Mr. Antonelli."

I started to deny it, but she shook her head emphatically.

"No, Mr. Antonelli, don't. But you can't judge him too harshly." She started to blink her eyes, trying to keep herself under control. "That's the way he was," she said, almost defiantly. "Or the way he became." Her chest heaved up and her hand shot to her eyes. "I'm sorry," she mumbled as she got to her feet. Pulling the sleeve of her dress around her hand, she used it to wipe her eyes.

"I thought I couldn't cry anymore," she said, trying to smile through the tears. "But, God, now that he is gone I wish they would just leave him alone."

I stood up and touched her gently on the shoulder. "Is there anything I can do?"

If she heard me, she ignored me.

"I told him he had to stop it. I knew there had been other women. But I told him he had to stop with her," she said, growing more agitated. "She was using him; and what was even worse—why it had to stop—Jeremy was using her. I don't mean what you think. He was using her—letting her think she was using him—so he could get to her father. Jeremy was obsessed. He wanted Lawrence Goldman, and the way to get to him was through his daughter; and he knew, you see, that she thought she could advance her own career—get what she wanted—by using him."

"Did he tell you this?" I asked without thinking.

"I knew Jeremy," she replied. "I knew what he was capable of doing. I didn't want him involved with those people, not like that, not that close. You have to keep people like that at a distance."

She stopped long enough to take a deep breath.

"Do you know why that happened that night—why I made a fool of myself in front of Jeremy and all those other people?"

She stared hard at me, as if she herself could still not quite believe what she was about to tell me.

"Because she's pregnant and had started a rumor that Jeremy was the father!"

It did not seem to make any sense. Why would a woman, pregnant by a married man, confide that fact to anyone other than someone she could trust to take her secret to the grave?

Meredith Fullerton wrapped her arms around herself, like someone trying to hold all her emotions in check. She lowered her eyes and for a long time gazed down at the floor. A shiver seemed to pass through her, and then, abruptly, the trembling stopped. A strange smile full of hard-earned wisdom passed over her troubled mouth.

"We don't live in Nathaniel Hawthorne's America, Mr. Antonelli," she said, lifting her head. "Women who commit adultery don't wear a scarlet letter. Ariella did not have to be pregnant if she didn't want to. She decided to have the baby because she thought if everyone knew she was carrying Jeremy's child, he would do—not the honorable thing; after all, he's a married man—but what most of these people would think was the smart thing to do. Don't you see, Mr. Antonelli: If you want to be president, a divorce is manageable; having a child out of wedlock is not quite so easy to handle. I don't know whether she intended to get pregnant, but she was perfectly willing to use it to get what she wanted once she was. She wanted Jeremy, Mr. Antonelli, because she wanted power; and now that Jeremy is gone, she finds out she can have the power on her own. But she's still pregnant, and enough people know it that she can't do anything about it. Ariella will have the baby, Mr. Antonelli—she doesn't have any choice—and they'll tell the world that Jeremy was the father and that if he hadn't been murdered he would have married the mother. By the time the Goldmans are through, everyone will think they were married all along and that with Jeremy's death Ariella became a pregnant widow."

Sliding past me, Meredith Fullerton sat down at the table and watched the night descend on the bay.

"What a strange irony," she said in a voice now heavy with fatigue. "To think that it should end like this, with someone trying to take advantage of Jeremy's death by telling the world Jeremy is the father of her child."

She watched out the window and for a while said nothing more. When she finally looked back at me, she smiled.

"Jeremy was not the father. Jeremy could not have children. Jeremy was sterile, Mr. Antonelli."

She lifted the cup of what was now lukewarm coffee to her lips. When she had finished, she turned again toward the window and the lights that twinkled in the darkness along the shore, just beyond the Golden Gate.

"We were living over there. We'd been married just a little more than a year. That's when we found out. That's when everything started to happen. Jeremy couldn't have what he had wanted more than anything, and it drove him crazy. He had always been ambitious; now he became reckless. He couldn't have children; he couldn't reproduce himself; and so he came to think of himself as unique, someone who wasn't like other people, someone indestructible, someone who because he couldn't leave anyone behind had to do something so that he would never be forgotten. Do you understand me, Mr. Antonelli? Jeremy wanted it all, because otherwise he didn't think he'd have anything.

"It was Jeremy's secret, his and mine. In a way, it destroyed us both. I loved him more than my own life, and I knew he loved me, too. We couldn't have a child, and after that, nothing was ever the same—for either one of us. And now, after everything else, I may have to tell everyone what we never told anyone, just to stop the Goldmans from telling any more lies."

"Your husband wouldn't have . . . ?"

"Told her he was sterile? No, she doesn't know. But of course in one respect it doesn't really matter, does it? Jeremy isn't the father, and that means someone else is."

She stood up and, with the same gracious look with which she had first greeted me, thanked me for coming to see her. She walked me out to the front door but, before she opened it, tried to warn me.

"Be careful, Mr. Antonelli. Whoever killed Jeremy is capable of anything. I'm sure they're not the least bit happy that there is going to be a trial."

As she opened the door, she glanced toward the elevator, then looked back at me.

"Have you considered the possibility that the police weren't shooting to stop that young boy, but to kill him? There would not have been a trial then, would there? Everyone would just have assumed that the boy must have done it."

Nine

Starting early the next morning, and without stopping for lunch, I worked my way through police reports, forensic reports, the notes of the pathologist, and the voluminous series of press clippings that summarized Jeremy Fullerton's well-publicized political career. With a pencil in hand, I forced myself through the burdensome prose of the official reports, stopping at the end of each page to jot down a word, a phrase, something that would remind me of what I thought I might need to remember. I was forever making lists.

When I turned to the faded chronicle of Fullerton's career, I put down the pencil and cradled the bulky scrapbook in my lap. This was not the first time I had read through the collection of press clippings that formed the fragmentary biography of a life led in full view of the public. I read it now, however, with a different understanding of what Jeremy Fullerton had really been like, and I saw something I had not seen before when I examined all those confident photographs of the victorious candidate standing next to his adoring wife in a long succession of election nights in which nothing seemed to change except the clothes they were wearing and the faces of the friends and supporters gathered around them.

As I glanced through the pictures of the last election, I could almost feel the excitement, almost hear the frenzied sensuous shouting of the crowd. And there was Jeremy Fullerton, unbeaten and, it appeared, unbeatable, smiling back at them with a grace and charm that made ambition seem a duty, knowing all the time that while he might one day become the most powerful man in the world, he would never have a child of his own.

Closing the scrapbook, I wondered whether Meredith Fullerton had been right that her husband would never have told anyone about his sterility. I scribbled a note to myself asking what Fullerton would have done had he lived and been told directly by Ariella Goldman that she was pregnant and that he was the father of her child. Another thought came to me, and underneath I scrawled: *Then who is the father?*

I went back to the beginning and started again. The district attorney, after all his posturing with the judge, had done what he was supposed to do and given me everything I had asked for about the police. It was not what I had hoped. I had been counting on finding something in the past history of the two officers that would point to at least the possibility of official misconduct; something that would allow the inference that the gun that had been used to kill Jeremy Fullerton, the gun that had been found inches from Jamaal Washington's outstretched hand, had been put there by the police. Marcus Joyner, however, had been on the police force for twenty-three years and had never been involved in a disciplinary proceeding. His partner, Gretchen O'Leary, had not been a police officer long enough to get in any kind of trouble. She had graduated from the academy less than six months before the incident. The night it happened was only her third night on patrol with Joyner.

Late in the afternoon, just as I was ready to throw up my hands in despair, my cousin stuck his head inside the door to my temporary office and asked if I wanted to go out for a drink.

We went around the corner to a place where everyone seemed to know Bobby by name, and sat at a tall table next to the wall across from the bar. The waiter, a gaunt-faced man in his sixties, bent close enough to hear our order under the constant din that rose up from the narrow, high-ceilinged room. We were in the heart of the financial district at the end of the day and all around us were middle-aged men in expensive suits and understated ties, exchanging the latest news and the newest rumors, some of them there for only one drink before they headed home, others there to drink their way into the evening and perhaps far beyond.

"If this cop—Joyner—has such an unblemished record," Bobby asked, "what's he doing in a patrol car after twenty-three years? Why isn't he a detective or something?"

I didn't know about Marcus Joyner, but I knew something about the police.

"Some cops won't play the kind of games you have to play to get ahead," I explained. "And some of them really like being on the street. Besides that, Joyner is black, and maybe, twenty-three years ago when he first started out, it wasn't that easy to move up."

The waiter brought our drinks. Before I could reach for my wallet, Bobby laid a twenty on the table.

"So what you have," he said with a grin as he sipped on a Manhattan, "is an honest cop who likes his work and a young virgin barely out of the convent."

I waited while the scotch I was drinking burned its way down the back of my throat.

"No," I replied, returning his grin with one of my own. "They have the honest cop and the virgin. I've got the black kid with the murder weapon found right next to his hand after he got shot by the police for fleeing the scene of the crime; the black kid, by the way, as I just read in a report, who turns out to have a juvenile record for assault."

Bobby turned down the corners of his mouth and lifted his eyebrows, teasing me, and at the same time daring me; the way he used to do when we were kids and he could get me to try just about anything once I thought it was something he had already done.

"The D.A. doesn't have a chance, does he?"

"Wouldn't think so," I agreed. I took another drink and let out a long, slow sigh. "The kid didn't do it. I'm sure of it."

Bobby did not shrink from the consequences. "Then the cops must have planted the gun."

There had to be another explanation, one that did not require proof of misconduct on the part of the police. I had been struggling with it all day long, and I thought I had the answer.

"It could have happened just the way the police said it did. He could have had the gun in his hand. The kid was scared, and don't forget, he was shot. Just because he says he didn't touch the gun doesn't mean he didn't."

In my mind I was watching it happen as I tried to describe what I saw.

"He hears someone coming. He knows someone is out there. It could be whoever killed Fullerton. He could have picked up the gun without thinking about it when he bolted out of the car, running for his life. He's running away; he has the gun; the cops think he did it; they see him, and they see the gun. He stops, or he hesitates, or he looks over his shoulder—and he still has that gun in his hand. They think he's going to shoot; they think he's going to shoot them; they fire first."

Everything I had read in the police reports, everything Jamaal Washington had told me, was starting to come together.

"He said he didn't hear any warning before they shot him, but maybe he just doesn't remember."

Bobby was looking at me, waiting for what I was going to tell him next, but that was all I had to tell, and I knew it was not nearly enough. I started to laugh.

"It's not very convincing, is it? Even if that is what happened, they still have him there: in the car, with the gun, running away."

I told Bobby what Mrs. Fullerton had said about how certain she was that someone else was responsible for her husband's death. I almost told him what she had said about Ariella Goldman's pregnancy and why Jeremy Fullerton could not possibly have been the father. Bobby was my cousin and I trusted him completely, but it was not my secret to share.

Bobby finished off his drink. "Though none of them would ever admit it, there are a lot of people glad he's dead." Pushing the empty glass to the side, he leaned forward. "I know somebody who can tell you a lot about him, somebody who knew him most of his political life. You want to meet him? Leonard Levine. I went to college with him; now he's a congressman and one of the most powerful members of the House Ways and Means Committee. When I first knew him he was just a skinny kid with a bad complexion still wearing braces on his teeth."

Bobby laughed and we got up from the table and he put his arm around my shoulder and laughed some more. We made our way through the tangled crowd around the bar and out the door.

"Let me tell you about Lenny," he said. "When I was playing football at Cal, everyone wanted to be my friend. Every fraternity wanted me to pledge. Lenny lived in a dorm. And while I and all my so-called good friends were going to parties and having what we thought was such a great time," he went on with a rueful grin, "Lenny was over at the library, studying his ass off. And while I was telling myself how hard I worked at football practice, going to college on an athletic scholarship, Lenny was putting himself through school. That's how I knew him: He was one of the guys who helped do the laundry for the football team and then handed out clean stuff to us each day before practice. You think any of us said a decent word to him? We thought we were the center of the universe. We thought life ended—that you just sort of retired and basked in all the glory—the day after the last game you played in college. You tell me who was smarter," he said, shaking his head as we trudged up the street, "us or the kid who was handing out the jock straps?"

Bobby tossed his head in that carefree way of his as we walked along, moving quickly and easily among the other pedestrians as I struggled to keep up. "Of course, Lenny doesn't seem to remember it quite that way. He talks like we were all great friends back then," said Bobby, looking at me over his shoulder as he moved on ahead. "He calls me at least three times a year just to tell me about all the great memories he has of when we were at Cal together. Then he asks me for money." Bobby shook his head and laughed again. "He's always running for reelection. He never stops."

The next morning, Bobby made the call he promised he would make, and the congressman agreed to meet us for dinner the following Saturday night. He wanted to meet in Chinatown.

A lot about San Francisco had changed, but once you passed through the red and green Oriental gate on Grant Street, everything you remembered was just the way it had been. Along the narrow, crowded streets of Chinatown, you still heard the discordant sounds of different languages jarring against each other in the cool night air. Waiters and shopkeepers still spoke a soft, gentle English with their customers and then talked to each other in a torrent of high-pitched unintelligible noise. Huddled together on the street corner, a gaggle of old women glanced at Bobby and me with suspicious eyes and then lowered their voices as they babbled along in a tongue of which I knew not even a single word.

When we arrived at the restaurant, Leonard Levine was shaking hands with a short, smooth-faced Chinese man with slick black hair. His other hand rested casually on his shoulder.

"Bobby," the congressman said as soon as he saw us, "let me introduce you to an old friend of mine, Herbert Wong."

With a polite smile, Wong shook hands first with Bobby and then, as Bobby made the introduction, with me.

"Any friend of the congressman is always welcome here," he said.

Before we could say anything by way of a reply, he shouted over his shoulder something in Chinese. Out of nowhere, a white-coated waiter appeared and waited obediently.

"Enjoy your dinner," said Wong, watching as the waiter, with a courteous bow, led his three guests into the dining room.

We sat on a deep red leather bench seat at a table in the back corner that gave us both the privacy to talk and an unobstructed view of the already crowded restaurant.

"Herbert owns the place," explained Levine. He carefully unfolded the linen napkin next to the empty plate in front of him and spread it over his lap. "Herbert owns a lot of places."

Levine placed his elbows on the tablecloth and laced his fingers together. Through half-lowered eyelids, he searched the room with the systematic gaze of an inveterate observer. The corners of his large, brooding mouth pulled back while the nostrils of his aquiline nose flared briefly.

"I like this place," said Levine, his eyes still moving methodically around the room. "Most of the people who come here, live here—in Chinatown. This is part of my district." For the first time, he turned to Bobby. "Did you know that?"

Leonard Levine was dressed in a light tweed sports jacket, tan slacks, a white shirt with French cuffs, and a pair of tasseled loafers. Long gray hair fell over his ears and curled up along the back of his neck. His face was weathered and his forehead deeply lined. The skin on the back of his hands was slightly mottled and heavily veined. If I had not known that he and Bobby had been in college together, I would have guessed him to be at least ten years older.

"How could I not know that?" I heard Bobby say as I felt the hard leather give against my weight. "I've paid for half your elections."

Levine was used to the give and take. He started to answer but instead suddenly got to his feet and stretched his hand across the table. An attractive middle-aged woman with intelligent eyes had come up to the table and I had not even noticed.

"I just wanted to thank you in person, Congressman Levine," said the woman, smiling. "We'll never forget what you did for us—all of us."

Levine remained on his feet until she had turned away and taken several steps back toward her table.

"It was an immigration thing," he remarked vaguely as he sat down. "I like being a congressman. Once in a while you ac-

tually do something that helps someone. Anyway," he added
with a shrug, "it beats handing out jock straps."

Bobby leaned forward. "Look, Lenny, let's get something
straight. We both know you had the better deal."

"The better deal!" repeated Levine incredulously. "You were
an All-American—a blond, blue-eyed all-American," he added
with a laugh. "I was a skinny kid so shy that if a girl had ever
noticed me long enough to say hello I probably would have
fallen down dead out of sheer embarrassment."

The waiter brought the congressman and I each a scotch
and soda; Bobby had a plain soda with a twist of lime.

"You were smart, Lenny. We all knew you were going to be
somebody. So you weren't the most popular guy on campus—
so what? All that meant was that you had the rest of your life to
look forward to. You think it was better to believe that you were
going to spend the rest of your life looking back on a football
field during your senior year as the best thing you'd ever do?"

Noiselessly, the waiter slid back in front of the table and
scribbled down our order. Just before he turned to go, Levine
asked for another scotch and soda. I had more than half mine
left.

"But you've done well," said Levine as he pulled one knee
onto the leather bench seat.

His voice seemed to fade away, and I started to imagine
what he had been like, the gawky kid with braces on his teeth,
sweating in the damp heat of a locker room, his arms flashing
like toothpicks as he took care of everybody's laundry, grinding
his teeth and squinting nervously each time some spoiled
muscle-bound clown shouted an obscenity if he wasn't quick
enough to do something the jock wanted. I didn't believe
Bobby when he told him that they had all thought Lenny
Levine was going to be someone later in life; I did not believe

they had ever thought about him at all. I wanted to believe that Bobby had thought about him, though; I wanted to believe that when everyone was crowding around him, telling him how great he was, he knew even then how ephemeral it all was, and that the next year, after he was gone, those same people would be crowding around someone else.

"Did you know that I never graduated from Cal?"

My eyes came back into focus, and I looked at Bobby, wondering if I had heard him right. Levine, a puzzled expression on his face, was again suddenly rising to his feet. With a broad smile he reached across and took the hand of someone Herbert Wong wanted to introduce.

"My apologies for the interruption," said Wong affably as he led away a prosperous-looking young man of not more than thirty.

"What do you mean—you didn't graduate? You went to law school," objected Levine.

"I didn't have enough credits to graduate at the end of my senior year, and then I played pro ball for two years—until I got hurt."

I suppose I had always assumed—and I think Levine must have assumed as well—that Bobby had in his youth led the kind of golden life most young men could only dream about. That the truth was somewhat different, that things had not always come to him so easily as we had imagined, changed the way we thought about him because it made him seem more like us. We pressed him for more detail.

"I didn't know what I was going to do then—after I got hurt and couldn't play anymore. Albert Craven suggested I become a lawyer. He was involved with the alumni association—that's how we first met. Albert knew everyone. He worked it all out. I enrolled at San Francisco State, took the courses I needed to get my degree. Then Albert talked to some people at the law school. That's how I got in—Albert Craven."

There was an awkward silence. Levine rattled the ice in his glass and finished what was left in it. The waiter came back, bearing a tray with steaming hot dishes. Bobby removed a pair of chopsticks from their paper wrapper and began to pick at his food.

"You may have had some help getting in," I reminded my cousin, "but nobody helped you get through it. You did that on your own."

Levine agreed and then added, "You're not the only one Albert Craven helped. He's always helped me—right from the start: first time I ran for Congress." Levine was starting on his third scotch. "Albert has been a great friend," he went on, turning his attention to me. "I tried to warn him against getting involved with Fullerton."

He studied me for a moment and then, with sullen eyes, followed the circle of his finger as he dragged it along the edge of the amber-colored glass.

"I've been in politics a long time," he said without looking up. "I've never seen anyone like Fullerton."

His finger kept moving around the edge, pausing only to reverse direction or to trace just above it the circle of the glass, in a contest with himself to see how close he could come without actually touching it at all.

"Fullerton was a fake," he said with a kind of grim determination. "He never told the truth about anything in his life. He lied about everything. He even lied about who he was."

Levine looked at me, then at Bobby. He wrapped his hand around the glass and lifted it to his mouth.

"He changed things," he explained. He set down the glass and searched the room for the waiter to order another. "His name, for example. It wasn't Jeremy," he reported with a mocking smile. "It was Gerald. He claimed his father had been an 'oil man'; his father ran a gas station out near Golden Gate Park. He said his mother had been involved with the theater; his mother was a cashier at an old movie house in the Sunset District."

"A lot of people try to make their backgrounds sound more interesting than they really are," protested Bobby.

"Yes," agreed Levine. "But they do it by emphasizing one thing more than another; they make something they did sound more important than it really was. They don't just change the facts when it suits them. Everything about Fullerton was dishonest."

Levine peered down at his nails, quickly brushing his thumb over the end of each finger. "He was worse than a fake," he said in a strangely solemn voice, uttering each word as if it were part of a formal judgment rendered by the living on the dead. "He was a thief, a crook."

Lifting his head, he gazed at me, waiting for a reaction. When he did not get one, at least not the one he wanted, he became annoyed.

"It's true," he insisted.

"What exactly did he do?" I asked, now studying him.

Leaning back against the cushioned wall, Levine folded his hands together in his lap. A thin, sarcastic smile started across his face.

"What did he do? I don't really know what he did—not the way a lawyer would want to know. I don't have any of what you might call provable facts. All I know is that on a salary that forces most members of Congress—I mean those who aren't independently wealthy—to share apartments in Washington because they still have to maintain a home back in their districts, Fullerton had a house in Georgetown you couldn't touch for less than seven figures, a co-op apartment here on Nob Hill, and a house across the bay in Sausalito."

He took another drink, swallowing hard. He put down the glass but did not let go of it.

"He didn't marry money, so you tell me—how did he get it all? The generosity of friends? Maybe. But then it might make you wonder who his friends really were—and what his friends really wanted—wouldn't it?" he asked, scowling at me.

"Do you have any idea who they were?" I asked.

"No," he replied, taking another drink. "Wherever he was getting his money, he kept it hidden."

Bobby had been watching with growing interest as Levine became more and more hostile.

"You drink too much, Lenny," he said as Levine, holding up his empty glass, signaled to the waiter.

Anger flashed across Levine's eyes. "What the hell business is that of yours?"

Calmly, Bobby eased forward and put his hand on Levine's wrist and held it down on the white tablecloth. "We're friends—remember? For some reason, just talking about Fullerton has you all upset. And you've just ordered your third—or is it your fourth?—scotch and soda."

The waiter brought the drink. For a while Levine just looked at the glass, as if he were deliberating with himself what to do with it.

"You're right," he said as he took a brief sip and then put down the glass. He looked at me, shook his head, and smiled. "Your cousin is right. I am angry. It has nothing to do with you. I meant what I said before: Fullerton was a fake—the worst I ever saw; and he always got away with it. There's nothing I can do about it, either," he went on, laughing at his own bewilderment. "Every time I turn around there's another reporter, another television camera, another interviewer who wants to know how we'll ever get over the loss. I have this sickening feeling that for the rest of my life I'm going to see Fullerton's phony smiling face on the cover of the tabloids every time I go through a checkout line at the grocery store."

He reached for the glass again, then banged it down and let it go.

"Do you know why I'm so damned angry?" he asked, his eyes flashing as he clutched the edge of the table with both hands. "The real reason? Because I could have had that Senate seat instead of Fullerton. It was mine for the taking. All I had to do was get into the Democratic primary. I would have won. You know why I didn't? Because I didn't think anyone could beat a Republican incumbent that year and because I didn't want to give up my House seat to find out. The truth—the absolute, unvarnished truth—is that I actually envied that crooked son-of-a-bitch."

He stared at us, a foolish grin hanging on his mouth. "Isn't that awful?" he asked with a haunted look in his eyes. "He was a fake; he didn't believe in anything; but despite that, somehow, deep down, he believed in himself a lot more than I did. The truth of it, Bobby," he said, turning to my cousin, "is that when I was a kid in college I wanted to be just like you, and now that I'm all grown up, I wanted to be someone just like him."

Beckoning to the waiter, the congressman handed him the scotch and soda and asked for coffee.

"Now that I've got that out of my system," he said, a broad, unforced smile on his face, "what can I do to help?"

I asked the most obvious question of all. "Do you know anybody who would have wanted Fullerton dead?"

He started to smile again. "I could give you a shorter answer if you asked me if I knew anyone who wanted him alive. But the answer to your question is anyone who knew him. Now, if you're asking me if I can think of anyone who might have had something to do with his death, then I suppose I have to say no."

"Would he have beaten Marshall—would he have become governor?"

Levine did not hesitate. "I don't think there's any question. You have to understand something. People who knew Fullerton—I mean really knew him—hated him. He was everything I said he was. But people who didn't know him, or who only met him at some political event, loved him the way you can only love someone you don't know, someone you can idolize, someone you can imagine is all the things you want them to be. He was like this great, magical mirror in which you always saw only the best things about yourself. I saw him in an auditorium speaking to thousands of people: Every one of them thought he was speaking only to them; and all of them felt better about themselves because of what he had said. Was he going to beat Marshall and become governor? Absolutely."

"And if he had won, would he have run against the president?"

"The president thought so. Before Fullerton decided to run for governor, the president was certain Augustus Marshall would be the Republican he would have to run against for a second term in the White House. As soon as Fullerton got into it, the president knew there would be a different Republican candidate and that he, the president, was going to have to fight for his political life inside his own party."

"Would Fullerton have beaten the president?"

Levine's eyes narrowed into a hard, calculating stare.

"That's not so clear," he said finally. "It would have been tough. No, it would have been brutal. They hated each other. I think it was because they understood each other. They had a lot in common, you know," he added with a cynical smile.

He remembered something. "Just before Fullerton was killed, I was starting to hear rumors that some of the people around the president were giving Marshall information about Fullerton that was supposed to be pretty damaging."

"What kind of information?" I asked, leaning forward.

But that was all he knew, and when I asked him if there was any way he could find out, he told me that it was not the kind of thing anyone was now likely to talk about. I had the feeling he did not want to ask.

"If Fullerton was that much of a threat, do you think the president could have had something . . . ?"

Levine put his hand in front of his mouth. I could see his jaw muscles working back and forth. His eyes looked tired. Then his hand dropped away and a sad smile crossed his mouth.

"We're not supposed to think that sort of thing is possible, are we?"

It was all the assurance I was going to get, and it told me more than perhaps I wanted to know. There was one more question I had to ask.

"What about the governor?"

"You mean, like what happened to the attorney general?"

It was the second time I had heard someone mention the fortuitous death of Augustus Marshall's first political opponent.

"He died of natural causes," Levine said, glancing at his watch in a way that told us he had to go. "If you want to know anything about the governor, all you have to do is go see Hiram Green."

I had no idea who Hiram Green might be, but instead of admitting my ignorance, I nodded as if I did.

Outside the restaurant, after we said good-bye to Leonard Levine, Bobby stood at the edge of the sidewalk, scraping the bottom of his shoe against the curb.

"Remember when he said he could have won the primary for the Senate seat instead of Fullerton?" he asked, shaking his head. "He wouldn't have had a chance."

We started to walk away, down the street toward the gate over Grant Street, on our way out of Chinatown. I had not learned much that was helpful from the congressman, and Bobby put his arm around my shoulder to cheer me up.

"Would you like me to tell you about Hiram Green?"

Ten

For those few archconservatives old enough to still remember, Hiram Green was the only real governor California had ever had. Green had exercised the veto more often than any governor in history and, better yet, had used it to keep higher taxes off the backs of the productive rich and public money out of the hands of the undeserving poor. Only an unfortunate series of scandals involving some of his closest friends and most trusted advisers had prevented him from winning election to a second term.

The former governor spent part of nearly every day in his offices in a small white stucco building with a dusty red tile roof on a palm-lined street not more than a block off Wilshire Boulevard. After he lost the governorship, Hiram Green could have joined any of a dozen of the larger law firms in Los Angeles, but he had even less interest in earning money for other people than he had in making it for himself. He had never worried about things like that. The same friends who had financed his political career bought him a house he liked in Beverly Hills and made all the arrangements for his partnership in a firm where, it was understood, he would never have to practice law. Set into the varnished black door, a polished brass plate listed the names

MARTIN, SHIFKIN, TOMLINSON AND GREEN. But no one who came to see Hiram Green came looking for legal advice.

I had taken an early morning flight down from San Francisco and arrived a few minutes before my scheduled appointment. There was no one else in the waiting room and no one at the desk behind the sliding glass window where the receptionist should have been. Two off-white sofas faced each other across a hand-knotted Oriental rug that covered part of the gleaming hardwood floor. On a glass coffee table, a dozen magazines were meticulously arranged in two perfectly parallel columns. Disturbing the order by picking one up to read would have been an act of malice. I wandered over to the far wall to examine more closely a watercolor hanging in an elaborate gold gilt frame.

"It was my wife's favorite," said a voice pleasantly. Hiram Green placed his hand gently on my arm. "I'm sorry to keep you waiting."

I turned toward him and we shook hands. He was taller than I was, not much, just an inch or so, but for someone already in his eighties, it was surprising. He must have been well over six feet tall in his prime.

"I'm glad you were able to come by," he remarked, as if this meeting had been his idea. "Let me show you around."

It quickly became obvious that there were few things the old man liked quite so much as showing someone around his office for the first time. His picture was everywhere: on the walls of the hallway that led down the center of the building; in the library; in the conference room, the copying room, in the coffee room; in every corner and cranny, pictures everywhere; pictures in black and white, pictures that depicted the political history of California, and in some cases of America and the world, for the last fifty years and more. It was as if nothing important had ever happened in the last half century that had not in some way involved the ubiquitous Hiram Green. In one framed photograph he was shaking hands with Barry Goldwater, and in another photograph, right next to it, with Richard Nixon; and then, next to that, with Ronald Reagan; and, a little farther on, with George Bush. The faces of the famous changed, but in every picture the face next to it was always the same; sometimes a little younger, sometimes a little older; sometimes wearing a dark suit, sometimes wearing a light one; but always the same face, with the same look, year after year after year, as if he had spent a life-time—more than a lifetime—staring into a camera, mesmerized into immortality the instant in which everything froze forever onto a single frame on a roll of a photographer's film.

Listening to Green's endless monologue, I walked beside him, watching his head, with its thinning strands of gray-white hair combed straight back from his domed forehead, bob up and down, like a crow pecking methodically at an insect trying to hide.

"Nixon was brilliant," he explained, nodding toward a photograph taken when the then-young congressman was running for the Senate against Helen Gahagan Douglas, the wife of the film actor Melvyn Douglas. "Brilliant," Green repeated as if he had known Nixon intimately. "But he never learned the difference between being a congressman and being president."

Green shook his head, whether from regret or something close to disdain it was impossible to tell.

"No class. When you get right down to it, no class at all," he said, shaking his head even more emphatically.

We had not taken more than two steps when he stopped again and pointed to another photograph, one in which he was shaking hands with a beaming Ronald Reagan.

"Reagan had class," he observed with a shrewd smile.

He paused to let me consider the comparison he had just

drawn between two Republicans, both of them from California, one of them driven from the presidency, the other long since retired. He held up his finger and looked me in the eye.

"But he was not brilliant," he said as if it were a secret he seldom shared. "Not even close." Green shrugged his shoulders. "It's too bad we don't have somebody with Nixon's mind and Reagan's manner. Well, who knows, perhaps one day we will."

He started to say something more but seemed to think better of it. Then, as if he had decided I could be trusted after all, he went ahead.

"And it won't be Augustus Marshall, though God knows the arrogant son-of-a-bitch thinks he's destined to one day be president. Christ," he muttered as he led me into his private office, "anybody who gets elected to anything in this state thinks they're destined to be president."

Green gestured toward a dark blue wing chair sitting at an angle to the front corner of his large walnut desk. Resting his head against the back of the maroon leather chair from which he had doubtless brokered some of his biggest deals, he looked at me, sizing me up in his mind, trying to determine how I might in the end be made more useful to him than he would be to me. It was moments like this, I realized, that made him glad to be alive. At an age when most other men were either in their dotage, saliva running out of their mouths and most of their memory out of their minds, or enjoying their last days in the tranquil embrace of family and friends, beyond the harm of fortune or the dangers of ambition, Hiram Green, fully lucid and forgetting nothing, continued to act as if the only important object of existence was the next political maneuver, the one he was just about to engineer, the one no one else had either the daring or the wit even to try.

"I think I know why you wanted to see me," he said finally, measuring as he spoke the effect he produced.

"I'm the defense lawyer in the Fullerton murder case. It would help to have some background on some of the major figures," I said as noncommittally as I could.

Green smiled pleasantly. "And someone suggested I could tell you what you need to know about the governor?"

"Yes."

"Because of how much I despise the bastard," he said, the smile still on his face. "Don't be embarrassed, Mr. Antonelli," he said, stroking the sleeve of his gray cashmere jacket. "Augustus Marshall betrayed me. It's nothing to feel bad about. When you've spent as many years in politics as I have, you learn that sooner or later everyone betrays you. Jeremy Fullerton, as I'm sure you already know, was fairly famous for that kind of thing. But he was a Democrat. I never knew him. I knew Marshall. Knew him? I practically invented him. But he betrayed me, and he did it the way they all do it. Shall I tell you how it happened?"

I could have said no, and he would have told me anyway. It was part of who he was. You have to be important to be betrayed by someone powerful or famous.

"It was on a Saturday morning, pretty much like this one," he said, though today was not Saturday, "a dozen years ago or so. I had invited Marshall over to discuss a little arrangement I wanted to make with him. You see, the attorney general— Arthur Sieman—perhaps you remember the name? No? Well, anyway, Arthur Sieman was brilliant." Suddenly Green laughed. "Unfortunately, that was not the only thing he had in common with Nixon."

Though it had taken place a dozen years before, the old man proceeded to recount the conversation he had had with the man who was now governor as if it had ended just a few minutes before I walked in the door.

"At first he didn't really want to admit what we were here to talk about, alone in my office on a Saturday morning," Green began. "They're all like that," he explained. "Ambitious men who try to hide their ambition. Finally, after I told him at least twice that he knew very well what we were here to talk about, he admitted—but only with a show of reluctance, you understand—that he thought it probably had something to do with 'this attorney general business.' "

Green looked at me, a smile of cynical detachment spreading across his worn-out mouth. " 'Yes, of course,' I said. 'We've had our eye on you for some time now.'

" 'I've never thought of myself as a politician,' Marshall began as he shifted around in his chair, crossed one leg over the other, and leaned forward. They all do that," Green explained, "when they want to look really sincere."

" 'I think I could be a good attorney general, but I could never bring myself to compromise on the principles in which I believe.' "

Green raised his eyebrows. "Do you have any idea how many times before I had heard that same pious disclaimer? I can't count that high."

" 'We don't want you to compromise on anything,' I told him. 'To the contrary, we want you to become the spokesman for the principles we share, Republican principles, principles the attorney general has betrayed.'

"Then I told him the truth—or something close to it."

Green closed his eyes and saw it all over again: the endless cycle of duplicity that, whether he knew it or not, had given meaning to his life—the long succession of betrayal and revenge.

" 'Arthur Sieman started out just like this,' I said to Marshall.

'Right here. He was sitting where you are now. He had never run for office, and I don't think he had ever really considered it. In a lot of ways he was just like you—a successful attorney, and about your age. He was interested, but reluctant—just like you. And he was afraid—just like you're afraid—that if he got into politics he would be forced to compromise, forced to let go of the things he believed in. He was completely sincere. He was also an idiot. No,' I said before he could object, 'I don't think you're an idiot. Far from it.' "

Green opened his eyes, a subtle smile lurking at the corners of his mouth. "I remember wondering at the time if he was going to be like everyone else and immediately accept as an unquestioned truth what was after all only a flattering lie. You would have thought I would have realized a long time ago that there really are no exceptions to the rule that vanity is universal. At least I haven't come across any. Have you, Mr. Antonelli?"

We exchanged a meaningful glance and in the silence he knew my answer.

" 'No,' I told Marshall, 'you are much more intelligent than Arthur Sieman. You see, what Sieman really feared—though he didn't know it then and doesn't know it now—is that there was nothing he believed in so strongly he wouldn't give it up the moment it became even the least bit unpopular. Anyone can believe deeply in whatever almost everyone else seems to believe; almost everyone does. But you aren't like that,' I assured him. 'You aren't like that at all. So, no, Mr. Marshall, we don't want you to compromise on your principles. That is the one thing we expect you never to do. Never.'

"Marshall sat straight up, looked me directly in the eye. 'You can count on that, Governor.'

"As you can imagine, Mr. Antonelli," said Green dryly, "that was a challenge I was not about to take up. I turned instead to more practical matters. I told him money would not be a problem. We could raise ten, twenty million—whatever we needed. And we had the right people to run the campaign. All he had to do was be the candidate. Then I put it to him directly. 'Well,' I asked, 'would you like to be our candidate?'

"There was no hesitation, not the slightest. He wanted it, all right, wanted it as much as anyone I had ever seen. Then I gave him the bad news.

" 'You do understand that you have no chance of winning?'

"He didn't want to believe it. 'I know it's a long shot,' he replied. 'But I certainly wouldn't say that I don't have a chance.'

" 'No, you don't,' I insisted. 'No chance, no chance whatsoever. None.'

"I tried to explain to him what I thought I had already told him: Arthur Sieman had given up every conservative principle he had ever supposedly had to curry favor with the public. He was the most popular politician in California, and the goddamn fraud would have sold his mother for a vote."

Green said it in a way that made me think this willingness to succeed at any price was something he envied.

"Sieman was animal-shrewd. I told Marshall that. I told him that Sieman would say whatever was most expedient at the moment and that when he said it, he believed it. Sieman had the greatest capacity for self-deception I had ever seen. At least," he added, lifting his eyebrows, "until I met Augustus Marshall."

A thin, sardonic smile settled on the old man's mouth.

"Sieman was all surface: there was nothing underneath. I think there was once, but it died, or got lost, or something. The surface was all there was anymore, and the surface reflected everything around him so perfectly that everyone saw what they wanted to see and heard what they wanted to hear. It was a form of genius, really."

Green thought of something. He looked at me as he scratched his chin.

"In a lot of ways, but in that way in particular, Arthur Sieman was just like Jeremy Fullerton. One was a Republican, the other was a Democrat, and one was supposed to be a conservative, while the other was a liberal, but those were just labels they used because they had to say they were something. They were both always inching their way toward that big amorphous middle where the only thing important is whether you can make everyone feel good."

Green waved his hand in the air as if to excuse his digression, or, more likely, to try to forget how disappointed he was in the kind of politicians that had taken his place.

"Marshall had no chance against Arthur Sieman. None. That was not the reason he was running. I tried to explain that to him—that he wasn't running to win, but to show that Sieman had lost the support of conservatives. If Marshall got just a quarter of the vote in the primary, we would have made our point; if he got a third of the vote, then Sieman, for the first time, would look vulnerable. But Marshall couldn't stand the thought of losing. He had to ask, 'And if I win?'

" 'You're going to lose,' I told him. 'But remember,' I suggested, 'there are losers, and there are losers. Sieman isn't going to stay in the attorney general's office. He'll run for governor, or if not that, senator.' "

Green looked at me with the bluff, affable manner with which, as soon as I saw it, I knew he had shaken a million hands and told a thousand lies.

" 'And then, next time,' I said, 'you can win the nomination, win the election, and I'll be able to call you Mr. Attorney General. I look forward to it.' "

Augustus Marshall did exactly as Hiram Green had expected.

Within weeks of his announcement, he moved from the category of political unknown to that of the almost famous challenger of the immensely popular Republican incumbent. The public opinion polls charted his progress: twelve percent at the end of the first month, seventeen percent at the end of the second, twenty-three at the end of the third. Then, after another month of exhaustive effort and exorbitant spending, it all came to a stop. He was stuck at twenty-three percent. Convinced he could still win, Marshall tried everything, but nothing worked. Two more months and there was still no change. Hiram Green had been right—he was going to lose—and though he never said it, Marshall was too intelligent not to have finally understood that he had never had a chance to win in the first place. And then, with only a few weeks left before the primary election, Arthur Sieman did something that no one—not even Hiram Green—had considered in all their political calculations as even a contingent possibility. He died.

Hiram Green did not know what to think. All he knew for certain was that in a single mortal instant the candidate he had put forward to lose had become the first conservative in years almost certain to win. Marshall was the Republican nominee, and because none of the Democrats who might have had a chance to win had wanted to run against Arthur Sieman, he became attorney general in a landslide. When it was all over and the only thing left was the victory speech in the ballroom of the Beverly Wilshire Hotel, Augustus Marshall had turned to Hiram Green, the man who had gotten him into the race he told him he could not win. Green remembered the way Marshall looked at him, the broad smile and the relaxed, friendly manner, and he remembered how certain he was that Marshall was about to thank him for everything he had done. Then Marshall started to speak and his eyes turned hard.

" 'If I had lost,' Marshall said to him, 'you would have found someone else to run the next time, wouldn't you?' "

The crowd was chanting Marshall's name, louder and louder, demanding what they always demand: that their new leader listen to them. Marshall stood there, his head held high, waving his hand back and forth, a triumphant smile flashing across his face.

"I remember wondering," Green mused aloud, "whether I might not just end up missing Arthur Sieman after all."

Two years after he was elected attorney general, and—more important in terms of the political calculations that had by now become instinctive—two years before the next election, Augustus Marshall divorced his wife after twenty years of marriage. She kept the home in Bel Aire; he kept the small one-bedroom condominium a block and a half from his office in the state capitol in Sacramento. It had become the only home he cared about.

The announcement of his divorce was made quietly and handled with all the discretion to be expected of what everyone would understand was a purely private misfortune. His marriage four years later to Zelda St. Rogers, the daughter of the owner of the largest newspaper in Los Angeles, received more attention than the inauguration of all but a few of California's governors. It was, as every columnist wrote and every commentator observed, a perfect alliance of new power and what in a place that worshiped the present passed for old money. As if to underscore their connection with California tradition, the bride and groom spent their honeymoon in Carmel.

"And I'll bet you anything," Green said, leering at the thought of it, "they spent most of their first night together watching the television coverage of the wedding. You think he didn't know what he was doing, marrying her? Three weeks later he announced he was running for governor. He got the support of his father-in-law's paper. And we used to think that only women slept their way to the top."

Hiram Green got up from behind his desk and walked over to a cabinet. He filled a glass with a chalky-white substance, stirred it with a spoon, and then, with a shudder, forced himself to drink.

"Ulcers," he explained, patting his stomach as he came back to his desk.

"Do you know how many times Augustus Marshall has called me during the eight years he was attorney general and the nearly four years he's been governor?" he asked, frowning as he drank a little more of his medication. "Not once. Not even a Christmas card, the ungrateful son-of-a-bitch."

He looked at the glass, then he looked at me. "I'd offer you something," he said, "but this is Saturday and there's no one here."

Just as I started to wonder again if I should tell him what day of the week it was, the buzzer on the console on the corner of his desk went off. The soft voice of a woman I assumed was the receptionist gently reminded him that he had a luncheon appointment in an hour. He thanked her and then went on with our conversation as if there were nothing inconsistent with what he had just said. Perhaps, at his age, when he spent most of his time thinking about things that had already happened, every day seemed like Saturday.

"There you have it, Mr. Antonelli," he said. "The short history of Augustus Marshall. There's really no getting around it: Some people have luck on their side and some people don't."

Green smiled, but it could not quite conceal the trace of bitterness in his voice, as if even now he still resented what had happened to the neophyte he had rescued from the anonymity of private life compared to his own undeserved political misfortunes.

"Arthur Sieman was as healthy-looking as any man you've ever seen. He'd just had a complete physical six weeks before. No history of heart trouble on either side of his family; he didn't smoke and hardly ever had a drink. He took care of himself: He jogged, he swam, played tennis—he was in superb condition. It's true that he would have betrayed his mother—and he betrayed me—but that isn't normally counted among the standard list of health risks. If it was," he added, quivering with silent laughter, "there wouldn't be a politician left alive in America and Augustus Marshall would now be at least ten years dead."

Green pressed his hands together in his lap and for a moment did not say anything.

"The odd thing is," he said presently, "people in politics hardly ever die—not while they're in office." An ironic smile, perhaps in acknowledgment of how much he had already cheated mortality, lingered for a moment on his mouth. Then he added, "Not from natural causes."

Gripping the arm of the chair, Green drew himself up to his full height. He looked past me, a hard shrewdness in his aged eyes.

"Arthur Sieman was one of the only men I ever heard of who dropped dead in what to all the world seemed like perfect health."

His eyes came back to me, and I thought I saw in them a kind of cheerful malice, as if he took a certain pleasure in having outlived any illusions he may once have had about how far anyone might go to get what they wanted. It was the look of someone for whom the beginning and the end of all wisdom was the knowledge that no one did anything for anyone without first asking what was in it for themselves.

"First Sieman, now Fullerton," he remarked. "Strange, the way things happen. Marshall could never have become attorney general if Sieman hadn't died; and he could never have been re-elected governor if Fullerton hadn't been killed. Either one of them alone would have seemed just a matter of chance—wouldn't it? One of those fortuitous circumstances which help explain the rise of nearly every successful man—or woman—in politics. But together—Sieman and Fullerton? That is an extraordinary run of luck, isn't it? Without precedent, I should say. If I didn't know better, I might begin to believe that Augustus must have had something to do with it—one or the other—or perhaps even both."

"If you didn't know better?"

An enigmatic smile circled over his lower lip. "Yes," he replied. "That sort of thing doesn't happen in this country, does it?"

He rose from his chair and with his hand on my sleeve walked me out of his office. He moved more slowly than when I had first arrived, and his voice, when he spoke, was now somewhat difficult to hear. As we entered the hallway, he stopped in front of a framed photograph of a very young Richard Nixon, taken while he was still a congressman from southern California, with his black wavy hair and nervous, darting eyes. The picture had been taken at a ground-breaking ceremony. Nixon stood together with five other men in a shallow semicircle, all of them bent over shiny silver shovels, staring straight ahead into the camera. Green's grip tightened around my arm.

"You recognize anyone in that picture—I mean besides Nixon and me?"

I examined the smiling faces of a half dozen men now either dead or a half century older.

"No, I'm afraid I don't."

"On the far left," he said, pointing toward a young man in his late twenties or early thirties, wearing a tan double-breasted suit. Like the others, he was smiling, but there was something different about the way he did it. He seemed more confident, more at ease, less interested in making an impression. I still had no idea who he was.

"He's the one who could have done it." Green saw the question in my eyes. "The one who could have been what I told you about before," he reminded me as if we had not spent the last hour and a half talking about anything else. "The mind like Nixon and the manner like Reagan. He had it all—maybe the most brilliant man I ever met, and one of the most engaging men I've ever been around. He could have gone all the way—governor, president. Nothing would have stopped him. He would have done whatever he had to do to win. He always did whatever he wanted. Maybe that's the reason he never wanted to run for anything," he added, squinting at the faded photograph. "Too many things about him that might come out, things I'm sure he wanted to hide—that and the fact that Lawrence always liked money too much," he said, shaking his head.

"Lawrence?"

"Yes," he replied, turning to me. "Lawrence Goldman. I'm sure you've heard of him. We were good friends once, back in the days when I could raise the kind of money we raised in Marshall's first campaign."

"What kind of things did he think he had to hide?" I asked, trying to conceal the intensity of my curiosity.

Green looked at me as if he were trying not to laugh at some great, delicious secret that was almost too good not to share.

"Everything," he said, as he led me away from the black and white framed photographs that, with all the hundreds of others that had been so carefully fastened to the walls, told the story of a life everyone else had managed to forget.

Outside, the sunlight shimmered off the sidewalk, and in the quiet shade of the tall sloping palm trees, the face and words of Hiram Green seemed like an old movie that kept playing over and over again in my mind. When I got to the airport, I took one last look around, wondering whether there was something in the languid scent of the air that had given him such a long life and the strange unreality in which he seemed to have lived it. Overhead, the planes kept coming in, one after the other, bringing more people with dreams of their own to become one of the famous names and faces that live in the dreams of people all over America, strangers they would never meet and would never know.

I caught the next plane to San Francisco and, after it leveled off for the short flight north, opened the newspaper I had bought at the airport. On the right column of the front page was a picture of Ariella Goldman, beaming like one of the faces in the long, darkened gallery of Hiram Green's office, the new Democratic nominee for governor. Though she had never run for office before, she was, according to the story, only seven points behind Augustus Marshall and there were still nearly three months to go before the election. I folded up the paper, and closing my eyes, remembered what Hiram Green had told me. First Arthur Sieman, then Jeremy Fullerton. Was it only chance?

Eleven

With all the resources of Albert Craven's firm and with the full-time services of three different detective agencies, every friend and every relative of Jamaal Washington, everyone who had known him at the university, and everyone who had known him at work was interviewed and, if there was so much as a single inconsistency between what one person said and what was learned from another, interviewed again. The gun, the bullet, the car itself—every piece of forensic evidence was examined, analyzed, discussed, and debated by one expert after another. The route Jamaal had taken from the Fairmont Hotel to the place where he had found Jeremy Fullerton dead in his car was measured to the last inch and timed to the last second. No expense had been spared; everything that could be done had been done. Now, finally, it was time for trial.

We waited in the monotonous silence, broken only by an occasional muffled cough or the shifting, shuffling sound of someone trying to find a place to sit. Dressed in a conservative gray suit, white dress shirt, and solid maroon tie, Jamaal Washington sat on the wooden chair next to me, the one closest to the jury box. The cane he now used to help him walk lay on the floor next to him. His soft light brown hands were folded in his lap. Under half-closed lids, his large deerlike eyes floated with a kind of languid indifference as he watched the court reporter fidget with a thick roll of stenotype tape.

Fifteen minutes after we were supposed to have begun, a quarter of an hour after the defense, the prosecution, and everyone else who had a function to perform in the trial had avoided judicial wrath by appearing on time, the door at the side of the courtroom swung open. The honorable and vindictive James L. Thompson walked mechanically toward the bench, his eyes fixed on the floor in front of him as if at any moment he might reprimand his feet for taking him in the wrong direction. Swatting the air with his hand as he plopped down an armload of papers and books, he ordered the bailiff to bring in the pool of prospective jurors.

A few minutes later, the door at the back of the courtroom swung open and two dozen men and women were herded like baffled sheep onto the two benches directly behind the wooden railing that, in a manner of speaking, separated the spectators from the players and the play.

Like most judges, Thompson thought it was his particular burden constantly to be plagued by lawyers and fools, categories that he by no means considered mutually exclusive. And, like most judges, his view of jurors was much more favorable. Because they were strangers he had never met, he could invest them with all the classic virtues of public-spirited citizens, eager to be impartial and determined to be fair. There was the additional advantage that as jurors they were required to listen to whatever he wanted to say and never question anything he told them to do.

Thompson greeted those two dozen prospective jurors like long-lost friends. With bright-eyed courtesy and exhaustive patience, he explained the important responsibility they were about to assume. Summoned from the relative anonymity of their lives, they concentrated on each word he spoke like grade school children listening to their new teacher on the first day of class. With a benevolent smile, he informed them that they were there to decide a criminal case.

The smile vanished and a trace of sorrow edged its way onto his mouth when he announced, "The defendant is charged with the crime of murder in the first degree."

Lingering over each word so they could grasp every nuance of meaning, Thompson read each word of the charging instrument. When he finished, he put down the document and, resting his arms on the bench, bent forward.

"The defendant has entered a plea of not guilty. That means that the defendant has denied the charge."

The judge paused; his eyes narrowed down into a searching stare; the furrowed creases in his forehead deepened. When he began to speak, there was a certain sense of urgency in his voice, as if he could not overestimate the importance of what he was about to tell them.

"Whenever anyone charged with a crime enters a plea of not guilty, it becomes the obligation of the prosecution to prove the defendant's guilt—to prove it beyond a reasonable doubt."

He gazed from one end of the front two rows to the other, his eyes boring in on first one juror, then the next.

"And that means," he went on, "that after you have heard all the evidence in this case, you must—and I repeat: you must—find the defendant not guilty, unless you decide that the guilt of the defendant has been proven—not by a probability, not to a reasonable certainty, nor to any other lesser standard, but beyond a reasonable doubt."

It was like the moment at the end of a service: that long,

clean, still silence in which there is no confusion left about what is important and what is not; that one moment of perfect lucidity in which something eternal speaks directly to the soul.

The judge kept looking at them, a last reminder of the gravity of the words that had been entrusted to his care and that only he could speak at the commencement of a trial to determine whether someone had committed a crime. Gradually, his gaze began to lose its intensity and the way in which he held himself became less rigid. As if to tell them that the lesson was over, he nodded and drew back.

"Let me now introduce the parties."

Introducing first the prosecution, then the defense, and finally the defendant, Judge Thompson asked if any of the prospective jurors were personally acquainted with any of us. No one raised a hand. No one knew Clarence Haliburton; no one knew me; and none of them had ever met the young man accused of murdering Jeremy Fullerton. The judge asked if any of them had formed any opinion about the case itself. No one said they had, and I wondered if any of them really believed they had not.

The clerk was directed to draw at random the names of twelve jurors. Each time a name was called, a man or a woman rose from their seat on the two front benches, gathered up their jacket or sweater or the book they had brought to help defeat the boredom of waiting every morning to see if they were going to be called, and made their way to the jury box. With slow, self-conscious movements each one took the chair next to the last one filled and then, with reluctant eyes, looked back at the room full of faces looking at them.

After the last name was called and the twelfth juror had taken the last seat left, the judge turned things over to the lawyers—but not before he made sure everyone knew whose side he was really on.

"The lawyers will now ask each of you some questions," he said, like a friendly neighbor having a chat over the backyard fence. "This process is called 'voir dire.' Don't ask me to translate," he said with a quick, self-effacing grin. "I don't know what it means, either."

Several jurors nodded; several others smiled; all of them laughed silently.

"The lawyers get to ask you questions to see if there is any reason why any of you should be excused from serving in this case. The questions are not meant in any way to embarrass you." Casting a sideways glance at the counsel tables, he added with a knowing grin, "And if they do ask you a question they shouldn't, I'll take care of it."

Chins went up, heads tilted slightly to the side; a few of them shifted forward in their chairs; one way or another they all signaled back that they knew they could count on him—he didn't trust lawyers, either.

Thompson sat back in the tall leather chair. "Mr. Antonelli," he remarked with casual indifference as he began to examine the contents of a thick folder he had carried into court.

I glanced at the makeshift chart on which I had written the names and numbers of each juror as the clerk had called them one by one to the jury box.

"Tell me, Mrs. DeLessandro," I asked, looking up at a middle-aged woman with a thick neck and short stubby arms, "how long have you lived in San Francisco?"

Voir dire was an art form lawyers kept trying to turn into a science. Psychologists claimed a knowledge of human behavior and an ability to predict what people were likely to do in any given set of circumstances. Jury consultants were the latest subspecies. Lawyers who thought there was more to be learned about the methods of persuasion from a thirty-second television commercial than from what used to be called forensic rhetoric paid small fortunes to have these supposed experts tell them what kind of people they should keep on a jury and what kind they should leave off. They wanted to rely on anything but their own judgment, but if they could not figure out for themselves whom they wanted as jurors, you had to wonder what business they had trying cases in a court of law.

"And where did you live before you moved to San Francisco?" I asked.

I had now begun the long, sometimes tedious march toward . . . I did not know what. I never knew, when it started, where it would go. I would ask them where they lived, what kind of work they did, where they had grown up, where they had gone to school, whether they were married, whether they had children—the same kind of questions strangers who happen to sit next to each other at a dinner, at a party, or on a plane might normally ask. One question led to another, and another after that—the same way it happens in every conversation, when two people start to get to know each other.

I was asking Mrs. DeLessandro questions, but we were actually talking to each other, back and forth. Her demeanor changed: Instead of that self-conscious reserve with which we typically address ourselves to people we have only just met, she became more relaxed, as if she had forgotten that there were several hundred spectators listening to everything we said.

I had a secret, which I only seldom shared, about the kind of juror I wanted to have. I was not particularly interested in people who might be thought to feel some sympathy toward the defendant; I was far more interested in jurors who would never dream of doing anything wrong. I wanted them willing to take the equivalent of a blood oath that they would never break the law, even if—or especially if—the law was one they did not happen to like. I wanted jurors who would vote to acquit someone they thought was guilty because the law said they had to.

"Have you served on a jury before?" I asked, smiling at her.

She smiled back and indicated that she had. I asked her if it had been a civil or a criminal case. She did not know which it was, only that it had been about an automobile accident in which someone who had been hurt brought suit against the driver.

"A civil case," I told her. "Perhaps you'll remember that in a civil case—when one person is suing another—both sides put on evidence. Whichever side has the better evidence, even if it's just by a little—what they call a 'preponderance of the evidence'—that side wins. Is that the way you remember what happened in that case?"

My eyes never left her as she told me that it was exactly the way she remembered it. We might as well have been the only two people in the room. We concentrated only on each other.

"Just a little while ago," I reminded her in the conversational tones used by people who are well acquainted, "Judge Thompson spoke about the burden the prosecution has to prove guilt beyond a reasonable doubt. That means the prosecution has to prove everything—we don't have to prove anything. This isn't like that civil suit you were involved with. They have to prove the defendant's guilt; the defendant doesn't have to prove his innocence." I threw up my hands, shook my head, and laughed. "We don't even have to put on a case. We can just sit here and watch the prosecution put on its case. We don't have to call a witness; we don't have to offer any evidence. The prosecution has to do all the work. I don't have to do anything. Now, the question I want to ask you is this: Do you think it's unfair to place this burden—this very heavy burden—on the prosecution? In other words, do you think it's unfair that the prosecution has to prove guilt beyond a reasonable doubt?"

There was only one answer she could give; there was only one answer anyone could give; but then, it was not the answer that was important—it was the question itself, because the question began to teach her the standard it was going to be her responsibility to enforce.

"Now, Mrs. DeLessandro, let me ask you a question that I'm going to ask all the other jurors as well."

For the first time since we had begun to talk, I took my eyes off her. I glanced slowly from one juror to the next until I had looked at them all. Then I leaned forward, my arm on the table.

"At the end of the case," I asked, searching Mrs. DeLessandro's trusting eyes, "after you've heard all the evidence—after you've deliberated with all the other jurors—if, after all that, you believe the defendant is probably guilty, but you don't think the prosecution has proven that guilt beyond a reasonable doubt, would you then return a verdict of not guilty?"

It was what the judge had told her; it was what I had told her; it was what the law required. Barely literate, a citizen for less than a third of her life, she believed—like nearly everyone believes—in the utter sanctity of the law. It was beyond reason: No one could decently argue against it. There was nothing else she could do, nothing else, now that she understood it, that she wanted to do. She agreed, willingly, eagerly, that if there was any doubt—any reasonable doubt—the defendant should go free.

By this time we were practically old friends. With relaxed self-assurance, I glanced at her jury questionnaire.

"I see from the form you filled out that you have three children. Are they still in school?"

Clarence Haliburton had apparently had enough. I had wondered how long it was going to take before he decided to object.

"You object?" Judge Thompson asked, a puzzled expression on his heavily lined face.

Turning away from Mrs. DeLessandro, I looked up, waiting to see what Thompson would do.

"What is it you object to, Mr. Haliburton?" he asked in a gruff, curious voice.

Haliburton was standing up, his feet spread apart and his hands on his hips. "I object to the way counsel is conducting voir dire."

Thompson bent forward. "You'll have to formulate a more specific objection."

Grinding his teeth, Haliburton looked down at the floor.

"I object to the last question," said Haliburton finally, raising his eyes just far enough to return Thompson's hostile stare with one of his own.

The judge almost laughed. "Whether her children are still in school?"

"Yes, your honor," Haliburton replied with a sneer. "The question has nothing to do with her qualifications as a juror," he went on, his voice rising, "and Mr. Antonelli knows it."

He waited for a response, but Thompson continued to stare.

"It's all part of a pattern," Haliburton complained. "He's simply trying to cultivate a relationship with this juror—and I've no doubt he'll try to do the same thing with all the others as well—because that way they might ignore the evidence in the case. I mean," he added with a sideways glance at me, "he's already spent half the morning talking to just this one juror. If he talks to her any longer," he suggested, turning toward the spectators behind the bar, "they'll have been together almost long enough for a common-law marriage!"

"Unfortunately for me," I shouted loud enough to cut him off, "Mrs. DeLessandro is already married."

Laughter swept over the courtroom and Thompson picked up his gavel. Then he changed his mind and instead of gaveling the crowd into silence let the noise die out of its own accord. When it was quiet again, he arched his eyebrows and looked at me.

"Do you wish to make any response?"

"I'm afraid I'll have to plead guilty, your honor. The more I talk to Mrs. DeLessandro, the more I like her." I paused, just for an instant, and then added, "But I'm not sure I'm quite ready for marriage. . . ."

This time Thompson used his gavel.

"And because I like her," I went on before he could say anything, "I probably do ask some questions that strictly speaking are not directly connected with her qualifications to sit as a juror." Flashing my best imitation of a bashful smile, I promised to try to do better.

We looked at each other, Thompson and I, and I knew that he did not believe a thing I had said, and I also knew that it made no difference at all.

"Objection overruled," he announced as he sank back into his chair like an old man eager to get back to his nap.

Haliburton was still standing, his arms straight down at his sides, clenching his fists so tight his nails bit into his flesh.

"But your honor!" he protested.

It was as if the chair had a catapult. One minute Thompson was barely visible behind the high wooden bench; the next minute he seemed to have shot right over the top of it like some crazy-looking pop-eyed jack-in-the-box.

"Overruled, Mr. Haliburton! Overruled! Don't you ever dare question a ruling of mine again!"

Haliburton stared hard at the shiny surface of the counsel table, clenching his teeth until his head began to vibrate.

"Yes, your honor," he said in a barely audible voice, raising his eyes just far enough to see Thompson smirk.

Shaking his head as he drew away, Thompson turned to me. "You may continue, Mr. Antonelli."

"Thank you, your honor," I replied with a show of formality. "Now, Mrs. DeLessandro, about those children of yours."

I did not hesitate to take what advantage I could from the way the judge felt about the district attorney and the way the district attorney felt about the judge. I could do whatever I wanted on voir dire, and Haliburton could do nothing about it. I asked more questions of the patient Mrs. DeLessandro than I had sometimes been permitted to ask of an entire panel; and when I could not think of anything new to ask, I asked her again some of the same questions I had asked her before.

Haliburton was no fool: He understood perfectly that I was far less interested in the answers I was given than I was in doing what I could to insinuate myself into a juror's confidence. When I was finally finished with Mrs. DeLessandro, he tried to do the same thing himself. He was still talking to her when the judge announced it was time for lunch. After the jury filed out, Thompson summoned us both to a conference at the side of the bench, where he admonished the district attorney to speed things up.

"I told you how much time I have to try the case. At the rate you're going, you won't have time to call your first witness. You both need to speed things up," Thompson added, as if the last thing he wanted to do was leave the impression that there was anything the least bit personal in any of this.

"I'll try to do better, your honor," I said as agreeably as I could, while Haliburton, glowering, gritted his teeth.

It was nearly a quarter past twelve by the time I finally got out of the courthouse. I was not meeting anyone for lunch and I was not particularly hungry. It was a gorgeous day, the kind that makes you wonder why you ever wanted to spend your life in the lamplight of dark rooms reading in the dismal, depressing science known as the law. The courthouse had emptied out onto the steps. Scattered all around, people were eating sandwiches and then closing their eyes as they raised up their faces to get a few minutes of the sun. I saw a place at the top of the steps, but then I remembered that there were reporters around. I did not want to talk to anyone, especially someone who was going to use what I said for a story. I decided to walk and without any destination in mind started down the steps.

A block away from the courthouse, I stopped at the same intersection where I had almost been hit by a car. This time I waited until I was sure the light turned green, looked both ways, and only then stepped off the curb.

"You learn caution quickly, Mr. Antonelli."

It was Andrei Bogdonovitch again, right next to me. I felt his hand take my arm and before I knew what I was doing found myself trying to keep up as he led me through the intersection to the other side of the street. He glanced in one direction, then the other.

"I have to see you. We have to talk."

He kept looking around, scanning the crowded sidewalk, as if he were afraid of someone he expected at any moment to see. I started to ask him what was wrong, but he grabbed my shoulder and stared at me with a strange, urgent intensity.

"There are some things you need to know. You may be in danger—very serious danger. I have to talk to you. Please," he begged. "It's very important. Could you come to my shop at the end of the day—about six?"

His eyes began to dart all around again, searching for God knows what, as he reached inside his coat pocket for a card, which he then shoved into my hand. He looked at me one last time.

"About six, then," he said. Without waiting for a reply, he let go of me and vanished around the corner.

If I had ever doubted that fear was contagious, I did not doubt it now. Bogdonovitch had disappeared, but whoever he had been so terribly afraid of seeing during our brief encounter on the street might have seen us. Gazing out over the swirling mass of pedestrians crowding the sidewalks in the noon-hour crush, I began to look all around, somehow certain I would recognize who I was looking for, though I had never seen them before and would not have known if I had.

I started to walk, and I kept walking, block after block, seeing over and over again the expression on the Russian's face, wondering what it meant and how it could have anything to do with me. I hardly knew anyone in San Francisco. I had not done anything. It was like being accused of a crime you have not committed: You know you didn't do it—or you think you know.

I walked long enough, and hard enough, finally to convince myself that I must have overreacted and that Bogdonovitch, who, after all, I did not know very well, had been overdramatic. I remembered the things he had said at dinner and the way in which he seemed quite willing to surprise, and even shock, Albert Craven's other guests. I also remembered that this was not the first time that instead of approaching me directly, he had followed me out of the courthouse and caught up with me in a crowd to tell me we had to talk. Even at dinner, when he

seemed so eager to question everyone's assumptions and contradict some of their most cherished convictions, I had thought
he was holding something back. After all the years he had spent
not only as a citizen but as a political operative of the Soviet
Union, perhaps it was only natural that he had become a deeply
secretive and suspicious man.

I slowed my pace and began to relax, looking in the windows of the shops, no longer concerned about whether I might
suddenly see someone's face reflected in the glass. When I
checked my watch, I found I had just enough time to make it
back to court.

Settled comfortably in my chair, I exchanged a few words
with Jamaal and waited for the jury panel to be brought back
into the room. As I began to get ready for the next round of voir
dire, I was almost ready to laugh at the exaggerated importance
I had attributed to the strange mannerisms of Andrei Bogdonovitch. Then I began to concentrate on trying to convince
the next juror I was someone he could trust.

We moved faster that afternoon than we had in the morning, though not by much. Instead of only one prospective juror,
we managed to question two. This was not nearly good enough
for the progressively impatient Judge Thompson. He refused to
waste any more warnings on two lawyers who seemed not to
understand the plain meaning of the English language. Instead,
at the end of the day, after he admonished the jury in the most
friendly way imaginable not to discuss anything about the case,
he told them that things always went faster on the second day
and that he could promise them that jury selection would be
finished no later than the end of the week. Without a glance at
either Haliburton or me, he picked up the papers he had
brought into court and left the bench.

It was a few minutes after five o'clock. I said good-bye to Jamaal and gathered up my things. I was outside on the court-house steps when I remembered. I found the card inside my suit coat pocket and checked the address, wondering what it was that Andrei Bogdonovitch thought so important.

Twelve

The address Andrei Bogdonovitch had given me was on Sutter Street, not far from Union Square and the St. Francis Hotel. I dropped my briefcase in my room and walked four blocks until I found it, a narrow storefront with the words IMPORT-EXPORT written in faded gold letters on the window. The sign in the door read CLOSED, and there were no lights on inside. I checked my watch to see if I was either a little early or a little late. It was exactly six o'clock, the time he had asked me to come. I was annoyed but also a little relieved. Whatever Bogdonovitch had wanted to talk to me about had apparently not been that urgent after all.

I turned to go, eager to get back to the hotel and get ready for a dinner date I had with Marissa Kane. I had not taken more than two steps when I heard the door open behind me and the remarkable voice of Andrei Bogdonovitch whisper my name. Half hidden in the shadows, he waved his hand, beckoning me to come in without delay. He shut the door quickly behind me and ushered me inside.

The shop had the stale smell of things that had never been moved from the place they had first been put. A long glass case held an assortment of cheap jewelry made from pounded copper and brass. Large Chinese vases were blanketed with dust. Oriental rugs, stacked on end, were tied with twisted hemp. A few undistinguished oil paintings hung high up on the wall, small white paper price tags attached with string to the bottom corners of wooden gilt frames. Everywhere you looked you had the feeling that nothing here ever sold and that some of these things had been here since they were first brought to San Francisco on the great high-masted sailing ships that once came from China and beyond.

In a pitch-dark alcove in the back, next to a door that presumably led to a storeroom—though why one would have been needed was itself a mystery—Bogdonovitch switched on a metal lamp atop a small wooden desk. Stacked neatly on the desk was a pile of what looked like order forms and invoices, and I assumed this tiny area must be his office. He nodded toward a chair on the side of the desk, waited until I sat down, and then took the one directly in front of it. Reaching inside a drawer, he pulled out a bottle of Russian vodka and two small glasses. Without asking me if I wanted one, he filled them both. He held his glass up, nodded toward me, and in one gulp tossed it down. I took a sip and put my glass on the corner of the desk.

"It should be kept on ice," he said, apologizing.

I was not certain why I had come, and now that I was here, I was beginning to regret that I had. I tried to get right to the point.

"You said you wanted to see me. You said you thought I might be in some kind of danger."

The light from the lamp fell in a small cylinder in the middle of the desk; everything above it, including Andrei Bogdonovitch, was bathed in darkness. Gradually, my eyes adjusted and I was struck again by the curious shape of his face and the strange way in which his eyes, covered with those heavy lids, seemed both to pull you in and to drive you away. He was, I thought, someone capable of both the most generous acts of friendship and the cruelest imaginable forms of brutality.

"We're both in danger, Mr. Antonelli. Since the night we had dinner together at Albert Craven's, the night I suggested to you that the murder of Jeremy Fullerton might not have been an act of random violence, people have been following me. I'm quite certain they're listening in on my telephone calls."

I took a deep breath and slowly let it out. For the first time I felt somewhat at ease. I understood everything: why he had followed me from the courthouse—not once but twice; why he had caught up with me, exchanged a few surreptitious words insisting on the urgency of something he had to say, and then vanished into the safety of the anonymous crowd. Despite his formidable appearance, Andrei Bogdonovitch was an old man, haunted by demons of his own invention, running away from a past he could not change, a past that no one else cared about or, for that matter, even remembered. The closer I looked at him, the more certain I became: He was an old man, losing the capacity to distinguish between his own identity and the lives of the people around him. He claimed I was in danger, but everyone was following him.

Bogdonovitch's large head jerked forward. He began to laugh, a deep, hammerlike laugh that reverberated all around the darkened walls.

"No, Mr. Antonelli, I'm not suffering the paranoid delusions of a lonely old man!"

The sheer strength of his outburst took me aback. "No," I protested, "I didn't mean to suggest anything of the sort."

"It isn't what you're suggesting," he said without the slightest trace of resentment. "It's what you're thinking. And why shouldn't you think it? It's a perfectly normal reaction." An ambiguous smile crossed over his mouth, and then, almost as an aside, he added, "Though I have to confess, I have myself seldom had the luxury of viewing things from the perspective of normal people."

The thought seemed to intrigue him. The smile lingered a moment longer. Then he blinked his eyes and nodded sharply.

"No, Mr. Antonelli, I know for a certainty that I'm being watched, and I have no doubt that this means danger for you."

He poured another shot of vodka into his glass and invited me to join him. Unlike the first time, when he downed it all at once, he drank just a little, not much more than I did.

"You see, Mr. Antonelli," he said, staring at the glass, "I believe I know why Jeremy Fullerton was murdered."

Had I been invited here to sit in this dismal dark back-store corner to listen to yet another discourse on the distinction between history and chance?

"I remember you said you thought it unlikely that a United States senator would have been killed in a random act of violence."

"I'm not speaking about theoretical generalities, Mr. Antonelli," he said as he raised his eyes from the glass. "I'm speaking about something quite specific. You see, Mr. Antonelli, I knew Jeremy Fullerton; I believe in some ways I knew him better than anyone else did."

How could he have known Fullerton, I wondered; and how could he have known him that well? Again, Bogdonovitch seemed to read my mind.

"I knew him from the time he was first elected to Congress, and I can tell you for a certainty that beneath that boyish charm of his, Jeremy Fullerton was utterly ruthless, without any conscience at all."

A tight cynical smile flashed across his mouth, and I had the feeling that Andrei Bogdonovitch would have once fallen into the same regrettable category into which he had just placed Jeremy Fullerton.

"It isn't as easy as most people think, Mr. Antonelli—to betray people who trust you. Most of us, I've found, do it, if we do it at all, only with reluctance, and then try to rationalize what we've done by telling ourselves that we had no other choice: that it was a matter of survival; a question of protecting someone else; that it was any one of a hundred other things that will give us some excuse for what we have done. Jeremy Fullerton never worried about any of that. He could betray someone without a second thought. He had a truly remarkable capacity to simply forget people, forget them as if they had never existed—once they had served his purposes."

I began gradually to realize what I was being told, though I had as yet no conception of what it meant or how far it might go.

"Are you suggesting that Jeremy Fullerton, a United States Senator, was recruited by the KGB?"

"No, Mr. Antonelli, I'm not suggesting anything of the sort. We didn't recruit Jeremy Fullerton; he came to us. It happened within a year of the time he was first elected to the House. He was a young congressman from California, without seniority, without any significant committee assignments—just another inconsequential member of the House no one outside his own district had ever heard of. But he had ambition to be more— much more—than just another congressman. And it was not just that he was ambitious—Washington is filled with ambitious people—he was impatient. He was the kind of man for whom everything is a means to something else. There is no doubt in my mind—none whatsoever—that even before he first knew he had been elected to the House he was already thinking about how he was going to get elected to the Senate.

"He came to us, Mr. Antonelli; we didn't recruit him. At first he said he wanted to open private discussions in the hope they might eventually lead to better relations between the two countries. It was quite the most astonishing thing I'd ever seen: a freshman congressman who talked like he was the American secretary of state engaged in back-channel negotiations. That may have been what first got my interest: how easily he assumed his own importance. He was also surprisingly well informed; not just about the current state of relations between the United States and the Soviet Union, but about Russian history, the Russian Revolution, the workings of Soviet economics. He tried to pass it off as a lifelong interest, and perhaps it was, but, as I came to learn, he was what you Americans call a 'quick study.' He was ruthless, but he also had an extraordinary intelligence.

"We began to have discussions—oh, dozens of them, Mr. Antonelli!—wide-ranging discussions over every conceivable topic, but never anything that would put him in a compromising position. Then, months after they began, he started talking about his frustration in the House, his inability to exercise any serious influence over policy, talking about how much more he could to do to bring about a better understanding between our two countries if he was in the Senate."

Bogdonovitch gave me a shrewd look. "We were not children, Mr. Antonelli. We knew he was spending a lot of time talking to people in California about a possible Senate campaign; we knew the only thing holding him back was money."

Pausing, Bogdonovitch took another drink. He set down the glass and slowly wiped his mouth.

"We were, I suppose, in what you might call a mating ritual: We danced around what we both knew we wanted and let things take their course. We gave him money; we gave him a lot of money—millions of dollars over the years. We financed his campaign, or rather we financed enough of it to make him the kind of credible candidate who could then attract money on his own. How much of what we gave him was always spent on his campaign, and how much he spent on himself, I don't know. It doesn't matter. From the moment he took the first dollar we gave him, we both understood that the dance had ended and that we were married for life. Fullerton had made his pact with the devil. Or perhaps we were the ones who had made a pact with the devil," he added, looking off into the distance.

"Do you read history, Mr. Antonelli?" he asked a short while later.

"Some."

"Thucydides?"

"Yes, but it's been a while."

"Do you remember how often Alcibiades did things for the enemies of Athens, but only so that he could eventually have the power to rule in Athens? That was Jeremy Fullerton. He made his bargain with us, but I think I knew that in the end he would find a way to turn on us without hurting himself."

"What was his part of the bargain?" I asked as Bogdonovitch took another drink. "You gave him money—what did he give you?"

"Something no one else could have given us: an understanding of the way things really worked inside the American government. We wanted to know everything we could about the people we were dealing with: their strengths, their weaknesses, who their friends were, who their enemies were. Fullerton gave us that. There were times I think we knew more about what was going on inside your government than we knew about our own. Fullerton was a brilliant observer."

"And in exchange," I summarized, "he got the money he needed."

"Oh, he got more than the money, Mr. Antonelli—though I admit that was what he wanted most of all. We also gave him the benefit of some of our own intelligence. It was no accident that after he was elected to the Senate, Jeremy Fullerton quickly became, by everyone's account, the best-informed member of the Foreign Relations Committee."

I could not think of any reason why Bogdonovitch should make this up; but neither could I see any apparent connection between what he had just told me and Fullerton's death.

"I'm still not certain that—"

"It's obvious, isn't it? Ever since the Soviet Union destroyed itself, people have been searching through the archives, trying to find out what really went on inside the Kremlin. It was only a matter of time before someone came across a report, a transcript, some file, something where Fullerton's name was mentioned or there was an accounting of the money that had been paid out to him. The point is that someone did find out, and that's the reason he was killed."

"But why—if he was working for the other side—and who?"

Bogdonovitch curled his lip in disdain. "Fullerton was never working for the 'other side,' Mr. Antonelli," he said sharply. "He was always working for himself—only himself."

It seemed a curious thing to say. He had just finished telling me that what Fullerton had given the Soviets had been invaluable; but now he seemed to have nothing but contempt for the motives that had made him do it. There was more than professional judgment involved in this. Whatever had happened between them, Bogdonovitch had for some reason come to think of it in deeply personal terms.

"He was on the Soviet payroll," I reminded him. "That

makes him a spy. The question is, who would want him dead because of it? If someone had learned about it, they could have turned him in to the government, they could have used it to blackmail him—but why kill him?"

Bogdonovitch thought I was an innocent. "What do you think would be the reaction in this country if it was discovered that not just a member of the United States Senate, but someone who might have become president, had for years been working with the Russians? The president hated Fullerton. He knew he was the only one who could defeat him for the Democratic nomination when he ran for a second term. Even if he defeated Fullerton in the primaries, he would be so weakened in the process that it would be next to impossible to win the general election."

He had just proven my point. "In that case, if they found out about Fullerton, they could have destroyed him with what they knew. The last thing they would have done is have him killed and make a martyr out of him."

Bogdonovitch picked up his glass and held it in front of his eyes, turning it first one way, then the other, as if he were searching for a flaw.

"Do you remember what happened in this country in the 1950s? Do you remember the great wave of fear and suspicion that began with a series of unsubstantiated accusations by your Senator McCarthy? I asked you before: What do you think would have happened if Fullerton had lived and all this had come out? Do you think that the public would have believed that Fullerton was the only high official to work for the Soviet Union? What do you think the political enemies of the president would have done with information that a major member of his own party had been a traitor? The Alger Hiss case poisoned politics in this country for a generation—and who was Alger Hiss compared to Jeremy Fullerton? No, Mr. Antonelli, they couldn't use what they had against him—they had to get rid of him, once and for all, and there was only one way to do it. It works out rather neatly, doesn't it? The president no longer faces a threat to his own survival and he becomes in addition the beneficiary of all the heartache and sympathy the public feels for a fallen hero."

He held the glass a little higher, twisting it back and forth in his hand. "There are only two people left they have to worry about." He put down the glass and smiled at me. "If they found out about Jeremy Fullerton, they know about me; and if they know about me, they can't take a chance with you."

"Me? Why would they have any reason to think anything about me?"

Bogdonovitch seemed almost sympathetic. "Because you're the defense attorney in the trial for Fullerton's murder, because you're the only one with a serious interest in proving that someone other than your client is responsible—and because they know you know me. They have to assume that you know something, and they can't take a chance on what that might be. You should know that as well as anyone, Mr. Antonelli. Isn't the first rule of murder not to let any witness live? You remember the car that almost hit you when you stepped off the curb that day I first tried to talk to you? Are you certain that was just an accident?"

It was logical, and insidious, and, I was now convinced, completely delusional. I might have believed what he told me about Fullerton—it would explain where the senator had obtained his money—but now I was being asked to believe that a conspiracy that went as high as the president himself was responsible for the murder. All the years of secrecy and deception, all the years of corruption and violence, had taken their toll: Andrei Bogdonovitch was a paranoid old man, scared of his own shadow.

I glanced at my watch, pretended I had not realized it was so late, thanked him for what he had told me, and quickly got to my feet. When we got to the door, Bogdonovitch put his hand on my shoulder.

"I know you don't believe me. I want you to know I don't blame you for that. But I can prove everything I told you about Jeremy Fullerton. In the meantime," he said as he cautiously opened the door, "be very careful."

Out on the sidewalk, I took a deep breath, trying to get out of my nostrils all the dust and dead air. At the end of the block, people were standing on the curb, waiting for the traffic light to change. I half expected to feel Bogdonovitch grab my arm as he caught up with me from behind, the way he had twice before. I stopped and glanced back over my shoulder.

It was the strangest thing. Everything seemed to stand still. The people walking on the sidewalk looked like cardboard cutouts, set there to fill up an empty space. Cars seemed to be parked in the middle of the street. Nothing moved; everything was frozen in time; and then, before I could blink an eye, there was an enormous, ear-shattering roar and a blinding orange flash that leaped all the way across the street and high up into the sky. I stood there, mesmerized, watching in utter disbelief as fire raged through the broken glass and jagged, twisted metal that was all that was left of the shop where less than a minute before I had said good-bye to Andrei Bogdonovitch.

I stood there, paralyzed, watching helplessly as a man and a woman, dazed and bleeding, wobbled aimlessly down the street. The sound of sirens—a mournful, insistent wail—grew louder and louder. A red fire truck with two firemen clutching the railing at the rear rumbled around the corner. From the opposite direction, a police car converged on the scene. A crowd had formed and I could hear all around me the voices of people asking each other what had happened.

Bogdonovitch was dead—nobody could have survived that blast. If I had not left when I did—if I had stayed just a minute longer—I would have been blown to pieces as well. Bogdonovitch had wanted to warn me, and I had not believed a word he said. He told me the same people who killed Fullerton would try to kill him, too—and not just him.

I could feel my pulse quicken. I began to search the faces of the crowd that swirled past me, looking for anyone who might be looking for me. Moving away from the street, I walked close to the buildings, trying to be as inconspicuous as I could. I thought about going back to the hotel, but anyone who had followed me when I went to see Bogdonovitch would know where I was staying. I thought about going to the office, but it was now nearly seven, and it was unlikely anyone was still there. I could think of only one place I could go, only one place where I would be safe.

With my head down and my hands shoved into my pockets, I walked as quickly as I could, forcing myself not to run. I turned on Powell Street, passed the front of the St. Francis, and kept going until I reached Market Street and the rapid transit station. I bought a ticket and took the escalator down to the platform where I waited for the train that would take me to Orinda, where Bobby lived. Things I never would have noticed before now took on a sinister significance: the passing glance of a stranger walking past me; the accidental bump from someone standing next to me each time the throng of weary commuters surged forward as an outbound train opened its doors.

Finally, the train I wanted pulled in. I dashed on board and then, certain that someone must be following me, watching me, waited until the doors began to close and at the very last moment jumped out. Ten minutes later, when the next one arrived, I wedged myself into the crush of standing passengers and, reaching between sweaty, tired hands, grabbed on to the overhead bar to keep from falling. The train rushed out of the station and into the black tunnel that passed under the city and under the bay. Swaying in tandem with the others, I peered through the tangle of lifted arms and drooping heads, wondering whether among all these strangers there was someone who meant me harm. As the train sped forward, the clicking cadence of the rolling iron wheels began to seem to my overheated imagination like the sound of my own heartbeat, the sound that when it stopped meant not only silence but death.

On the other side of the bay, the train shot out of the darkness and into the burnished bronze light of the evening sun. The train slowed down, and my heartbeat with it; the fear that had twisted every certainty into a doubt, and every doubt into a certainty, began to dissolve of itself, replaced with a growing sense of relief. I was safe; I had nothing to fear. At the next stop, I got off, walked underneath to the other side, and waited on the platform for the train back to San Francisco. When it arrived, nearly empty, I took a seat next to the window. On the seat next to the aisle, someone had left the front section of the afternoon paper. Halfway down, just below the fold, a picture of Jeremy Fullerton caught my eye. The lead line in the story announced that the Democratic candidate for governor, Ariella Goldman, the former "top assistant" to the murdered senator, had gradually narrowed the gap between herself and the incumbent, Augustus Marshall. They were now in a statistical dead heat.

As the train slid down into the tunnel under the bay, I wondered when someone first put together the plan that left only one man between Lawrence Goldman's daughter and the governor's office. Jeremy Fullerton's widow was certain that it had begun the moment the death of her husband first became known. After everything that had happened, I wondered if it might not have begun even earlier than that.

My arms folded across my chest, I slouched against the corner of the seat, watching my own reflection in the glass as the train raced through the enveloping darkness. Nothing made any sense, and I was ready to believe that it was because I was trying to find a meaning where there was not any. It was like the feeling I used to have when I found myself walking down some deserted street in the gray silence just before dawn, after drinking for days with people whose faces I could not remember and whose names I had never known. All the late-night enthusiasms and all the great, grandiose plans had died their deaths and turned to ashes, leaving behind nothing except a dim sense of embarrassment and a feeling of loneliness so vast that, once I fell down inside it, I knew I might never be able to pull myself out of it again.

Thirteen

I dashed up the steps to the St. Francis and saw her waiting in the lobby.

"I'm sorry," I began to apologize as she got up from a chair and began to walk toward me.

She had every right to be furious, but there was not a trace of annoyance in her eyes. She seemed much more worried about what might have happened to me.

"I waited at the restaurant for a while, but then, when you didn't come, I had this strange feeling that something might have happened," she said as she came close to me and looked in my eyes, searching to see if something was wrong. "I don't know why, but when I heard what happened tonight to poor Andrei Bogdonovitch—"

"You heard . . . ? On the news? Do they know what happened?" I asked. "Was it an accident?"

Ignoring my questions, she took my hand. "Are you all right?" asked Marissa intently. "You don't look right. What's the matter? What happened?"

I let go of her hand and took her by the arm. "I'll tell you all about it," I said as I guided her toward the entrance I had just come through. "Now tell me: Was it an accident, a gas line, something like that?"

She shook her head. "No, they think it was some kind of bomb. Someone did it deliberately."

"And Bogdonovitch?" I asked, just to be sure.

At first she could not bring herself to say it. "They found his body," she said finally. "Or what was left of it."

We walked two blocks down the street to the restaurant where we had had dinner several times before. Beginning the day nearly four months ago when we had driven through the Napa Valley, we had gradually become in our middle-aged way very good friends. That was all, just friends. I was not looking for a new romance; and, so far as I knew, neither was she. I liked being with her, and I was glad that she seemed to like being with me. Marissa saw the absurdity in the things most people thought important; and, in what only seemed a paradox, understood there were some things so serious they had to be taken lightly.

As soon as we sat down I ordered a scotch and soda. I started to drink it straight down.

"What happened?" Marissa kept asking, growing more alarmed.

"I was there when it happened. I was with him, talking to him."

Reaching across the table, she put her hand on my arm and held it there until I put down the glass.

"Who were you with? Who were you talking to?"

"I was with him—when it happened," I said, wondering why she did not seem to understand.

"Slow down, Joseph. Just tell me. Where were you?" she asked in a calm, measured voice.

I realized that nothing I had been saying could possibly have made any sense; and I wondered how I could describe to her even a little of what I had seen and what I had felt.

"This afternoon, after I left the courthouse at lunch, Andrei Bogdonovitch showed up. He said he had to see me; he told me I was in danger. I didn't believe him—at least not after I thought about it for a while. But he said he had to see me, and he asked me to come by at the end of the day—six o'clock."

Marissa's eyes grew larger. "That's where you were? That's who you were with—Andrei Bogdonovitch?"

"Yes. That's where I was: with him. I left—I was just at the corner—when it happened. It was awful. I could not believe it was happening, especially after what he had just finished telling me. That's what happened. That's why I thought I had to get away."

Marissa tilted her head to the side, a look of doubt in her eyes. "Get away?"

I was thinking about something else, something I had started to think about while I was still on the train, coming back to the city.

"How much do you really know about Jeremy Fullerton?"

Surprised by the intensity with which I had asked, she had to think a moment about the question, and even then did not know quite how to answer.

"Just what I told you before," she began tentatively. "I knew him, but not very well. I met him when he first ran for Congress. I did some volunteer work in his campaign. I knew him well enough that whenever I saw him at some event—like the night at Lawrence Goldman's—he remembered me. But that isn't what you're asking, is it?"

"When you first knew him—when he was running for Congress that first time—did he have money?"

Marissa drew her eyebrows close together and pursed her lips, trying hard to remember.

"No," she said finally. "They had enough to get by, but they didn't have what you would call money. He drove around in an old car, a four-door; I remember because the back seat was always filled up with boxes of campaign literature. They owned a house, but it was a small one—nothing special. Why? Why is it important?"

The waiter came to take our order. I handed him my empty glass and asked for another scotch. Marissa gave me a worried look.

"I never have more than two," I assured her. "Not for a long time, anyway."

Marissa knew I had not told the whole truth. She opened those large mysterious eyes of hers and with her lips slightly parted waited for me to tell her what I had left out.

"A year ago," I admitted. "For a while before that I was drinking quite a lot."

The waiter came back with our order and with my second scotch. I took a sip but discovered I had suddenly lost the taste for it. As I put it down, I remembered the way Leonard Levine had first reacted when Bobby told him he was drinking too much; and I remembered how the congressman seemed to blame even that on Jeremy Fullerton.

My mind, which for the last few hours had been racing from one thing to the next, began under Marissa's calming influence to grow less frantic. I suddenly realized I was famished.

"How do you think Fullerton came by the kind of money he ended up with?" I asked as I shoveled a forkful of spaghetti into my mouth.

I took three mouthfuls in succession before I paused and waited for her to answer. With a steady and fastidious hand, she reached across the table and with the corner of her napkin wiped the tomato sauce from my lips.

"I don't know how the Fullertons got their money. I suppose I just assumed that when you're in that position—a United States senator—you have helpful friends, people who put you into the right kind of investments, that kind of thing."

"Bogdonovitch told me Fullerton got his money from the Russians, that they paid him millions," I said, the words tumbling out. "Do you think that's possible? You knew him—do you think it's possible he would have done that: sold himself to the Soviets?"

Her first reaction was to deny it, or at least to doubt it; but then, reluctantly, she changed her mind.

"I told you once how he reminded me of that boy I knew in school—that with both of them you thought they had poetry in their soul, but you also thought that they might turn out to be frauds. If Jeremy Fullerton thought it was the only way . . ."

Marissa slowly raised her chin. A melancholy smile floated across her mouth.

"Or maybe if he just thought he could get away with it. There was that about him, you know: that sense that the rules didn't apply to him. It may have been part of who he was: the need to show himself that he could get away with things most other people would not think of doing, or think of trying if they did."

She smiled again, but there was a different meaning in it now, something I could not quite grasp.

"I think you're a little like that," she said. "Aren't you?"

I suppose because I thought it made me sound more interesting and enigmatic, I did not deny it; but neither did I want to talk about it.

"Bogdonovitch thought that was the reason Fullerton was

killed—because someone found out. That's why he wanted to see me. Bogdonovitch was convinced that whoever killed Fullerton was going to kill him—and anyone else they thought knew that Fullerton had taken money from the Russians. He thought the murder of Fullerton was a political assassination. He thought the government—the White House—was behind it."

I ate some more and then put down my fork.

"I didn't believe him. I thought he was a paranoid old man who thought there was a conspiracy behind everything that happened. You remember that night at Albert Craven's—the night we first met—all the things he said, all those allusions to the Kennedy assassination? You remember the way he suggested—at least seemed to suggest—that J. Edgar Hoover and the FBI were behind it? So when he started telling me about Fullerton and why he was killed and how we were both in danger—"

"Both in danger?" she asked with a startled look.

"Bogdonovitch tried to tell me that he was in danger because he was the only one left who knew what Fullerton had done and might be able to prove it."

"Why did he think you were in danger?"

"Because I'm the defense lawyer in the Fullerton murder trial and would try to find out everything I could about who might really have done it; and because, if they were following him, they had to know we had met and they couldn't take a chance he might have told me what he knew. I didn't believe any of it."

"But you believe it now, don't you—after what's happened?" asked Marissa as she pushed her plate aside.

"I didn't have any doubt of it, not when that bomb went off and I saw the glass flying and the fire ripping up into the air. I didn't have a doubt about it when all I could think about was where I could go and how fast I could get there."

Suddenly I thought of something and laughed because it

seemed so completely ludicrous that I had not thought of it before.

"All I could think about was getting away. That's what Jamaal Washington told me the first time I talked to him. He's
right: That's what you think, that's all you think. At least that's
all I thought. He thought he could do something, help somebody. He wasn't any less afraid than I was, but he beat his fear; I
didn't."

She disagreed, or tried to.

"It isn't the same. I don't doubt he was brave, terribly brave,
braver than most; but he didn't have any reason to think someone was trying to kill him, too; not until he was inside the car
and the light suddenly shone. Then he thought he was in danger and then he did what anyone would have done: He tried to
get away."

The waiter came and we ordered coffee and sat in silence
while he cleared away the dishes. When he left, Marissa raised
her chin and tilted her head. For a while she just looked at me,
as if she were trying to tell me that whatever I did, or whatever
I had done, it was all right.

"You didn't tell me—and you don't have to—but why were
you drinking like that, a year ago, before you stopped?"

I had never talked about it with anyone, except for a few
fragmentary remarks by which I told one or two people all they
needed to know. But I suddenly found that I actually wanted to
tell Marissa what had happened.

"I was in love with the woman I had first fallen in love with
when I was just a kid, still in high school. We had not seen each
other in years, and then we did, and it was like nothing had ever
changed. We were going to get married, after all that time, and
then something terrible happened. Jennifer became ill, seriously

ill; she just sort of disappeared inside herself, closed off the world the way someone pulls down a shade to darken a room.

"I used to visit her, once a week, at the hospital. Sometimes, when the weather was good, I'd take her for a drive. I kept thinking that something would happen, that she would suddenly come back to herself, that everything would be like it was before. When I finally knew that the doctors were right—that she was never coming back—I started to drink. It was all quite deliberate: I wanted to get drunk; I wanted to get lost, to disappear—the way she had. Maybe I thought I could find her there. And there were times, when I was in some drunken stupor, when I almost thought I had. I remember finding my way home late one night, blind drunk, tearing through the house, screaming at the top of my lungs, telling her to quit hiding and to come out from whatever room she was in."

I paused and looked around the crowded restaurant, watching the way everyone seemed to be having such a good time.

"I also drank because I felt sorry for myself, and because, to tell you the truth, I did not much care if I lived or died. I suppose I was already dead and just didn't know it yet."

Marissa touched the side of my face with her hand. For a long time she did not say anything.

"What made you finally stop?" she asked presently. "How did you find the strength?"

"I don't know. Maybe it was instinct, a sense of survival—maybe it was because I knew Jennifer would have blamed herself for what was happening to me. I had a friend who had been in AA for years. He knew about Jennifer and what had happened. He tried to get me to go, but I was not going to talk about any of this with anybody, certainly not with people I didn't know. He found me one time—after I really tied one on—stayed with me until I was sober, and made me promise that next time I felt like having a drink I'd call him instead. I called him a lot."

"But you didn't quit. You put a limit on yourself, instead. I thought—"

"I wasn't going to call myself an alcoholic; I wasn't going to go around reciting the twelve steps like a child repeating the ten commandments; I didn't really believe that the only alternative to getting drunk was not to drink at all. Flynn—that's his name: Howard Flynn—was too smart to try to talk me into it. Instead he made me promise that I'd never have more than two."

It was inexplicable, the effect Marissa produced with that look of hers. Staring into her eyes was like staring at my own conscience.

"He went with me one day to the hospital. He sat there with me while I told Jennifer what I had done, why I thought I had been doing it, and the promise I had made. Crazy, isn't it? She did not hear anything I said, but in another way I thought she knew; I thought she knew before I ever told her. Howard knew that I would try to keep any promise I made him; but he also knew I'd die before I broke a promise I made to her."

That was all I was going to say, but then I added something I had not, at least consciously, thought before.

"Howard was wrong. I can imagine doing it again—trying to lose myself in a bottle—but so far, at least, I've kept my word."

I was starting to feel the effects of everything that had happened, a kind of delayed reaction. The energy seemed to flow out of me. I felt tired, more tired than I had felt in a very long time.

"You need to get to bed," said Marissa with sympathy, but also worry, in her voice. "But I don't think you should stay at the hotel anymore. Your first instinct was right: You should have gone to Bobby's."

I started to object, but she stopped me with a look.

"You didn't want your cousin to think you were afraid?" she asked, gently mocking me with her eyes.

Outside the restaurant, Marissa took my arm and we started to walk up the block toward the hotel. We passed in front of the open door of a bar, and above the noisy laughter heard the wailing smoky sound of a saxophone. All the shops were still busy as shrewd-eyed merchants leaned over counters and pointed out various, never to be repeated, bargains. Weary, dull-eyed tourists and overweight women hanging on to their young children picked through piles of sweatshirts and T-shirts, bright-colored caps and cheap plastic mugs; pencils, pennants, and postcards; all of them bearing the name San Francisco or a picture of Coit Tower or the Golden Gate or one of the half dozen other things that had come to symbolize the city. We crossed the street to the hotel and at the corner Marissa stopped and tugged on my sleeve and told me again she did not think it was safe.

"I'm parked just up the street. Get what you need out of your room. I'll meet you in front of the hotel. I'm going to take you to Bobby's."

Before I could object, she added, "I'll feel better if you do it."

I threw a few things in my overnight bag and grabbed my briefcase. I was in the lobby before I remembered that in my hurry I had not thought to check for phone messages. I stopped at the desk and was told that Albert Craven had called. I thanked the clerk and turned away.

"You also had two visitors."

I looked back. "Visitors?"

"Two gentlemen came by, about an hour ago. They said they were reporters."

"Did they leave their names?"

The clerk shook his head. "They said they would try later."

I stepped close. "Do you remember what they looked like?"

"In their forties, I think. I'm sorry, but we were fairly busy at the time."

"Did you see them leave?"

"I assume they must have left," he replied as he glanced over my shoulder to another guest who had a question.

Reporters called all the time, trying to get me to say something about the case, but none of them had ever just shown up at the hotel.

Marissa was waiting outside, the engine running.

"Are you all right?" she asked as she pulled away from the curb.

"Yes, I'm fine."

"You don't think they were reporters?" asked Marissa when I told her what had happened.

"I don't know. But I don't think they were assassins, either. If they were coming after me, why would they let the hotel clerk get a good look at them?"

When we got onto the Bay Bridge, Marissa called Bobby on her cell phone.

"No answer," she said with the phone still at her ear. "Maybe he's out." Then she smiled. "Hello. This is Marissa. I'm bringing your cousin over. He needs a place to stay tonight. I offered," she said with a quiet laugh, her eyes straight ahead, "but I think he's a little shy."

With a mirthful, teasing look, Marissa handed me the phone. "He wants to talk to you."

"It isn't true, Bobby. She didn't offer," I said, looking at her while she pretended to concentrate on the road. "The truth is, I asked her, but she turned me down. Look, I hope you don't mind," I said, becoming serious, "but there's been a little problem. I'll explain when I get there. Marissa doesn't think I should stay at the hotel, and she might be right."

Bobby said he was glad I was coming and renewed the invitation to stay as long as I liked. "The longer, the better," was the way he put it.

Marissa knew her way; though, as she explained, she had not been to Bobby's house since his wife died.

"I used to come out here once in a while to see her."

"How did Bobby handle it when she died?"

I am not quite sure why I asked her that. Perhaps because I was not any longer quite so confident that my cousin had always done everything better than I could have done. It was, I suppose, inevitable that the more I got to know him, the more I would find that, like everyone else, he had made mistakes and done things of which he was not particularly proud. No one who lives beyond his boyhood years finds himself without something he regrets having done or having said, no one who still has a conscience.

Marissa did not reply until we left the freeway and drove past the golf course on our way into the Orinda hills. Then she said something about Bobby that surprised me.

"Bobby has never talked about it, at least with me. Frankly, I'd be surprised if he ever talked about it with anyone. He doesn't talk about personal things. He never has. He's always been kind of a lost soul."

Marissa steered the car through one twisting turn after another, but the driving had become automatic, instinctive. Her eyes were on the road, but she was seeing something else.

"Things didn't turn out for Bobby the way he thought they would. Or maybe he didn't think about how things were going to turn out until it was too late and there was nothing he could do about them. There are people like that, you know," said

Marissa, glancing at me for just a second to see if I understood. "They just go along with things, day by day—accept whatever comes along. It doesn't mean they don't become successful people, at least in terms of what the world thinks is success; but it doesn't mean that much to them. My father was like that. Maybe that's the reason I always liked Bobby so much: They were a lot alike. I think they both knew before they got out of college that nothing in their lives would ever be that good again. My father played football at Yale in the years right after the war. He was the captain of the team that won the Ivy League championship his senior year. He had a very successful career on Wall Street. He made what most people would consider a fortune, but I think he spent his whole life looking back, wishing he could do it all over again. I think Bobby is like that. He's cheerful, charming, but underneath it all he doesn't care very much about anything, except getting through it—getting through his life—the best way he can."

Bobby had turned on the outside lights. When he heard the car in the driveway, he opened the front door.

"Why don't you come in?" Bobby asked Marissa as he took the bag from my hand.

"I should go," she replied, looking at me.

Bobby said good night to her and turned toward the door.

I started to follow him, then changed my mind. Marissa was just looking over her shoulder, ready to back out of the drive. Laughing, I rapped on the window. She rolled it down and looked up at me, waiting. I bent down and kissed her gently on the mouth.

"Thanks—for everything," I whispered.

I let her go and stepped back. She tossed her head and laughed.

"Tell Bobby," she said as the laughter faded into the night, "that I'm becoming rather fond of his cousin."

I started to say something, but the words came out in an awkward stammer that made her laugh again.

"Better go," she said, rather pleased that she had managed to turn me into a tongue-tied fool.

Bobby began to tease me as soon as he shut the door. "I think she's after you."

I insisted we were just good friends; he insisted I was lying through my teeth.

"I could hear it in her voice. She may not have asked you to stay at her place, but if you had suggested it, she wouldn't have said no. Trust me," said Bobby with a confident look. "I know her."

"What does that mean?" I asked, a little annoyed at what I thought he might be suggesting.

"Not what you're thinking," he said as he took the bag out of my hand and led me down the hallway toward the guest room. He put the bag down on the bed and pointed toward the door to the bathroom so I would know where it was.

"Come on," he said, "let's get a beer."

We sat at the kitchen table, drinking out of two bottles. The tan cotton robe Bobby was wearing fell open over his leg, exposing the jagged scar that ran three-quarters of the way around his kneecap. It was the injury that had ended his football career and, if Marissa was right, marked the moment when he began to think of his life as something that was for the most part already behind him.

"Marissa has been with a lot of men, but not that way," explained Bobby as he put down the bottle. "She's never been with anyone very long. All I can tell you is I've never seen her look at anyone the way I saw her looking at you, just now when you were getting out of the car.

"She'd be good for you," he remarked as he lifted the bottle back to his mouth. "You should have somebody in your life," he added after he had taken a drink.

He looked at me for a moment to let me know he meant it; then he asked me what had happened and why Marissa did not seem to think it was safe for me in the city. I told him everything: how I first met Andrei Bogdonovitch; how he had twice approached me on the street; what he had said to me about Fullerton and the danger the two of us were supposedly in; how I had not believed a word of what he said until the explosion seemed to prove it. We talked for hours, or rather I talked and Bobby listened, late into the night, until I could not talk anymore.

Fourteen

The next day, and the day after that, I went on with voir dire the way I always had, asking one question after another, trying to convince each juror in turn that I was someone he or she could trust. They were the same questions I had asked before, questions about how the jurors lived and what they believed, and always whether they would insist on proof beyond a reasonable doubt before they thought about voting to convict; the only difference was that under the baleful eye of Judge Thompson I asked them more quickly and tried not to cover the same ground twice.

When court convened Friday morning, the day by which we had been ordered to finish jury selection, we were right on schedule. An hour after we began, both sides, the prosecution and the defense, exercised the last peremptory challenges we each had left. Unless there was a challenge for cause, that is to say unless there was a clear case of bias, the next person called to the box would be the twelfth and last juror needed. There was only one question I wanted to ask, and as I very well knew, it was perhaps the strangest question any juror had ever been asked.

"Tell me, Mr. DeWitt, who do you think killed John F. Kennedy?"

The district attorney shot out of his chair. "Objection!" he cried. "This is an outrage! That question has no relevance to anything: not the qualifications of the juror, not the charge in the case, not to anything conceivably connected to the case!"

If Clarence Haliburton had been someone he liked, or even someone he could tolerate, Thompson would have told me to move on to something else and that would have been the end of it. But he hated Haliburton, hated him so much he could not bear to do anything that might help him until he was convinced he had no other choice.

"It is a rather unusual question, Mr. Antonelli," observed Thompson with a perplexed frown.

"Really?" I replied as if I had not thought there was anything unusual about it at all. "Well, perhaps it was. Let me try to rephrase it."

I smiled at the juror. He was in his mid-thirties with greasy black hair plastered to his scalp. An enormous belly protruded from under a tight-fitting faded red short-sleeved shirt.

"Let me ask the question this way: Do you think Lee Harvey Oswald acted alone, or do you think he was part of a conspiracy?"

Haliburton threw up his hands. "Your honor! This is . . . well, I don't know what this is!"

It was plain from the look on Thompson's face that he did not know what it was, either. But he still was not ready to tell me to stop.

"Mr. Antonelli, would you mind explaining what it is you think you're doing?"

"Your honor, this is a murder trial. The defendant," I said, glancing down at Jamaal Washington, who was sitting impassively in the chair next to mine, "entered a plea of not guilty."

Thompson gave me a blank look. "Yes, and . . . ?"

"And, your honor, we know that a crime has in fact been committed. The victim, Jeremy Fullerton, a United States senator, was murdered. The defendant insists he did not do it. Obviously, then, someone else did."

Thompson tried to follow, but the harder he tried, the more befuddled he became. He squinted his eyes and twisted his mouth until it was almost entirely on the left side of his face.

"What possible connection is there between the defendant's contention that someone else killed Senator Fullerton and the assassination of John F. Kennedy? To say nothing else about it, the two events are separated by almost forty years."

"Quite right, your honor," I replied while the district attorney shook his head. "And we still don't know for sure who was really responsible. But leaving that aside, the point I was trying to explore with Mr. DeWitt here is whether, in a case like this, where a member of the United States senate, a candidate for governor of California—a man considered a serious future candidate for the presidency—it really makes sense simply to assume that his murder was nothing more than just another random act of violence."

Haliburton was beside himself. His face was red; his eyes were practically bulging out of their sockets.

"Your honor," he said with so much anger he could barely get the words out, "first he asks a question that has no conceivable relevance to the case, and now he starts to argue his case to the jury!"

Thompson saw it as a minor victory. He bent toward Haliburton and formed his mouth into the illusion of a sympathetic smile.

"Try to keep yourself under control, counselor," he said in a calm, soothing voice that, in Haliburton's present state, was almost an invitation to violence.

"May I see counsel in chambers?" asked Thompson before Haliburton, still speechless, could catch his breath.

When we sat down in front of Thompson's desk, the color in the district attorney's face had returned to normal, his anger hidden behind a mask of studied indifference. Now that we were out of the courtroom and out of public view, Thompson changed as well. Without the same incentive to make life difficult for his old nemesis, he turned on me with a vengeance.

"Listen, Antonelli, I've been on the bench a long goddamn time, but that's got to be the strangest goddamn question I've ever heard anyone ask. 'Who do you think killed John F. Kennedy?' " he said in a singsong voice, mimicking what I had done. "Maybe you don't know this," he went on, squinting at me like a physician examining a patient, "maybe they do it differently up there in Oregon, but down here the insanity defense only works when the defendant is nuts—not when his lawyer is crazy!"

If Haliburton took a certain satisfaction in what Thompson said about me, he was not given any time to enjoy it.

"And as for you!" the judge sneered. "All you had to do was stand up and say you had a matter for the court. But no—you had to show everyone all your righteous indignation. And what do you get out of it? Antonelli gets to make his little speech in full view of the jury. You better understand something, Mr. District Attorney: I'm not going to do your job for you. If you don't care if the jury hears a speech about how the defendant must be innocent because—if I follow what Antonelli was trying to insinuate—this must have been some kind of political assassination, that's all right with me!"

The color drained out of Haliburton's face. Tight-lipped, his hands trembling, he struggled not to say what he felt.

"I'll keep that in mind, your honor," he said finally, taking refuge in the formalities of courtroom behavior.

"All right," said Thompson with a quick, decisive nod. "Enough of this. We have to get down to business. Now that we've finally finished with jury selection—"

"I haven't examined the last juror," Haliburton reminded him.

"Don't worry, you'll have your chance," said Thompson impatiently. "But it shouldn't take long, unless," he added with a look of disgust, "you follow Antonelli's lead and start asking questions about the assassination of Abraham Lincoln."

Pausing, Thompson stared grimly at the floor. Shifting around in his chair, he raised his eyes and looked at me. Shaking his head, he muttered, " 'Who do you think killed John F. Kennedy?' And I thought I had heard it all."

We returned to the courtroom and acted as if well-mannered civility were the only way we knew how to behave. I had no more questions to ask of the last juror, and the district attorney asked only three or four. The jury was sworn. In friendly, conversational tones, Judge Thompson informed them that their first order of business was to take the rest of the day off. With the usual enjoinder against discussing the case, he dismissed the five men and seven women until Monday morning, when the trial would begin in which they, and no one else, would decide if Jamaal Washington would live or die.

When the jury had filed out of the room, Jamaal asked, "How are we doing, Mr. Antonelli?"

It was the same question I had been asked a thousand times before, asked in every case I had ever taken to a jury, asked by defendants desperate to find some meaning in the arcane procedures that were dull as dust to the lawyers who spent half their lives in a courtroom but a strange, incomprehensible mystery to the poor unfortunates who found themselves put on trial. They always asked, and I always gave them the same answer, the answer that gave them the assurance they were so eager to have. They wanted me to tell them that things were going well, that everything was fine, that there was nothing to worry about. That was really what they wanted: to believe that they did not have to worry; that though they might have to worry tomorrow, or the next day, or the day after that, right now—today—they could relax and feel almost normal again, if only for a little while longer.

"How are we doing?" asked Jamaal again, a hopeful look in his large, guileless brown eyes.

I started to say, "We're doing fine," but only the two first words came out. I smiled. "Actually, we're getting killed," I said instead.

For a second he was not sure what to make of it; then he knew—or thought he knew—that I was kidding. He laughed, and I could see how relieved he felt. Everyone wants to hope.

I could not leave it like that. I patted him on the shoulder.

"I think it's a pretty good jury. They seem fair-minded, and they seem interested. Sometimes that's the most important thing. It means they're curious: They want to know. They haven't already made up their minds."

The deputy was waiting to take him back to jail.

"Will I see you before we come back to court?" asked Jamaal.

Before I could answer, his eyes looked past me, the expression on his face changing in a way I had not seen before. Jamaal was always polite and never—with me, at least—unfriendly, but there was also a certain reserve, a kind of intelligent formality that preserved a slight, but definite, distance. In an instant, all that had vanished, and he had the look of someone who has just found his way back home.

I turned around, following his eyes, and found myself staring at one of the most remarkable-looking women I had ever seen. It must have been the way she was looking at Jamaal that told me she was his mother. They did not look that much alike, or perhaps it was that they seemed so different that I did not at first see the resemblance that was surely there. They were almost a different color. Jamaal had light brown skin, his mother dark black. Her face practically glowed. Her skin, stretched taut across high cheekbones, glistened like polished ebony; her coal-dark eyes smoldered and shone. Her hair, raven-black, was pulled back from her temples and tied behind her head. She had broad thin shoulders, long graceful arms, and long tapered fingers. She was as stunning as any woman I had ever seen, and I could hardly take my eyes off her.

Mary Washington had made her way through the crowd and was standing patiently behind the bar, a few feet from her son. I caught the eye of the deputy.

"Give her a minute with him, will you?"

Jamaal's mother leaned across the low railing and wrapped her arms around him. The deputy looked away and waited until they had had a chance to exchange a few private words. Then he cleared his throat, stepped forward, and put his hand on Jamaal's shoulder. It was time to go.

I introduced myself and told Jamaal's mother I was sorry we had not met before.

"I've been trying to get in touch with you for weeks. I've left messages. I've asked Jamaal to tell you that I wanted to see you, but perhaps . . ."

Suddenly I felt like a fool. I was running on about the way we had finally met as if we were two people discussing at a party how much we had heard about each other from our mutual friends, when she was a mother whose son was on trial for murder. With her head held high, she waited until I stopped talking.

"Thank you for helping Jamaal, Mr. Antonelli," she said in a low clear voice.

"Perhaps we could go somewhere and talk," I suggested as I turned back to the counsel table and started to put my things in my briefcase.

"I really can't," she said.

I looked over my shoulder, ready to ask when we could get together, but she was already moving past the last few stragglers on their way out of the courtroom.

Through the open door I heard the voice of Clarence Haliburton calmly answering the questions shouted at him from the pack of journalists jammed tightly together in the corridor. I decided to leave through the side door that led to the clerk's office. Before I had taken two steps, the reporters outside surged forward, the harsh, strident lights of the television cameras close on their heels. The cameras were not allowed inside the courtroom, but with the judge gone there was nothing to hold them back. I glanced at the closed door to the clerk's office. It was still tantalizingly close, just a few quick steps away; but if I made a dash for it, the only picture that would be seen in the papers or shown on the local television news was the back of the defense attorney, running away as if he had something to hide. I turned around and walked right at them and kept moving until we were out in the corridor and the doors to the courtroom were shut behind me. Everyone had a question, all of them variations on the same theme.

"Do you really believe that the murder of Jeremy Fullerton was a political assassination?"

I tried to be careful, but I had the feeling that things were already slipping out of my control.

"You seemed to suggest that it was more than just a possibility," another reporter insisted skeptically.

"In a murder case," I replied, staring back at him, "you always ask who had anything to gain by the victim's death. There are a number of people who had a great deal to gain by the death of Senator Fullerton."

The same reporter looked up from the note he was jotting. "As in the governor or the president?"

I was already on dangerous ground. I could not afford to get drawn into that kind of speculation. I started to take another reporter's question, but it was too late.

"Is that why you've subpoenaed Governor Marshall to testify at trial—because you think he had something to do with Fullerton's death?"

There was a dead silence. Everyone waited to hear how I was going to reply. The reporter, whoever he was, had remarkable sources of information. The subpoena had been issued only the day before, and I did not know until this moment that it had yet been served. I tried not to show my surprise, but the reporter, a small, wiry man with a crooked mouth, sniffed the air with satisfaction. We had never met, but I could tell he did not like me; he did not like me one bit.

"The governor has been subpoenaed because the defense believes he has evidence relevant to the case," I said quickly, hoping no one would notice that I had not said anything at all. It did not work.

"What evidence is that?" shouted someone from the back.

"Do you think the governor had Fullerton murdered?" yelled another reporter.

"Is that the only way Marshall thought he could get reelected?" added another voice.

"What about the president?"

I held up my hands and refused to answer anything until they stopped.

"I know the following things: The defendant, Jamaal Washington, did not kill Senator Fullerton. That means someone else did. I also know that Jeremy Fullerton was a very ambitious man who threatened the political careers of a number of other important, very powerful people. The defense intends to offer evidence about who those people were and what they had to lose so long as Jeremy Fullerton was left alive."

Before any of them could ask another question, I held up my hands again and shook my head. "That's all I can say at this time."

I turned and, as quickly as I could, walked away.

I grew angrier with each step I took, quickening my pace as if I could outrun the way I felt. I was so caught up in my own emotions that I did not notice until I reached the courthouse doors that Bobby was right behind me.

"I came over to watch. You were terrific," said Bobby with an encouraging grin. "Why are you so upset?"

"Because I shouldn't have put myself in a position where I had to answer questions from reporters."

"Isn't that why you asked that question about the Kennedy assassination—to get everyone to think that this had to be an assassination, too? You didn't say anything back there that wasn't implicit in what you asked that juror."

He was right, of course; and I realized I was not angry because of what I had been asked, but because I did not have an answer to the only two questions that counted: Who murdered Jeremy Fullerton and why?

In the sunlit air outside, my mood began to change and the burden of what I was doing, or trying to do, did not seem quite so intolerable. A few blocks from the courthouse we found a small restaurant and, though neither of us was particularly hungry, went inside. Pencil in hand, the waitress flashed a vapid smile, which vanished immediately when we told her we only wanted something to drink.

"She's about as pleasant as the Honorable James L. Thompson," I said with a laugh. I sank against the back of the booth and with a grim smile shook my head. "What a piece of work he is."

Bobby never went to court, not to try a case of his own. He was intrigued, and he wanted to know what had happened while, with everyone else who had come to watch, he had been forced to sit, waiting, while something presumably important was being discussed in the rarefied language of legal scholars debating a fine point of law.

"In chambers?" I asked, laughing at the way we all imagine that the things we did not hear were always so much more interesting than the things we did. "Nothing much. Thompson told me I was crazy and told Haliburton he was a fool. You can't really blame him for thinking that about me. That question I asked about Kennedy . . ."

"Couldn't you feel the effect it had?" asked Bobby eagerly. He bent toward me. "Everyone just sort of tensed, all their attention on you, waiting to see what would happen next."

"I almost didn't do it," I confessed. "I planned to do it; I thought I had to do it; but it was like one of those things that seems like such a great idea at two o'clock in the morning, when you're all alone. You wake up the next morning, all the dull prosaic facts of everyday life staring you right in the face, and it doesn't sound anything like as good as it did late at night, when you imagined things were so much different than what they really are."

"And without those late-night thoughts, the day wouldn't be

worth much, would it?" asked Bobby with the knowing glance of someone who had spent some late nights of his own. "It worked," he insisted. "It made everyone wonder how likely it could be that someone like Fullerton could have been killed in—the phrase you kept using—'a random act of violence.' "

The dour-faced waitress brought an iced tea for Bobby and a cup of coffee for me and dropped the check on the table.

"And the next thing everyone is going to start wondering is why I don't have any evidence to prove that it wasn't," I replied, brooding as I sipped on the coffee.

"Do you know how I first thought about asking that question? When you reminded me of one of the things you taught me when we were kids, something you said you learned from our grandfather: That you never start a fight; but when someone starts one with you, especially when they're bigger than you are, you have to throw the first punch; because, if you don't, you may never get the chance to throw one at all. I had to ask that question, because it was my only chance to get that thought in front of the jury—my only chance to let them know that what happened to Fullerton was not just any murder. But there was another reason, and it had nothing to do with the case—or maybe it had everything to do with it. If Bogdonovitch was right—if he was killed because of what he knew about Fullerton, and if they think they have to kill me for the same reason—then I thought that maybe they'd have second thoughts about doing something that would make people wonder if I wasn't right after all: that it was an assassination and that there was a conspiracy to cover it up. So you could say I asked the question more out of cowardice, more because of how scared I was about what might happen to me, than because of what I thought might help the defense."

Raising his chin, Bobby gave me a skeptical look. "And is that the reason you subpoenaed the governor—cowardice?"

"No, stupidity. I did not know what else to do. I could not subpoena the president, and I had to do something. I have to have a witness I can use to show the jury just how much a threat Fullerton really was. The truth is, I don't have a case. I don't have any evidence about anything, except motive. Everyone from the president down seemed to have a motive to want Fullerton out of the way. With Fullerton dead, the president won't have a fight for the nomination and the governor isn't facing sure defeat in November."

"And Ariella Goldman has a chance to become governor," added Bobby.

"That would not explain Bogdonovitch's death," I rejoined.

"But you don't know for sure why he was killed. All you know is what he told you, and you did not believe him—remember? What if you were right—what if he made the whole thing up? What if he invented that story about Jeremy Fullerton and the money? And even if that part was true, how do you know anyone else ever found out about it? Andrei Bogdonovitch could have been killed by anyone—not just some White House assassin. Think of all the people he must have harmed during all the years he was with the KGB. Don't you think some of them might have wanted revenge? And if a government was involved, why not the Russian government? Perhaps they did not want one of their former spies telling what some of the new Russian democrats were doing when they were all still communists."

I paid the check. We left the restaurant and started walking to where he had left his car.

"You haven't forgotten about tomorrow, have you?" asked Bobby when we reached the entrance to the parking garage.

I had not forgotten but found myself wishing that I were going to be doing something else than spending the afternoon on Albert Craven's boat circling the bay.

"By the way," he said as he handed his ticket to the parking attendant, "who was that striking-looking woman talking to Jamaal Washington?"

"You don't know her? She's Jamaal's mother—Albert Craven's friend, the one he has known for years."

Bobby just shrugged his shoulders.

"Albert has a lot of old friends. But that woman? No, I've never seen her before in my life."

Fifteen

Albert Craven was waiting on the dock when Marissa and I arrived. I could not help but smile and hoped I would not laugh. Every time I had seen him before he had been wearing a dark suit, a silk shirt, an obviously expensive but understated tie, and soft, gleaming Italian shoes. Dressed like that, he had the look of a self-made man of wealth and influence, a man who could afford anything he wanted and had the taste to know what he did not need. I had not realized how much of the way I thought of him had depended on what he wore.

He was dressed in a dark blue polo shirt, which, though it was not yet quite noon, clung to him like a second sweat-soaked skin, and a pair of white shorts that exposed two knobby knees and two pale white spindly legs. With his smallish head, sloping shoulders, and sagging waistline, Craven looked like an aging old man, tottering out for a weekend walk.

Bobby was already there, standing behind the wheel, talking to Laura, a young woman he had been seeing for a while. She had short brown hair and a dark tan that made her eyes seem dark as well. She moved quietly and, when we were introduced, smiled and did not say anything at all. I knew I was going to like her when I watched her talk to Marissa and saw the way her eyes kept coming back to Bobby.

Craven collapsed in a canvas deck chair, mopping his brow, as Bobby took us out of the marina and, gradually increasing speed, out into the bay.

"You really put a subpoena on the governor?" asked Craven, blinking his eyes against the salt spray. "I heard it on the news yesterday, but I still couldn't quite believe it." Suddenly he brightened. "How do you like my boat?" he asked eagerly. "I used to want to have a sailboat—sail 'round the world, that sort of thing—but I couldn't. I get seasick. Wouldn't you know it? Anyway, I got this instead. I go out on the bay once in a while— when it's nice and calm the way it is today. Other times I just sit in it at the marina and feel the water rolling under it. It's a nice feeling, really quite soothing."

Craven's eyes grew distant. He tilted his head back to feel the wind against his face.

"I was extremely sad to hear what happened to Andrei Bogdonovitch. Poor man. I liked him, you know," said Craven firmly as he bent forward in his chair and looked directly at me. "The police don't seem to have any idea who killed him or why. I suppose he must have had a lot of enemies."

Bobby was at the wheel, just out of earshot. Marissa and Bobby's friend, Laura, had gone below. There was something I had to know and this might be my only chance to ask.

"Who is Mary Washington?"

Craven tried to give me a blank look, as if he did not understand what I meant.

"You told me she was an old friend, a good friend," I said, bending close. "Someone you wanted to help."

"She is," he said. He hesitated, waiting to see if that would be enough or if I was going to insist on being told something more.

"Then why hasn't she come to see me? Why wouldn't she even return a phone call? She came to court yesterday. It was the first time I had ever laid eyes on her, but even then she couldn't talk to me. I'm trying to defend her son, for God's sake, and she can't be bothered to see me?"

"Don't be too hard on her," he replied. "She's a little different than most people."

He started to say something more, but Marissa came up from the galley. Holding on to a metal handle with one hand, she clutched her tan floppy hat with the other.

"Can you go any faster?" she shouted gleefully, daring Bobby to show her what the boat could do.

The stern fell lower in the water as Bobby gave it more power. A long wake, like a double furrow turned up by a plow, blew out behind us. Opening the throttle all the way, Bobby put the boat into a quarter turn and then pulled back, forcing a long rolling motion that Marissa seemed to love. Albert Craven closed his eyes and groaned.

As he slowed down, Bobby, with Laura standing next to him, looked back over his shoulder and pointed toward the shore at a long promenade of stucco homes. Painted pink, yellow, blue, green, and white, they were built tight together, wall to wall, curving along the street that edged along the bay.

"Can you recognize your house from here?" shouted Bobby to Craven.

"Of course," replied Craven without bothering to look.

"Everything looks different when you're out here," added Bobby.

Reducing speed, we moved closer to shore and crawled past the abandoned piers of Fort Mason, watching the Saturday

crowds swarm between the shops and settle into the lines starting to form outside the restaurants.

"You really did that?" asked Craven as he tapped me on the
shoulder. "Subpoenaed the governor?"

"I called his office for a week. No one returned my calls. It's
an old rule, Albert: If they won't talk to you in private, they can
talk to you in court."

Snapping open a hard leather case, Craven removed a pair of
gold-rimmed sunglasses and slid them carefully onto the tender
bridge of his reddened nose.

"It's a little different with the governor, don't you think?"

Bobby had taken us away from the shoreline of the city. We
were moving faster now, the wind rising all around us. I had to
shout my reply.

"You'd think so."

Craven leaned closer and turned his ear toward me. "I beg
your pardon?"

"You'd think so," I yelled.

He did not try to say anything more; he just nodded to indicate that he had heard and settled back into the deck chair.

A dull, thudding sound reverberated through the hull as the
boat crashed across the crest of one wave and then the next. We
passed under the Bay Bridge, and through the steel grillwork
high above I could see tiny cars moving along like the playthings
of a child, and I remembered what Bobby had told me about
what our grandfather had told him. I felt a strange, wistful smile
cross over my mouth.

"Long way to fall," I said out loud, though no one, not even
Albert Craven, who was sitting right next to me, could hear.

We passed under the bridge, circled around Yerba Buena Island, and then, on the eastern side, passed back under it again
and ran parallel to the tan flat-roofed buildings along the low-

lying shore of Treasure Island. Out beyond the island we hit rough water. The bow rose high in the air and then came smashing down, over and over again, wave after wave washing over us, drenching us in cold salt water. Mesmerized by the cruel monotonous rhythm of the sea, I gazed at the milky green color of the bay, wondering what it must have been like when there was nothing else here, nothing but the wind and the water and the open sky and the lonely vacant hills.

Bobby turned north, away from the Golden Gate, and headed toward Angel Island, less than half a mile at its closest point from the Sausalito shore. The island broke the current that flowed from the Pacific and the boat slipped through the water on an even keel. Marissa stood up and shook her head, laughing at the way the water sprayed all around her. She disappeared into the galley and then, a moment later, rubbing her face with a thick fluffy towel, came back up just long enough to throw me one I could use myself. A few moments later, she was back again, the towel draped around her neck, with a dark green bottle and some empty glasses.

"Ready for lunch?" she asked as she began to hand everyone a glass.

Bobby had slowed the engine and turned toward shore. Twenty yards from a cement pier, he dropped the engine into neutral and let it idle. The dwindling wake of a boat that was vanishing into the distance slapped gently against the hull. Ahead of us, even closer to the shore, a half dozen kayaks, their double-bladed oars flashing, raced furiously against each other. At the edge of the muddy shore, a young Hispanic woman was briskly handing sandwiches to three shirtless eager-eyed children.

Rising up behind them, looming so large that the eye could not take it in all at once, was one of the bleakest buildings I had ever seen. You could scarcely look at it without a shudder. It stood there, an enormous four-story complex, a kind of perverse tribute to the soulless efficiencies of nineteenth century industrial architecture, each blackened yellow brick speaking the same depressing story a million times over.

"I didn't know that was there," remarked Marissa as she handed a glass to Craven and then handed two glasses to me. "Hold them for me, will you?" she asked as she went below.

I had put my feet up and slipped down until my head was leaning against the side of the seat. Taking off my dark glasses, I turned my face to the sun and listened to the laughter of the children playing onshore. The rough pounding rhythms of the crossing had taken away the tension that had built up inside me, and I was left alone with the things I could feel: the warm sun on my face as the fading wind rippled over my skin; the easy rolling motion of the boat; the sound of my own breath, drawn in from the clean salt air.

I heard Marissa's voice, though I could not make out the words. I wondered whether I should try to open my eyes or think of something to say. There did not seem to be any hurry to decide. Then I felt on my forehead the warm touch of her fingers.

"What exactly do you propose to do with him?"

I sat up and looked around. Reclining in the canvas deck chair, Albert Craven balanced on his ample stomach a paper plate heaped with food.

"You can't just put him on the stand like he was any other witness, can you?"

"The hell I can't," I grumbled, winking at Marissa as she handed me a plate of my own.

Albert Craven liked having people around him. He especially liked having women around him. Their company seemed to heighten his sensibilities and inspire his more generous impulses. He was an inveterate tease and a harmless flirt.

"This is Antonelli's case," he said, glancing first at Marissa then at Laura. "But I end up doing all the work. All he has to do is go to court, while I have to take all the telephone calls from really important people that your friend Joseph here doesn't seem to have time to talk to."

Craven's pinkish face glowed with pretended self-pity. He took a bite of a sandwich and then wiped his mouth.

"It's about all I do anymore," he said with a long sigh. "I'm beginning to feel like a receptionist—or a press agent."

"Take long lunches," said Bobby with a wry grin.

Craven dismissed it with a wave of his hand. "This case is all anyone wants to talk about at lunch. It has the whole city by its ears. Especially now that you've gone and subpoenaed the governor," he added with a shrewd glance. "His people, by the way, are very upset about it."

"Those are probably the same people who wouldn't return my phone calls. The governor and his people seem to think that a murder trial is some kind of personal inconvenience," I objected.

Craven nodded. "More like a political inconvenience, I should say."

The boat rose and fell in the long gentle swells. Albert Craven sipped on his wine, then held the long-stemmed glass upright in the palm of his hand, watching pensively as the surface level inside traced the undulating movement of the bay below.

"You wanted to know what that was," said Craven suddenly, looking up at Marissa. He waved his hand lazily toward the shore and the dreary grime-covered building about which she had earlier asked.

"It looks like something you might expect to find in the valleys of Manchester or the hills of Pennsylvania, doesn't it—one of those factories built at the beginning of the industrial age: brick-walled prisons for the wage-earning poor, places where whole families—whole generations, men, women, and children—spent all their waking hours, working for nothing more than enough to keep them alive long enough to work again the next day, and the next, and the day after that. But it's not a factory at all."

Sitting at an angle, one leg crossed over the other, Marissa gazed across to a part of the island hidden from every landbound perspective. "I've been out on the bay, and this isn't the first time I've sailed around this side of Angel Island, but if I ever saw it before, I don't remember it."

Craven was intrigued. "How far do you think it is from where you live?"

"In a straight line—across the water? Less than a mile, I suppose."

"And you didn't know it was here; though when you look at it now, you must wonder how anything this massive, this substantial, could have been here all this time, less than a mile away, just out of view, and you never knew anything about it."

Bobby took a swig from a can of Coca-Cola. "What's your point, Albert? I didn't know it was here, either."

"Point? I don't know if there is a point," drawled Craven amiably. "I just find things like this curious—how little we notice things that are around us, how different things are from the way we imagine them to be, how much goes on right in front of our eyes that we know nothing about."

"From the look of it," said Bobby as he surveyed the stark rectangular lines of that dismal forgotten place, "not much has gone on there in a very long time."

"What is it?" asked Laura shyly. "Or, rather, what was it?"

"It was Ellis Island," replied Craven. "It was the western version of Ellis Island. It was where a generation of immigrants had their first introduction to America. Instead of the Irish and the Italians and the Germans and the Russians and the Poles, the immigrants who entered here were Asian—Chinese, mainly— and instead of heading for homes on the lower east side of Manhattan and work in the sweatshops of New York, they were herded into camps and then sent off to help build the railroads."

Pointing vaguely toward a spot farther up the shore, he added, "The ships used to come in every day."

Sipping slowly on his wine, Craven stared at the quiet vacant place, which had once been filled with the ruthless movement of sailing ships and steam ships, teeming with masses of huddled Chinese blinking under the assault of sounds they had never heard before and sights they had never seen.

"It's all part of the great illusion—or, if you prefer, the great mystery—of San Francisco. People who come here now think they can become whatever they want; they think everything is possible. The Chinese came here because it was the only way they could survive. They could not blend in, pass unnoticed the way white people could; they were treated like foreigners and they lived that way, separate and apart. Some of them still live that way. Chinatown is part of San Francisco, but I'm not at all sure San Francisco is any real part of Chinatown."

The spreading wake of a fast-moving ferry rolled under the boat. A little of the wine that had just been added to Craven's glass sloshed over the top and onto his hand. Laughing, he switched the glass to his other hand and licked his thumb.

"Oh, I know," said Craven, returning to his subject, "things are different now. The Chinese aren't treated like indentured servants. But for a long time they were, and in those days the city belonged to people like my good friend Lawrence Goldman, people who spent their lives pretending they were someone they were not."

Craven's eyes were fixed on the dreary brick complex where every Asian immigrant was quarantined to protect against the invasion of exotic diseases from the Orient.

"Can you imagine? The Chinese talk about—or at least they used to talk about—their ancestors, a line going back thousands of years. I don't know half a dozen people who can tell me the names of all four of their great-grandfathers, and Lawrence Goldman certainly isn't one of them. Lawrence claims to be 'old San Francisco.' He isn't just someone with a lot of money. No, Lawrence had to be part of a tradition. And he is, though it isn't the one that gets told in the newspapers."

"Wasn't his grandfather the chief of police?" asked Marissa alertly.

Craven took another sip of wine. A shrewd, knowing smile creased his small round mouth.

"Yes," he replied, peering down into the glass, "and that is so to speak the respectable core of Lawrence's achievement; the basis, if you will, of his claim to inclusion among the established families of San Francisco. Of course," he went on, raising his eyes, "none of the families that considered themselves established at the time would have been caught dead having a police chief in their homes. But leave that aside. Lawrence's grandfather was the police chief of San Francisco, and every time he attends some ground-breaking ceremony for a new hospital, or a new museum, or a new gallery, or anything else that benefits the city, he dismisses the importance of his own contribution by insisting that he is only trying to follow the example of public service first established by his grandfather."

That same shrewd smile appeared again on Craven's mouth as he looked at each one of us in turn.

"What that does, of course," he explained, "is to give Lawrence a status he could never have achieved with money alone.

"Lawrence Goldman's grandfather was Dan O'Brien, who became police chief in 1920 after twelve years on the force. The interesting thing is that when he first became a cop—in 1908—he was already thirty-three years old. Where he came from, what he did for the first thirty-two years of his life—no one knows. He was chief of police for about a dozen years. He had one child, a daughter, Kate, a fiery, headstrong girl who always did exactly what she wanted. What she wanted more than anything else was to become an actress, a movie star.

"She went to Hollywood, became a bit player, and then, after a while, began to get better parts. She starred in a dozen or so silent movies, but her career only really took off with the arrival of sound. She had a voice you could never forget: silky, sensual, it slipped into your mind and stayed there, playing over and over again like a record you can't stop, don't want to stop. She was in the first all-talking picture. *The Jazz Singer* was the first talkie, and Al Jolson spoke the first words a movie audience ever heard, but the first full-length picture in which talking was a regular, normal part of the story was made a few months later that same year—1927, I think it was. Kate O'Brien was in it, and so was Lawrence Goldman's father.

"That's how they met, Lawrence's parents, on the set of the first real movie." Craven caught himself. "Real movie!" he exclaimed, laughing quietly.

"Tim Cassidy. Ever heard of him?" he asked, looking at Bobby and then at me. "He was a restless, earnest sort. He grew up in New York. Cassidy was his stage name. His movie name, I should say. His real name was Goldman."

"Why did he change it?" asked Marissa, carefully refilling his glass.

"Everyone changed their names for the movies," he replied. "It was all part of the illusion, part of being something else. And if you were Jewish," he said, patting her hand as they exchanged a meaningful glance, "well, America wasn't ready for a Jewish cowboy.

"Nathan Goldman—that was his real name—grew up in New York and dreamed of becoming a surgeon. But he spent two years in the army during the First World War, saw active duty in France, and when he came back no longer knew what he wanted to do. The war had changed him, unsettled him, made it impossible for him to get back into the routine of everyday life. The war—that war—seemed to do that to a lot of people. He left New York and went to Los Angeles. He made dozens of silent movies, and then, when sound came, he became a star. From that first all-talking picture until the beginning of the Second World War, Tim Cassidy guaranteed the success of any movie he was in. They were all westerns, and of course he was always the hero.

"He married Kate O'Brien in 1928 or 1929—I've forgotten which. For a few years—really into the mid-1930s—they were one of the best-known couples in America. The San Francisco papers were full of stories about them, stories that always mentioned she was the daughter of police chief Daniel O'Brien. It seemed they were here almost every weekend. In those days, there was very little nightlife in Los Angeles. Everyone from Hollywood came here. There was a train—the Starlight—that left L.A. every Friday afternoon and returned Sunday night. San Francisco was filled with nightclubs, and on weekend nights they were filled with Hollywood stars. That's when Errol Flynn and Melvin Belli became such good friends, on two-day drunks, when they did things that today would put them in jail or worse. But everybody loved it: the glamour, the celebrity, the harmless escapades of famous people who mixed with everybody else and, like everybody else, just wanted to have a good time.

"You see, that's really the point: Everybody wanted to have a good time, and you could have it here. San Francisco was a wide-open town. You could do anything you wanted, as long as you had the money to pay for it. The cops looked the other way—for a price. Everybody was great friends, as long as the police got their share. Everybody understood the game, and everybody followed the rules. One of the rules was that no one ever publicly questioned the integrity of the police."

Rising slowly, Craven balanced himself on wobbly legs and stood next to me at the side of the boat, watching the light move up the side of the island and disappear into the deepening shadows of the dark green trees.

"The great illusion of civic duty was perpetuated right to the end and even beyond. When O'Brien died, the newspapers called him 'the most beloved policeman the city has ever known.' Everyone attended his funeral, and everyone believed—or pretended to believe—the astonishing story of how on a policeman's salary he happened to die with an estate worth nearly a million dollars."

Taking a deep breath, Craven filled his lungs with the brisk salt air. Stretching out his arms, he twisted his small round head from side to side. With an affable grin, he looked down at the two women.

"A million dollars, mind you, in 1934. Do you have any idea what that would be worth today? Neither do I, but I wouldn't think ten or twenty million would be out of the question."

I spread my feet apart and let go of the side of the boat. "That's where Lawrence Goldman's money started?" I asked. "Police corruption?"

Craven stared at me with owlish eyes. "Oh, no. There was no corruption. The police chief accumulated all that money as an act of 'unselfish devotion.' Yes, that was the phrase the newspapers used: the 'unselfish devotion' of a father to his daughter and her husband. You see," said Craven, reaching for the glass Marissa had just refilled, "the good chief had become terribly concerned about the lavish spending habits of his daughter and her husband, and he was afraid that they might find themselves penniless when their careers came to an end. So he began to borrow money from them, large amounts of money: money for a new car, money for a new house, money for this investment, that investment, whatever excuse he could invent at the moment. And of course," he added, raising his wispy eyebrows, "they always said yes, because, after all, what did money mean to them?"

With a puckish grin, Craven settled back into the canvas deck chair. He crossed one leg over the other, trying to hide the purplish varicose veins that ran behind his knee.

"According to the story," said Craven with a sly glance, "Dan O'Brien borrowed a prodigious amount of money over the years. And because the chief was really a saint in policeman's clothing, he never spent a dime of it on any of the things for which he had supposedly borrowed it. No, he saved it, all of it. He put it in a trust fund, nearly a million dollars, and the beneficiary was his only grandchild, Lawrence Goldman.

"It's a wonderful story, isn't it?" asked Craven, shaking his head in wonder. "Except, of course, there is not a word of truth in it. O'Brien never borrowed any money from his daughter or his son-in-law. He stole it, all of it—kickbacks, bribes, payoffs: the tariff charged by the police to protect all the illegal operations that let everyone who could afford it have the kind of good times they wanted. The chief must have died laughing. He lived well, died rich, and did it all on other people's money. And even though they knew what he really was—because they were all in some sense in it with him—both the people who paid him off and the judges and the politicians who were paid off with him had no choice but to sing his praises and build monuments in his name.

"No one seemed to notice, or if they did, no one seemed to care, about the way he had used his own daughter to cover his crimes. She and her cowboy star husband were left to smile and nod and grow teary-eyed at the way he had schemed to save them from themselves. They had to stand in front of all the photographers and reporters and newsreel cameras and fill in all the blanks in the story of how irresponsible they had been in the way they had spent their own money, the way they had given him whatever he had asked for and somehow never even noticed that the new car he wanted had never been purchased and the new house had never been built. They had to do the best acting job of their lives to convince everyone that they were thoughtless, irresponsible fools who on their own would never have bothered to save anything to take care of their only child. They had to look into a camera and show how deeply grateful they were that thanks to Daniel O'Brien their only child would never have the misfortune to have to rely on his own parents."

"What happened?" I asked, urging him to go on.

"The daughter and the son-in-law? Nothing good, I'm afraid. A few years later, sometime in the late thirties, Kate O'Brien died under rather mysterious circumstances. There were rumors the police suspected her husband, but, mind you, the police never said that. They never said anything. The studio probably had something to do with that. No one wanted that kind of scandal. But Tim Cassidy never worked again. His career was nearly over anyway, and no one really noticed that he was gone. He just disappeared. I don't mean he went into hiding, or even left town. He didn't do anything, really. He stayed in the same Beverly Hills house until he died, almost twenty years later. But he might as well have left the country. He was never in another movie."

Craven stood up and stretched.

"I don't know why it all happened. Perhaps he resented the way he had been dragged into a lie. Perhaps," he added, his voice subdued, "he resented the fact that this corrupt old man had in a certain sense replaced him in the eyes of his only son. I've always thought there was something slightly incestuous about it, the way O'Brien used his daughter to establish himself as the dominant male in the life of his grandson.

"Well," he said briskly, his eyes coming back into focus, "that all happened a long time ago. The only thing certain is that thanks to the crimes of his grandfather, Lawrence Goldman started out a very rich young man."

"Do you think he knows? About his grandfather, I mean," asked Marissa.

"There was a story, years ago, that his father told him all about it and that Lawrence then left the house and never saw his father again. All I know for sure, however, is that I have never once heard him mention his father's name."

An enigmatic smile flickered on Marissa's mouth. "I wonder if he finds it ironic that, like his grandfather, he's about to become the male parent to his daughter's fatherless child."

"Lawrence has never been much given to irony," replied Craven dryly as he settled behind the wheel. "My turn to drive," he remarked with a sideways glance at Bobby.

There was a loud gurgling sound as he pushed forward the

accelerator lever and began to steer the boat away from the island shore. The desolate brick building receded into the distance and then vanished from view as Craven took us around the far end of Angel Island.

We passed along the other side and made our way beyond Sausalito and out into the current that flowed in from the sea. The yellow face of the sun stared straight through the reddish rust-colored Golden Gate. Clinging to the single masts of their boards, wind surfers, clad in black rubber suits, darted across the rolling chalk-green waves like some strange species of winged insects that had been here long before the first primitive movements of man and would be here still after the last man had died.

Sixteen

The boat moored safely at the dock, Marissa and I left the others at the marina and drove across the Golden Gate to her house in Sausalito. While she showered and changed, I sat on the back deck and gazed out across the bay, retracing our journey past the city, beneath the Bay Bridge, around Treasure Island, and behind Alcatraz to that abandoned place on the other side of Angel Island. All I could see of it now, in the dim purple light of dusk, was a saddle-shaped silhouette just across the narrow waterway. You could live here forever, look out at it every day, and never know that there was anything on the opposite shore, much less those grim, haunting ruins.

I felt Marissa's hand on my shoulder.

"Do you like my house, Joseph Antonelli?" she asked as she held out a glass of wine.

I stood up and leaned back against the wooden railing, surveying the chocolate-brown shingle-sided house. Dark green shutters were nailed permanently in place next to white-trimmed paned windows. Copper gutters with their own green patina stretched under the edge of the steep wood-shingled roof. The railing on the deck was painted white, and orange clay pots filled with red geraniums were scattered off to the side.

"It's a great house." I turned around and, with my elbows on the railing, looked down over the steep hillside and along the narrow street that ran through the center of town and then out along the shore of the bay. Just beyond the yacht harbor below, the few sailboats still on the water raced home against the night.

"How long have you lived here?" I asked, dangling the glass from my fingers as I stared at the bay.

"Eighteen years," replied Marissa. She was standing next to me, watching the water grow dark. "Seven years since the divorce."

She lifted the glass to her lips and then, when she had finished, a bittersweet smile crossed her mouth.

"He got his girlfriend, and I got the house."

It was hard to think of her as a woman anyone would have left. She was really quite beautiful. More than that, she had the kind of imagination that could make things you always thought trivial and commonplace seem somehow mysterious and unique. She was one of the most remarkable women I had met, but Marissa was not young anymore, and when it came to the difference between youth and the power to enchant, men were often fools.

"What were you thinking just now, when I first came out? Were you thinking about what is on the other side?" asked Marissa, looking across at Angel Island.

"Yes," I replied, no longer surprised when she knew what I was thinking. I had almost come to expect it.

She had changed into a white blouse and a flowing cotton skirt. She was wearing Moroccan sandals. Her hair had the scent of jasmine.

"And about what Albert said about Lawrence Goldman?"

"Yes, about that, too."

She bent down and snipped off a dead geranium from a terra-cotta pot, then held it in her hand, twisting the stem so that it spun first one way, then the other.

"Remember what Albert said about his grandfather?" I asked, reminding her of the way the police chief, Dan O'Brien, had once run things in the city. "I think my grandfather was one of the people who paid him off."

I told her what Bobby had told me, about the choice our grandfather had made between prison and bribery, and how, to our pretended regret, he had chosen honor over money. She put her hand on my arm.

"So part of Lawrence Goldman's fortune comes from money stolen from your grandfather. Do you see where this could go? If your grandfather had not been so good at what he did, had not made all that money, he would not have been able to bribe his way out of prison, and Dan O'Brien would not have had as much money as he did. And if he didn't have that much money, Lawrence might not have done nearly so well; and then Jeremy Fullerton wouldn't have been that interested in getting close to him and might never have had anything to do with his daughter. So you see, it's all your fault, Joseph Antonelli. At least, it's your family's fault."

Stepping back, Marissa gave me an appraising glance. "But that isn't what you're thinking, is it? You're thinking, wouldn't it be wonderful if you could somehow get even—do something to Lawrence Goldman—to make up for what his grandfather did to yours."

"Even before I knew about his grandfather, Lawrence Goldman didn't sound like someone I'd like. But I'm really not much interested in him; I'm much more interested in his daughter. She seems to be right in the center of all this, and the only thing I know about her—other than the fact she's Lawrence Goldman's daughter—is that she worked for Fullerton, was having an affair with him, and thinks she's carrying his child."

Marissa looked at me, a puzzled expression on her face. "'Thinks she's carrying his child'? You mean, she isn't?"

I had not told anyone what Jeremy Fullerton's widow had told me about her husband, but I had come to trust Marissa implicitly. Talking to her had become as easy, and as private, as that inner dialogue we carry on with ourselves. With a few disconnected words, a change of expression, a barely perceptible alteration of tone or emphasis, we understood each other perfectly.

"Jeremy Fullerton couldn't . . ."

"Have children? Meredith Fullerton told you that? She must have trusted you a lot to tell you that."

Reflected off the black water, the lights of the city seemed to reach across the bay. I remembered the way Jeremy Fullerton's widow kept looking out the window, drawn back to the place where she and her husband had still been free to imagine things the way they wanted them to be.

"She asked me if I had ever read *The Great Gatsby*. She said that when they were first married, they used to walk late at night down to the water and look across at the city and that it reminded her of the way Gatsby used to stare across the Sound at the green light on the dock where Daisy lived."

"He had the eyes for it," Marissa said after she had thought about it, "the eyes of someone always dreaming about something, something deep down they know they can never have, not really, not the way they want to have it."

Marissa lifted her face and with her hand brushed back her

hair. "In a way, everyone does that about something, don't they? When I was a girl, I used to think about things that would happen, things I was going to do."

She laughed, a self-deprecating laugh, but her eyes sparkled with the memory of what she had been like, a young girl dreaming about what she would be. And she had no regrets about the life she had wanted.

"I used to think about the things that would make me noticed, the things that would make other people want to be with me."

Taking her arm, I pulled her close and slipped my hand into hers. In the darkness I looked down at the wooden deck and moved my foot until it touched the tip of her sandal. In the breeze that whispered up from the bay, the end of her skirt wrapped around my knee.

"That's what Jeremy was doing, wasn't he? Dreaming about what he would do, about the things that could happen, so that what he loved would love him back. It's not that hard to understand. It's the oldest story there is: the young man who loves something he can't have because he isn't thought to be good enough, or rich enough, or prominent enough, or from the right family. And so he goes off and does whatever he has to do to become the kind of man he thinks he has to be. Gatsby became a thief; Jeremy became perhaps something worse; because they both thought they had no other choice. We all do that, too, don't we? Do things we never thought we would because we don't think we have any other choice."

Marissa kissed me gently on the side of my face, then wrinkled her nose and laughed.

"You taste like salt. Why don't you take a shower, and instead of going out, let's just stay here. I can throw something together for dinner. It won't be too bad. I promise."

She took two steps toward the sliding glass door and stopped. "And over dinner I'll tell you what I can about Lawrence Goldman's daughter."

Because we had planned to go out, I had brought a change of clothing. Half an hour later, dressed in gray slacks and a blue oxford shirt, I sat barefoot at the dining room table, twisting my fork into a second plate of some of the best linguini I had ever tasted.

"Feel better?" asked Marissa from the other side of the gleaming black table. Sliding her plate to the side, she raised a glass of gray Riesling to her lips.

I was hungrier than I had thought, and I kept on eating, nodding my response. She watched me with a kind of amused satisfaction until I finished and put down my fork.

"Ariella Goldman," I reminded her after I wiped my mouth with a napkin.

The candle on the table between us flickered for a moment, the small flame bent by a sudden rush of air as the nighttime breeze passed through the screen door. Marissa sat quietly, a pensive expression on her face, as if there were something she wanted to tell me but had not decided she should. I looked at her, a question in my eyes.

"I haven't told you quite everything about the reason I was divorced," she said presently.

The base of the wineglass was balanced on the fingers of both hands. She stared at the clear crystal as if somewhere just on the other side of it were the answer to a riddle, the riddle, I suppose, of the things that happen between two people who live together for any appreciable period of time.

"I had breast cancer," she said, her gaze fixed on the crystal glass. "I had a mastectomy. That was not the reason for the divorce—or perhaps it was. I'm not really sure. I think it actually prolonged the marriage. I think he felt an obligation to stay, to try to make it work."

A strange smile drifted across her mouth.

"Have you ever wondered about that kind of thing?" she asked, raising her eyes to mine. "Someone wants a divorce—goes home that night to say so—but before they can say anything, the other one—the husband, the wife—tells them they have some very bad news. They have cancer, but it isn't terminal, at least not yet. They have a chance, a very good chance, the doctors say, if they get immediate treatment and if—and this if changes everything, doesn't it?—they keep up their spirits and stay in the right frame of mind. What do you think must go through that other person's mind? Guilt, remorse, regret? And if regret—for what? For what they were about to say, or because they had not said it earlier, before they knew about the illness, before there could be any question that they were being selfish about what they wanted? It isn't such an easy question, is it? Because, of course—in most situations at least—he must have felt something for her once; he married her, didn't he? And probably—in some situations, at least—he must still care for her, still care for what happens to her.

"My husband tried. He really did. But, to tell you the truth, I wish he hadn't. It would have been easier if he hadn't. It would have been easier if I'd known he was in love with someone else than to have him go through this charade that what was happening to me didn't change the way he felt. I wish I had known. I wouldn't have told him. I would have had at least that much dignity left."

I reached across the table to take her arm. She shook her head.

"I'm all right. Really. I'm only telling you this because I have to explain something that happened. If I don't, I can't tell you how I know what I'm going to tell you about Lawrence Goldman's daughter.

"After the divorce, I met someone. It was right after I opened the first store. She worked for me. We became good friends. We're still good friends."

Marissa searched my eyes, not only to find the understanding she needed, but also to let me know it was important that she could find it in me.

"I didn't feel very attractive in those days; and I was lonely, more lonely than I could ever have imagined. Paula—Paula Hawkins—was very sympathetic. One night . . . well, I had never done anything like that before. It happened just that one time."

A flash of something like defiance passed briefly through her eyes.

"I don't regret what happened—I'm not ashamed of it—but I knew I didn't want it to happen again. Paula understood. There were no recriminations or anything of the sort. Paula wanted me to be happy; besides, she was in love with someone else, had been in love with someone else since college."

I read it in her eyes. "Lawrence Goldman's daughter?"

It was as if some weight had been lifted off her shoulders. Marissa had told me something about herself I was certain she had never told anyone. She trusted me, now more than ever, and what I think was at least as important to her, she knew I trusted her. With a casual smile, she reached across the table, filled up my empty glass, and then filled her own. Holding it with both hands around the rim, she watched the way the color changed in the shadows cast by the candle's dim flickering light.

"Paula said Ariella was the most self-sufficient person she had ever known. The way Paula told it, she almost had to be.

Her mother made sure of that. Lawrence Goldman was in his mid-forties when Ariella was born. He was of that generation for whom children, as they used to say, were 'made to be seen, not heard.' She once told Paula that her earliest memory was of her mother holding her hand as they walked down the long curving staircase from the upstairs bedroom to the living room below. Her hair had been curled and powder put on her cheeks; the smell of lavender was all around her. Wearing a little pink dress, all starched and stiff, she stood right next to her mother, staring at a roomful of bright smiling strangers, all the men in black tie. Then, the moment her mother squeezed her hand, she performed the brief curtsey she had been taught, and in a tiny, tremulous voice remarked with earnest delight, 'I'm very glad to meet you and I hope you all have a lovely evening.' She thought those must have been the first words she had ever learned to speak."

Marissa drank from her glass, then put it down on the table and draped her long slender fingers across the top of it. As the candlelight danced in her eyes, she began to trace along the edge the circle of the glass.

"From the very beginning, you see, she was Lawrence Goldman's daughter. Even when she grew up and was no longer an amusing sidelight at dinner parties for adults, that still set her apart. Everyone wanted something from Lawrence Goldman—his approval, his permission, something. And of course everyone went out of their way to be as helpful as they could to his daughter."

Her fingers stopped their movement around the glass. She tossed her head back and fixed me with a quizzical look.

"Have you ever known anyone who grew up like that?"

I shook my head and chuckled as I took another drink.

"When I was growing up, the only tuxedo I ever saw was

the one worn by the guy who took tickets at the movie theater downtown."

She studied me a moment longer before she asked, "You don't like people with money, do you?"

"I know a few people with money I like."

"What is it you don't like about the rich?" she persisted.

"Other than the fact that money is all they think about and that they tend to have the attention span of a gnat, I haven't seen that it has any very direct connection with character."

"Money can buy you freedom," countered Marissa.

"To do what—spend it? Earn more of it? Go on a cruise? Play golf? Retire? Buy a new house, a new car? How much of anything do you need? But you can always use more money, right? If a man ate so much at every meal he became ill, everyone would call him a glutton; if he drank every day until he passed out, we'd call him a drunk. But if he acquires more wealth than he'll ever be able to use, we call him—what? Smart, successful, a born genius, and someone everyone else could take a lesson from, but we don't anymore call him greedy."

She was ready for me. "And what do you call a lawyer who charges a small fortune to defend someone wrongfully accused of a crime?"

"Smart, successful, a born genius, someone everyone else could take a lesson from," I drawled as I reached for the narrow-necked green bottle.

"Ah!" she exclaimed with the satisfied look of a small triumph.

"Where was I?" she asked. "Yes, growing up with all the money in the world. Whatever it did or did not do to her character, Ariella seems from a very early age to have understood exactly what the money meant. Not just what it could buy, but what it meant. She knew that because of the money—her father's money—everyone would always try to do everything they could for her, and she understood why."

Leaning on her elbow, Marissa spread her fingers and raised her chin. "Think about that. Your father was a doctor; I came from very comfortable circumstances; but when we were growing up, neither of us would have been considered rich—not like that. No one tried to get on our good side because of the money our parents had. When we found out someone we had a crush on, or someone we just wanted to be friends with, didn't like us the way we wanted them to, it might have been devastating, but at least we knew it was all about us. Ariella always knew there was something else involved. The odd thing is, she seemed not to mind—apparently she even thrived on it. Before she was even old enough to think about it, she understood that it was up to her to decide how close anyone would get. In a way I suppose it was like being royalty: When you have an inherited power, I don't imagine you very often doubt that it's a power you ought to have.

"Paula was convinced that the reason Ariella chose her as a friend was because when they first met at school, she was the only one who did not know who she was. Paula had never heard of Lawrence Goldman," said Marissa, her large eyes narrowing as she concentrated on what she was trying to describe.

Outside, the lights of the city danced across the darkness from the other side of the bay. The sky had turned midnight-blue, and Angel Island, cut off from the inhabited world by a half mile of water, loomed up like a ghost ship thrown on shore by some great underwater upheaval.

Slouched against the back of the black lacquered art-deco chair, I watched the way Marissa's mouth formed each word in a smooth flawless harmony with the small, nuanced movements of her hands and the slight, subtle change of expression in her eyes.

"Early last spring, Paula asked me to lunch. She wanted to tell me about something that had happened during a weekend she had spent with the Goldmans. Ariella had just gotten back from Europe—some small place in Italy not far from Monte Carlo—where she had been with Jeremy Fullerton. Paula had known about them from the very beginning. Ariella always told her everything—or almost everything. They were very good friends; closer than friends, really. Anyway, Paula picked her up at the airport late Friday afternoon and they drove to the Woodside house."

Listening to Marissa, I could see it all: Ariella, the house—everything. The Tudor mansion on twelve secluded acres was apparently the closest thing Lawrence Goldman had to a permanent home. A few years after he built it, the area had become some of the most expensive real estate in the world. Houses that had stood for half a century—the unpretentious summer places of comfortably well-off San Franciscans—were torn down and replaced with structures designed less for the convenience of the people who owned them than to advertise the fact that they were the kind of people who could afford to have them. Goldman's house was too far away from the narrow, winding road that ran past it to tell anyone much of anything, except that whoever lived under that steep slate roof, barely visible through the tangle of live oak trees, wanted his privacy.

Paula had been a frequent guest. They walked in the front entrance without knocking or calling out to see if anyone was home. Closing the heavy wooden door behind them, she and Ariella put the bags down on the smooth white marble floor. The muffled voices of women working in the kitchen faded in and out as the two of them made their way down a broad paneled hallway that led to the wing opposite the dining room. A door stood partially open, and from somewhere behind it came the unmistakable voice of Lawrence Goldman.

Ariella pushed open the door just far enough to reveal the profile of her father. He was sitting in an upholstered chair, his long, angular head jutting forward as if poised to ask a question, a barely perceptible smile of almost feminine encouragement flickering across the thin lips of his rather broad mouth. Both elbows on the leather-topped antique desk, he was staring straight ahead, talking on the telephone, calmly, quietly, as if this were the only conversation he could possibly want to have.

"I've pledged a million and a half to the new museum project," he was saying, "and I'd like it very much if I could count on you for two hundred thousand of it."

Goldman saw them standing in the doorway. He put his hand over the receiver.

"Welcome home," he said, gesturing for his daughter and her friend to come in.

He ended the conversation in the same slow, unhurried way in which he had doubtless begun it. "Yes, thank you, Charles. I was certain you'd want to be involved."

As he hung up, he scribbled a note to himself on a cheap tablet of lined paper that lay next to the telephone. He kept careful track of every transaction.

"Hello, Paula," he said with the pleasant smile he bestowed on close friends and perfect strangers alike. "Did everything go well?" he asked his daughter as she bent down to kiss the side of his reddish tan face.

"Yes, Father, it went very well," replied Ariella confidently.

Goldman nodded silently. "It's a bit of a gamble," he said

presently, "but not that much. He has a better chance than Marshall."

"Much better," agreed Ariella.

"I hope the flight from Nice was all right and that you were able to get some sleep. Our guests will begin to arrive in about an hour. Christopher Borden is already here. He's in his room making some calls. You remember what we talked about," said Goldman as his daughter turned to go. "We need his help on the downtown development project."

Borden was a partner in a New York investment house with which Goldman had frequently done business. Considerably younger than Lawrence Goldman, he had the reputation of a man who liked women almost as much as he liked money.

A dozen couples had been invited to dinner, and within ten minutes of each other all twenty-four people arrived, some of them forced to cancel long-standing commitments to be there. The dining room, like the living room, faced out through tall lead-paned windows to the patio and the pool and, beyond that, to the tennis courts and the stables far below. An oblong table ran the length of the room. Lawrence Goldman, as always, was seated with his back to the wall, so that when he spoke nothing outside might disturb the attention of his guests. Directly opposite him, Ariella was seated next to Christopher Borden.

A round-faced woman in her mid-forties expressed her disappointment that Goldman's wife, Amanda, could not be there. His eyes swung around to where she sat.

"She wanted to be, but she's up at the vineyard getting everything ready, and she just couldn't get back."

Without expressing an opinion or asking a question, Lawrence Goldman deftly brought together the threads of several different desultory conversations into a discussion that affected them all. Among those gathered around his table were some of the most successful venture capitalists in the Bay Area and the heads of some of the most famous technology companies in the world.

"As we all know," remarked Goldman, lifting his blizzard-white eyebrows, "Moore's Law claims that the computing power of the microprocessor will continue to double until a physical limit is finally reached."

He paused, and the silence was so complete that the only sound heard was the hushed warble of a dove huddled on the roof outside, watching the dark blue sky fade to black.

"I don't know if Moore's Law is right," said Goldman, his large head moving in a slow, methodical arc as he looked around the table, "but I do know something about Goldman's Law, and I can assure you, that law is never wrong."

Wrapping his broad smooth fingers around the beveled mouth of his glass, Goldman took a drink of water. He dried his lips with a linen napkin and continued:

"Goldman's Law says that ultimately economics always prevails over politics. When government becomes the major impediment to economic progress, sooner or later government has to change. Let me be more specific. We are now for all practical purposes out of buildable land."

Leaning back, Goldman spread his fingers and began slowly tapping them together.

"Economic expansion now depends on our ability to convince government to allow private development of some small part of the public lands it controls."

Goldman glanced one last time around the table, nodded once, then picked up his knife and fork and began to eat. He did not speak again until dessert was served.

"The company, as you probably know," he began, shoving

aside the chocolate mousse after only one bite, "owns a very substantial tract of land near Arcadia, immediately adjacent to the national redwood park. I have begun three-way negotiations to trade it for a much smaller parcel of state park land just north of here, which would, according to our estimates, provide enough space to meet the development requirements for the next twenty years. We would of course want each of you to be involved in the project from the very beginning, from planning to completion."

Turning up his soft hands, Goldman raised his head, waiting for the first question.

Thomas Malreaux, thirty-six years old, the founder and head of a software company worth more, at least on paper, than all but a handful of the corporations included in the S&P 500, spoke up. "Lawrence, you said you had begun negotiations. How long do you think it might be before you actually know?"

Only someone who had known him for a very long time, someone who had learned to detect the almost invisible signs of his displeasure, would have noticed the slight twinge that formed at the corner of Lawrence Goldman's mouth. Paula, who had visited so often that her presence went practically unnoticed, caught it right away. Thomas Malreaux, on the other hand, assumed that what for just an instant had flashed across the old man's face was nothing more than the abbreviated beginnings of a smile.

"The federal government, as you might imagine, is eager to increase the size of its holdings," explained Goldman, peering at his guest through half-closed eyes. "The state government, on the other hand, is not quite so eager to release the land we want."

With a derisive laugh, Malreaux wagged his head. "The

government can't even add right. They're going to get—
what?—ten, twenty times more land in this deal, and they can't
even figure that out!"

With his hands under the table, Goldman slowly arched his
eyebrows.

"Size is of course not always the sole measure of value," he
remarked dryly. "But beyond that, there is the political problem always faced when you deal with two governments, a problem compounded in this instance by the fact those two
governments are controlled by two different political parties."

He let his eye linger a moment longer on the young Mr.
Malreaux, and then, turning his attention to his other guests,
explained, "In the past, as you know, I have done what I could
for Augustus Marshall. But, given the choice we have now, I'm
throwing my support to Jeremy Fullerton. I hope all of you can
do the same."

He looked around the table, a benevolent smile on his face.
Then, with the same deliberate ambiguity with which he had
so often wrapped a threat inside a promise, he added:

"It will make all the difference in the world if you do."

He let everyone contemplate for a moment the meaning of
what he had just said, before he laughed good-naturedly and
exclaimed, "And it isn't because the senator had the great good
sense to hire my daughter."

Goldman looked directly across the table to Ariella.

"Though the fact she writes most of his speeches gives me
some reason to hope that he will at least say all the right
things."

After the last guest had gone and Christopher Borden had
said good night, Paula joined Ariella and her father in his
study. The long flight back from France and the long evening
of disciplined affability had taken their toll. Ariella sank into a

square brown leather chair at the side of her father's desk. She began to unfasten her earrings. With his back to them, Goldman ran his hand along the bookshelf behind the desk.

"Here it is," he said, pulling out a slim volume. "You should read this," he remarked, turning to his daughter. "Aldous Huxley: *Brave New World.*"

Sitting down, Goldman crossed his legs and opened the book. A wry smile curved across his wide mouth, stretched down at the corners, and turned into a look of almost amused disdain. He shook his head and then, glancing up, closed the book and nodded once.

"You really should read it," he said as he set it down on the desk. "It goes a long way toward explaining all this."

"All this?" asked Ariella wearily as she removed her other earring.

Goldman turned away from her to stare out the window at the dark impenetrable night.

"The world run by engineers. That's what has happened, of course. Those people tonight—engineers. They don't build bridges anymore, they build computers; but it's the same mentality. They see everything in such simple, rigid terms. They go from point to point, making everything smaller, faster, more repetitive. There is no depth, no nuance, no understanding, nothing like a comprehensive view of things—just that same, deadly addiction to making everything a numeric function. They talk about improving the overall level of intelligence—the social IQ, some of them call it—by connecting everyone with everyone else. They're not smart enough to see that as what 'society' supposedly knows goes up, what an individual understands goes down. In this 'new economy' of theirs, everyone will become a specialist who knows more and more about less and less. It is going to be one great ant heap, everyone working together to produce astonishing efficiencies, and everyone will be essentially the same. There won't be any individuals anymore. There won't be anyone interesting, much less unique. There will be a great, all-embracing sameness, all the more oppressive because no will feel in any way oppressed."

For a few moments, he stared in silence. Then, as if he had only now become aware of her presence, he swung his head around to Paula, who was sitting on a davenport next to the fireplace on the other side of the room.

"I hope you had a nice evening," he said warmly.

Paula started to respond, but Goldman's eyes swept past her and settled on his daughter.

"And such astonishing greed!" he marveled. His mouth grew hard, a crafty, cynical expression on it. "It almost makes it too easy, doesn't it?"

"They haven't had money long enough to understand it," remarked Ariella shrewdly and, Paula thought, a little impatiently. "They know only how to count it."

Goldman nodded. "Yes, precisely."

He moved his chair until he faced Ariella directly. "Now, tell me all about our future governor and would-be president."

Ariella was so tired she could barely keep her head up. "What would you like to know?" she asked, her voice a dreary monotone as she reached down to remove her shoes.

"Well, I really don't have much interest in what kind of lover he is," said Goldman sharply. "Unless, of course, that's the only thing you care to talk about!"

With her shoes in one hand and her earrings in the other, Ariella got to her feet. "I didn't deserve that," she said, her eyes flashing.

He apologized immediately. "Yes, you're right—you didn't.

Please," he went on, gesturing toward the empty chair, "stay just a while longer."

Her annoyance at the way he had spoken to her was still evident as she rather reluctantly sat down on the edge of the chair.

"There isn't much to tell. You were right. Jeremy is running for governor because he wants to take the nomination away from the president in two years. He thinks that if he waits until the president finishes a second term, the vice president will get the nomination. You were right: He wants to beat an incumbent governor so he can turn right around and use the momentum to beat an incumbent president."

Watching her as she again rose from the chair, Goldman nodded. "He never struck me as the kind of man willing to wait for anything. Tell me," he asked as Ariella started to turn away, "will he leave his wife for you?"

Ariella looked back at him, her chin raised high. On the side of her mouth was that same slight twitch Paula had observed on Lawrence Goldman's face earlier at dinner.

"It wouldn't be the first time someone left his wife for me, would it?"

Ariella took a step toward the door, then stopped and came back. Bending down, she kissed him on the forehead.

"It's late. I'm dead tired. I'm going to bed. You should be going yourself."

Goldman got to his feet and patted her on the arm. "I have to make a call to New York, then I thought I'd read for a while." He pointed toward a hardbound book with a brightly colored jacket. On the cover was a drawing of the Golden Gate Bridge. "Another book about San Francisco," he said with a sigh. "I read them all," he explained, glancing across at Paula as if she had just entered the room. "I don't know why. They never get it right."

Ariella looked at the clock on the corner of her father's desk.

"You're calling New York at this hour? It's quarter past four there," she said, thinking he must have reversed the time difference.

"Yes, it really can't wait."

Picking up the receiver, he began to dial. His eyes moved from his daughter to Paula and back again.

"Either of you remember the name of that company our good friend Malreaux owns?"

With his hand over the receiver, he thanked Paula when she told him and then said good night to them both. Both elbows on the desk, Lawrence Goldman stared straight ahead.

"Hello, Herbert. This is Lawrence. Sorry to call so late," he said, talking slowly, never changing the tone or the pitch of his voice.

With Paula right behind her, Ariella made her way to the doorway and then waited to hear what her father was planning to do. He was quite explicit.

"Start the usual rumors: bad management, falling demand, worse-than-expected earnings. Start selling what we have of it, and then, when the price is as far down as it is going to go, buy enough so we have a position sufficient to force out Thomas Malreaux."

The guest room where Paula stayed was right next to Ariella's bedroom. They said good night at the door and Ariella reminded her that they were scheduled to ride at eight the next morning. Paula woke up before six and, unable to get back to sleep, decided to go into the kitchen and have coffee. Throwing on a robe, she stepped out of her room and began to make her way down the hallway. As she passed the other guest bedroom, the one where Christopher Borden was staying, the door opened and Ariella, wearing nothing but a silk nightgown, was suddenly standing right in front of her. Startled, Ariella's expression seemed to change from one of fear and embarrassment to one of defiance and contempt. Without a word, she swept past Paula and disappeared into her own room down the hall. It had all happened so quickly that for a moment Paula had to wonder if she had seen her there at all or whether it had not been a trick of her own early morning imagination.

Marissa poured into my glass the last few drops of wine left in the bottle.

"Paula was never judgmental. She knew that Ariella had been having an affair with Jeremy Fullerton; but she thought that was because Ariella was in love with him. She also thought Ariella loved her; perhaps not as much as she, Paula, loved Ariella, but enough," said Marissa with a melancholy smile. "But when she saw Ariella coming out of Christopher Borden's bedroom—when she knew Ariella had been sleeping with a man she had only just met—she knew she was doing it because her father needed Borden's help; then everything changed. Paula was not just hurt; she was angry, angry at herself. She should have known from the beginning that no one had any value to the Goldmans except as a means to whatever they wanted to have."

Marissa stared out the windows at the lights of the city, silhouetted on the dark waters of the bay.

"Paula was supposed to meet Ariella at the stables to go riding," she said presently. "Instead, she packed her bag and left. She hasn't talked to Ariella since."

I helped Marissa clear the table and straighten the kitchen. As she put the last glass away, she turned to me.

"That's enough about Lawrence Goldman and his daughter. Let's talk about something more interesting. Let's talk about you and me."

A mirthful, teasing smile crossed her mouth.

"You can stay here tonight—if you want. I'd like it if you did."

Seventeen

If I had been born less of a coward, or if I had learned to control the sometimes irrational workings of my mind, it might not have taken quite so long to recover from the fear that had seized upon me the moment Andrei Bogdonovitch was blown to bits in that explosion and fire. I had checked out of the St. Francis Hotel and had become the household guest of my cousin; I traveled by different routes and at different times; I studied the faces of the strangers I passed in the crowd on the chance I might have seen them somewhere before. I was as careful as I knew how to be, and yet, despite all my precautions, despite the absence of even a single tangible fact to suggest that I was in any more danger now than I had been before the death of that strange, enigmatic Russian, I could not escape the feeling that something was not quite right. Whenever I looked over my shoulder, at the people on the sidewalk behind me or the people packed in the courtroom every day at trial, I had the uncanny sense that someone was not only watching me but knew that at that very moment I was thinking of him.

Clarence Haliburton was near the end of his opening statement, but instead of thinking ahead to what I was going to tell the jury, I sat with my chair at an angle to the counsel table, searching the faces of the crowd.

"And when you've heard all the evidence," I heard the district attorney droning on in the background, "I'm sure you'll agree that the People have met their burden and that the guilt of the defendant, Jamaal Washington, has been proven beyond a reasonable doubt."

I looked from face to face, wondering who they were and why they were here. One of them was here because of me. I was sure of it. But who was it, and, more important, who had sent him?

"Mr. Antonelli," said Judge Thompson with his practiced courtroom familiarity, "do you wish to make an opening statement at this time?"

"What?" I asked, startled out of my reverie.

Thompson turned his head toward the jury and smiled.

"Oh, nothing, Mr. Antonelli," he drawled. "We just wondered whether after sleeping through Mr. Haliburton's opening statement you had decided to sleep through your own as well."

A bashful grin spread over my face as I ambled up to the railing that ran the length of the jury box and tried to turn my inattention into an advantage.

"For a while there, I thought I must have somehow fallen into a coma. One minute we were at the beginning of the trial and then, what seemed just a moment later, I heard the voice of the district attorney giving what I was certain was his closing argument. I wondered why I could not remember what any of the witnesses said or even what they looked like. Then, when I heard the judge ask me if I wanted to make an opening statement, I realized I had not been in a coma after all. While I'm relieved about that, I'm afraid I now have to find some way to convince you that this really is just the beginning of the trial and not, as Mr. Haliburton seems to think, the end of it."

With my head down, I moved slowly across the front of the jury box. When I reached the end of it, I turned around and looked back to the district attorney.

"Mr. Haliburton has told us a great deal about Senator Fullerton, and so far as I know everything he told you is true— everything, that is, except the way he died."

My gaze moved to the defendant. Jamaal Washington sat at the separate table he shared with me, in the chair closest to the jury box. The jury followed my eyes.

"The district attorney also had some things to say about the defendant. By my count he called him a 'cold-blooded killer' seven different times during his opening statement."

I paused long enough to allow them a good look at Jamaal's fine features and intelligent eyes.

"He doesn't look much like a cold-blooded killer, does he?"

For the next twenty minutes, while Jamaal, wearing the same dark suit and the same solid-color tie he wore every day to court, sat in an attitude of respectful attention, I told the jury what it was like for most of the black children who grew up in San Francisco, reciting all the well-known statistics that seemed to suggest they were born to die of either gunshot wounds or drugs. The odds against survival were shocking; the odds against a normal life next to impossible. Yet Jamaal Washington had done more than merely survive: He had accomplished more in his short life than most of us had ever tried to achieve. Without a note, I recited his academic record and reminded them that there had never been a time, not from the day he began high school to the day when, an honor student at Berkeley, he was arrested for a crime he did not commit, that he was not working to help support himself.

"And so, Jamaal Washington was on his way home from work."

I faced the jury and, with an ironic smile, remarked: "This 'cold-blooded killer' had just finished working at a dinner at the Fairmont Hotel, the dinner where nearly a thousand people paid thousands of dollars to listen to what would be the last speech Jeremy Fullerton would ever give. Jamaal Washington never heard that speech. There was too much noise in the kitchen where he washed pots and pans to allow him to hear much of anything.

"When he was through washing dishes, he joined the crew that clears the room after one event and gets it ready for the next one. He worked more than eight hours that night, and he did it after spending the whole day—from seven in the morning until sometime after three in the afternoon—studying physics, and chemistry, and all the other subjects a 'cold-blooded killer' spends his time trying to master."

I shot a caustic glance across the courtroom. Haliburton pretended not to notice.

"This 'cold-blooded killer,' " I went on, my hand on the back of my neck as I stared down at the floor, "who the prosecution told you was willing to kill for however much money he might find in a dead man's wallet, studies all day and works all night and then goes home."

My hand dropped away from my neck. I raised my head.

"Only this night he never got home. He never got home because he tried to help someone. He never got home because, for all his trouble, he got shot in the back."

The words came without conscious effort, freely, voluntarily, of their own accord. The copious notes; the long lists of things I had spent days preparing so I would not forget; the dozens of tattered-cornered, bent yellow lined pages filled with my longhand illegible scrawl—all of it had been left at the counsel table, locked away in my briefcase.

"How many of us would have done what Jamaal Washington did that night? How many of us would have done what he did had we been walking along, late at night, on a city street in fog so thick you could barely see your hand in front of your face, and we heard a gunshot just a few short yards away? We like to think that if we ever had to, we'd do the right thing; that if someone were in danger—real danger—we'd do everything we could to save their life. We dream about being the kind of people who run into a house on fire to save a child. We dream about hearing an explosion and without a thought for our own safety diving into the wreckage to see if someone is still alive. We dream these things and some of us, put in that situation, do them; but most of us do not. Most of us look the other way, wait for someone else—the police, the fire department, the paramedics—and then feel we've done our best if we made the call that brings them.

"Jamaal Washington heard a shot. He didn't turn on his heel, the way you or I might have done. It might have been better if he had," I added, slowly searching their eyes. "If he had been more a coward and less a hero, he would not have been shot; his life would not have been put in danger; he would not have spent nine hours on an operating table while surgeons struggled to save first his life, then the use of his legs. He would not have been here, forced to defend himself against the charge of murdering the very man he went to help."

Hunched forward at the end of the jury box, I rested my hand on the railing.

"But he wasn't thinking of what might happen to him—only that someone else might need help. He didn't hesitate—not for an instant. He went to help and he went right away. He saw someone slumped over the wheel. He opened the door on the passenger side and got in. He put his hand on the man's throat, searching for a pulse. The man was dead. He tried to find out who he was. He took his wallet out of his coat pocket. Then he noticed a gun lying on the floor."

Dragging my hand along the railing, I began slowly to move across the front of the jury box.

"Suddenly a light broke through the fog. Now, for the first time, he was scared, really scared. Someone had just been murdered. Maybe the killer had never left; maybe the killer had been there the whole time, just on the other side of the car; maybe the killer was going to kill him!"

I reached the other end of the jury box, seized the railing with both hands, and leaned across.

"He bolted out of the car! He ran as fast as he could! It was the only way to save his life! That's all he could think about—getting away! That's all anyone would have thought about. And then everything went dark. He was hit by a bullet in the back. He never heard the shot. He never heard anything."

Only the shuffling of my leather-soled shoes broke the silence as I turned away from the jury box and headed toward the empty chair next to Jamaal Washington. At the other table, Clarence Haliburton was busy jotting a note to himself.

The first witness called by the prosecution was the city coroner. Thin and stoop-shouldered, with sunken cheeks and hollow, deep-set eyes, Dr. Rupert C. Hitchcock slumped into the witness chair. Haliburton took him through the usual questions about his training and experience, questions that the coroner answered in a voice so listless and dull that Haliburton more than once had to ask him to speak up.

It was only when the issue became that of death itself that the good doctor began to rouse himself from his lethargy. Asked to describe the fatal wound, he became almost manic as he charted the bullet's progress as it penetrated Jeremy Fullerton's right temple and tore into his skull, carrying behind it sharp fragments of bone as it sliced through his brain. Death had been instantaneous. Jeremy Fullerton had died from a single gunshot wound to the head.

"Mr. Antonelli?" asked Judge Thompson. "Do you wish to cross-examine the witness?"

Bending forward, Dr. Hitchcock squeezed the fingers of first one hand, then the other, open and shut. An eager, self-confident smile began to spread across his narrow mouth.

"No, your honor," I said, shaking my head with indifference. "I have no questions for this witness."

Rupert Hitchcock's hands went limp; his nascent smile faded into oblivion. He dragged himself off the witness stand and out through the courtroom doors.

Like a spectator at a tennis match, I watched the prosecution and its expert witnesses volley questions and answers back and forth, the same, predictable way they did it every time they were called into court. The burden of proof, as everyone had been reminded so often it was difficult to know if the words still had any meaning, was on the prosecution. They had to make their case; they had to prove every element of the crime; nothing could be left out. I had learned a long time ago seldom to stipulate to anything. Let the prosecution bore everyone with the kind of tedious detail no one would remember and, if it went on long enough, some jurors might start to resent. Besides, the more witnesses the prosecution put on, the greater the chance one of them would make a mistake or be easy to dislike, like the coroner, and therefore easier to discredit.

The prosecution's case was simple: Jeremy Fullerton had been killed by a bullet fired at close range from a handgun found on the sidewalk next to the defendant after the defendant had been shot by the police. Nothing could be more straightforward. It had taken only seven witnesses and less than three days of testimony. I had not asked a single question.

Thursday morning, Judge Thompson settled into his chair, smiled affably at the jury, and told the district attorney to call his next witness.

"The People call Officer Gretchen O'Leary," announced Haliburton routinely.

Opening a black loose-leaf notebook, I turned the pages until I found the place I was looking for. While the witness took the oath, I glanced quickly over the extracts I had made of the police reports and of the background information I had managed to assemble.

Even though she was wearing her black police officer's uniform, sidearm buckled down in a heavy leather holster on her belt, Gretchen O'Leary did not really look like a cop. With short brown hair, freckled face, and large hazel eyes, she seemed more like a college girl dressed for a part in a play. That impression began to vanish, however, as soon as she took her place on the witness stand. Stiff and erect, her mouth drawn tight, she focused on Haliburton with the same intensity with which, it was easy to imagine, she measured the movements of a suspect she was about to take into custody. She sat as still as a cat. No one watching her could have had any doubt about how quickly she could move.

As I listened to her answer the first few preliminary questions asked by the prosecution, I remembered something I had learned about her first night on patrol. Responding to a domestic disturbance call, she and her partner found the husband in a drunken rage and his wife, beaten bloody, cowering on the floor.

The husband pulled a knife. With one swift blow of her baton, O'Leary fractured his wrist.

Haliburton took her through the events of the night Jeremy Fullerton was murdered. O'Leary's voice was steady, midrange, betraying just a trace of conscious self-control. She spoke in simple, straightforward terms, without emphasis or enthusiasm. Whatever color was added to the bare recitation of what she had seen and heard was put there by the mind of the listener.

She testified that on routine patrol, she and Officer Marcus Joyner heard what they both were certain was a gunshot. Activating the overhead lights, Joyner pressed down on the accelerator.

"Where did it come from?" Joyner shouted over the noise of the siren.

O'Leary looked all around, searching through the fog.

"Behind us!" she yelled. "Somewhere down the block. Back there!" she cried, grabbing the back of the seat as she craned her neck.

According to her testimony, Joyner looked back to his left as the car skidded around the corner. At the next intersection, he turned left again. As they neared the next street, he stared diagonally across the Civic Center, trying to get a fix on the location of the shot. Something broke through the fog. He rammed his foot on the brake pedal. O'Leary hit the dashboard with her shoulder as her head flew backward against the passenger-door window. The patrol car careened over the sidewalk, grazed a lamppost, and jolted back into the street. Out of the corner of her eye, she saw a pedestrian they had nearly hit scrambling for safety.

They went all the way around the two-square-block Civic Center. At the last intersection, Joyner pulled the car into a hard right.

"Where?" he yelled, breathing hard. "How far down?"

"I don't know," O'Leary yelled back. "Can't be too far."

Joyner slowed down until they were barely moving. A moment later, he extinguished the blue flashing overhead light and stopped the car in the middle of the fog-bound street. There was nothing, not a sound. The street was still.

"You see anything?" whispered Joyner tensely.

O'Leary leaned as far forward as she could, searching along the line of cars parked on her side of the street, barely visible in the thick white fog. Her hand fumbled with the leather strap that held her gun snugly in its leather holster until she had it free.

"No, nothing," said O'Leary, her eyes peering vainly into the fog.

Joyner let the patrol car slide a few yards farther down the street.

"What's that?" he asked urgently, pointing straight ahead.

O'Leary had seen it, too; or thought she had. The fog was playing with her imagination. One moment, it seemed to lift; then, a moment later, they were in it again. Now, just for an instant, it cleared once more. Across the intersection, on her side of the street, a large, dark-colored Mercedes was parked against the curb. Someone was bent over the wheel. Joyner stopped the car, reached for the flashlight that was fastened under the dashboard, and opened the door.

Getting out on her side, O'Leary watched Joyner walk cautiously toward the Mercedes. She saw him hesitate halfway across the intersection, draw his weapon, and turn on the flashlight. The narrow funnel of yellow light slashed through the light gray mist until it hit the driver's-side door. A man's head was tilted against the window, the side of his face pressed up against the glass, thrown against it with such force that it was stuck there, held fast by the sticky red blood that was spattered all over.

Joyner moved closer. O'Leary began to move forward, keeping to the right, gun in hand, looking past the passenger side of the car in case someone was still lurking in a doorway nearby. Joyner reached for the handle of the driver's-side door. Someone jumped up on the other side of the front seat and bolted out the passenger door. Startled, Joyner fell back, the ribbon of light from his flashlight jerking crazily through the gray silk fog. O'Leary immediately dropped into a crouch, both hands on her gun. The light from the flashlight swept past someone in a black leather jacket, a black wool cap pulled down to his eyes, running right in front of her, running toward the corner, trying to escape.

Testifying in open court, there was no trace left of the emotions that must have surged through Gretchen O'Leary and concentrated every instinct, every impulse in a way that no one who has never faced that kind of danger can begin to imagine. She spoke in a quiet, conversational tone, calm, in control, waiting to the end of each question before she began to answer, and always turning to face the jury when she did. Slowly, meticulously, every word was put in perfect order.

"I had begun moving closer," she explained, describing the events immediately preceding her decision to fire. "When the suspect started to run, I was halfway across the intersection. He saw me. He started to turn toward me. He was raising his gun. I knew he was going to shoot. I discharged my weapon and the subject went down."

It was curious. She did not say she "fired" or that she "pulled the trigger." She said she "discharged" her weapon. She might as well have been reading aloud from a police training manual. I could almost see the section where she must first have learned it:

"An officer whose life is in danger may discharge his weapon to protect himself."

Haliburton finished his direct examination. Thompson asked if I had any questions I wanted to ask on cross.

"Just a few," I replied almost apologetically as I got to my feet.

Under Haliburton's patient encouragement, O'Leary had gradually become, if not relaxed, at least comfortable on the stand. But now, as I moved around the end of the counsel table and started toward her, she sat erect, with a slight forward lean, tense and expectant.

"The district attorney asked you a lot of questions. Certainly more than I can remember," I added with a helpless shrug. "So I wonder if you'd mind helping me out just a little. Could you, in your own words, just tell me again what happened that night? I don't mean everything that happened: just what happened from the time Officer Joyner got out of the patrol car."

Her eyes never left me. When she was sure I was finished, she began the slow, methodical recitation of what she had seen and what she had done.

"Officer Joyner approached the subject vehicle. He shined the light on the driver's-side window. I could see someone's head. Then I could see blood on the glass. Then, all of a sudden, there was another head—on the passenger side. It just popped up. And then the passenger door shot open and he was running down the sidewalk, heading toward the corner."

She paused and took a breath. There was no change in her expression, nothing to reveal what, if anything, she felt.

"I had begun moving closer. When the suspect started to run, I was halfway across the intersection. He saw me. He started to turn toward me. He was raising his gun. I knew he was going to shoot. I discharged my weapon and the subject went down."

Not a word out of place, not a word left out. I tried to act as if there were nothing out of the ordinary about what she had just done.

"Yes, yes, I see," I said, peering down at my shoes.

As if I had forgotten what I wanted to ask next, I went back to the counsel table and began to thumb through the pages of my black loose-leaf notebook.

"We've never met before, have we?" I asked, looking up.

"No," she replied evenly.

I smiled. "But we have spoken before, haven't we?"

She seemed not to understand the question.

"You remember, don't you?" I asked, still smiling. "I called you. I asked if it would be possible to talk to you about the case."

Guardedly, she nodded her head.

"I'm sorry, but you have to answer out loud. The court reporter has to take these things down."

"Yes," replied O'Leary reluctantly. "I remember your call."

I looked down at the notebook to the page my finger held open.

"And do you remember your answer?" I asked, glancing up.

There was a slight, almost imperceptible tightening of the muscles around her jaw. "I believe I indicated I did not wish to discuss it with you."

"Yes, I suppose you could describe it that way. Although," I added with a short, self-deprecating laugh as I looked at the jury, "all I remember is the sound of the telephone being slammed in my ear."

O'Leary sat still as stone, glaring at me.

"Oh, well, it doesn't really matter. We get to talk about it now. And the way my memory has been working lately," I said with a rueful grin, "I probably wouldn't have been able to remember anything you might have told me then anyway."

I shook my head, like someone embarrassed because he can no longer do the things he used to do, or at least not do them quite so well.

"Let me ask you this," I began tentatively. "How long had you been a police officer that night you rode with Officer Joyner—the night of the murder?"

"Three months."

"Three months? So this was one of your first assignments as a police officer?"

"Yes, it was."

"And, of course, you were riding in the patrol car with a much more experienced officer, weren't you?"

"Yes, Officer Joyner has been on the police force for more than—"

"We'll find out about Officer Joyner's experience later," I said, interrupting her before she could finish. "Right now we're only concerned with you."

I had made my way across the front of the courtroom to the jury box. Leaning against the railing, I folded my arms across my chest and stared hard at the witness.

"Was this the first time you shot anyone?"

"Yes."

"And you testified the fog was very thick that night?"

"Yes, it was."

"And you testified that you first saw the figure in the driver's side of the car only when the patrol car was just a few yards away?"

"Yes, that's correct."

"And yet you testified that you could see plainly not only

that the defendant had turned toward you while he was running away, but that he had a gun in his hand and—"

"Yes," she replied before I could finish, "I did."

I threw up my hands in apparent frustration. "I'm sorry. I was going too fast. I got ahead of myself."

Walking toward her, I apologized: "I'm afraid I've lost track of where I was. Would you mind? Could you just tell me again—in your own words, of course—exactly what happened, from the point at which Officer Joyner left the patrol car?"

It is strange sometimes, the way memory works. I had not read the case since law school and, despite what I had heard from the witness, I might still not have remembered if I had not heard Albert Craven, when he described that abandoned building on the far side of Angel Island, mention the tenements and sweatshops of New York. The case I had read in law school, the case everyone reads in law school, was about a fire in a sweatshop: the Triangle Shirtwaist Company. Dozens of women were killed. At the trial, a lawyer had a witness for the other side go back through the story she had told on direct. When she repeated it word for word, he had her do it again. When she repeated it a third time word for word, everyone knew she was telling a lie.

This was Gretchen O'Leary's third time, but she was so concerned that I not catch her in an inconsistency that it never occurred to her that there was an even greater danger in staying too close to the same script.

"Of course," replied O'Leary confidently. "As I testified, Officer Joyner approached the subject vehicle. He shined his light on the driver's-side window. I could see someone's head. Then I could see blood on the glass. Then, all of a sudden, there was another head. It just popped up. And then the passenger door shot open and he was running down the sidewalk, heading toward the corner.

"I had begun moving closer. When he started to run, I was halfway across the intersection. He saw me. He started to turn toward me. He was raising his gun. I knew he was going to shoot. I discharged my weapon and the subject went down."

When she finished, my eyes were wide with amazement.

"Tell me, Officer O'Leary, who was it who helped you rehearse the testimony you have given here today?"

"No one!" she snapped.

"Ah! You did it all by yourself." I shook my head in disgust. "No more questions," I announced as I headed toward the counsel table, trying hard to conceal my delight.

Eighteen

"Call your next witness," Judge Thompson ordered the next morning with a peremptory wave of his hand as he stepped to the bench.

Clarence Haliburton waited until the judge was seated in the high-backed leather chair.

"Your honor, the People call—"

Raising his hand, Thompson cut him off.

"Good morning, ladies and gentlemen," said the judge, smiling at the jury.

Thompson began to arrange the papers he had brought with him. A moment later, he glanced up and asked irritably, "Are you going to call a witness or not?"

Haliburton's crooked mouth hung open, an expression of bewildered contempt flashing in his eyes.

"The prosecution calls Officer Marcus Joyner to the stand," he said finally.

His hands folded together as he leaned forward on the witness chair, Marcus Joyner appeared attentive, alert, and, so far as I could tell, completely at ease. Well over six feet tall, with round shoulders and long arms, he had a short wide neck and a broad pockmarked face. Narrow almond-shaped eyes slanted toward pudgy cheekbones and his heavy mouth turned down at the corners. Everything about him gave the impression of relentless strength, and yet Joyner's voice was surprisingly gentle and soft.

"In answer to one of the questions asked by Mr. Haliburton," I inquired when it was time for cross-examination, "you indicated that you instructed Officer O'Leary to stay at the patrol car when you approached the Mercedes. Did I understand you correctly?"

Joyner was a courtroom veteran. Some witnesses start to answer a question as soon as they understand it; he waited until the last echo of the last word had died away.

"Yes, that's correct," replied the officer.

I stood at the far end of the jury box, directly in front of the witness. One hand was shoved down into my pocket; with the other I fumbled with a button on my coat.

"And what was the reason you asked her to do that?"

"Standard procedure," replied Joyner, looking right at me. "If there was a problem, one officer should be in a position to request assistance."

I filled in the blank. "By summoning help on the patrol car radio?"

"Yes."

"But instead of remaining at the car, as you requested, Officer O'Leary began to move toward the other vehicle, correct?"

He did not hesitate. "Yes, but she was still close enough to get assistance if we needed it."

"But that wasn't what you told her to do, was it?" I persisted. "You told her to remain at the vehicle."

"She did what she was supposed to do," he insisted.

I took my hand out of my pocket and stepped closer. "Before she fired the shot that struck the defendant, did you hear

her issue any kind of warning, any kind of command, anything
that told the defendant you were police officers?"

"There wasn't time."

"There wasn't time? You mean because he pointed a gun at
Officer O'Leary?"

"Yes. She didn't have any choice."

I moved even closer. "Did you see the defendant point a gun
at Officer O'Leary?"

For just an instant, Joyner's eyes narrowed. "No. I was on the
other side of the car. My view was obstructed, and," he added,
"it was very foggy."

"In fact, the fog was so thick you couldn't see the body of
Jeremy Fullerton until you were just a few feet away. Isn't that
correct?"

"Yes. As I said, it was very foggy that night. I mean, that
morning."

I kept my eyes on him while he answered and watched him
a moment longer after he finished. Then I shoved my hand back
in my pocket, turned away, and walked across to the counsel
table.

"So," I said, peering down at an open page of the loose-leaf
notebook, "you didn't hear a warning, and you didn't see the defendant point a gun at Officer O'Leary." Closing the notebook,
I looked up.

"At the moment she fired, which of you was closest to the defendant?"

Joyner thought about it for a moment.

"I'd have to say I was, at least a little closer. But, as I say, my
view was obstructed by the car."

"Yes, that's what you said," I remarked as I drummed my fingers on the corner of the table. "How tall are you?"

"Six-foot-two," he replied. He knew where I was going and

added almost immediately: "But when he jumped up from the front seat and threw open the passenger-side door, I dropped down onto one knee."

"How long have you been on the force?"

"Twenty-three years."

"You were the senior officer?"

"Yes, I was."

I moved behind the counsel table and rested both hands on the back of my empty chair.

"You must have wondered why Officer O'Leary fired, did you not?"

"Yes," replied Joyner without any change of expression.

"Yes?" I repeated with a puzzled smile. "Yes? Is that all? Didn't you inquire—didn't you at least ask why she had fired?"

"Yes," he said, staring back at me. "I asked."

I waited, letting the jury draw from his silence an implication of reluctance, before I finally asked, "And what answer did she give you?"

"She said she fired because the defendant," he said, stretching out his bulky arm to point across the courtroom at Jamaal Washington, "had turned to fire at her."

"You gave the defendant first aid until the paramedics arrived and took him to the hospital, didn't you?"

"Yes," replied Joyner.

"You saved his life."

It was not a question and Joyner made no answer. I let go of the chair and patted Jamaal on the shoulder as I passed behind him.

"Now, the reason you were there," I asked as I stopped in front of the jury box, "the reason you found Jeremy Fullerton in the first place, is because you heard what you thought was a gunshot?"

The tight black leather in Joyner's gleaming knee-high boots creaked as he shifted position in the witness chair.

"Yes," he replied.

"You immediately started to drive toward where that shot had come from, correct?"

"Not quite. The shot seemed to come from some point behind us, so I—"

"So you drove to the next corner—at the Civic Center—turned left, then drove around the center until you came out on the street where you thought the shot had been fired," I interjected impatiently. "How much time would you estimate elapsed between the shot you heard and when you first found the car with the body of Jeremy Fullerton inside it?"

Before he could answer, I added, "And I understand from previous testimony that after getting all the way around the Civic Center you slowed to a crawl, searching for the location in the fog that everyone agrees was so incredibly thick that night."

Twisting his head to the side, Joyner moved his closed mouth back and forth across his teeth as he tried to calculate the time.

"I'd say something less than two minutes," he said tentatively. "Yes, I'd say that," he added more confidently.

"Nearly two minutes!" I exclaimed, shaking my head in astonishment. "I guess I just don't understand. Nearly two minutes," I repeated, throwing a puzzled glance at the jury.

As I began to pace in front of the jury box, I looked at Joyner out of the corner of my eye.

"In your experience, Officer Joyner, when someone robs someone at gunpoint, doesn't the victim usually give them the money?" I stopped still, a look of incredulity on my face. "If someone had a gun in my face, wouldn't I ordinarily do whatever I was told to do?"

"Sometimes people try to resist, but you're right: That's what someone would normally do."

"Resist?" I asked in disbelief. "With a gun right in their face?"

For the first time, Marcus Joyner smiled. "It happens. It isn't the smart thing to do, but it happens."

"All right," I said. "Let's assume for the moment that Jeremy Fullerton was shot as part of a robbery. Either he resisted or he did not. Now, if he did not resist, then he was shot after he gave up his money—his wallet. Is that fair?"

"That makes sense," Joyner agreed.

"But if he was shot after he gave up his wallet, whoever shot him would have run away as soon as the shot was fired. He would not still be there two long minutes later, would he?"

Joyner leaned forward and rubbed his hands together. "No, probably not."

"But the defendant was there—wasn't he?—when you got there, two minutes after you heard the shot. Which means that if he did it, Jeremy Fullerton must have resisted. But if he resisted, and if he got shot while he resisted, is it likely that the defendant would have just hung around—for two whole minutes—after he shot him?"

Before Joyner could answer, I asked, "Isn't it a fact, Officer Joyner, that when a robbery goes bad and someone gets shot, whoever did it might grab whatever was in sight, but they would never just stay there for—how long did you say it was?—two minutes, before they tried to get away?"

"It would be unusual," Joyner had to concede.

"Quite unusual," I added. "Especially when it would have taken only a few seconds at most to reach inside a dead man's jacket to get his wallet."

Haliburton was on his feet. "Objection! Mr. Antonelli is giving a speech instead of asking a question."

I did not wait for the judge to rule. My eyes never left the witness.

"Were the keys in the ignition?" I asked as the district attorney, shrugging his shoulders, sat down.

"Yes, they were."

"Was the engine running?"

"No."

"Had the engine been running? Did you check the hood of the car?"

"I checked. It was cold. The engine hadn't been turned on in some time."

"The car doors were unlocked, correct?" I asked rapidly, ready with the next question before the last one had been answered.

"That's correct."

"All four of them?"

"Yes."

"In that model Mercedes, when you open the driver's door, do the others open at the same time? In other words, do they all unlock at once?"

Joyner shook his head. "We checked that. Only the driver's door unlocks. There's a button on the console if you want to unlock the others."

I looked at him as if I wanted to make sure I had it exactly right.

"In other words, the driver unlocks his door and gets in. The other doors—all three of them—remain locked?"

"Yes."

"So no one could simply have slipped in the passenger-side door when the driver got in, could they?"

"No," he admitted, "unless the driver was compelled to open the other door."

I turned toward the jury and drawled, "Because, I suppose, if you're going to mug someone, you're more likely to tell him to let you in instead of forcing him to get out; because, I suppose, you'd rather not do it in the dark when you can do it in the well-lit leather-lined interior of a late-model Mercedes?"

"Your honor!" cried Haliburton from the other side of the courtroom.

"Sorry," I said, waving my hand in the general direction of the bench. "All right, Officer Joyner," I went on, brushing back the thatch of hair that had fallen over my eye. "Let's go back to the weather that night. It was foggy—correct?"

"Yes."

"You could barely see in front of your face?"

"It was quite thick at times."

"You could barely see the car across the intersection?"

"That's correct."

I was in front of the counsel table, almost sitting on it, one foot crossed over the other. My left arm was wrapped across my stomach, my right elbow resting on it, while with my thumb and forefinger I stroked my chin.

"And neither you nor Officer O'Leary shouted any kind of warning—not even once—to the defendant before she shot him?"

"As I said, there wasn't time. He raised his gun—"

"But you never actually saw that happen, did you?"

"No, but—"

"In fact, neither one of you ever said anything before that shot was fired, did you?"

Joyner did not understand the question. He looked at me, a

blank expression in his eyes, waiting for me to explain what I meant.

"You never announced your presence as police officers, did you?"

"There wasn't any time. He jumped out of the car the moment my flashlight hit the dead man's face."

Pushing off from the table, I quickly closed the space between us. "And there wasn't any way that the defendant could have known you were the police instead of the killer, was there?"

"He was the killer!" Joyner shot back.

My eyes darted toward the bench. I was about to ask that the answer be stricken as nonresponsive. Then, in an instant, I realized what he had given me.

"That was your assumption, wasn't it? From the moment he jumped from the front seat of the car, you assumed—didn't you?—that he was the killer."

"He ran away from the scene," said Joyner.

"So far as you know, he was running away from the killer—isn't that possible, Officer Joyner?" I asked as I turned away from him.

"No," he insisted vociferously. "It is not. He had the gun."

"Oh, yes—the gun," I said, turning back. "Isn't it just possible, Officer Joyner, that this young man opened the unlocked door—unlocked because someone else had just left—and tried to help? Isn't it possible that he saw the gun on the floor, heard you coming, saw the light flash through the fog, and—afraid the killer was coming back—panicked and ran? And isn't it possible, Officer Joyner, that in his panic he picked up the gun as he bolted out of the car and tried to get away?"

Tossing back my head, I searched Joyner's eyes.

"Isn't it possible that instead of pointing the gun at Officer O'Leary, he turned for a split second to see who was after him, to see how close they were, and that Officer O'Leary just thought he was turning to take a shot?"

Reluctantly and without conviction, like someone forced to answer a question with no obvious connection to the only reality he knows, Joyner agreed that it was at least a possibility. My hand resting on the railing, I did nothing to disguise my disapproval.

"You're a trained police officer, aren't you?" I asked sharply.

He fixed me with a contemptuous stare. "Twenty-three years."

"When you're investigating a crime, aren't you supposed to consider all the alternatives?"

"I'm not a detective, I'm—"

"You're a street cop. You drive a patrol car. Yes, yes . . . we know all about that," I interjected with a show of impatience. "When you arrive at the scene of a crime, do you interview all the witnesses—or only those who agree with what you assume must have happened?"

With sullen eyes, Joyner replied tersely, "All the witnesses."

"Very good. Now, once again, indulge me. Assume that the defendant did not kill Jeremy Fullerton. Assume instead that, like you, he heard a shot, but instead of being blocks away, he was just a few yards away. Assume that he heard the shot and went to help. That would explain why he was in the car, wouldn't it?"

Joyner had been on the stand a long time and he was getting tired. His manner became more irritable; he was not so willing to ignore questions about his competence or his character. As he listened to the question, a cynical smile formed at the drooping corners of his mouth.

"Yeah, I suppose it would."

"And given how thick the fog was, and given that you never

announced you were police officers—that would explain why he tried to run away, wouldn't it?"

A corrosive smile spread over his face. "Yeah," he grunted.

"And the panic he must have felt—that anyone would have felt—that would explain how he happened to pick up the gun he found in the car, wouldn't it?"

"Yeah," replied Joyner, his voice filled with derision.

I looked at him for a moment, then stared down at the floor as if I were trying to understand the reason for his skepticism. Slowly, I raised my eyes and studied him again.

"But if that doesn't explain it, Officer Joyner, there's only one other way the gun could have ended up there on the sidewalk next to his body, isn't there? Either you or Officer O'Leary put it there."

Angrily, Joyner began to deny it.

"No more questions," I announced, waving my hand in disgust.

Before the judge had finished asking if he had any questions on redirect, Haliburton was on his feet, trembling with anger.

"You were about to answer the defense attorney's question when he cut you off," he began, the words coming one on top of the other. "Finish the answer you were going to give! Did either you or Officer O'Leary move the gun from the car?"

"No, sir, we did not."

"If neither of you moved the gun," asked Haliburton, his voice dropping into a more conversational tone as the color of his face returned to its normal shade, "then how did it get to where it was found?"

Joyner sat back in the witness chair and turned to the jury. "The defendant dropped it there."

Haliburton waited until Joyner's eyes came back around to him.

"After he was shot running away from the murder?"

"Objection!" I shouted, jumping out of my chair.

The judge hesitated, then looked at me, waiting for an explanation.

"The question either assumes the conclusion or it's a compound question," I insisted. "Either way it is impermissible; both ways it is ambiguous."

Thompson smiled. "In plain English, Mr. Antonelli."

"The district attorney said: 'running away from the murder.' That assumes what he has to prove: It assumes the conclusion. If he isn't doing that, then he's asking two questions: First, did the defendant drop the gun after he was shot; and, second, did the defendant commit the murder."

Pulling his head to the side, Thompson thought about it for a moment.

"I don't know if I agree with that," said the judge finally. "But I don't want to spend any more time on it." Turning to Haliburton, he instructed him to rephrase the question.

Haliburton shrugged his shoulders and muttered something under his breath.

"Officer Joyner," he asked, "was the gun found where the defendant dropped it after he was shot?"

"Yes," replied the witness. "We found it just a few inches from his hand when he was lying on the sidewalk."

A faint smile on his lips, Haliburton rubbed his thumb over the crystal of his watch. He turned to the jury.

"Mr. Antonelli took you through a number of alternatives," said the district attorney while he continued to stare at the jury. "Why don't we go through the same alternatives again, but in reverse order?" He faced the witness and asked, "The gun was found where it fell after the defendant was shot, correct?"

"Yes."

"In other words," said Haliburton, casting a withering glance at me, "you didn't do what defense counsel suggested—plant evidence?"

"No," said Joyner, grim and defiant as he slowly shook his head. "We did not."

"Then if we assume—as Mr. Antonelli insisted—that the defendant was just an innocent bystander, then panic is left as the only alternative explanation as to how he happened to have the gun in his possession at the time he was shot."

Haliburton had moved close to the jury box, grazing it with his hip as he looked ahead to the witness stand.

"Based on all your years as a police officer, is it likely—even in a state of panic—that someone would pick up a gun, a loaded gun, a gun just used in a murder, and then run into the street waving it around?"

"No, not likely at all," agreed Joyner immediately.

"But if you didn't 'plant' the gun, and if he didn't pick it up in his 'panic,' then there is only one explanation left, isn't there?"

Joyner did not need to be told what that explanation was. "The gun belonged to the defendant. He used it to shoot the senator and he still had it in his hand when he jumped out of the car and tried to get away."

Haliburton turned his head to the jury. "Yes, exactly. Now," he went on, looking back at the witness, "let's get back to something else Mr. Antonelli asked you about: the time it took to get to where the shot had been fired. Mr. Antonelli said—more than once, I think—'two minutes.' But I believe I heard you say something like a 'little less than two minutes.' Which was it?"

"Less than two minutes."

"Good," said Haliburton, as if the truth were the only thing he was after. "Now, how much less than two minutes, do you imagine?"

"I'm not really sure," admitted Joyner.

Head down, Haliburton started to walk toward him and then, halfway between the jury box and the witness stand, stopped.

"Have you ever been in a high-speed chase?" he asked, looking up.

"A number of times."

"Is it like being in an accident?"

"I'm not sure I know what you mean."

"Everything seems to move in slow motion," explained the district attorney.

"I see. Yes, that is sort of how it is."

"Because you're concentrating with such intensity on what you're doing. Isn't that the way it is?" asked Haliburton as he stepped closer to the witness stand. "You see things in such vivid detail that it seems like it's all taking place over a long period of time. No," he said, suddenly correcting himself, "it's more like time stops, isn't it? And what actually takes seconds—or sometimes even a fraction of a second—seems like it takes forever. Is that what it's like?"

Joyner had started nodding his agreement with the first sentence. "Yes, exactly," he said, remembering just in time to turn to the jury as he gave his answer.

Now less than an arm's length from his witness, Haliburton laid one hand on the arm of the chair and placed his other hand on his hip. He looked across at the jury box.

"So when you say you think it took something less than two minutes," he said in an ingratiating tone, "could it actually have taken a lot less?"

Joyner was more than willing to agree.

"Perhaps not much more even than a minute," suggested Haliburton, casting a meaningful glance at the jury.

Joyner now thought that was a definite possibility.

"You were driving as fast as you could," said Haliburton, reminding him. "So fast that you came very close to hitting a pedestrian, didn't you?"

Joyner tucked his chin and let out a sigh of relief. "Too close."

"You were driving as fast as you could—you got there as fast as you could," prompted Haliburton. "Mr. Antonelli talked a lot about panic and the things it can make people do. Tell us, Officer Joyner, do only 'innocent bystanders' panic, or do criminals sometimes panic as well?"

"Anyone can panic," replied Joyner knowingly.

"If someone were in a state of panic, might they lose track of time? Let me be more specific. Based on your experience as a police officer," asked Haliburton as he turned and began to walk toward the jury box, "is it possible that in the heat of the moment, after he shot him, he started looking for the victim's wallet, fumbling through it, looking for money, credit cards, anything of value—and didn't stop to consider how much time was passing?"

"That certainly could have happened."

At the far end of the jury box, Haliburton stopped and looked back at the witness. "In other words, Officer Joyner, if you've just murdered someone, you might be so panic-stricken that you might forget almost anything except getting something—a wallet, a watch—anything that would make what you had just done all worthwhile, isn't that correct?"

I was on my feet, angrily shouting an objection. "That question is inflammatory, calls for speculation, is—"

"Withdrawn," announced Haliburton with a flourish as he whirled away from the jury box. "No more questions."

Still on my feet when the judge asked if I wished to recross, I made straight for the witness stand.

"You just testified that the gun was found where the defendant dropped it after he was shot. You never saw the gun in the defendant's hand, though, did you?"

"No, but—"

"Do the police ever plant evidence, Officer Joyner?"

"Objection!" cried Haliburton from the counsel table behind me.

"The prosecution just asked this witness if either he or Officer O'Leary planted evidence, your honor," I said, my eyes still locked on Joyner. "The witness said no. I'm entitled to ask if this is because it never happens."

"I'll allow it," ruled Thompson, "but be careful."

"Officer Joyner," I asked again, "have you ever heard of the police planting evidence in a criminal investigation?"

"Sure," he admitted, "I've heard of it happening, but I've never—"

"Eight years ago you had a partner—an Officer Lawton—who was found guilty of doing precisely that. Tampering with evidence was the specific charge. Isn't that true?"

Shifting his weight around in the witness chair, Joyner nodded glumly. "He wasn't my partner when it happened."

I looked at him through narrowed eyes. "You wouldn't tamper with evidence and you would never change your testimony. Yet, when I asked you how long it had taken from the time you heard the shot until the time you found Jeremy Fullerton slumped over the wheel of his car, you said it was nearly two minutes. But now, with the helpful assistance of the district attorney, you want us to think it was really not more than a minute. Tell us, Officer Joyner, were you in a state of panic that night when you heard the shot?"

The question took him by surprise. "Me! No, I don't think so."

"So then it wasn't quite the same way someone feels when they're involved in something like a car crash, was it?"

Without so much as a breath in between, I added, "Nothing further, your honor," and walked away.

Thompson looked around the courtroom and then turned to the jury.

"Ladies and gentlemen, it's nearly twelve o'clock. Because the court has other matters to attend to, we will simply adjourn for the day and begin again Monday morning."

Nineteen

Surrounded by the throbbing noise and swirling color of the city, my senses seemed to wake from a week-long slumber. For days I had done nothing but listen to words and try to make sense out of them: words spoken by witnesses; words, the invisible signs of intangible thoughts, grasped like ghosts caught in a net, all their first-heard clarity gone the moment you tried to remember them long enough to compare them with other words spoken by the same witness or words spoken by someone else. I was tired of hearing them, tired of using them.

I started walking, without any particular place I wanted to go and with no other aim than to get as far away from the courthouse as I could. I wanted to put the trial out of mind; I wanted to forget everything that had happened; above all, I wanted to stop thinking about what the witness had said and what the witnesses were going to say. It was a close question which was worse: going over again and again what had already been said, wondering what you could have done to make it come out better; or playing over in your mind the endless variation of questions you planned to ask, and the answers you might possibly be given, by the people who had yet to be called. The prosecution had one more witness, then it would be my turn to put on the case for the defense. All I had was the defendant; that, and the assertion, which I was in no position to prove, that someone else, someone powerful, someone whose every ambition was threatened by Jeremy Fullerton, was responsible for the murder.

I kept walking, block after block, following the crowd, without any thought where I was or where I was going. Then, suddenly, I stopped. Whether drawn there by instinct or purely by chance, I was standing directly across the street from the burned-out ruin where just a week before I had watched Andrei Bogdonovitch die in that awful blast. A temporary plywood barricade had been erected in front of it to protect the public from falling debris. Behind it, a crew was busy demolishing what was left. Dodging traffic, I crossed the street and for a while watched them work, trying to remember the way it had looked the evening I was there, when Bogdonovitch had been hiding in the shadows, waiting for me to come.

My eye traced the path we had taken to the back of the shop, to the tiny alcove next to the storeroom door. At first I could not believe it. The door was still there, hanging by a single broken hinge from a single wooden post, but there all the same. It was the only thing left, amid all that twisted steel and concrete rubble; the only thing that had somehow escaped the blast. It was like looking at a photograph of the path taken by a tornado that leveled everything flat except, unaccountably, a single brick chimney of a house no one can find.

I heard a voice shouting and realized someone was shouting at me. Standing next to a pile of broken dusty bricks, a burly man in a hard hat was pointing at the scoop of a steam shovel high up in the air and with his other hand gesturing for me to move away. I waved back, acknowledging his warning, and turned to go.

At the corner, as I waited for the light, I looked back, the way I had that evening, and saw it all over again: the reddish orange ball rising into the sky; the deafening roar that seemed for that one moment to silence forever all the noise of the city; the bone-chilling certainty that Andrei Bogdonovitch had been killed with the kind of ruthless indifference associated normally with an act of war.

Bogdonovitch was dead, and I had as little idea who killed him as I had who murdered Jeremy Fullerton. And though Bogdonovitch had been convinced that whoever had killed Fullerton wanted him dead as well, I could not be sure the same person was responsible for both murders or that, despite my suspicions, there was even a connection between the two. As I wandered down the street, I could not get rid of the vague feeling that there was something I was missing—not the fact that I had no proof of anything, but something more basic: a different way of looking at things, a different perspective, something I had not considered that would put everything in a new light and make sense of things in a way nothing else had. It was like trying to remember a face you had seen only once or a name you had not heard in years: the strange sense that you know something precisely because you cannot remember anything about it.

I was too tired to walk anymore and went back to the office on Sutter Street. I started to tell Bobby about the feeling of uncertainty that was nagging at the back of my mind, but as soon as he looked up from his desk I could see in his eyes there was something he wanted to tell me first.

"Leonard Levine is dead," said Bobby, shaking his head in disbelief.

I sank into a chair in front of his desk. "What happened?"

Bobby leaned forward on his elbows and nodded toward the telephone. "Lenny told me to call him today. I called him after we talked. Remember? I told him what Bogdonovitch had told you about Fullerton. Lenny said he knew a few people in the White House he thought he could trust. He said he'd find out if they knew anything about it."

My throat started to tighten up. My mouth went dry.

"Was he murdered?"

Bobby did not know. "He was hit by a car, late last night, in Georgetown, just as he was leaving a restaurant."

"It was a hit-and-run, wasn't it?" I asked, for some reason certain I was right.

He nodded toward the telephone. "That's what they told me."

"It was murder, Bobby. Levine called the White House, told them what he had heard about Fullerton, and now he's dead. They killed him for the same reason they killed Bogdonovitch: They can't afford to have anyone find out that Fullerton—a member of the president's own party—was a Russian spy."

I saw the skepticism in his eyes and I could not blame him for it.

"No," I said as I got to my feet, "I can't prove it; I can't prove any of it; but it's true, Bobby, I know it."

Suddenly I thought of something that alarmed me. "He wouldn't have said anything about you, would he? Whoever he talked to at the White House—he wouldn't have told them who had told him about Bogdonovitch?"

"No," replied Bobby, smiling at me because I was concerned about him. "Lenny told me he'd keep my name out of it."

"Do you know who he was going to talk to?"

"No, just that there were a couple of people he trusted."

We looked at each other and in the silence I knew that Bobby now realized that while someone else had betrayed

Leonard Levine, it was only because he had trusted Bobby that he was now dead.

"I asked you to make that call," I reminded him. "I'm the one who wanted to know what Levine could find out about what the White House knew."

Bobby turned and stared out the window, his hands resting in his lap. Across the bay, under a perfect blue cloudless sky, the Berkeley hills shimmered in the early autumn light of a late afternoon.

"I didn't pay attention to him at all when we were in college together. I was too caught up in my own life to spend any time with a kid who worked in the laundry. The truth is, I didn't even know his name until years later, after he was elected to Congress and he reminded me who he was. I thought it was funny at first, that this guy I barely remembered, remembered so much about me. Then I started to think about the way things were then, and I started to see him, not as the kid who worked in the laundry room, but as the kid who worked his way through college on his way toward becoming someone really important, a lot more important than I ever became. But he still thought about me the same way he did then. You heard him that night," said Bobby, glancing back at me. "You should have heard him on the phone. When I told him what Bogdonovitch had said about Fullerton, you would have thought I had done him some enormous favor. Remember what he said about Fullerton being a fake and a fraud? This proved it, and for Lenny that meant that all the resentment he felt about Fullerton was not just jealousy and his own disappointment. Fullerton was a traitor, and I don't think anything could have stopped Lenny from proving it to the world."

Bobby rocked back and forth in his chair, thinking about

Leonard Levine and the odd ways in which their paths had crossed.

"I almost forgot," he said as I turned to leave. "Albert asked me to tell you that the governor's office called. The governor wants to see you."

"Where? When?"

"Tonight. Six-thirty at your old hotel. He's in town for something," explained Bobby. "That's all I know."

Bobby came around the desk and put his hand on my shoulder. "I'm sorry I got you into this," he said with an anxious look.

"I'm not," I replied, surprised at how confident I sounded. "And besides, you didn't get me into it. I did."

Bobby smiled and searched my eyes. "Maybe you're not as smart as I always thought you were."

I was at the door when he said, "Listen, Joe, I meant what I said. I'm sorry I got you into this. You're like a kid brother to me. I don't want anything to happen to you. I don't know if you're right about Lenny or not. All I know is I want you to be careful. I'm not going to tell you how to do your job, but don't take any chances you don't have to take."

I stayed in the office until a little after six, trying to think through the cross-examination I planned to conduct of the last witness the prosecution intended to call, but I could not concentrate. I kept thinking about Leonard Levine and the intensity of the hatred—there was no other word for it—he had felt for the man who had won the position he thought he should have had. Was there anyone whose life had been touched by Jeremy Fullerton who was not the worse for it? His wife had loved him, and look what he had done to her: made her a martyr to his own infidelity, her only comfort the perhaps fraudulent belief that he would always eventually come back to her. The astonishing thing was that she had accepted it, accepted him for what he became and perhaps had always been, and seemed to love him even more because of it. I did not know whether Meredith Fullerton was one of the greatest women I had ever known or a fool. But there was one thing about which I had no doubt at all: She had always remained faithful to him. It was the way in which she had been able all those years to remain faithful to herself. All the others, including the unfortunate Leonard Levine, forced to define themselves, at least in part, by what Fullerton had done or might yet decide to do, had not been left with even that much dignity. No wonder they all hated him so much.

At quarter past six I took a cab the short distance to the St. Francis Hotel. As I walked through the lobby, I glanced at the entrance to the bar where for several weeks I had been in the habit of having a late-night drink before I went up to my room and tried to sleep. In front of the bank of brass-door elevators, I checked the scrap of paper on which I had written the suite number and then stuffed it back in my pocket. When I reached the floor on which the governor was staying, I looked at my watch. It was six twenty-nine. Adjusting my tie, I tugged on the lapels of my suit coat and then knocked on the door.

An angular young man in his early thirties with a shock of light brown hair parted just below the center answered.

"Come in, Mr. Antonelli," he said.

He had a flat, slightly nasal voice that made him sound a bit like a snob. Without offering his hand or bothering to introduce himself, he stepped aside. The suite was enormous and littered like the aftermath of a week-long binge. The cloying smell of alcohol and stale tobacco was everywhere. An ashtray on the coffee table was cluttered with cigar butts. Crumpled cocktail napkins and glasses full of melting ice were scattered over the top of the chrome-sided bar.

"The governor had a few people up earlier," explained the

young man with a fleeting tight-lipped smile. "Would you like something?"

I sat in the middle of a pale yellow sofa. Through the open bedroom door I could see out a window that looked over Union Square and down the narrow streets to the Bay Bridge in the distance. Standing next to the bar, the young man picked up a glass from which he had apparently been drinking and with a slight movement of his wrist jiggled the ice.

"The governor would like to know why you have put him under a subpoena."

Slowly, I turned my head until I was looking straight into his eyes.

"I'll be glad to tell him."

He did not blink, nor did he look away. He was young, and he was important, and if I was too stupid to know it, that was not his problem.

"I'm afraid the governor won't be able to meet with you after all," he said without a hint of apology.

"What's your name?" I asked as I rose from the sofa.

"Cavanaugh. Richard Cavanaugh. I'm the governor's administrative assistant."

"Well, Dick, I didn't come here because I wanted to see the governor; I came here because your office called and said the governor wanted to see me."

"Unfortunately, the governor's schedule got changed at the last minute, and he asked me to take the meeting instead."

I did not believe a word of it.

"You're not under subpoena, Mr. Cavanaugh," I replied as I moved toward the door, "and I did not come here to talk to you. Next week the governor can come to see me—in court."

"Tell me, Mr. Antonelli," he said as I opened the door. "Did

Hiram Green really tell you the governor was an 'ungrateful son-of-a-bitch' who's never even sent him a Christmas card?"

I looked back to see a derisive smile crossing Richard Cavanaugh's slightly off-center mouth.

"He was on the phone to us probably before you had reached the sidewalk in front of his office. He wanted to be sure we heard it from him first, especially the things he had said about the governor. You made his day, Mr. Antonelli. He got the chance to be important, first to you, then the governor. Hiram Green doesn't get many chances like that anymore. I'm surprised the governor even remembers his name."

I smiled back. "From everything I've heard about the governor, so am I."

As I rode the elevator down to the lobby, the anger I felt at the way I had been used began to dissipate. I started to think of how I was going to describe to Marissa what had happened. I knew she would find it funny and make me think it was as well. She would remind me that I had probably myself suffered from the same vain imaginings of my own importance when I was as young as the governor's insufferable assistant.

I walked through the marble-columned lobby, glancing swiftly at the people I passed and down the carpeted steps to the front entrance. My hand was pushing open the door when I changed my mind and went back inside.

"The usual?" asked the bartender as I slid onto the leather stool. I nodded and asked him how he had been.

"Fine, Mr. Antonelli," he replied as he mixed a scotch and soda. I laid a bill on the bar.

"This one's on the house," he said as he picked up a glass from the stainless steel sink behind the bar and began to wipe it with a towel. "It's been a while. Glad to see you back."

At the other end of the bar a well-dressed middle-aged man

was idling over a drink. At a table on the far side of the room, two women with graying hair were chatting together, several shopping bags on the floor next to them.

"Slow night," I remarked as I took a drink.

"It'll be a mob scene later," he said as he held the glass up for inspection. "You know how those political things are. They're having a fundraiser for the governor. Afterward, they'll all show up," he explained with a shrug as he put the glass down.

He started to pick up another one, but instead he leaned across the bar and whispered scornfully, "The governor comes in for a drink, and they all come in. He finishes his drink and leaves, and they all leave. They're all a bunch of lemmings. No one wants to be out of step. The governor tells a joke—they all laugh. Someone says something and the governor stops smiling and they all look at the poor bastard who said it like he's got leprosy. I think the son-of-a-bitch does it on purpose—embarrasses someone like that—just to let everyone know who's in charge."

He straightened up and picked up a glass. At the other end of the bar, the well-dressed gentleman glanced at his watch, put some money down next to the empty glass, and left.

"I would have voted for Fullerton," said the bartender, wiping the glass clean. "He didn't play that kind of game."

Holding up the glass, he twisted it around in his hand, admiring his work.

"When he came in that night, it was only after nearly everyone else had already left."

I was supposed to meet Marissa for dinner and I did not want to be late. I checked my watch and started to get up.

"What?" I asked suddenly, gripping the bar. "What did you just say?"

He gave me a blank look.

"You said Fullerton came in that night. Which night? The night he was killed?"

"That's right. It was late. About half past midnight. The place had pretty well cleared out by then."

I sat down again and bent forward.

"Was he alone?"

"No, the two of them. They sat over there," he said, nodding toward the corner farthest away from the bar, just beyond where the two women were sitting now.

"The two of them?"

"Right. The one who worked for him; the one who's running in his place. You know—Goldman's daughter."

"You're sure?"

"Yeah, it was her, all right. She had on a long coat, and her hair was up, and she had on dark glasses—like she didn't want anyone to recognize her. I didn't know who she was, not until later when I started seeing her picture in the papers and on television. It was her, all right."

"How long did they stay?" I asked, wondering what it could possibly mean.

The bartender had tossed the towel over his shoulder and was leaning on his elbows. "I don't know—twenty minutes, maybe. They each had a drink, then they left."

"Together?"

"Yeah, together."

"Tell me this: How did they seem?"

His brittle iron-gray eyebrows lifted slightly and drew together just above the bridge of his straight thin nose.

"You mean, did they look like they were a couple of lovers? Not exactly. Something was going on between them, but whatever it was, they didn't seem too happy about it."

"But they left together?"

"Yeah," he replied as he turned his eyes to a couple who had just sat down at the bar.

I picked up the ten-dollar bill I had left on the bar and put a twenty in its place.

"Thanks," I said as I turned to go.

Under the awning outside the front entrance to the hotel, I waited for a cab, wondering what Jeremy Fullerton and Ariella Goldman had been talking about late the night he was murdered and why they had come to the St. Francis instead of the Fairmont.

"Mr. Antonelli," said a voice from somewhere just ahead of me.

I looked up and found myself under the watchful eye of a muscular, square-shouldered man wearing dark glasses and a dark blue suit. He was standing next to a black limousine. As he talked, his hand moved to the handle of the door.

"Someone would like a word with you."

I could not see his eyes, but there was something distinctly ominous in his voice, and he was less than an arm's length away.

"And just who might that be?" I asked, glancing up the street as I got ready to run.

"See for yourself," he said as he opened the door.

All I could see were the legs of someone sitting on the far side of the back seat. A moment's curiosity got the better of my fear. I took a half step forward and bent down to see his face. Suddenly a hand was on my arm and another one on my back. I was shoved inside and the door slammed shut behind me. I scrambled back around, reached for the handle, and in the same motion hit the door with my shoulder. The door was locked, and the car was screeching away from the curb.

Twenty

Settled against the darkened corner of the back seat, peering at me through tiny eyes that seemed to float under the heavy eyelids of his round, full face, a man I had never seen before insisted I had no reason to be alarmed.

"I just wanted to have a little talk with you."

I looked at him in astonishment. His suit coat was unbuttoned and his white dress shirt bulged out in the middle and covered his belt. His stomach was so large that his tie looked more like a napkin he had tucked in at the collar and forgotten to remove when he finished his meal. He was so huge that for a moment I forgot that I had been taken by force and made a prisoner in his car.

"If you want to talk to me, call my office and make an appointment. Now tell your driver to stop this car and let me out immediately!"

The expression on his face did not change; or, rather, there continued to be no expression on his face at all. Perhaps there was simply too much of him to allow it. His eyes were barely visible behind the thick folds of skin that engulfed them; his mouth was burdened with so much flesh that it would have been almost impossible to detect a smile, either of benevolence or malice.

"Just relax and enjoy the ride," he suggested. "We don't have far to go."

My heart was beating too fast, my mind racing too far ahead; but even had I been able to, I did not want to relax. I wanted to stay angry, because I did not know how otherwise to beat back the fear that was crawling up my spine, testing, pulling at my nerves.

"All right, then," I half shouted, "what is it you want to talk to me about?"

"About Jeremy Fullerton," he replied with labored breath. "And about you, Mr. Antonelli."

He seemed almost immobile, the only motion he made an endless, irritating circling of his thumbs as he moved them around each other while his hands, the other fingers clasped together, rested in his lap. The thought flashed through my mind that I could seize him by the throat and squeeze the life out of him. Out of the corner of my eye, I noticed the square-jawed passenger in the front seat, the one who had shoved me into the car, watching me closely in the rearview mirror.

"Who the hell are you, anyway?" I demanded, trying to keep up my courage.

His mouth was closed, and the breath that passed through his nostrils made a high-pitched sucking sound.

"Let's just say I'm an interested observer."

"And what exactly is it you observe?"

"Human behavior. It's a fascinating subject, don't you think, Mr. Antonelli? Your behavior, for example. People who were only familiar with the bare outline of your biography would think you had led a very enviable life: an enormously successful lawyer, famous for never—or almost never—losing a case. And yet you come here, to San Francisco, to take a case we both know you have no chance to win. It's a sort of pattern with you, isn't it, Mr. Antonelli? To push things to the edge, to take risks, just because it's something most other people would not do. You don't want to see yourself as just like everybody else, do you, Mr. Antonelli? You want to see yourself as somehow different from other people. You've never married, though we both know—don't we?—you're attracted to women. You were engaged once, but that ended badly, didn't it?"

I was angry now and fear had nothing to do with it. "What do you know about that?"

"I know that, quite unfortunately, the woman to whom you were engaged was institutionalized. I told you, Mr. Antonelli, I'm an interested observer."

His thumbs stopped moving around each other in that insane rhythmic circle and his hands went limp in his lap. He turned away and stared for a while out the window. We had just reached the top of a hill. The lush green outline of Golden Gate Park stretched out toward the ocean in the distance below.

"You asked a very interesting question during jury selection. Do you remember?" he asked, his small half-hidden eyes swinging in a slow lazy arc back around to me. "You asked one of them who he thought killed John F. Kennedy. I thought it was quite effective."

In the darkened shadows, his silhouette was a series of descending circles, each one larger than the one above. It did not seem possible that he could have been in that courtroom, even before I had begun to study the faces of everyone there, without my noticing him.

"You've been watching the trial?" I asked, pretending that it was at most a matter of mild curiosity.

"We've kept an eye on it," he said in what struck me as a

strange tone. It was as if he were amused, and also a little ag-
grieved, by the enormous disparity in what we knew.

Whatever doubts I may have had about what Andrei Bogdonovitch had told me, whatever hesitation I may have felt
about believing that people had been following him and that I
was in danger as well—all of that had now vanished, defeated by
the absolute certainty that the large figure who sat opposite me
was somehow responsible for at least the death of Bogdonovitch
and perhaps the death of Fullerton as well.

"Do you know why that question was particularly effective,
Mr. Antonelli?" he asked, each word echoing slowly into the
night. "Because ever since that day in Dallas, everyone in this
country believes that behind everything that happens—every
apparently 'random act of violence,' as I believe you put it—
there must be a conspiracy of some kind that gives the reason
why."

"Are you trying to tell me that there was not some kind of
conspiracy? That Fullerton's death was a random act of violence?"

"I'm not here to tell you anything, Mr. Antonelli. I don't
know who killed the senator, and, to be quite blunt about it, I
don't really care. Both of us know what Jeremy Fullerton really
was."

He was guessing. He did not know what I knew about
Fullerton or whether I knew anything at all. Or did he?

"I'm afraid I don't know what you're talking about," I
replied, doing what I could to appear indifferent.

He looked at me with open disdain, an expression that even
he could show.

"I was hoping we could have a serious conversation, Mr. Antonelli. I've been quite impressed with you. I was certain you
were a serious man. Please believe me when I tell you there is

nothing to be gained by treating me as if I were some kind of fool. I am anything but that, Mr. Antonelli."

With that warning, my anonymous companion leaned forward and whispered something in the driver's ear. At the next corner we turned left onto a two-lane road that ran under the cover of a long line of cypress trees bent by the winds that swept in from the Pacific. It was the entrance to Golden Gate Park.

"You know all about Jeremy Fullerton, Mr. Antonelli. Don't try to tell me otherwise. Andrei Bogdonovitch told you. Why bother to deny it? We know you talked to him; we know you met with him at his shop. You were there, Mr. Antonelli; you were there just before Bogdonovitch was killed in that unfortunate accident."

"Accident!" I cried. "You told me not to treat you like a fool, but you don't seem to have any hesitation treating me like one!"

There was no change, at least none I could detect, in that expressionless face. In the only visible manifestation of his reaction, he closed his eyes and slowly shook his head.

"Perhaps it was not an accident," he said as he opened his eyes again, "but if he was murdered, I certainly had nothing to do with it. Bogdonovitch was no threat to anyone. What could he do? Tell the world what he told you—that Jeremy Fullerton had once taken money from the Russians? Who would have believed him? What kind of proof could he have offered?"

He was overlooking the obvious.

"You found out," I reminded him. "And it wasn't because Bogdonovitch told you. There are records in Moscow—KGB files."

His nostrils flared open as he took a breath. His moist lips seemed to tremble with condescension.

"If any such records ever existed," he said with satisfaction, "I think you can probably assume they don't exist anymore."

The road, not much wider than a paved footpath, opened onto a broad expanse of rolling lawn and artfully sculpted ornamental trees. Straight ahead, at the far end, row after row of vacant wooden benches ran back from the front of a large circular band shell. Off to the left, the last few stragglers were leaving the gray stone buildings that housed the aquarium and the Museum of Natural History. Quietly, the limousine rolled to a stop.

"But I'll bet they weren't destroyed until after Fullerton was dead, were they? Because until he was, they would have been extremely valuable to anyone who wanted to destroy any chance Fullerton might have had to become president—isn't that right?"

He looked hard at me, and the fear I had almost forgotten started up my spine again.

"Whoever killed Jeremy Fullerton did everyone a favor. It would all have come out—everything. And what would have happened then? It would not have been like any other political scandal; he couldn't have just retired in disgrace and then, a few years later—or perhaps just a few months later—" he added, a glint of amusement in his eye, "apologized for his indiscretions and enjoyed first forgiveness and then a new rush of popular approval. No, this was different. Fullerton would have been charged with treason. There would have been a trial with God knows what kind of testimony, and he would have been sent to prison. What do you think that would have done to this country? But now, fortunately, we've been saved that entire trauma, all that unnecessary unpleasantness. He's dead. What good would it do for anyone to find out now what he really was? Because even though there isn't any evidence to prove it, the allegation alone—the mere suggestion that Jeremy Fullerton might have sold out his country for money—could be enormously harmful. That kind of thing can destroy people, Mr. Antonelli.

Surely you know that. It would destroy his wife, his friends, all those millions of people who believed in him. It's better just to leave it alone, don't you think?"

I turned around and looked across at the stranger I knew I could never trust to tell the truth about anything.

"You didn't grab me from in front of the St. Francis Hotel to tell me that now that Fullerton is dead we should hide the truth about him so that no one's feelings get hurt."

"I wanted to talk to you, Mr. Antonelli, to let you know that certain people would be extremely grateful if you took a somewhat larger view of things as you conduct the defense in the trial of Jeremy Fullerton's murder. Extremely grateful."

I stared intently at him, searching his eyes for an answer. "These people you tell me would be so grateful: Do they include the White House?"

He made no response, but it did not matter. Even if he had denied it, I would not have believed him. The White House was behind it, all of it.

"You're going to lose, Mr. Antonelli. Surely you know that. You're too good a lawyer not to know that all the evidence points to your client. You're going to lose; it's how you're going to lose that is important. That question you asked—that question about the Kennedy assassination—that kind of thing makes people uncomfortable; it makes them start to wonder about things. It has to stop. Conduct the defense any way you want; but you are doing no one any good—and you could be doing yourself a great deal of harm—by these unsubstantiated allegations of conspiracy and cover-up."

"Do myself a great deal of harm?" I asked, glaring at him.

For the second time he whispered something in the driver's ear. The car started up again and a few minutes later we were out of the park, heading toward the bridge.

"I have no idea whether the death of Andrei Bogdonovitch was an accident or a murder; and, if it wasn't the young man who's now on trial for it, I have no idea who killed Jeremy Fullerton. But make no mistake, Mr. Antonelli: The same people who are willing to be quite generous if you just do your job and let the law takes its course would not hesitate for a moment to punish your refusal to act as you should."

"In other words," I said as I felt my mouth go dry, "you had nothing to do with the death of Fullerton or the death of Bogdonovitch, but you would not mind killing me?"

He threw his head back and laughed. "You have a gift for summation, Mr. Antonelli."

The grim laughter faded into the silence and he stared straight ahead. I did not know where we were going or what was going to happen when we got there. He did not say a word until we started across the Golden Gate.

"Death, by itself, is quite overrated as a punishment, don't you think, Mr. Antonelli?" he asked as if we were engaged in a friendly dinnertime conversation. "It's the manner of death that's important, don't you agree? Discovering what someone fears the most, that one way of dying that makes him want to do anything, including killing himself, or perhaps even killing someone else, to avoid it. That's what is at the heart of it. Did you ever read Orwell's *1984*? Do you remember the way Winston feared rats? Do you remember what Big Brother did to him with that knowledge?"

He turned his eyes until he was again gazing straight ahead. "I've never forgotten that," he added quietly.

The driver edged the limousine over to the outside lane and began to slow down.

"What are you afraid of, Mr. Antonelli?"

I made no answer, and I thought I saw a smile pass over the

otherwise indistinct features of his massive gelatinous face. Other cars were hurtling past us as we slowed to a crawl. I tried to hide my fear, and the harder I tried, the greater the terror I felt.

"A great many people are afraid of heights, Mr. Antonelli. Did you know that?" he asked, turning toward me again. "They can walk in a straight line for miles; they have perfect balance—but put them on a flat surface as wide as any sidewalk high up in the air and they think every second they're about to fall. It's not a fear I share, but I don't mean to dismiss it on that account; I have fears of my own—everyone does. Shall I make a confession? What I fear the most? Being buried alive. The thought of it alone makes me shudder."

The car came to a stop. The lock on my door suddenly snapped open. We were at the middle of the bridge, hundreds of feet above the cold black water of the bay. The tinted window next to me slid partway down and the wind outside whipped the side of my face.

"Are you afraid of heights, Mr. Antonelli?" he asked with a kind of dreadful anticipation.

It was not so much a sense of honor as anger at my own cowardice that made me refuse to tell him the truth.

"No, I'm not," I replied, though there was no doubt in my mind that he knew I was lying.

"Then you won't mind walking the rest of the way," he said as he reached in front of me and pushed open my door.

"I'm not walking anywhere. You can take me back to where you got me."

Suddenly the silent passenger in the front seat had a gun pointed in my face. Slowly, carefully, my eyes on the pistol, my hands in plain sight, I got out of the car. A gust of wind hit me hard and I stumbled to catch my balance.

"Here, Mr. Antonelli, this is for you," said that now-familiar voice. He was reaching through the open window, holding a thick manila envelope in his fat puffy hand. "You're going to lose the case, Mr. Antonelli. Nothing Fullerton did can help you win it." As the car began to move away, he added, "We'll meet again, Mr. Antonelli; you can be sure of it."

I stood there watching the taillights of the limousine, and then, at the sound of a horn, jumped back as a car came bearing down on me from behind. Once I got onto the pedestrian walkway, I clutched the railing and tried to steady my nerves. I knew better than to look down, and so I looked back toward the city. It was less than a mile away, but it made me feel like I was circling the earth and that at any moment the city was going to roll back below the horizon as the planet rotated around the sun. I looked the other way, toward the dark obscurity of the hillside at the northern end of the bridge. I began to walk toward it, never for a moment letting go of the railing.

Each time the wind blew up in a sudden gust, each time the bridge moved beneath my feet as the traffic rumbled across, I felt myself tense. I taunted myself with the knowledge that, as the schoolbooks teach, a coward dies a thousand deaths and laughed out loud at how utterly useless when you needed them all those lessons were. Anyone passing must have thought me mad, waving my arm around, shouting into the wind, angry at the man who had taken me, angry at being threatened with something worse than death, angry at the cowardice without which those threats would have had no effect.

The anger concentrated my mind and made me think about something other than how terrified I was of being out here, high up in the air, on a bridge that was moving beneath my feet and, billowed by winds, swaying from side to side. I wanted revenge; I wanted that obese obscenity to know what it was like to live out your worst fear. I began to see myself with a shovel, throwing dirt on his grave, listening while he beat with his bare hands on the lid of his coffin, knowing he was going to be buried alive.

There is a certain cathartic effect in graphic thoughts of revenge. I felt better than I had before. I began to walk faster and after a while even found the confidence to let go of the railing. The wind subsided, and as I neared the end of the bridge that sickening sideways motion finally came to a stop.

Once I was off the bridge, I caught a ride with an old man in a pickup truck who, because he had seldom seen anyone hitchhiking in a coat and tie, thought my car must have broken down. He insisted on taking me to the door, and I gave him directions to the house where I now sometimes spent the night.

Marissa came to the door when she heard the pickup come down the drive. She stood there, laughing with her eyes, while I stepped out of the truck.

"What happened to you?" she asked, smiling at my disheveled appearance as I waved good-bye to the old man.

We went inside and she made me a drink while I told her what had happened. It was little more than a bare recitation of events with next to nothing of the way I had felt. I did not want to admit to her that I had been terrified. Seeing myself the way I wanted her to see me, I began to think that not begging for my life had been a little on the side of bravery.

"You must have been scared out of your mind!" she exclaimed when I told her that at one point I thought they were going to kill me.

Now that it was over, now that I was safe, the fear I had tried so hard to fight no longer seemed quite so real.

"I was angry, mainly," I replied.

She tilted her head the way she did whenever she was revolving something in her mind. Her eyes seemed to draw me closer.

"Angry at yourself because you were afraid? Or angry because you thought it was the only way you had to keep your fear under control?"

She did not want an answer; that was not why she had asked. She wanted to let me know that there was nothing I had to hide from her, and perhaps to tell me that I could not keep anything hidden from her if I tried.

"What was in the package he gave you?" asked Marissa, gesturing toward the manila envelope that lay on the dining room table in front of me.

I had not thought of it since it was handed to me. I had not looked inside; I had not even wondered what it might contain. When I opened it now, my first reaction was that I was glad I had not opened it before. It would only have fed my fear.

"Look at this," I said as I emptied it out on the table.

There were photographs, dozens of them, and I was in every one of them. It took only an instant to recognize the chronology in which they had been taken. I spread them out, beginning with the earliest and ending with the most recent.

"They've had me under surveillance since the first day I appeared in court," I said, nodding toward the first photograph. "From the moment I officially became the defense lawyer in the case."

There were photographs of me in front of the building on Sutter Street where Albert Craven had his office; photographs of me at the St. Francis; more ominously, there were photographs taken on both occasions that I spoke with Andrei Bogdonovitch in the street. They even had pictures of Craven's boat, the day we went out on the bay.

"They have everything I've done, everywhere I've been," I

said, shaking my head. "They've got a picture of Bobby's house, and look at this," I said, stabbing my finger at a black and white photograph taken less than a week before. "They have one of us standing together on the deck outside."

There were also two photographs taken the evening I went to see Andrei Bogdonovitch at his shop: one when I entered, the other just as I was leaving.

"What do they tell you?" asked Marissa.

"That they just missed getting me, too," I replied with a cynical shrug.

She shook her head vigorously. "No, don't you see? They knew you were there. If they were the ones who set off the bomb, why did they wait until after you left? Maybe they were telling you the truth about that—maybe someone else killed Andrei Bogdonovitch. Either way, one thing is clear, isn't it? These people don't want you dead." She waved her hand over the photographs scattered all around the table. "What do these pictures prove, except that they could have killed you anytime they wanted? Isn't that the question—why they haven't?"

I thought I knew the answer. "If I were killed, the judge would have to declare a mistrial. Another lawyer would take the case. Everything would have to be done all over again. But it's more than that. There would be another murder, the murder of the lawyer who claimed someone else, someone powerful, was responsible for the death of Jeremy Fullerton. It would start an investigation."

Marissa cocked her head and bit her lip. There was a worried look in her eyes.

"They don't want to kill you; they want to scare you. They want to make you think about them instead of the trial. They want you to worry more about what might happen if you win than about what will happen to that boy if you lose."

Twenty-one

"The People call Ariella Goldman," announced Clarence Haliburton, rising from his chair.

Dressed in a simple dark blue skirt and jacket, her auburn hair swept above the soft back curve of her neck, Lawrence Goldman's daughter, the last witness for the prosecution, entered the courtroom. The door shut behind her, blocking the television lights and the flashbulbs of the cameras in the corridor outside. Conscious that every eye was on her, she remained completely composed. Ariella Goldman was used to the undivided attention of people she had never met. She let herself through the gate in the wooden railing.

The district attorney did not waste a minute. He elicited the length of time Ariella Goldman had worked for Senator Fullerton and what her principal duties had been. Then he asked, "And was it in that capacity that you were with him the night he was killed?"

Sitting at an angle, her knees pressed primly together, she allowed herself an indulgent smile. "Yes, for the most part. As his speechwriter I would certainly have been with him when he spoke that evening at the dinner. I'm not sure I would have been at the gathering later on at my father's apartment."

"Yes, I understand," remarked Haliburton, smiling back. "You were there—at your father's apartment—until the senator left?"

"Yes."

Haliburton dropped his eye to the list of questions he had laying open in the notebook in front of him. Though the testimony of several of his witnesses had involved technical terms not easily remembered, this was the first time I had seen him do this. The district attorney was not going to leave anything to chance, not even the order in which he asked the questions he had written out in advance, during the direct examination of Lawrence Goldman's daughter.

"And were you the person who drove Senator Fullerton to his car?"

"Yes, I was," she answered in an even tone.

"Would you tell us, please, the reason why you did that— drove the senator to his car?"

Leaning to the side, Ariella Goldman delicately rested her elbow on the arm of the witness chair and glanced toward the jury.

"Mrs. Fullerton had left early, and the senator needed a ride to the Civic Center where he had left his car."

While she was speaking, Haliburton checked his list.

"And why was his car there instead of at the hotel where the dinner was held or, for that matter, at the senator's own residence just a few blocks away?"

Dropping her hand, she extended her arm out across the arm of the chair. She sat perfectly straight, her back arched slightly, her chin tilted up. Each time Haliburton asked a question, she waited, smiled politely, and then, her eyes fixed on a point directly in front of her, turned and faced the jury.

"The senator had an office in the Civic Center. We were there together, going over the speech he was going to give that evening. The senator was something of a perfectionist; he always wanted everything to be just right. We went over it and over it, making one change, then another. It was time to go, and he still wasn't satisfied. I drove my car so he could keep working on it until we got there. That's why he needed a ride back."

"Approximately what time did you drop him off at his car?"

"Right around one o'clock, I think."

"What did you do then?" asked Haliburton, raising his eyes from the list.

"After I dropped him at the car? I went back to my father's apartment and went to bed."

Haliburton closed his notebook. "When you dropped him off, did you actually see the senator get into his car?"

"Yes," she said, then changed her mind. "No. I saw him open the door as I drove away," she explained.

Her lower lip began to tremble. She pulled it taut, shaping her mouth into a grimace of self-accusation.

"I should never have done that, just driven off like that—in that fog. I should have stayed there, waited until he was safely inside with the door shut and the lights on," she continued, her voice rising. "I should have waited until he turned on the engine; I should have waited until he pulled away from the curb; I should have waited until I knew he was safe. None of this would have happened!" she insisted, gamely trying to hold back the tears.

Haliburton had moved in front of the counsel table. He waited until the witness regained her composure. In a deep, rich voice, full of solemn sympathy and understanding, he announced that he had no more questions to ask.

There is a point in almost every trial when the routine inquiries from the bench become abbreviated and the answers to them dispensed with altogether.

"Mr. Antonelli?" was all that Judge Thompson now said by way of asking if I wished to cross-examine the prosecution's witness. My only response was to get to my feet.

Touching Jamaal Washington on the shoulder as I moved behind him, I made my way to the front of the counsel table. My arms folded across my chest, I tilted my head to the side, looking at the witness as if there were something about which I remained quite perplexed.

"The reason you drove Senator Fullerton to his car," I said hesitantly, "was that Mrs. Fullerton had left early. Isn't that what you told Mr. Haliburton?"

My apparent confusion seemed to give her even more confidence than she had before.

"Yes, that's right," she replied with a civil smile.

It was more than just a smile. She did something with her eyes I had not noticed before, something quite extraordinary. Without any movement of her lashes—at least none I could detect—her eyes flared open in a way that seemed almost to dissolve the physical space between us.

I furrowed my brow as if I were still confused. "And what was the reason Mrs. Fullerton left early?"

She did it again, that flash of light that came from her eyes at the precise moment the first word was formed on her soft-sloping mouth. It was like watching someone trying to take her own photograph.

"I believe she wasn't feeling well."

Arching my eyebrows, I slowly tilted my head to the other

side. "And do you have any idea just why it was she might not have been feeling well?"

Her eyes blazed again, but the word that was already on her lips never came. She lowered her eyes and for a moment stared pensively at her hands.

"No, I'm afraid I wouldn't know."

"You're sure you 'wouldn't know'?" I said, lowering my voice as if there were some hidden secret in that otherwise conventional phrase. "The party was at your father's apartment, wasn't it?"

"Yes," she replied, looking up.

"Your father is Lawrence Goldman, correct?"

"Yes."

"It's fair to say that your father is a very wealthy man, is it not?"

Her eyes flashed the way they had before. "Yes," she replied, looking directly at me. "It would be fair to say that my father is rather well off."

"Your father was one of the principal fundraisers for Senator Fullerton's campaign for governor—isn't that correct?" I asked. I began to drag my foot back and forth as if I were keeping time to her answers.

"Yes, that's correct."

"And that was the reason he had this gathering in his apartment after the dinner at which the senator gave the speech you helped write—is that correct?"

"Yes, it was a fundraising event, if that's what you're asking."

I stopped swinging my foot and raised my eyes. "Yes, that's what I'm asking. People paid for the privilege of attending this gathering at your father's apartment—is that correct?"

"I think I just answered that," she replied with a brief smile more condescending than she intended.

"Humor me," I shot back. "Answer it again."

"Yes, those who came made a contribution."

I took two quick steps toward the jury box and stopped. With my hand on the back of my neck, I stared down at the floor.

"So everyone made a contribution. Good. What was the size of those contributions? Fifty dollars? A hundred dollars? How much, Ms. Goldman?" I asked, glancing up at her. "What was the price of admission to your father's apartment that night?"

"Fifty," she answered.

"Fifty?" I asked with a blank expression.

"Fifty thousand, Mr. Antonelli."

"Oh, I see," I said, facing the jury. "Fifty thousand dollars to say hello to the senator."

"Fifty thousand dollars a couple," she added hastily.

My eyes were still on the jury.

"Yes, I see, fifty thousand dollars a couple. Well, for those of us who don't normally spend fifty thousand dollars to go to a party," I said as I swung around to face her, "is this what is usually charged at an event of this sort, or was this perhaps at the high end of things?"

Though she tried not to show it, she was now in a state of intense annoyance.

"It was a very exclusive event," she explained curtly.

"How many people—I'm sorry, how many couples—were there that evening?"

"Seventy-five or eighty."

"That means you raised in the vicinity of four million dollars?"

"About that, I suppose."

I stood next to the jury box, my hand on the railing.

"And you were at this rather expensive event, not because

you were the senator's speechwriter, but because—as I believe you testified in response to a question asked by Mr. Haliburton—you are, if you don't mind my putting it this way, your father's daughter?"

"Why should I mind?" she replied, her eyes flaring open. "I am my father's daughter, and proud of it."

"And that was the reason you were there?" I asked as I began to pace.

"Yes, that was the reason."

I stopped abruptly and looked up.

"Not because you were there—let us say—as the senator's date?"

"No, of course not," she replied, raising her chin ever so slightly. "I was there because I'm Lawrence Goldman's daughter."

"Your father was there, but your mother was not?"

"She was at our ranch outside Santa Barbara, getting it ready. Unfortunately, she was not able to get back."

"You took her place, didn't you? When the guests arrived, you were there with your father—and with the senator—to greet them, correct?"

"Yes, along with Mrs. Fullerton."

"Until she had to leave?"

"Yes."

"Because she wasn't feeling well?"

"Yes."

Nodding thoughtfully, I wandered back along the jury box, away from the witness. I put my hand on the railing and looked back.

"Now, approximately how long did it take to drive the senator from your father's apartment to the Civic Center where he had left his car?"

Crossing her legs, Ariella Goldman let her hands dangle down over the ends of the arms of the witness chair. On one wrist she wore an understated watch of impeccable taste and extravagant expense; on the other she had a gold bracelet with a gold leaf cluster and a single gold heart. She considered her answer.

"I suppose, from the time we got into my car in the garage . . . ten, maybe fifteen minutes. I had to drive very slowly. The fog was as thick as I've ever seen it. At least twice I had to stop and lean my head out the window to see where I was going."

"Other than that, did you stop anywhere after you left the garage?" I asked, sliding my hand along the railing as, step by step, I moved closer toward her.

"No," she insisted. "As I just told you, it took ten or fifteen minutes to get to the Civic Center."

I opened my eyes wider and smiled as pleasantly as I could. "So you didn't stop anywhere?"

"No," she replied, unable to suppress a trace of annoyance.

I raised an eyebrow and studied her. "You didn't stop anywhere to have a drink with the senator?"

She clutched the arm of the chair as she bent forward. "I've already told you: We didn't stop anywhere. I took him directly to his car."

I stared at her with amusement and said nothing. Clenching tightly the wooden arms of the chair, she stared back, waiting for the next question. Finally, I turned away and walked the few short steps to the counsel table. When I looked up, she had let go of the chair and was sitting back, confident and at ease, her hands held lightly in her lap.

I opened a file folder that lay next to the loose-leaf binder and ran my finger down a sheet of paper. When I found what I was searching for, I glanced up, my finger still on the spot.

"Are you acquainted with someone by the name of Paula Hawkins?"

Startled, she tried to hide her surprise behind an eager smile. "Yes. We're good friends. We went to college together."

"Several months ago—early last spring—she picked you up at the airport. I believe you were returning from a trip to Europe?"

"Yes," she said tentatively.

I lifted my finger off the page and let the file folder close. "She spent the night with you at your father's house in Woodside—correct?"

Ariella Goldman moved her face slightly to the side and crossed her legs the other way. "Paula has often been a guest. So I'm not sure I particularly remember that she stayed that night, but she might have."

I put my hands in my coat pockets and stared at her again. "I believe it was the same time that Christopher Borden was an overnight guest at your father's home. Does that help remind you?" I asked.

Her head snapped up; a look of distaste swept across her mouth. "I don't know what any of this has to do with—"

"Objection, your honor!" cried Haliburton before she could finish. "The question is irrelevant. What difference can it possibly make when the witness last had as a guest an old friend from college?"

Judge Thompson turned up the palms of his hands. "Mr. Antonelli, where is this going?"

"I'll withdraw the question, your honor," I replied, my eyes still on Ariella Goldman.

Thompson sank back into his high leather chair and resumed his habit of picking with the back of his thumb the rough edges of his fingernails.

"On that trip to Europe—the one at the end of which Paula Hawkins picked you up—you were traveling with Jeremy Fullerton, weren't you?" I asked with a stern glance.

"I was one of the staff people on that trip. So yes, in that sense, I was traveling with the senator."

"How many other staff people were there?"

"The senator's administrative assistant, Robert Zimmerman, was there."

"So there were two staff people. Where exactly in Europe did you go?"

"London and Paris. The senator spent several days meeting with British officials, then several more with members of the French government."

"Did Senator Fullerton make this trip alone, or was he part of a larger delegation?"

"No, there were four members of the Senate Foreign Relations Committee."

"That's counting Senator Fullerton?"

"Yes."

"After the delegation finished its official business in Paris, did you return directly to the United States, or did you spend a few more days in Europe?"

"I came home directly."

"To Washington or to San Francisco?"

"San Francisco."

"And Senator Fullerton—what did he do? Did he come back directly as well?"

"No, I believe he stayed behind a few days," replied Ariella with a vague expression.

"You're not sure?" I asked, raising my eyebrow. "Isn't it true, Ms. Goldman, that you both stayed in Europe a few days?"

Haliburton was out of his chair, waving his hand in the air. "Asked and answered, your honor!"

Thompson scratched his chin as he thought about what he should do.

"Sustained," said the judge finally.

I took my hands out of my suit coat pockets and shoved them deep into my pants pockets.

"So the senator stayed, and you came home. Why? Why didn't you just stay there with him?"

"I'm not sure I understand the question," she replied.

I looked at her and then, after a moment or two, gazed at the ceiling.

"Mrs. Fullerton left the party because she wasn't feeling well," I said, sighing with impatience. "Isn't that what you said?"

"Yes, that's what I said."

My eye traced a horizontal line from the ceiling to the corner where the two walls met and then began a slow descent.

"And isn't the reason she wasn't feeling well because the two of you had just exchanged words?" I asked, my eyes resting once again on hers.

She began to fidget with her hands. She shifted around in her chair. There was a cold, scornful look in her eyes.

"Mrs. Fullerton said some things that—"

"She accused you of having an affair with her husband, didn't she?"

"Yes, she did, but—"

"And you didn't deny it, did you?"

She sat bolt upright, her eyes flashing with anger. "No, I didn't deny it, but—"

"And it was because of what you said to her that she walked

out and that later on you left your father's apartment with Jeremy Fullerton and you drove him—not to the Civic Center—but to the St. Francis Hotel, where you had a drink together. Isn't that right, Ms. Goldman? Isn't that what you really did that night, and isn't everything you've said here today—under oath—a blatant, bald-faced lie?"

Haliburton was on his feet screaming an objection. Startled by the ferocity of my interrogation, Thompson had stopped what he was doing and raised his head. He started to say something, but I beat him to it.

"No more questions," I announced, waving my hand toward the bench as I shot one last angry look at Ariella Goldman.

Peering over the bench, Thompson looked at Haliburton. "Redirect?"

Haliburton shook his head. There was something he wanted first.

"Could we have a short recess, your honor?"

Haliburton waited until the jury was out of the room and then moved right next to the witness stand and began an intense whispered conversation with Ariella Goldman. Ten minutes later, when Judge Thompson returned to the courtroom, they were still talking. With the jurors back in their places, the district attorney stood at the corner of the counsel table and said to the witness:

"Mr. Antonelli asked you a number of questions and then cut you off before you could finish your answers. Rather than go back through each one of those and give you the opportunity to say what defense counsel apparently didn't want the jury to hear, why don't you just tell us what was said that night between you and Mrs. Fullerton?"

Every eye was on her, and not just the jury; everyone in the crowd behind me was watching with that rapt attention reserved for the rumored misbehavior of the famous and the wellborn. And it was on them, not the district attorney or the jury, that Lawrence Goldman's daughter now lavished her attention.

"I don't remember the exact words," said Ariella firmly, looking out over the crowd. "I just remember that it was very unpleasant."

She started to say something more, stopped, and swallowed hard, as if she had to make a conscious effort to keep control of herself. A faint, apologetic smile flickered for a moment on her mouth. Determined to go on, she lifted her chin.

"Mrs. Fullerton accused me of ruining her marriage. I was so taken aback, so shocked—we were in a receiving line with dozens of people standing there—and then this sudden outburst! Well, I'm afraid I said something back; and again, I don't remember exactly what it was—I only know I should never have said it, not to anyone, but especially not to her. It was unforgivable of me, and I can't tell you how ashamed I am of having done it."

The expression on Clarence Haliburton's face as he stood there, hands folded in front of him, had gone from compassion to something close to bereavement.

"Why do you say 'especially not to her'?"

Ariella Goldman lowered her eyes. The courtroom was enveloped in a profound silence. When she finally looked up, you could hear her breath escape.

"Because," she replied in a voice heavy with regret, "Mrs. Fullerton is a very disturbed woman. Most of the time," she added immediately, "she can function perfectly well. You wouldn't know there was anything wrong with her."

Like a consulting physician, Haliburton pressed his lips together and asked judiciously, "Do you know the nature of this disorder?"

"No," she said, sadly shaking her head. "Just that she suffers from bouts of depression and at times can become quite paranoid."

It was not anything I would have thought about Meredith Fullerton. I did not believe it; but it was uncannily close to something that had happened to someone I loved, something I had told only Marissa, something that the man who had taken me captive and then left me in the middle of the Golden Gate Bridge had told me. Ariella Goldman was lying about Jeremy Fullerton's widow, and she was doing it in a way that made me wonder how much she had found out about me.

"And was that the reason—her condition—that you were reluctant to discuss what happened that evening in your father's apartment?"

"Yes. After everything that's happened, after everything she's had to go through, I didn't want to do or say anything that might cause her any more pain."

Nodding sympathetically, Haliburton proceeded to clarify the next point of inconsequence on which she had, for all the right reasons, said something not strictly speaking correct.

"Mr. Antonelli asked you whether you stopped to have a drink with Senator Fullerton before you dropped him at his car. You said you did not. Is that true?"

"No," she replied with an earnest expression, "we did stop. We had a drink at the St. Francis. Jeremy—I mean, the senator—wanted to talk about Mrs. Fullerton."

"And was the reason you didn't say so when Mr. Antonelli asked you the same question the same reason you just gave—you didn't want to cause Mrs. Fullerton any unnecessary distress?"

With a grateful smile, she agreed.

"Thank you, Ms. Goldman," said the district attorney, the

soul of understanding. "Nothing further, your honor," he said with a cursory glance toward the bench.

I was standing at the corner of the counsel table, glaring at her, before Haliburton had taken his seat.

"So because of your concern for the well-being of the senator's wife, you came in here today and committed a criminal act—is that what you want us to believe, Ms. Goldman?"

"Criminal act?"

"You lied under oath. I asked you if you had stopped anywhere when you drove Senator Fullerton to his car. You said no. That's called perjury, Ms. Goldman; and perjury, if you didn't know it before, is a criminal act. People go to prison for that, Ms. Goldman."

She smiled, the way a mother might smile at the understandable stupidity of a child. "I didn't mean to lie," she explained in a soft voice trained to cover treachery with benevolence. "I didn't think it really mattered that we stopped for a drink. And as I tried to explain, Mrs. Fullerton has been through so much already that—"

"During the break—while the jury was out of the room—where did you go?" I asked sharply.

"Why, nowhere," she replied, surprised. "I stayed right here."

"In conversation with Mr. Haliburton, isn't that true?"

"Yes," she responded, watching me closely.

"Did you talk about anything in particular?"

Halfway out of his chair, Haliburton thought better of it and sat down.

"Yes," she said, her eyes flaring open. "He told me I should not hold anything back; that I should tell the whole truth—no matter whom it might hurt."

I looked at her and smiled. "Did he really? Had he not told you that before?"

This time Haliburton did not change his mind.

"Objection!" he shouted as he sprang out of his chair.

"Withdraw the question," I said, waving at Haliburton to sit down. "So," I went on without a pause, "you and the district attorney have now decided to tell the truth—the whole truth—no matter whom it hurts—is that correct?" I demanded with an air of disbelief.

Bristling at the suggestion of impropriety, she exclaimed, "I don't need a lawyer to lecture me about honesty!"

"Then tell us this," I said, lashing back. "Just what was it Jeremy Fullerton wanted to talk to you about that night? Just what was the reason you stopped at the St. Francis—because he wanted to talk about Mrs. Fullerton? Isn't that what you said?"

She exploded. Clenching its arms with all her might, she pushed herself straight up until she was barely touching the chair.

"All right!" she cried fiercely. "If you really have to know everything—if you really don't care about who gets hurt—I'll tell you! Jeremy wanted to talk. He wanted to talk about how things had become intolerable. He wanted to tell me that he had finally decided that no matter what the consequences he was going to leave her. He was going to divorce her, Mr. Antonelli! He was going to divorce his wife and marry me!"

The floor seemed to sink beneath me as I was buried under a solid black wall of noise. Instinctively, I looked up at the bench. Thompson was sitting there, glassy-eyed, like someone locked in a trance. Then, suddenly, his eyes blinked and began to dart all around the room. Furiously, he beat his gavel, louder and louder, until finally it began to be heard over the dwindling clamor of the crowd.

"I'll clear the courtroom if I have to!" he threatened.

Collecting myself, I waited until the last, lingering murmur had died away. I was not sure what I was going to ask Ariella Goldman next, but looking at her tear-stained face, I knew I could not afford to let it end there.

"You didn't come back directly from Europe, then, either, did you?"

"No," she replied, trembling.

"You stayed there for a few days, along with Jeremy Fullerton, didn't you?"

She settled into the chair, rubbing her eyes with the back of her hand. "Yes."

"That wasn't the first time you had been alone with him, was it?"

"No," she said, the streaks on the side of her face beginning to dry.

"You'd been having an affair with him for some time, hadn't you?"

She shook her head, as if there were something I did not understand. "I didn't want to have an affair. That was the last thing I wanted to happen; but I fell in love with him, desperately, completely. And he fell in love with me."

"And how long ago did this happen?" I persisted.

"We fell in love about a year ago," she said, as if she were glad finally not to have to hide the way she felt.

"Is that how you happen to know that Mrs. Fullerton was, as you put it, disturbed—sometimes depressed, sometimes paranoid?"

"Yes. Jeremy told me. It's something she's had for a very long time. It's the reason Jeremy was never going to leave her."

I was in control again, following each word of her answer, ready before she finished with the next, logical question.

"But you just said that he told you that night he was going to get a divorce and marry you."

"Something had changed."

"Something had changed?" I heard myself repeating before I had taken the time to think.

"Yes, something had changed. I'd just found out I was going to have his baby."

Thompson beat his gavel again, but it was like throwing pebbles against the sea. The courtroom was in chaos as every reporter tried to be the first to fight his way out to call in the biggest story any of them had had since the night Jeremy Fullerton was murdered.

Twenty-two

It was the headline in the late edition of the afternoon paper, the lead story on every local news show; it was the only thing anyone wanted to talk about. Under the "relentless"—a word used so often it seemed like the only word any reporter knew—cross-examination of Defense Attorney Joseph Antonelli, the Democratic candidate for governor, Ariella Goldman, admitted that she and Jeremy Fullerton had been planning to marry as soon as he obtained a divorce.

" 'In tearful testimony,' " read Albert Craven aloud from the newspaper he was holding in front of him, " 'the former speechwriter of U.S. Senator Jeremy Fullerton . . .' "

Craven stopped and looked up. " 'Tearful testimony.' That's a good touch," he remarked with a droll smile.

Slouched on one of the gray upholstered chairs in front of Craven's grotesque Victorian desk, I unfastened the top button of my shirt and loosened my tie. I was exhausted, too tired to do or say anything except look from Craven to my cousin, who was sitting next to me, and wearily shake my head. I knew what had happened; I knew it the moment Ariella Goldman announced she was pregnant with Fullerton's child; but I was still stunned—

not by what she had done, but that with my eyes wide open I had walked right into it.

Bobby patted me on the shoulder and tried to tell me it was going to be all right. Silently, Craven went on reading. When he reached the end of the column on the front page, he spread open the double sheets, folding one back on the other, and continued the story. Though he apparently had been working without a stop since lunch, he looked as if he had just gotten dressed for dinner. His gray pin-striped suit was perfectly pressed, his pale blue silk shirt hung at just the right length beyond the sleeves of his coat. When he finally finished, he set the newspaper on the desk, off to the side of the stack of documents over which he had been laboring when we first walked in, and looked up.

With a rueful smile, I looked down at my feet stretched out in front of me.

"That 'relentless' cross-examination was maybe the best thing I've ever done."

I raised my eyes, glancing first at Bobby, then at Craven. Neither of them had ever tried a case to a jury; neither of them had ever had to make the instantaneous decision to go one way or the other with an answer just given by a witness.

"I took her—Lawrence Goldman's daughter—all the way around a circle, over and over again, each time making it just a little tighter. I was not just one question ahead of her: I was at least a dozen questions ahead. With each answer she gave, I was already thinking about the way I was going to ask her the same question again—the second time, and the third time—questions I would not ask until I had first asked her seven, eight, nine other questions in between. It was like a dance—a tango—where each step has a meaning, but a meaning that only becomes completely clear when you reach the end of the dance. She was the perfect partner: She went with me every step."

I shoved myself up until I was sitting almost straight, and then bent forward and rested my arms on my knees.

"She testified that she drove Fullerton to his car because his wife left early. On cross, I asked her why Fullerton's wife left early. She said it was because she wasn't feeling well and that she didn't know why she wasn't feeling well. I dropped it and asked her how long it had taken to drive from Goldman's apartment to where Fullerton had left his car. I asked her if they stopped anywhere, and when she said they had not, I asked her again, this time whether they had stopped somewhere for a drink. She denied it again."

I was watching it all over again, watching myself, confident and self-assured, as I led her step by step to where I wanted her to go, a study in self-deception.

"I let her answer go and asked her instead about Paula Hawkins, her friend from college, her lesbian lover who knew everything about her affair with Jeremy Fullerton, and about the fact that she slept with other men as well. I wanted to let Ariella Goldman know that I knew things about her, things she didn't know I knew, things I was certain she didn't want anyone to know. Then, after I asked her that, I asked her about what she and Fullerton had been doing together in Europe. Then, after all that, I went back to the party at Lawrence Goldman's apartment and asked her again why Fullerton's wife left. She repeated her answer again that it was because she wasn't feeling well. I hit her with the question whether the reason she wasn't feeling well was because she had just accused her—Ariella Goldman—of having an affair with her husband."

Peering into Albert Craven's pale blue eyes, I shook my head in chagrin at my own inexcusable mistake.

"I took her all the way back around, one question right on

top of the other—closed it right down on her. Everything she had said had been a lie. I had her dead."

Leaning against the arm of the heavily upholstered chair, I let my eye wander across the room to the oil painting above the fireplace that depicted the earthquake and fire of 1906 that destroyed one San Francisco and gave birth to another.

"If it had just ended there, she would have been destroyed as a credible witness; more important, she would have become the best possible witness for the defense. I could have brought in the bartender from the St. Francis to testify that she was there that night with Fullerton. I could have brought in someone—Marissa or either one of you—to testify about what she really said to Fullerton's wife. I had Fullerton's administrative assistant, Robert Zimmerman, under subpoena to testify that she did not come back directly from Europe the way she said she had.

"Don't you see? That was all I would have needed. I could have asked the jury: Why was she lying? What was she trying to hide? What did she know that she didn't want them to know? She was the last person to see Jeremy Fullerton alive, and if she was lying—lying under oath—then . . ."

I looked again at the painting and felt a certain strange kinship with people who without warning were suddenly struck by disaster.

"I should have seen it coming," I said as I slowly turned away from the earthquake and fire. "It should have been obvious. If I hadn't suspected anything before, I should have known something was going on when she lied about stopping somewhere before she dropped him off. The St. Francis is a public place, for God's sake!" I said with a helpless, self-deprecating laugh. "She might not have been famous then, but Fullerton was. She couldn't have thought that no one noticed or that no one was going to remember that he had been in a bar with a woman just a few minutes before he was murdered."

I glimpsed at Bobby and tried to remember what it was like when we were both still young and everything was a game and we could play only the ones we liked.

"Meredith Fullerton—the senator's wife—told me the Goldmans would manage to arrange things like this. I didn't pay much attention to it at the time; but even if I had, it never would have occurred to me that they'd figure out a way to use a criminal trial to do it."

Albert Craven pressed his small manicured fingers together under his smooth-shaven chin. "Figured out a way to do what?"

"To let everyone know that Ariella Goldman is having Jeremy Fullerton's baby. She said it would be like this. She said by the time the Goldmans got through, everyone would think that Ariella was the one left behind as the grieving widow."

Craven tried to be helpful. "Well, even so, it hasn't done you any real harm."

I was looking right at him and I barely heard a word he said. I had worked myself into a state where all I could think about was the sheer effrontery of what had been done.

"And the most astonishing part is that she was still lying, right up to the end: lying when she said Fullerton was leaving his wife; lying when she cried through those false tears of hers that she was having his baby. My God, that woman could lie!"

I looked around at Bobby and with a pained expression threw up my hands. "It takes a certain kind of genius to understand that the best way to tell a lie is to make it appear that you're being forced into telling the truth. She knew what she was doing right from the beginning. She let me catch her in a lie so that everyone would think she wanted to protect Jeremy Fullerton's reputation and save his wife any more pain."

"How do you know she was lying—about having Fullerton's child?" asked Craven.

I realized what I had done. Until that moment I had not shared Meredith Fullerton's secret with anyone; no one, that is, except Marissa. But if I could justify telling her—and I was not sure I could—there was no excuse for telling anyone else. Or was there? What was it that Meredith Fullerton had said? That she might now have to share with the world the secret that she and her husband had shared only with each other, as the only way to keep Ariella Goldman from getting away with a lie.

"Jeremy Fullerton could not have children. His wife told me. She told me what she had never told anyone before because she had heard that Ariella was telling people that she was pregnant and that Fullerton was the father."

"But if Ariella didn't know Fullerton couldn't have children," said Craven, picking up the thread, "what did he tell her when she told him she was pregnant and that he was the father?"

"Who knows what Fullerton might have told her? But if that's what they were talking about that night in the bar at the St. Francis—if he told her he couldn't possibly be the father of her child, or if he just insisted he wasn't the father and that he wouldn't marry her—what do you think she would have done about it?"

"Are you saying you think Ariella Goldman murdered Jeremy Fullerton?" asked Craven in a way that suggested he would not be entirely surprised if I was.

Before I could answer, Bobby asked a question that seemed to settle the matter.

"Where would she have gotten the gun? If he told her at the bar, how could she suddenly find a cheap untraceable Saturday night special? It isn't very likely she always kept one on her or that Fullerton carried one around in the glove compartment of his car."

"Perhaps he had already told her he wasn't going to marry her, and so she brought the gun with her that night, thinking she would give him one last chance to change his mind," I said without conviction.

"What I really don't understand," said Bobby, "is why she decided to go ahead and have the child. She could have had it aborted. Anyone to whom she had told that story about Fullerton would have drawn the logical conclusion: She got pregnant by a married man and handled it discreetly."

"Perhaps she really did love Fullerton," suggested Albert Craven. "Perhaps she really wants to have his child. But whether she loved him or not, I think Meredith Fullerton was exactly right about one thing at least: Everyone is now going to believe that Ariella is the one Jeremy Fullerton loved and left behind, and that the proof of that is the child she's carrying, the one whose parentage she had apparently been at such pains to conceal. Yes, I think Meredith Fullerton understood the Goldmans perfectly. This isn't the same country it used to be. Divorce, infidelity, a child born out of wedlock—none of that means anything anymore; the only thing that matters is how people feel about each other. I'll bet if you did a poll two weeks from now, you'd find a surprising number of people who believe that Fullerton and Ariella were really married."

A shrewd look came in his eyes. He put his arms on the desk and bent forward.

"Lawrence Goldman would have recognized immediately the advantage he had. There are two kinds of people who can run for governor or senator in this state without having run for anything before: those who can spend millions on their own campaign and those with the kind of celebrity that makes everyone think they already know them. Ariella Goldman is the first one I can remember who has both. She always had the money; and now, because of what happened today, she has acquired the kind of celebrity status money alone could never have given her.

"Think what this does for Lawrence Goldman. He decided to abandon his old friend, Augustus Marshall, because with Jeremy Fullerton he thought he could influence, and perhaps control, not only a governor, but eventually, perhaps, a president. Now his own daughter steps into the role Fullerton was supposed to play."

We sat in the faded light of the late afternoon, the sun shielded from the narrow street outside by buildings in which the always overriding thought was money and how to make more of it, while Albert Craven, who had made his share, talked about things on which it was not so easy to set a price.

"I don't like Lawrence Goldman. I never have. Remove all morality, all sense of good and evil, as nothing more than a personal preference—everything becomes not just possible, but inevitable. There is a sense in which, like a line I once read, all of America conspired to produce Lawrence Goldman and his daughter. The murder of Jeremy Fullerton must have seemed to him almost too good to be true. Forget what it did in terms of his daughter; think what it will do for his grandson—if it's a boy. Think of the enormous advantages to which that child will be born! In the eyes of the world, the son of a martyred senator, a man thought destined to become president, murdered at the height of his powers; the child of a beautiful, gifted mother, a woman so decent, so honorable, she was willing to conceal the identity of the child's father to protect both his reputation and the feelings of the woman he was about to leave. All that, plus all the power and all the money and everything else Lawrence

Goldman could do. Like his grandfather before him, Lawrence Goldman would become the father to the child."

Craven looked at us a moment longer; then he sat back in his chair and folded his hands into his lap.

After a while, Bobby cleared his throat and asked, "Who do you think is the father?"

"I don't know," I replied. "It could be anyone." I thought about the way Ariella Goldman had handled herself on the stand and then added, "Anyone her father had wanted her to sleep with."

Bobby thought of something. "You said before that if you could prove she was lying, you could use that to argue that she was trying to hide something and that that might be enough to establish reasonable doubt. Why not put Fullerton's wife on the stand? She can testify that her husband couldn't have children."

I did not want to do it. I admired the way that, despite everything, Meredith Fullerton had never stopped loving her husband. I did not want to put her through any more embarrassment unless I had to.

"Maybe I should put her on the stand—and maybe I will—but the danger isn't just that she'll be humiliated again. The jury will think that she is so embittered by what happened that she's willing to say or do anything to get back at them both, not only Ariella, but her husband as well. The district attorney will ask her two questions on cross:

" 'You were aware your husband was having an affair with Ariella Goldman, weren't you?' "

"And then, after she admits she was, he'll ask: 'And that night, at the gathering at Lawrence Goldman's apartment, when you were in such a rage about it, you accused her of trying to take your husband away, and then you left—but he stayed, didn't he?' "

It was getting late. There were other things I had to do. Wearily, with one hand on the corner of Craven's enormous desk and the other on the arm of the chair, I got to my feet.

"After seeing today just how effective a lie can be, I have to go out to the jail and convince Jamaal Washington that all he has to do tomorrow is take the stand and tell the truth."

Craven seemed surprised. "You start tomorrow? The prosecution rested?"

"About the very moment Ariella Goldman started crying," I said, my voice betraying the resentment I still felt. "Haliburton didn't even look at Thompson. He just looked at the jury and said, 'The People rest, your honor.' It was all he could do to keep from laughing."

I started to say good-bye, when I noticed again the pile of documents on which Craven had diligently been at work.

"It looks like I'm not the only one who is going to be working late tonight."

Craven was just picking up his fountain pen. "It's the estate of Andrei Bogdonovitch, poor devil. It's rather more complicated than I had anticipated," he added as he reached for the stack of papers.

"You were his lawyer?" I asked for no other reason than to let him talk after he had spent so much time listening to me.

"Yes, well, there was never much work involved. I drew up his will—more as a personal favor than anything else. And then, because of the business he was in—import-export—we had to have a complete inventory to establish a proper basis for an accurate valuation—for insurance purposes, you understand. Well, trying to get two people to agree on the value of an Oriental rug or a Chinese vase is far more trouble than I could have imagined."

We said good night and I followed Bobby to the door.

"Where is it going?" I asked, looking back from the doorway.

The pen dangling from his hand, Craven stared at me, a blank expression on his round face.

"The estate," I explained. "Whatever it's worth."

"Oh, that," he said as he raised his wispy eyebrows and began to nod his head with animation. "Yes, well, it's worth quite a lot, as it turns out. And oh, yes, it's all going to a brother of his. Lives somewhere in Europe—somewhere in Italy," he said absently as he began to rummage through the documents. "It's in here someplace."

"Don't bother," I insisted. "It doesn't matter. I just wondered. Good night," I said as I closed the door behind me.

As soon as I left the building, I tried to think what I could tell Jamaal that would give him the confidence he was going to need. Everything depended on him now. He had to make that jury believe him; he had to make them believe not just that he did not murder Jeremy Fullerton, but that he could not have murdered anyone. By the time he was finished, they had to look at him and know that he could not possibly have done what he was accused of doing. They had to know it, the same way they would have known it about a child of their own: not by the evidence, but by an instinct, the instinct that tells us who we can trust and who we cannot. Jamaal Washington had to be as good at telling the truth as Ariella Goldman had been at telling the lie.

There had been times when I was afraid that Jamaal might be on the verge of sinking into the mind-numbing lethargy that often comes with prolonged confinement. It had been a difficult adjustment, more difficult than it would have been for someone less intelligent, less curious about the world around him. Gradually, and not without periods of depression, he had become, if not reconciled to his situation, at least willing to tolerate it for as long as he had to.

Jamaal was waiting for me in the small conference room. He was sitting at a metal table, his hands clasped together in front of him, a lively expression on his fine straight mouth.

"How long had you been practicing law before you learned to do that with a witness the way you did today?"

I looked up from the legal pad I had just taken out of my briefcase, struck not for the first time by how astonishingly quick he was.

"I don't know," I said. I thought it was an honest answer, but he did not.

"You could do it right from the beginning, couldn't you? It isn't something you learn how to do, is it? Either you can see things coming before they get there or you can't—isn't that right?"

It was true what he said, but it was only a part of it, and perhaps not the most important part.

"I think I could do it right from the beginning, but it isn't like sitting down at a piano and without being able to read a note of music play anything you hear. You try to anticipate everything anyone—any possible witness—might say. You go over it again and again in your mind; you see it as if you were already in court. Somehow you absorb it all, so that even when something you did not anticipate happens you know what to do. You don't think about it; you don't say to yourself: 'He just said x instead of y, so now I should ask him z.' You just ask the question; it just happens. But it never would have happened—you would not have had a question to ask—if you had not just about driven yourself crazy going over again and again all those questions you did not ask and all those answers you were never given."

Jamaal seemed to understand completely. "I think that must be what it's like to practice medicine. After a while you know what's wrong with a patient before they've finished describing their symptoms."

He was only nineteen years old, but there were times I felt myself drawn to him the way I had been drawn to few other people before. Perhaps what I saw in him was a reflection of myself, what I was like when I was still as young as that and still thought that nothing could ever go wrong.

"How long did it take," I asked, watching his eyes, "before you figured out I was taking her in a circle?"

"I don't know," replied Jamaal modestly, "maybe when you came back for the second time about why the senator's wife had left."

"You ever think about becoming a lawyer instead of a doctor?" I asked, laughing.

He glanced at the barred window on the door, a wry smile forming on his mouth. "I may have to live with criminals," he said as his eyes came back to mine. "That doesn't mean I have to work with them."

"You won't have to live with them too much longer," I promised as we began one last time to review the testimony he was going to give the next morning.

It was nearly ten o'clock when I closed my briefcase and got ready to go. There was only one more thing I wanted to ask. I had brought it up several times before, but each time he had made it clear that it was not something he wanted to discuss. It was more than simple curiosity, though that was certainly part of it; I needed to know because I wanted the jury to know.

"Jamaal, what can you tell me about your father?"

He looked at me for a moment, hard, almost threatening, the way someone does when you have asked something you had no business asking. Then, because he knew I was only doing what I had to, his gaze softened and he nodded apologetically.

"Nothing," he said. "I never knew him."

I could not let it go at that. "But surely your mother must have told you something about him."

"Never," he insisted, but without any animosity. "When I was old enough to understand, she told me my father was someone she had known, someone she liked, but someone she could never have married."

"And you never asked for more, later on, when you were older, than what she told you then?"

Jamaal smiled at me, as if he were certain I knew the answer myself.

"You've met my mother. She's an extraordinary person. I always knew that about her. I knew that if she wanted me to know more, she'd tell me. And I also knew that if she didn't, she had her reasons."

He got up from his chair and banged once on the door to summon the guard.

Outside, under the clear dark sky, I stood on the sidewalk next to the street and took a long deep breath. I wanted to purge myself of the stagnant air that festered inside like a strange premonition of death. When I reached the car, I looked up and down the street. When I got inside and turned on the ignition, I checked the rearview mirror before I pulled away from the curb. If anyone was following me, they were too good at it for me to know.

Twenty-three

As soon as I called his name I could feel the intensity of the crowd. Every face in the courtroom was pressed forward, straining to get a closer look. Jamaal Washington, a slender figure in a dark suit bent over a cane, dragged one leg behind him as he hobbled toward the clerk, waiting impassively just below the bench. The surprisingly delicate fingers of his left hand curled around the handle of the plain wooden cane as he held his right hand shoulder-high and took the oath. Then he lowered himself onto the witness chair and slowly looked around. His gaze came to rest on the juror who sat closest to him in the jury box, a short blond woman with deep-set suspicious eyes and a small pugnacious mouth. He glanced at the juror next to her, and then the next, and did not stop until he had looked in the eye all twelve of the strangers who were there to decide if he would live or die.

Not one of the twelve tried to look away. A few of them seemed to offer, by a nod of their head or the way they changed position in their chair, a silent form of encouragement. On an impulse, I led with the question I had told him would come only at the very end.

"Did you kill Jeremy Fullerton?"

He was one of the most intelligent people I had ever defended. I had explained to him the importance of looking at the jury when he answered my questions: "Let the jury see your face; let them see you have nothing to hide; let them see you telling the truth and that you don't have to look at me to know what that is." We had gone over it so often, it had become an automatic, almost Pavlovian response. But now, the only time it counted, he forgot.

"No, I did not," he said without hesitation, and without so much as a glance at the jury.

Why could he not have remembered to do that? It was something I had been able to train even barely literate defendants to do without difficulty. I started over, at the point we were supposed to have begun, with the story of how he had been raised and the difficulties he had overcome, but it made no difference. Whatever the question, whatever the answer, his eyes followed me everywhere. I moved to the end of the jury box farthest from the witness stand.

Though I had told the jury something of Jamaal's background in my opening statement, it had a much more striking effect when it was repeated, refined, elaborated, given context and color by the defendant himself. Nothing was left out. Though I knew he would not say, and perhaps could not say, much more than what he had said to me before, I made him admit that he had never known his father and never even known his name. I made him talk about how he had often been beaten up when he was still just in grade school by teenage gangsters because he was carrying a book instead of a gun. I made him talk about how well he had done in high school and how he hoped to go to medical school after he graduated from college. Everything I asked, everything he said, was designed to paint a picture of a young man who had come too far suddenly to do something so completely out of character. It took us all morning.

"Did I do all right?" he wanted to know before the deputy took him back to jail for lunch.

"You did fine; but remember: Look at the jury when you answer my questions."

He was embarrassed that he had not, and he promised that he would.

"We'll start this afternoon with what happened that night," I said as the deputy took him away.

I began to put my things in my briefcase. With a strange premonition, I turned around and searched the faces of the vanishing crowd. At the very back, his hand resting on the corner of the bench nearest the double doors, the grossly corpulent stranger who had left me in the middle of the bridge was glaring at me through the narrow slits of his puffy eyes. A crooked smile crept over his soft wet lips. He nodded curtly and then, with an agility that belied his size, disappeared out the door.

He was there to throw me off, to make me think about him and what he said he could do, instead of concentrating on what I had to do to keep Jamaal Washington from the hands of the executioner. Angrily, I grabbed my briefcase and went down the hallway to a private conference room where I could work undisturbed.

The more I thought about it, the more I remembered the way I had been picked up off the street, pushed headfirst into the car, held hostage, and made to think I was being driven somewhere to die, the angrier I became. Anger became defiance, defiance became determination: I was going to do everything I could to win; not only that, I was going to do everything I could to expose these people for what they were. I sat in that small windowless room, reveling in thoughts of revenge, and it was only when I started to congratulate myself on my courage and resolution that I realized that it was already time to go back to court. I had not done any of the things I had come here to do.

"You heard a shot?" I asked Jamaal after he described what he had done at work that night and the route he had taken on his way home.

"I heard something. I thought it was a gunshot, but I wasn't completely sure."

Despite his promise, he had done it again: forgotten to look at the jury when he answered. His eyes were still focused on me. I stared at him, saying nothing, hoping by my temporary silence to remind him what he was supposed to do. It had no effect.

"Did you hear anything else?" I retreated to a position at the far end of the jury box. If he was going to look at me, it would at least be as close as possible to the jury.

Pushing his head forward, Jamaal squinted, as if he were back on that street, trying to see through the fog.

"I heard a car door open, then slam shut. Then I heard the sound of footsteps, someone running away."

There was a certain breathless quality to his voice that seemed to reflect a kind of insistent curiosity.

"The fog was so thick," he continued, "that just before I heard the shot, I remember looking down and laughing to my-self because I could barely see my shoes. It was like walking through snow."

The smile on his face lingered a moment longer, then faded away.

"At first, I was not sure where it had come from—the shot, the sound of the door, the footsteps running away—except that it was somewhere real close. Then, for just a second, the fog lifted. That's when I saw it—just a few yards in front of me—a face in a car window, all twisted around."

With my left hand on the railing of the jury box, I studied him intently. "Why didn't you just run away; get out of there before something happened to you?"

He gave me a puzzled look, as if even now, after everything that had happened to him, he could not understand how anyone could suggest that he not try to help someone in trouble.

"I thought he had been shot and that he might still be alive."

"So you opened the passenger door and got in?"

"Yes. I checked his pulse; but I could not find one. There was a phone in the car, and I picked it up and started to dial 911; but then I thought I better find out who he was. I don't know why I thought it would make any difference: Maybe it seemed too impersonal to report a death without a name," said Jamaal, strangely absorbed in his own reaction.

"I put down the phone and reached inside his suit coat for his wallet. That was when I saw the gun, laying there on the floor."

"Did you pick it up?" I asked.

"No. A light came flashing out of nowhere. I crouched down as far as I could. I was afraid whoever had shot him had come back."

Jamaal had not once looked anywhere but at me; now, as he recounted the fear that had taken him over, his eyes started to roam all around.

"I was scared; I didn't know what to do. All I could think about was that I had to get out of there, I had to get away. I shoved the door open as hard as I could and jumped out of the car and started to run fast as I could."

"You were afraid," I said, taking a step toward him. "Afraid you might be killed?"

"Yes."

"And because you were afraid you might be killed, you panicked?"

"Yes," he admitted. "I panicked."

"And in your panic, you might have picked up the gun, held on to it without even knowing you had it?"

"No, I didn't touch the gun."

We had been over this more times than I could count. He had told me that he did not think he had taken the gun—that he could not remember taking it. But I had pressed him, pressed him hard, until he agreed that he might have picked up the gun and not retained any conscious memory of it.

I tried not to betray my own sense of panic. I asked the same question a different way.

"Yes, but because of your fear, because of that panic you felt, isn't it possible that you might have picked it up, had it in your hand, and now, after the trauma of being shot, simply don't remember?"

His gaze once again rested on me. Beneath the surface of his eyes I detected what I thought was a faint glimmer of regret. Most of us jump at the chance to find an excuse for something we should not have done or an explanation that removes any suspicion that we did something we did not. I should have known better than to think that he would testify to something he did not really believe. He was going to tell the truth, and the only concern he had was that he might have misled me into thinking he might do something else.

He answered my question directly and without the slightest ambiguity.

"No, it's not possible. If I had touched that gun, I wouldn't have forgotten it, no matter what happened."

We looked at each other across the length of the jury box. Silently, I nodded my approval.

"Very good. You didn't have the gun. You didn't have it when you left the car; you didn't have it when you were shot. Did you hear anyone shout a warning once you started running?"

"No, I didn't hear anything. I was running as fast as I could. I remember thinking I was safe: that no one could see me in the fog. It was like being inside a cloud—a big gray cloud—and then everything went black. That's all I remember."

I had no other questions to ask. As I took my seat, I glimpsed the impenetrable expressions on the faces of the jury and tried to guess what they were thinking. They must have understood that I had given him the perfect excuse by which to explain how the gun could have been found inches from his hand after he was shot. Why would anyone have said what he did unless he was telling the truth? It was a point the district attorney understood quite well and wasted no time trying to turn to his own advantage.

Placing his hand on his hip, Clarence Haliburton studied for just a moment longer the notebook lying open on the table below. With his other hand still on the page, he looked up and greeted the witness with a dismissive smile.

"So you did not pick up the gun at all?" he asked in a mocking tone.

"I never touched it," insisted Jamaal politely.

With a theatrical gesture, Haliburton opened his eyes wide. "You never touched it." He lowered his eyes and dragged his finger across the open notebook to the edge of the wooden table. The corners of his mouth turned down as he seemed to revolve in his mind the answer he had just been given.

"You never touched it," said Haliburton again as he looked up. "Then perhaps you can explain," he asked, his voice beginning to rise, "just how that gun managed to end up next to you?"

Jamaal shook his head and looked straight at the district attorney. "I don't know," he said firmly.

Haliburton's eyes shone with malice. Standing at the corner of the table, he crossed his arms over his chest and put one foot slightly ahead of the other.

"You needn't be so modest, Mr. Washington. You must know. You heard your lawyer explain it to us. If you didn't pick up the gun in a 'state of panic,' there is only one way it could have gotten there—isn't that true?"

Jamaal refused to be drawn in. Again he shook his head, though this time without quite the same emphasis.

"I don't know," he said calmly.

Haliburton flashed a derisive smile. "The police put it there, Mr. Washington. Do you remember now? That's exactly what your lawyer said—isn't it? That if you didn't pick up the gun in a 'state of panic,' then the police must have planted it next to you. My only question is why?" He began to pace in front of the table, smiling to himself in a manner calculated to irritate all but the most self-possessed witness. "Why would they have done that, Mr. Washington?" Haliburton stopped still and raised his eyes to Jamaal. "Why, Mr. Washington? Why would they have done that to you?"

"I don't know."

Haliburton took two steps toward him, staring at him with open contempt. "You don't know? You just said you never had the gun in your hand. Is that right?"

"I never touched it," insisted Jamaal. "I don't know how it got out of the car."

Haliburton's head snapped up. "Perhaps the police were just out to get you. Have you ever been in trouble with the law, Mr. Washington?"

I flew out of my chair. "Objection! Your honor, I have a matter for the court!"

Thompson was already on his feet, glowering at Haliburton. "In chambers!" he thundered as he stalked off the bench.

Thompson was so enraged that he forgot to send the jury out of the courtroom. They were left to sit quietly in the jury box, while Jamaal waited, silent and alone, on the witness stand.

Drumming his arthritic fingers, Thompson sat behind his desk, glaring at Haliburton.

"Do you want me to declare a mistrial, Antonelli?" asked the judge without moving his eyes from the district attorney.

I had learned from the beginning that it was best to go along with anything the honorable James L. Thompson suggested, especially when it supplied him the means to embarrass the district attorney. This time, however, I was genuinely angry. I did not want to try the case all over again from the beginning, but I had no choice but to ask for the chance to do precisely that.

"Yes, your honor; I do want a mistrial. The district attorney—"

His eyes still on Haliburton, Thompson held up his hand, letting me know there was no need to tell him what he already knew. Not without pleasure, the judge asked, "Can you think of any reason I shouldn't give it to him, Mr. District Attorney?"

Haliburton met Thompson's stare with a blank wall of indifference. "You must be kidding," he sniffed.

The steady monotonous drumming of Thompson's fingers suddenly stopped.

" 'Kidding,' " repeated Thompson. "You think I'm kidding?" he said as he cocked his head to the side. "Kidding? Let me explain the facts of life, counselor. I denied your motion to introduce the defendant's juvenile record. I denied it a week ago. You knew you weren't allowed to bring it up. So what do you do?" he went on, jutting out his chin. His mouth quivered belligerently. "You go ahead and ask him if he's ever been in trouble with the law! Who the hell do you think you are? Nobody does that in my courtroom!"

Nothing he said, nothing he did, made the slightest impression. Haliburton sat there, undisturbed and implacable, the only change in his expression a thin, patronizing smile that seemed to become more flagrant the angrier Thompson became.

"I don't know what you're so upset about," grunted Haliburton. "I may have asked a question that could have elicited an improper response, but no answer to the question was given."

"Only because I stopped it with an objection," I reminded him.

Haliburton shifted back in his chair, crossed one leg over the other, and began to swing his foot back and forth.

"That's exactly right," he said as he raised his eyes to mine. "And by preventing an answer, that objection of yours removed any conceivable ground for a mistrial."

"The question left the impression the defendant had something to hide," I said as forcefully as I could.

Haliburton leered at me, a sarcastic grin that grated more on my nerves than I wanted to show.

"And he does, doesn't he?" he said, arching his eyebrows. "But we're the only ones who know that. The jury doesn't know he has a juvenile record for assault."

"A juvenile record for assault!" I cried, letting my anger get the best of me. "He was fourteen years old; another kid called his mother a name—not just any name, Haliburton—the kid called his mother a whore! Anyone ever call your mother a whore, Clarence?" I asked, shaking my head with contempt. "Jamaal Washington broke the kid's jaw; I would have killed him—and so would you!"

Haliburton tried to dismiss it. "I don't care what he did—the point is, the jury doesn't know anything about it."

"You asked him if he had ever been in trouble with the law. If he doesn't answer the question, the jury will be convinced that he has."

"All right!" exclaimed Haliburton, throwing up his hand. "I'll rephrase the question. I'll ask if he's been in trouble with the law as an adult. He can answer that."

Astonished at his temerity, I explained what he knew already. "Everyone will know that means he had trouble before he was an adult."

Haliburton was not interested in listening to anything more I might have to say. He turned to Thompson.

"Why don't I just withdraw the question?"

"Antonelli is right," insisted the judge grimly. "Without an answer, that question, whether you formally withdraw it or not, leaves an inference—an impermissible inference—about his prior criminal record."

Thompson sat back in the cushioned metal chair. With a shrewd glance at the district attorney, he tapped his fingers together.

"You have a choice: We treat the question as limited to whether he's had any convictions as an adult or we walk back into court and I declare a mistrial. And just so you understand," he added, the sound of his voice the echo of a threat, "I'm going to allow Antonelli to advise the defendant privately that the question does not include his juvenile record. That way he can truthfully answer the question in the negative. It's your choice, counselor."

Haliburton shrugged his shoulders. "I have no objection. He can take the question that way."

Haliburton was already on his feet when Thompson said,

"There is one other thing, Mr. Haliburton. I'm finding you in contempt for your failure to follow a ruling of the court. We'll put that on the record, along with the sanctions I'm going to impose, after the case goes to the jury."

As soon as we were back in court, Thompson directed the clerk to take the jury out of the room. The clerk, a portly woman, smiled vacantly at each juror as they filed past her into the jury room. When the last one entered, she leaned in just before she closed the door and, in the same meaningless way she had doubtless said it thousands of times before, promised, "It won't be long."

Whether or not Thompson had seriously entertained the possibility of a mistrial, he was already beginning to regret the compromise solution he had imposed. Visibly agitated, he flapped his hand in my direction.

"Take a moment to confer with your client, Mr. Antonelli."

Thompson had told Haliburton he was finding him in contempt and that he would put it on the record after the case went to the jury, but there were too many years of built-up resentment to wait that long for revenge. It was not enough that he knew, or that Haliburton knew, what was going to happen. Driven to distraction by this thing that was always eating him away inside, Thompson suddenly lurched forward.

"Now, as for you," he said, glowering at Haliburton. "The court ruled on your motion to allow the introduction of the defendant's juvenile record: The court denied that motion. Yet, despite that ruling, you proceeded to ask a question clearly designed to elicit the information you were strictly prohibited from bringing to the attention of the jury. The court has no alternative but to find you in contempt. At the end of this trial, after the verdict, the court will hold a hearing to determine the appropriate sanction for your flagrant misconduct!"

Finally content, Thompson dragged his arms back over the bench until he was sitting comfortably in his chair. He glanced down at the witness stand, where I was exchanging a few final words with Jamaal, and asked me if I was ready to begin. Then he ordered the clerk to bring in the jury. While we waited, Thompson looked around the courtroom, a blank, vitiated expression on his face. He began to scratch, over and over again, the back of his wrist.

The district attorney began where he had left off.

"Let me ask you again, Mr. Washington: Have you ever been in trouble with the law?"

Jamaal understood the limitation that had been placed on the question. "No, I haven't."

Haliburton lifted his chin slightly and opened his eyes wide. A smug, knowing smile drifted across his mouth. He did not say a word until, drawn by the silence, the eyes of the jury had turned from Jamaal to him. When they were all watching, he raised his head a little higher still and opened his mouth as if he were about to bury the witness in a lie so blatant that no one would ever forget it. Then, as if he had to force himself not to do it, he clenched his teeth and, with a taunting smirk, muttered aloud, "Really?"

I was halfway out of my chair when I heard him ask, "Then is there any reason you can think of that the police would want to blame you for a crime you didn't commit?"

As Jamaal began to shake his head, Haliburton wheeled away from him and faced the jury. A glimmer of triumph flashed in his eyes.

"I'm sorry. You'll have to answer out loud."

"No," admitted Jamaal. "I can't think of any reason why they would do that to me."

A corrosive smile spread across Haliburton's broad face as he turned again to confront the witness. "Neither can anyone else."

Haliburton looked one last time at the jury. Then he stared down at the floor, a kind of grim finality on his face. It had the effect, which I have no doubt he intended, of reminding everyone who was watching—and no one was watching more intently than the members of that jury—of the somber reality of the reason we were there. A man had been murdered, and even the defendant could not explain why he had been caught with the murder weapon right next to his hand as he lay unconscious, shot in the back as he fled from the scene of the crime. Three times Haliburton stroked his chin. Then, without raising his eyes, he waved his hand in the air.

"No more questions," he said as he walked slowly toward the empty chair at the table.

I could not let it end there. On redirect, I asked the same question Haliburton had asked and one more besides.

"You can't think of any reason why the police would want to blame you for a crime you did not commit?"

"No," replied Jamaal with a helpless look.

"Do you believe it's possible that the police, certain you must be the killer because they saw you run from the car, wanted to make certain there wasn't any question about your guilt—and about their innocence—and so they put the gun next to your hand after they shot you?"

For the first time, he remembered. He turned and faced the jury directly.

"It must have happened like that. I never touched the gun."

Twenty-four

The next morning, a few minutes before ten o'clock, in a courtroom packed with reporters, I rose from my chair, ready to call the last witness for the defense. The district attorney, his black dress shoes polished to a hard shine, rose at the same time. I glanced across at him, wondering what he was up to, but though the only reason to stand was to address the court, he made no attempt to speak.

"Your honor," I said, watching Haliburton out of the corner of my eye, "the defense calls Augustus Marshall."

The moment the name of the governor was out of my mouth, Haliburton raised his eyes to the bench. "Your honor, I am obligated to inform the court that the witness Mr. Antonelli intends to call is not available at this time."

"And just how is it you happen to know so much more about my witness than I do?" I asked.

Refusing to look at me, Haliburton continued to address himself to the judge. "I was advised by the governor's office earlier this morning that because of a legislative emergency, it will be impossible for the governor to leave Sacramento."

"He's my witness and he's under subpoena!" I shouted at Haliburton.

It did no good. He treated me as if I were some heckler in the crowd, a minor annoyance best to ignore.

"It appears," he went on, "that the governor won't be able to be here until next Monday at the earliest. He's asked me to extend his apologies to the court for any inconvenience this may cause."

There was only one thing Thompson wanted to know, and it had nothing to do with the effect the governor's absence might have on the conduct of the trial.

"Perhaps you could explain, Mr. Haliburton, why you, and not the court, were advised of this?"

"To say nothing of the defense attorney," I grumbled under my breath, loud enough for Haliburton to hear.

As often happens with those who find themselves entrusted with the confidence of someone powerful and well known, the demeanor, and even to a certain extent the physical appearance, of the district attorney had undergone a significant change. He was relaxed, confident, his movements more fluid, his voice deeper and far less hurried. He was entirely self-possessed. He was important.

"It was the opinion of the governor's general counsel that it would be inappropriate for a witness—no matter who that witness was—to attempt direct contact with the court, your honor. That was the reason they communicated with my office instead. I can assure the court that was the only reason," he said with the generosity the recipient of a gift can afford to lavish on someone from whom that gift has been withheld.

Haliburton condescended to turn his head for a quick glimpse at me before he looked back at Thompson.

"The governor's office has tried in the past to work out a mutually acceptable way for the governor to testify in this matter, but the defense has refused to do anything except insist on a personal appearance."

I was beside myself and did nothing to conceal it. I threw up my hands in protest.

"Governor—president—the janitor down the hallway: a witness is a witness, and a subpoena is a subpoena. This is a murder trial, your honor. My client is on trial for his life, and the district attorney, who has taken an oath to do justice, wants to talk about convenience, and whether a witness I subpoenaed likes the fact that I want him here in court where the jury can see him in flesh and blood instead of on a piece of videotape taken in his office a hundred miles away!"

I turned on Haliburton with a vengeance. "And if you want to play to the jury and the press—if you want to come in here, in open public court, and not in chambers where this matter should have been discussed . . ."

I thought of something that made me madder still.

"You knew this before court convened this morning. Why don't you explain to the jury and to the media why you didn't tell me—more important, why you didn't tell the court?"

Haliburton was staring at me with a cynical dismissive grin.

"You want the jury to think I've been unreasonable? Why don't you tell them the truth: that I had no choice but to subpoena the governor because he would never so much as agree to have a conversation with me? Why don't you tell them that, Haliburton?"

For a moment I thought he was going to come after me. He wanted to—I could see it in his eyes—but he stopped himself before it was too late. I felt a pressure on my wrist. Jamaal was looking up at me, and I realized that without knowing it I had formed my right hand into a fist.

"Your honor," said Haliburton, his voice the voice of reason, "perhaps we should discuss this in chambers after all."

Thompson turned up his palms and glanced around the courtroom, a wry sparkle in his vindictive eyes. "And miss all this? Besides," he added, lowering his gaze until his eyes met Haliburton's, "what else is there to talk about?"

His head snapped to the side. He looked directly at me.

"How do you want to proceed, Mr. Antonelli? My own view," he went on without a pause, "is that unless you have other witnesses you wish to call, we simply reconvene Monday morning. At which point, relying on the representations of the district attorney—and I can assure you, Mr. Haliburton," he said with a glance full of menace, "the court is relying on your representations—the witness will appear as scheduled. I don't see that there is anything else we can do, do you?"

Hidden between the lines, where it would not be noticed except by someone who understood all the intricacies of legal procedure, was both a question and, if I had the wit to grasp it, an answer. The question was whether I wanted him to order sanctions, which could include even the arrest of the governor, for the failure to obey a lawful subpoena; the answer, implicit both in what he said and the way he said it, was not to ask because he would not do it if I did.

"I agree, your honor," I replied, trying to hide the bitterness I felt at what had happened.

Jamaal had made an impression. I was sure of it. The jury liked him and wanted to believe him. The strategy, if it is permissible to call something so obvious and straightforward by that name, was simple. The defendant denies he did it. The next witness, following immediately, helps to show that there were other people—a lot of other people—who had more to gain from Jeremy Fullerton's death than the theft of his wallet. But now, with the trial suspended for the rest of the week, the momentum built up by Jamaal's testimony would begin to dissipate. It was Wednesday, and by next Monday, when the governor finally testified, he would do so free of the shadow of Jamaal's insistent denials.

The governor might not have thought of this, but the district attorney would have. I had by now become so suspicious of everything connected with the case, I was not prepared to accept anything at face value. It would not have surprised me at all if the governor's decision to thumb his nose at the court had been made for him, if not by the district attorney, then by someone else, someone with an even more direct stake in the outcome.

There was also, I have to admit, a certain sense of relief that I did not have to be back in court until the beginning of the following week. It was like an unexpected holiday. The moment I was out of the courtroom I could feel the tension begin to ease away. For the first time since the trial began I started to feel free.

I left the city that afternoon and did not come back until Monday morning when the trial resumed. I did not go far, just across the bridge to Sausalito, where I stayed at Marissa's brown shingle house on the hill, coaxing her into long conversations in which she talked about things in ways I had not heard before. It did not matter what she talked about: She could have talked about nothing at all and I would have been quite content to listen. Just the sound of it—that rich exotic humid hothouse voice of hers—had an effect. Sometimes, in the quiet of the early evening, when we sat alone on the back deck overlooking the bay, her voice seemed like a wind whispering somewhere just around the corner, something you feel and may not even hear.

"Sometimes," said Marissa as she stood at the railing, gazing out at the white-sailed boats sliding through the blue-gray water, "you think everything is upside down and the sailboats are clouds scattered across the sky."

Stretched out on a chaise lounge, I looked up. She sensed I was watching and turned to me, a little embarrassed.

"Why?" I asked. "What were you thinking?"

"What we were talking about last night: Ariella and Jeremy Fullerton—what they must have talked about that night, the night he was killed. Whatever they said to each other, I imagine it was a good deal more interesting, and a good deal more surprising, at least to her, than what she said in court."

"More surprising? What could be more surprising than what she said in court: He was going to leave his wife and marry her because she was going to have his child?"

Her long black lashes slowly closed and then sprang open; her eyes started to dance.

"It's not as surprising if you don't know he can't have children. It isn't surprising at all when you consider who they were—or who everyone who had never met either one of them thought they were," she added with a cunning smile. "Jeremy was a United States senator who was going to be president. Ariella was the beautiful and intelligent daughter of a rich and powerful man. People like that are forgiven anything they do, if they sin for love and their sins are private. They're not just forgiven; they're applauded in some measure for being so much like the rest of us: no better, no worse. It proves, I suppose, how democratic we all are: Nobody much cares anymore when a husband leaves his wife for another woman, do they?"

She said it without bitterness, though it had happened to her; and perhaps because she had not made it personal to herself, I thought of someone else. I was surprised I had not thought of it before.

"If Fullerton had left his wife to marry Ariella, it would not have been any different than what Augustus Marshall did. He divorced his wife and married the daughter of the man who could do the most—and did the most—for his career."

Marissa brushed her hair back over her shoulder. "Men with power, women with wealth and influence, each using the other," she said, summarizing my effort to draw the parallel. She gave me a look meant to tell me that it was only good for as far as it went.

"Jeremy was different," she began, as her gaze drifted back toward the boats that scudded over the shiny silver surface of the bay. "Augustus Marshall had always been a part of that class of people who have everything and always want more; the people who have wealth and want power or have power and want wealth. Jeremy was not like that. Even when he seemed to have it all, he was still an outsider. He would always have been an outsider."

She turned around, a pensive look in her large dark eyes, as if she were inviting me to share her thought. She twisted her head a little to the side, pausing for a moment before she asked, "Do you know what I mean? I think you must. You're a bit like him in that respect: someone who is always an outsider, a kind of stranger in whatever society, whatever group he happens to find himself."

She straightened her head and looked directly at me, a smile, whether of sympathy or amusement I could not quite tell, flickering at the corners of her mouth.

"It's rather enviable, in a way. Things look better when they're seen from the outside. Imagine looking in, on a cold, wintry night, from outside a restaurant, peering through the ice-glazed window, watching well-fed people dining, laughing, having such a wonderful time; and you never for a moment suspect—you're too cold, too hungry, to suspect—that all these people you're looking at are going through the motions of a meaningless life; wishing, many of them, they were somewhere else; wishing, some of them, they could go back to the beginning and become someone else."

She smiled at me, half embarrassed, but only half embarrassed, by the passion with which she had said this.

"Would you rather have been that poor, cold, hungry wretch, staring through the window?" I asked, wondering at the tendency of people to romanticize the life they never led.

"I suppose I'd like to think so," admitted Marissa candidly. "Things came too easy for me; everything was given to me. I chose my parents well, and I was not unintelligent. School was easy; friends were easy—too easy. I became a dilettante, afraid to make a serious effort at any one thing—not because I might fail, but because there was no reason to try. I had everything: What was there to sacrifice for? What do you have to dream about when there is nothing left to have—nothing except the sense that you were doing something worthwhile? I lived on the surface of things, always more interested in saying something clever than doing anything important. Everyone liked me," she added with a quiet, irrepressible laugh.

"Maybe that's why, despite everything I now know about him, I still can't quite help . . . I don't know—not admire, exactly, but in a way respect what Jeremy Fullerton was able to do. He was an outsider, a stranger, and he changed the way everyone thought about everything. He became the one person they could not ignore. He did what he wanted, and all those other powerful, ambitious people—all those important, well-established people—did what they had to. He had nothing in common with someone like Augustus Marshall. If there was anyone who was a little like him, it was Lawrence Goldman," added Marissa with a shrewd glance. "They both lived a lie about who they were and where they came from."

"And both of them extremely intelligent," I remarked.

Marissa tossed her head. A warm smile flashed across her full mouth.

"Shrewd, ruthless, and engaging. But extremely intelligent? No, I wouldn't call either of them that."

I thought she was wrong—about Fullerton, at least. I reminded her what his wife had told me about how he read everything and about the way he had used the quotations of famous men—and invariably blamed it on his speechwriters—to say something serious in a way that made his audience believe they were just as serious as he.

"I don't know what Meredith Fullerton had in mind when she said he read everything, but I doubt that Jeremy Fullerton had a mind trained in any more rigorous discipline than an occasional weekend perusal of *Bartlett's Quotations*. Which isn't the worst thing anyone can read. It does give you a certain breadth of vision," said Marissa, laughing with her eyes. "And, with people who have never read a book and seldom look up from their television sets, perhaps a reputation for profundity.

"You know what I'm talking about. There was nothing deep about Jeremy Fullerton. You didn't get the idea he was someone who ever wanted to be left alone to think through a difficult problem. He did not have that kind of intelligence; he had something much more valuable, much more useful. He had the ability to grasp things only half understood; the ability to pick up the thread of someone else's thought and follow it out. He could do something else as well: He could supply the word, the phrase, that clarifies the thought, that gives it the expression the person who first struggled with it immediately believes is exactly what he was trying to say all along. Jeremy Fullerton was a thief who made you think that he had given you as a gift what he had just stolen from you."

The last light of day glimmered soft and golden on the side of her face. She folded her hands in front of her and lowered her eyes. Whatever she was thinking, I knew it was not about Jeremy Fullerton or Augustus Marshall or any of the other people who had figured so prominently in the trial. It had something to do with us. With a distant, modest look, she lifted her gaze and waited for me to say something.

"I like being here—with you," I said, as I swung my legs around and sat up on the edge of the chaise lounge.

"I like your being here," she replied, waiting for something more.

There was a short, awkward silence, before she finally asked what, until that moment, we had almost gone out of our way to avoid discussing.

"What are you going to do when this is over?"

I was still trying to avoid it, not so much because I did not want to talk about it, as because I was not sure what I wanted to say or even where to begin.

"You mean if I don't get killed?"

A look of disapproval darkened her gaze. "You'd like me to think you were a coward, wouldn't you? Why? So you can surprise me with an occasional act of bravery? You're not scared of those people, whomever they are. I think you're more scared of me than you are of them."

"Scared of you?" I asked, sitting straight up, more than a little astonished.

She brought me through her eyes deep inside her, a kind of intimacy that, if it lacked the intensity of passion, produced a kind of wonder I am not sure I had ever known before.

"Scared of hurting me," whispered Marissa softly. She

touched the side of my face and slowly drew her fingers down to the edge of my mouth. "Don't be," she said with a trusting smile. "I want you to do what's right for you."

Her eyes started to glisten, and her hand dropped away from my face. "It's late," she said with a self-conscious laugh. "I have to get ready." She opened the sliding glass door to go inside. "We have reservations—remember?"

In the middle of the living room, she spun around on her heel.

"Of course you don't remember. I made them myself—this afternoon. One of the things to know about Sausalito is that we have one restaurant that was started by a madam and another that was originally a whorehouse. That's where we're going tonight; but don't worry," she added, making an attempt at a sly grin. "Tonight all you have to pay for is dinner."

I started to reach for her, but she left me with a quick shake of her head. Three steps later, each one echoing sharply on the gleaming hardwood floor, she stopped.

"I bought you something. It's on the table next to the CD player. Mozart: the violin concertos. Itzhak Perlman." She lifted her chin, her eyes flashing. "I like Mozart better than Beethoven, and I like Beethoven more than anything that came after. Do you know why? Because Mozart is full of clarity and light, and Beethoven is full of passion, and because the twentieth century was just full of noise. I imagine, if you put your mind to it, you could trace the same downward spiral in other things as well," she added before she vanished down the hall.

We went to dinner together and then we came back and made love in the night and slept late in the morning. We did the same thing the next night and the night after that. We spent our time talking about what had happened in our lives and what had happened to the people we had known best. We talked about everything, but we never once talked again about what might happen later on, when the trial was over and there was nothing to keep me here, nothing except how much I liked being with her and how much I wanted to stay. She stayed home, and I never left at all, until Saturday, when, because I had promised him weeks before, I had to go with Bobby to a football game at Cal. When I left, Marissa kissed me good-bye, and for just a moment I had the strange but comfortable feeling of what it must be like to be a happily married man.

It was homecoming; Cal was playing USC; and Bobby was afraid we were going to be late. As soon as he gave the tickets at the gate, he started jogging up the steep cement steps that led up to the back side of the stadium. The weather was dry and hot, and when we found our seats, high above the field, where the stadium curved around the corner of the end zone, the teams were lining up for the kickoff. I was still trying to catch my breath when Bobby nudged me hard with his elbow.

"Watch this kid," he said, as the ball sailed five yards deep into the end zone. The Cal player who caught it knelt down for a touchback. The referee blew his whistle, took the ball, and walked briskly out to the twenty-yard line.

"Did you see that?" asked Bobby. Nothing had happened. There was no return of the kickoff. It was a touchback. Cal would take possession on the twenty-yard line.

"It was the third game of my sophomore year. Freshmen didn't play then. I was the second-string halfback and I was the backup kickoff return man. During warm-ups, the guy who was ahead of me, a senior, Charlie something, pulled a muscle. He couldn't play. Funny how things happen. If that had not happened—if he had been able to play—I might not have played all year. We won the coin toss, elected to receive. We were playing USC, just like today; only then USC was great, and we weren't.

We elected to receive, and I stood back there, just where that kid was standing—same end of the stadium—waiting for the ball to come down out of the sky. It seemed to take forever, and I remember thinking that maybe this guy had actually managed to kick it right over the stadium wall. I caught it five yards deep in the end zone. I didn't hesitate for an instant; as soon as I had it in my arm I was gone.

"I knew I was going to go all the way, a hundred and five yards. I knew I was going to score. I knew more than that: I knew there were at least three different ways I could do it. I could see the whole thing out in front of me, the same way you can see a map spread out on the floor in front of you."

Bobby described it to me, every part of it: the way he moved, the way he changed pace, how he cut back and the angle he took, what he did each time an opposing player tried to stop him. It was like listening to someone describing to a blind man everything going on that very moment. He had not forgotten anything. It was extraordinary. He could sometimes not remember the plot of a movie he had seen just a week before, and by his own admission he had nearly flunked out of law school because he had such difficulty recalling the things he had read; but when it came to what he had been able to do better than anyone else at the time, he possessed a memory that was as close to perfect as any I had encountered. He dismissed it as unimportant and explained it as unremarkable.

"The dumbest guy in the world can tell you what happened to him in a car wreck. You remember things that happen to you."

I went along, but only to a point. "Because when they're happening to you, you're concentrating on it with everything you have."

"Sure," he agreed. "Like you do during a trial."

That was the problem. I had not been concentrating enough on what I was doing. Whether it was the distractions—Bobby, Marissa—that normally did not exist; or—though I did not want to admit it—the threat of death or something worse if I persisted in doing everything I could to win, there was something I was still missing, a piece of the puzzle I still had not found. I knew it was there, right in front of my eyes, and I still did not see it.

At the end of the game, as we filed out of the stadium, Bobby nodded toward an area under the stands where a crowd had started to form. It was the home team locker room.

"They used to stand around and wait for me like that," he said, a glint of nostalgia in his eyes. "We stood around inside, celebrating when we won, talking to reporters about the way we had done it. We didn't have any doubts about anything: who we were, what we were. You'd peel off your uniform, take off your cleats, get out of your pads—throw it all on the floor near your locker and, tearing the tape off your ankles, walk naked into the showers. You'd stay there for a long time, the water pounding off your back, laughing about the game, bragging a little about what you'd done. Then you'd get dressed in a clean shirt and a nice pressed pair of pants and your best brown loafers and go outside into the crowd, where your girlfriend—the prettiest girl in school—was waiting, and everything was just the way it was supposed to be, and it never once entered your head that things were ever going to be any different. You were young, and you were going to be young forever, and everything would always take care of itself. We'd walk away from the stadium, shiny with our own earned wisdom, covered already with the nostalgia of our own autumn glory. And so we'd go on to one party and another, a slowly dying chorus of approval, and never give a thought to who was still back in that dingy, dirty locker room, picking up our things, cleaning up after us."

We were out of the stadium, moving with the scattering crowd down the middle of a university street. Bobby turned his head just far enough to catch my eye.

"I meant what I told Lenny: He had the better deal. I hope he believed me."

For a few minutes we walked in silence in the yellow and orange bittersweet light of the late afternoon, lost in our own thoughts of vanished youth and things we wished we could change and knew we never could.

"Albert has started a fund to endow a chair in Lenny's name at the law school. I think that's a good thing, don't you?"

Twenty-five

Augustus Marshall had begun to testify before I reached the doors to the courtroom. Surrounded by reporters, the governor was standing at the far end of the corridor, his tanned face flushed with color under the hot glare of the television lights. If the questions I heard were any indication, the media was treating his appearance more like a campaign stop than as part of a trial. They asked about the latest polls showing that he and Ariella Goldman were running head and head. Relaxed and confident, he insisted he was not worried; and, though anyone who had thought about it might have wondered at the apparent inconsistency, he claimed he had known all along that it was going to be a close race.

Pushing herself forward, a young woman with a handheld microphone demanded to know how much of his challenger's recent rise in the polls was due to the revelations, made during her testimony as a witness for the prosecution, that she was pregnant with Jeremy Fullerton's child. Marshall became distant and reserved.

"I've been asked that question before, and I'm going to give you the same answer," said the governor firmly. "I'm not interested in, nor am I going to comment on, the private lives of other people. I will only say this: I think it's very unfortunate that some lawyers seem to think that the only way they can defend their clients is by trying to attack the integrity and the credibility of people who quite obviously had nothing whatever to do with the crime in question."

I knew little about politics, but I knew right away that Marshall was as shrewd as they come. He had been hurt by what Ariella Goldman had done—upstaged while she became the object of public sympathy—but he had immediately understood that the worst thing he could do was to raise questions about the morality of what she had done. There were others who would eventually do that. He could not attack her with advantage, so he made her in a curious way indebted to him for his support. He would not condone her adulterous affair, but he would defend her from the cheap tricks and intrusive questions of some unprincipled lawyer willing to do anything to win.

"Why were you subpoenaed to be a witness for the defense?" shouted another reporter.

The countenance of Augustus Marshall, one minute so solemn and austere, became suddenly cheerful and almost jovial. The left side of his mouth pulled back as a wry grin formed on his lips. His eyes moved in the direction from which the question had come.

"You'd have to ask the defense attorney . . ." said the governor, hesitating as if trying to remember the name.

"Antonelli," someone yelled out.

"Yes," said Marshall, and then lapsed into a silence that let everyone know he did not think the name worth repeating or the man to whom it referred worth remembering.

"Perhaps the defense attorney," he went on, "could tell you.

I'm afraid I have no idea at all. I don't know anything about what happened the night Senator Fullerton was murdered."

The expression on the governor's face once more turned grave. "All I know is that this was a great tragedy. Jeremy Fullerton and I were of course political rivals; but we were also good friends. There are few people in public life that have contributed more and have had more to offer. His death is a very great loss for us all," he said with a sincerity so well practiced he had perhaps come to believe it himself.

In the presence of the governor, Judge Thompson lost his nerve. Normally a strict disciplinarian, ready to enforce with removal any breach of conduct by the crowd, the judge now without protest permitted reporters to pack close to the bar, kneeling behind it like parishioners waiting to take communion.

Impeccably dressed and meticulously groomed, Augustus Marshall, sixty years old and as trim and fit as the best-conditioned man fifteen years his junior, sat on the witness stand surveying, and probably counting, the faces turned toward him. There was something highly efficient and well measured about him; a certain precision that was reflected in the way he looked and the way he moved. Thinning black hair, graying at the temples, swept back from a high-domed forehead; jet-black eyes, alert, active, intense, peered out from behind an expensive pair of steel-rimmed glasses. He had on a double-breasted dark blue suit and a crisp white shirt with French cuffs. A gold pin pulled both sides of his collar tightly together under the double knot of a muted paisley tie. His black shoes were freshly polished, but there was a single, barely detectable scuff mark on the front of the left one. I wondered if earlier that morning he had for some reason tried in anger to kick open a door.

Standing at the side of the counsel table closest to the jury box, I glanced at a single piece of paper as if I were engaged in a last-minute review of a typewritten list of questions I intended to ask. When I looked up, ready to begin, Marshall wore the expression of someone who knew he had the advantage. He was used to people afraid of making a mistake in the limited time he was willing to give them.

"How long have you been governor?"

As soon as Marshall had been sworn, he had taken a moment to smile at each juror. Before I had finished asking the question, he was looking at them again, bending forward at the waist, his elbows on the arms of the witness chair, trying to get as close to them as he possibly could.

"I'm in the last year of my first term," said Marshall with a modest grin. "Four years this coming January."

"And before that you were the state attorney general?"

He could not keep his eyes off them. I was standing right in front of him and I don't think he saw me at all, not once he had started to concentrate all his energy on making those twelve jurors—those twelve voters—believe whatever he was going to tell them.

"Yes, I was privileged to hold that office as well."

"When you ran for governor four years ago, you were elected by a fairly substantial margin—is that correct?"

He left the jury and turned toward me, but only to look past me to the hundreds of people jammed into the courtroom.

"Yes," replied the governor in the subdued, respectful tone of a grateful servant. "It was a very gratifying victory," he added with a narrow smile that managed to be both humble and benevolent.

"Though it was not quite as large as the margin of victory in your second election as attorney general, was it?" I asked rather sharply. "As a matter of fact, it was a full nine points less, wasn't it?"

He stared at me, bristling. Then he remembered where he

was and how many others were watching, and how many of those would later report everything he said to the public at large. He became once more earnest and amiable. Cocking his head to the side, he flashed a bashful grin.

"Every election is different."

I took a step toward the jury box, raised my head, and gave him a searching look. He smiled.

"It would be hard to find an election more different than that first election—the election for your party's nomination—the first time you ran for attorney general, wouldn't it?"

The district attorney had risen from his chair. He stood there, his head bowed and his hands folded together in front of him, like a respectful petitioner politely waiting his turn, until I finished.

"Your honor," said Haliburton, "I don't see that this line of questioning has any relevance to the issue before us, and—"

I waved my hand as if none of this mattered in the slightest to me.

"If the governor would prefer not to answer my questions, if there's something he would rather not talk about—"

"No," said Marshall, exchanging a glance with the district attorney. "I'll be glad to answer anything you care to ask."

Thompson looked at Haliburton to see what he wanted to do, but the district attorney, with ambitions of his own, was not about to contradict someone who could either help or hurt him later on.

"No objection," said Haliburton, almost apologizing for the interruption.

Marshall knew what I had asked but, because he did not want to give it any more importance than he had to, pretended he did not.

"Let me repeat the question." Then, engaging in a pretense

of my own, I changed my mind. "No, let me ask you something entirely different. Next to being governor, isn't attorney general the most important office in the state?"

"I wouldn't disagree with that."

"And so you held the second most powerful office before you became a candidate for the most important office, correct?"

"Yes, that's a fair way of putting it."

He was watching me carefully now, a little puzzled by where I might be going with these seemingly innocuous questions.

"And what office did you hold before you ran for the second most important office?"

He turned toward the jury again. "I had never held office before. I had not been involved in politics at all. I only became involved because a number of people convinced me that politics was too important to be left in the hands of the politicians."

"There was one person in particular who convinced you to become a candidate for the Republican nomination, wasn't there?"

He gave me a blank look and did not answer.

"Surely you haven't forgotten Hiram Green, who once held the same position you do now."

He was just about to say that of course he had not forgotten. I did not give him the chance.

"That first campaign of yours—you were running against an incumbent, weren't you? Wasn't Arthur Sieman the attorney general then, and wasn't Arthur Sieman a Republican?"

"Yes, that's correct: He was."

"And wasn't Arthur Sieman by all accounts the single most popular public official in the state—more popular than the governor at the time or either of the two United States senators?"

"Yes, he was popular, but—"

"So the reason that former Governor Green wanted you to

run wasn't because he thought you would be a stronger candidate against the Democrats?"

Nothing is a greater threat to the belief that others have of your strength than to be reminded of your former weakness. Marshall tried to bluff his way through it with the kind of ambiguous response that no doubt worked when he was questioned by reporters and had not sworn under oath to tell the truth. He insisted that it had happened years ago—more than a dozen years ago, to be precise—and that he could not speak about what, if any, political calculations might have been made by any of the people who had decided to support him. In politics, he explained with a certain regret, the last election is ancient history after six months; and the next election, even if it is still four years off, is just around the corner. I almost laughed.

"The real reason Hiram Green asked you to run is because Arthur Sieman had betrayed him and he wanted to embarrass him. He did not think you had any chance to win, did he?" I asked, taking a step toward him. "In fact, he told you to your face you wouldn't win. He told you if you got twenty or twenty-five percent of the vote, you'd have done everything he and his conservative friends wanted. He wanted to embarrass Sieman. That was the reason he wanted you to run; that was the reason he raised millions of dollars for your campaign—wasn't it, Governor Marshall?"

Haliburton was on his feet. Without taking his eyes off me, Marshall motioned for him to sit down.

"In politics, as in life altogether, there are as many motives as there are people to have them."

"But the motive that drove Hiram Green was the desire for revenge, wasn't it?"

He just looked at me and waited.

"Arthur Sieman betrayed Hiram Green—or so at least Hiram Green believed—correct?" I asked rapidly.

"I suppose that's true," Marshall reluctantly agreed.

"No, you don't suppose that's true. This isn't some rally on the steps of the capitol; this isn't some press conference in the hallway of the courthouse. This is a court of law, and this is a murder trial, and you're a witness sworn to tell the truth. Now, did Hiram Green believe Arthur Sieman had betrayed him?"

"Yes, I believe he did."

"And did you in turn betray Hiram Green?"

"I most certainly did not," indignantly replied the governor.

"He says you did. He says that once you were elected, he never heard from you again—not even a Christmas card. Is that true?"

Marshall's features seemed all to soften at once. His voice became gentle and confiding.

"Governor Green is a very old man and his memory isn't what it used to be, I'm afraid. It's true we haven't always agreed on everything, but I've tried not to ignore him. I probably should have done more to make him feel that people still remember him."

I walked back to the counsel table, picked up the piece of paper on which no list of questions had been typed, and acted as if I were trying to find something I had forgotten.

"Arthur Sieman died, didn't he?"

"Yes."

"He died just before the primary election, didn't he?"

"Yes."

"That's the reason you won that primary, the reason you were able to run in the general election, the reason you became attorney general, the reason you were later able to run for governor—because Arthur Sieman died, correct?"

His face grew rigid; his lips were pressed tight together; he stared hard at me.

"Arthur Sieman died. No one can know what would have happened if he had not."

I stared back at him.

"And now Jeremy Fullerton has died, and no one will know what would have happened if he had not—except that for the second time, someone you could not otherwise have defeated no longer stands in your way!"

The district attorney was on his feet; the judge had bolted forward; Marshall was halfway out of the witness chair. The courtroom was bedlam. Haliburton screamed an objection, but even when he finally heard it, Thompson seemed too dazed to know what to do. I saved him the trouble.

"No more questions, your honor," I announced as I left Augustus Marshall sputtering with rage.

I waited at the counsel table, staring down at my hands, while Clarence Haliburton used the formalities of cross-examination to express his indignation at what I had done and his apologies for what the governor had been forced to endure. With an ingratiating smile, meant no doubt to constitute an apology of his own, Judge Thompson had already begun to excuse Marshall as a witness when I startled him by suggesting we were not quite finished.

"Redirect, your honor."

Marshall raised his eyes and waited.

"What was the reason Jeremy Fullerton was running for governor?"

Augustus Marshall had not gotten as far as he had without knowing how to defuse a situation that threatened to blow up in everyone's face. He smiled as if despite what had happened just a few minutes before we were still good friends.

"Because he wanted my job, I imagine."

There was an almost audible sigh of relief. An undercurrent of laughter moved through the courtroom. Everyone began to relax. I crossed one foot over the other, nodded my head, and smiled back.

"But isn't it also true that he was running because he thought it would help him to become president?"

Marshall studied me for a moment. "It was hardly a secret that the senator wanted to be president. And yes, I believe he thought that if he could defeat me, an incumbent governor of the largest state in the union, he'd be in a far stronger position if he then decided to try to take the Democratic nomination away from the president two years from now."

"So, politically speaking, Jeremy Fullerton was a threat to both you and the president?"

"Politically speaking."

"Is that the reason the White House offered to give you information that was damaging to Fullerton—to help you win so Fullerton would not have a chance to run against the president?"

Marshall did not hesitate for a moment. "No one from the White House ever offered me any such thing."

He said it with such sincerity, such conviction, that I almost thought he was telling the truth.

"Does the name Andrei Bogdonovitch mean anything to you?"

He shook his head and said it did not. There was nothing more I could do, so I dropped it and went back to where we had been.

"At the time of his death, who was leading in the polls—you or Senator Fullerton?"

"He was, but it was early, and—"

"And if Jeremy Fullerton had defeated you—become governor—then two years from now, he would have tried to run against the president?"

"As I said, I believe that's what he wanted to do."

"So it would be fair to say, then," I asked with a polite smile, "that both you and the president had something to gain by Jeremy Fullerton's death, wouldn't it?"

Outrage loses its force by repetition. Haliburton objected; Thompson sustained the objection; but the only noise from the crowd was a subdued murmur that died away the moment the judge raised his eyes.

I had no more questions to ask and neither did the district attorney. With a half embarrassed smile, Augustus Marshall glanced one last time at the jury and then quietly left the courtroom. As I watched him go, the rush of emotion that had driven me forward, flying at him with one question after another, began to dissipate; and what had seemed so obvious to me no longer appeared quite so clear. Instead of simply pointing out that the death of Jeremy Fullerton had been an advantage to any number of powerful people; instead of suggesting that these were motives far more powerful than that which the prosecution had tried to attribute to Jamaal Washington; instead, in other words, of sticking close to the indisputable facts, I had for all practical purposes insisted that both the governor and the president were capable of murder.

The courtroom doors swung shut behind the governor. I turned back to the bench, an empty feeling in my stomach, worried that I had just made one of the worst miscalculations of my career. But if I had just started to realize it, the district attorney had known it all along. The moment he began his closing argument he tried to take advantage of my mistake.

"I have to credit Mr. Antonelli with one thing at least," said Haliburton as he strolled toward the jury box. "From almost the first question he asked on voir dire to the last question he asked at trial, he's been nothing if not consistent in his theory of the case."

He halted in front of the jury box, glanced briefly at me over his shoulder, and shook his head as if he still could not believe what he had heard. He tapped the fingers of his right hand on the wooden railing.

"The defendant, Jamaal Washington," he began in a deep voice filled with derision, "did not kill United States Senator Jeremy Fullerton. Why? Because someone that important could only have been killed by 'powerful people,' political enemies, people so ambitious they're prepared to murder rather than risk defeat in the next election. I don't know what country Mr. Antonelli has been living in, but it can't have been the United States. We've had presidents killed, and we've had senators killed, but so far as I know this is the first time anyone has ever tried to accuse our highest officials of murder."

Haliburton stepped back from the railing and looked at me again.

"You remember during voir dire," he asked, still staring at me, "when he asked one of you who you thought killed John F. Kennedy?"

He looked around, his eyes settling on the juror I had asked.

"I wondered at the time what he meant to do with that. Well," he went on with a shrug, "who can blame him? When your client is caught in the act—and especially when the act is murder—what else can you argue except that nothing is what it seems and that a conspiracy was responsible for the death of the victim; because, after all, we all know—don't we?—that there is a conspiracy behind everything!"

It was not enough to paint me as a charlatan; the district attorney still had to prove his case. With workmanlike precision,

Haliburton condensed and carefully reviewed the testimony given by the witnesses for the prosecution. The technicalities of death had been explained by the city coroner; and no one, he reminded the jury, not even the defense, had objected to the description of the way in which the life of Jeremy Fullerton had been brought to a sudden, violent end. Fullerton had been shot to death, and the bullet that killed him had been fired from the gun that was found by the hand of the defendant when he was shot by the police while trying to escape.

Everyone, insisted Haliburton over and over again, agreed on all the essential facts. The defendant was in the senator's car: Everyone agreed. The defendant removed the senator's wallet: No one denied it. The defendant ran away as soon as the police arrived: The defendant himself admitted it. Everyone agreed that the gun was the murder weapon, and everyone, including the defendant, agreed that it was found on the sidewalk right next to his hand. The defense had no facts to argue, so the defense, he added with a withering sidelong glance at me, had decided to argue fantasy.

"Mr. Antonelli," continued Haliburton with an exaggerated and malicious sigh, "tried to tell us, not only that 'powerful people' are behind all this, but that, in addition, the police are to blame. The defendant testified—swore—that he never touched the gun; even though, as I hope you noticed, Mr. Antonelli asked him repeatedly whether he might have picked it up while in a state of panic and then, because he had been shot, forgotten that he had done it. The defendant insists he did not touch the gun, and that means, according to the defense, that the police must have put the gun next to his hand. What we have is yet another conspiracy. First one of the officers shoots him; then the two of them conspire together to plant the gun so it will look like the officer fired in self-defense."

Haliburton was talking faster, his face getting redder, as he paced in front of the jury box. Suddenly he stopped still and leaned across the railing.

"And what evidence are we offered to support this outrageous allegation? The testimony of the police officer herself. Are there any contradictions, any inconsistencies—are there any provable falsehoods—in anything Officer O'Leary said? On the contrary, under the insistent and sometimes almost fanatical questioning of the defense attorney, she repeats her testimony over and over again; and no matter how hard he tries, he can't get her to change a word of it. What does the defense lawyer make of his own failure? Not that she was determined to tell the truth, but that she must be lying!"

Haliburton went through everything, summarizing with subtle distortions all the evidence that had been offered on both sides of the case. Then he stepped back from the jury box and glanced quickly around the courtroom.

"When anyone dies," he said, lowering his eyes, "especially someone with so much more life left to live, there is always enough suffering to go around without deliberately and for no good purpose inflicting more."

Slowing lifting his gaze to the jury, he furrowed his brow, a sign that what he was about to say had been much on his mind.

"Ariella Goldman was in love with Jeremy Fullerton. After he died, all she wanted was to protect his good name. Instead, she was not only forced to admit that she loved him, and to admit that he loved her, but forced to tell you and to tell the world that he was going to get a divorce; that they were going to get married; and that she is going to have his child. She was forced to tell you all this because there was no limit to how far the defense was willing to go in its single-minded attempt to convince you that 'powerful people' had something to hide. He made his point. Ariella Goldman, as we all know now, did have something she wanted to hide. I leave it to you to decide whether any of us is really better off because she was not allowed to keep it hidden."

I knew when I stood up that unless I could win it on closing argument, the case was lost; and I knew that the only way I could win it on closing argument was to forget all about conspiracies and talk only about what had been proven and what had not. I had to make an argument so compelling in its apparent simplicity that the jury would have to believe that there was at least some doubt, some reasonable doubt, about the guilt of the defendant. It was the last chance left.

"We've heard the same events described so many times," I began, still in my chair, "that we start to see it as if we had been there ourselves, watching the whole thing unfold, like the narrator of a novel who knows everything about everyone."

With both hands I pushed myself up. Standing at the table, I moved my finger back and forth across the empty page of a yellow-lined legal pad.

"We hear the noise at the party at Lawrence Goldman's apartment, where people paid small fortunes to attend. We see them, all those wealthy, well-dressed people talking, laughing, drinking champagne, smiling at each other as they lined up to have their pictures taken with Jeremy Fullerton, the bright, good-looking young senator who everyone thought might one day soon be president."

I moved around the table into the opening between the bench, where Judge Thompson sat staring blankly at the ceiling, and the jury box.

"We watch Meredith Fullerton, the senator's wife, lashing out at her husband's mistress and then, in tears, run away. And we're not entirely surprised that the party goes on as if nothing had happened. Then, after midnight, when the party is finally over, Jeremy Fullerton and Ariella Goldman go have a drink together, just the two of them, in a quiet corner of the bar at the St. Francis Hotel. We can hear what they talk about as if we were sitting at the next table; and then, when they finish their drink, we go along with them when she drives him to his car."

I watched the faces of the jury watching me. They were seeing it again, just the way they had before.

"We watch him get into his car, and then we watch her drive away, disappear into that thick, enveloping fog. Then, a moment later, we hear it, and we know immediately that it's a gunshot, and we know—don't we?—that Jeremy Fullerton is dead. And now we see something else: a police car, blocks away; and two police officers, Joyner and O'Leary. We watch the way they react; the way Joyner's huge hands grip the wheel; the way O'Leary's eyes move first one way, then the other as she tries to see in that impenetrable fog just where the shot must have come from. We watch the car race 'round one corner, then another; and we sit up fast and hold our breath as that unfortunate pedestrian just manages to jump out of the way."

Unbuttoning my coat, I slid my hands down around the small of my back as I hunched forward and peered down at the tips of my shoes.

"Now we see them, out of the patrol car, Joyner and O'Leary, guns drawn, creeping toward the Mercedes. Then, suddenly," I said, slowly raising my head, "someone jumps out of the car and starts running down the street, moving through fog so heavy you can barely see him. Then, somehow, it's clear enough that we can see he has a gun, that he's looking back, that he's ready to fire. But Officer O'Leary fires first and, as she put it, 'the subject went down.'"

I looked from one end of the jury box to the other.

"We've heard it so many times we think we were there. We know Jamaal Washington killed Jeremy Fullerton because we saw it happen, didn't we? We heard the shot; we saw him jump out of the car; we saw him run away. We know what happened. We saw it with our own eyes, didn't we?"

Shoving my left hand into my pocket, I rubbed the back of my neck with my right, a puzzled expression on my face.

"Or did we? We saw Fullerton's face pressed against the glass on the driver's side of the car; we saw Jamaal Washington dash out of the car. But we never saw the murder, did we? No one saw the murder, did they? The prosecution paraded out a long line of witnesses; but none of them was a witness to the only thing that is really important: Not one of them witnessed the crime."

Turning until I was face-to-face with the district attorney, I continued: "The single most important fact in this case is that there were no witnesses to the crime. The entire case is built on circumstantial evidence, and only circumstantial evidence. The prosecution is asking you to convict Jamaal Washington of murder, not because anyone saw him do it, but because of the circumstance in which he had the misfortune to find himself when, in a remarkable act of courage, he decided someone had been shot and he might not be too late to help."

I turned away from Haliburton and back to the jury, pleading with my eyes, begging them to do the right thing.

"He was there, in the senator's car, when the police arrived: We admit that. He tried to run away: We admit that as well. He explained to you why he did that. The prosecution tells you he had the murder weapon in his hand when he was shot by the police: He insists he never touched the gun. I confess I don't know if he did or not. Perhaps in his panic he picked it up and, after the trauma of being shot, blocked it out of his mind. I don't know. But he believes he did not, and that is what he testified.

If it's true—that he never touched it—the question becomes: How did it get there, next to his hand, after he was shot?"

Pausing, I looked over at Jamaal. He was sitting straight in his chair, his hands folded in his lap, following me with his eyes.

"The district attorney tells you that Officer O'Leary was just trying to be accurate when she repeated word for word the same story three different times. But if you're going to tell the truth, just going to describe what happened, why do you have to memorize your testimony down to the tiniest detail? The truth doesn't change. It's only a lie you have to be careful not to forget.

"But you must have asked yourselves: Why would she lie? What motive could she possibly have?"

I placed my hand on the railing and peered into their open faces.

"To cover a mistake, a mistake that at the time did not seem to matter much. Just like the district attorney, she knew—she was certain—that Jamaal Washington was guilty. She had just seen her first homicide victim, his blood-covered face shoved against the glass. A split second later, someone in a leather jacket and a wool cap, a young man, a black man, bolts out of the car. She's scared out of her mind, just like you or I would have been scared. He hesitates, looks back. She thinks the only thing she can think: He's going to kill me! She fires, and 'the subject went down.' Then, but only then, she discovers that he didn't have a gun after all, nothing, no weapon of any kind. But he's just killed someone, and not just someone: a United States senator. He's a murderer. He might not have had a gun, but the gun was in the car and he was in full flight from the police. The gun is an irrelevance, an inconvenient detail, a minor omission. What difference does it make! He did it! He's a killer, a cold-blooded killer, and he's lucky he's not dead. They take the gun from the car and put it next to his outstretched hand while he's lying there, sprawled on the sidewalk, unconscious and barely alive. What difference does it make? He did it. No one will ever know.

"No one, let me repeat, witnessed the murder of Jeremy Fullerton. The only witness to what Jamaal Washington did that night before the police arrived was Jamaal Washington himself. He testified under oath. He told you what he did. He heard a shot; he went to help; he saw a light cut through the fog; he was afraid the killer had come back and he ran away—not because he was guilty, but because he was afraid. And there is not one witness that has been able to tell you anything different."

When I finally finished, I sank into my chair, my heart racing, my hands full of sweat. I knew I had won.

Twenty-six

Everything that happened after the verdict, everything that took place after the jury pronounced Jamaal Washington guilty of murder, was lost in an alcoholic haze. I never did remember where I had gone or what I had done during the three days and nights that I apparently wandered, a drunk without a memory, lost somewhere in the city. Because of my own astonishing incapacity, a young man of exemplary habits and character was going to pay with his life for a crime I knew he had not committed. He was going to spend years on death row, growing old in the narrow confinement of a cell, waiting through a long series of losing appeals for the date that nothing could now avoid, when the executioner would finally come. I had known the moment I heard the verdict that every day he lived like that a little bit of me would die; and so I drank myself into oblivion in a stupid, self-indulgent attempt to walk away from my own grave.

I was on the Golden Gate Bridge in the middle of the night, gripping the steering wheel of the car so hard that my knuckles turned white. Cars were racing by me, honking their horns. I had to force myself to take my eyes off the road in front of me and look in the rearview mirror. Long parallel rows of dim yellow lights were rushing up behind me, shooting past me as if I were not moving at all. My eyes had become intolerably heavy and kept trying to close. I rolled down the window and opened my mouth to gasp the cold midnight air, hoping it would keep me awake. Focusing on the road, I gradually increased my speed. Cars still shot by me, but not quite so fast as they had before. My right hand was frozen to the wheel. I had to loosen it, one finger at a time. Once it was free, I shook it and shook it again, trying to get the circulation back.

I could not remember why I had come, why I had crossed the bridge in the first place. All I knew was that I wanted to go home, and I could not remember where it was. Beneath the swirling surface of my mind, something, some instinct, pulled me on until I was parked in front of a shingle-sided house on a narrow street on a steep hillside facing the bay. All the lights were out.

Carefully, methodically, afraid I might not remember each thing I was supposed to do, I switched off the ignition and turned off the lights. I opened the car door, started to get out, and then, because I had forgotten, reached back behind me to set the hand brake.

I shut the car door, quietly, using both hands, so I would not wake anyone up. In the distance, the lights of the city danced upside down on the bay. I tried to turn my head to make them come right side up again, but I started to stumble, and then, spinning around, I started to fall. Laughing at it all, I rolled over on the ground until, with my hands spread behind me, I stared at a sky full of stars and wondered if I was looking up or whether I had landed on my head and was watching their reflection on the water far below.

Just as I was struggling to my feet, the porch light came on and the front door opened. I could feel a stupid grin cut across my godforsaken face as I pointed an unsteady finger and wobbled toward the woman in the doorway.

"I know you!" I exclaimed as if I could not really be sure that I did.

"Where have you been?" asked Marissa, gently and with relief, as I draped one arm over her shoulder and let my face collapse against the warm smooth skin of her neck. She put her arm around me to help me stay on my feet.

"Everybody's been looking all over for you."

That idiotic grin had pasted itself on my face. I raised my head, just enough to see the worried expression in her eyes.

"Did they find me?" I asked, grinning even more broadly at what I was sure was the funniest thing I had ever heard in my life.

When I woke up, some fifteen hours later, my head throbbed with a dull, constricting pain; even the late afternoon light was too harsh for my exhausted eyes. Wrapped like an invalid in a soft cotton robe, I stayed inside, sitting motionless on the davenport, protected by the shadows that lengthened across the living room floor. Cradling in my feeble hands the cup of coffee Marissa had given me, I blinked, in measured intervals, the blank verse of my empty, desolate mind.

"I lost," I said presently, as if I had just remembered something terrible that had happened a long time ago.

"I know," she said, consoling me with the gentle, soft sympathy of her eyes.

My mouth hung open and I tilted my head toward her, trying to remember if I had told her before. Marissa bent forward and crossed her arms over her knees.

"The trial was over four days ago."

I had no memory of any of it, nothing between the verdict and late last night, coming over the bridge.

"Four days?" I mumbled, everything a blank. "I left the courthouse," I said, trying to remember. "I came here, went to bed—last night. Didn't I?"

"Yes, you came here last night," she said as she stroked my hand. "But the trial was over four days ago. No one knew where you had gone. You just vanished. Everyone was worried: Bobby, Albert . . . me."

For the next few days I did nothing except what I was told. I slept late every morning and sat outside every afternoon with Marissa, basking in the lazy warmth of the October sun, talking aimlessly about things of no importance. The better I felt, the more ashamed I became of what I had done.

"I've never lost a case before," I tried finally to explain. "Not a case I should have won; not a case where I knew the defendant didn't do it. The truth of it is, I didn't think it could happen to me. Arrogance, pride—call it what you want—I didn't think I could lose."

There was at times a certain ruthless clarity about the way her mind worked, an unwillingness to pretend things were better than they were.

"You must have known it could happen, though. I wouldn't know how often it happens, but people do get convicted for things they didn't do. What is it that really bothers you: that you don't think he murdered Jeremy Fullerton, or that you think you did something wrong?"

"You think it wouldn't bother me if someone was convicted of something he didn't do, so long as it wasn't my fault that he was convicted?"

"Of course you'd be bothered, but not like this."

She paused for a moment and then said, quite seriously, the

way someone might counsel her closest friend, "The greatest sin is self-pity, and you have less right to it than almost anyone I know. Listen to yourself. You didn't think you could ever lose a case you should have won. Of course that's arrogance, but it's something else as well, isn't it? You've never lost before; you never had to hear a jury say someone you were certain was innocent was guilty. You're incredibly good at what you do; Bobby says you're the best. If you made a mistake—if you really believe it's your fault—what do you think it's like for all those other lawyers out there who aren't half as good as you and lose cases all the time, cases you would have won? If you made a mistake, do what everyone has to do—learn from it. What else can you do—quit? Things don't always turn out for the best. You're old enough to know that. We're both old enough to know that," added Marissa with a smile that tried to appear indomitable but could not conceal the look of vulnerability that lay only half hidden in her eyes.

She was right, of course: There was nothing I could do except face up to my own responsibilities and somehow learn to live with the awful fact that I had not been able to save an innocent man from the death penalty. Early Monday morning I forced myself to go back into the city and try as best I could to explain to Albert Craven why I had lost. Though he had never tried a criminal case in his life, he seemed to have a pretty good idea of what I was going through.

"You can't blame yourself," he insisted firmly as we sat in his darkened office discussing the case.

I had come not only to say good-bye and to thank him for everything he had done, but to say I was sorry.

"When I finished my closing argument," I said, still astonished at how badly I had judged the effect of what I had done, "I was certain they'd have to acquit. I may have made—no, I'm certain I made a mistake in the way I handled Marshall. I shouldn't have treated him like that—like someone with a criminal record lying to save himself. I shouldn't have thrown around accusations without having something more specific I could prove. I was so certain—I'm still so certain—that someone desperately wanted Fullerton dead that I thought everyone else would believe it, too. And then I thought that after they had seen Jamaal, listened to him, heard how intelligent he is, they'd know it couldn't possibly have been him.

"As I say, I made a mistake; but during that closing argument, as I took them through each step of what they thought they had seen, reminded them that no one had been able to tell them what had actually happened—no one besides Jamaal—because there was no other witness, I thought everything had fallen back into place and that they could not possibly find him guilty."

Craven rested his small hands in his lap as he leaned against the chair. He was dressed as he always was in the office: a dark suit, silk tie, gold cuff links; but the cheerful demeanor of easy exuberance and quick intelligence that made what he wore seem impeccable and made him seem distinguished had vanished. He looked old, old and tired; more like a man resigned to a few last years of quiet contemplation than someone who had either the energy or the patience for the kind of bright, free-wheeling, and perhaps inconsequential conversation that enlivened his table and made him one of the few seemingly indispensable members of San Francisco society.

"I was there," he said in a voice strangely subdued. "I saw what you did with the governor."

Craven paused long enough to smile at me, and I knew then that whatever he thought about me, he did not blame me for what had happened.

"I'm not a trial lawyer, so I can't speak from any direct experience; but I've been a lawyer for a very long time, and I've watched some of the great lawyers—names that everyone still remembers. You're as good as any of them ever were. I don't think what you did with Marshall was a mistake at all, and your closing argument was one of the best things I've ever seen done."

A pensive expression on his face, he rubbed the back of his head. Then he put his hand back in his lap and looked at me.

"The case wasn't lost because of anything you did, or didn't, do. The case was lost because of who the victim was. It would have been an enormous responsibility for that jury to decide that the person the police arrested for the murder of Jeremy Fullerton, a United States senator, the next governor, and maybe the next president, should be let go. They couldn't let a murder like that go unpunished. It was not enough to show them there was a reasonable doubt about his guilt. I think you would have had to have shown that there was no reasonable doubt about his innocence."

I was not sure Craven was right, and on one point in particular I was almost certain he was wrong.

"Do you think any of this would have happened if he had been some white kid in a coat and tie walking home from a date, instead of a black kid in a leather jacket and a wool knit cap? I don't mean just whether that cop would have fired without first shouting a warning, but whether the jury would have believed that he only tried to help."

Craven pressed his fingers together in front of his small round mouth. Pursing his lips, he stared straight ahead, a look of intense contemplation in his eyes as if he were weighing in his mind something of unusual importance.

"You could also ask," he said presently, "whether any of this would have happened if I'd married his mother, twenty years ago, when she told me she was pregnant."

He seemed surprised by the stunned expression on my face. "I thought you might have guessed."

His voice became stronger. The color began to return to his face.

"We had what I suppose might have been called an 'arrangement,' " explained Craven in a tone that seemed to mock the sensibilities of those who would have used the phrase. "She was what used to be called a courtesan. She sold herself—that's true—" he added as if to forestall the objection of some invisible third party, "but not just to anyone, and never except under conditions she set herself. And it was never any kind of direct exchange—nothing like it. I paid for her apartment, and I saw her once a week. She saw other men, of course—and I knew that—though who they were and how often she saw them was none of my business and was never discussed. Now, you may be wondering why I did that: why I had this fairly elaborate arrangement. All I can tell you is that she wanted it that way and I was prepared to do whatever she wanted. She was quite the most extraordinary woman I've ever known. You've seen her. Imagine her twenty years ago. She was exquisite, and, without wanting to embarrass you, let me just say she could do things—she could make love in ways—I had never imagined. That was only part of it. There was a depth to her, an honesty, I had never known before."

Craven stopped and smiled to himself.

"I never saw her anywhere except at that apartment. She was very discreet; and I never really knew why, though I think now that it might have been a matter of pride. But one day she called me at the office and asked me to meet her that afternoon. We sat on a bench outside the Palace of Fine Arts and she told me, quite calmly, that she was pregnant and that she was almost certain I was the father. Yes: 'almost certain.' That was honest to a fault, wasn't it? She told me, again quite calmly, that she had decided to have the baby, that she wanted nothing from me, and that she had told me only because she was not going to see me again. She gave me the keys to the apartment, and I knew then that she meant it: that I was never going to see her again and that neither would anyone else she had known in the way she knew me. I did not know what to say, or even what to do."

Craven sat forward, his arms on the desk, looking at me with the gratitude of someone who wants not so much to unburden his soul, but simply to explain fully and without fear of disapproval something he had done.

"I would have asked her to marry me if I had thought there was a chance in the world she would have said yes. I was quite in love with her—more than I ever was with any of the women I married—but she didn't feel that way about me."

His small delicately formed head snapped up and a confident friendly smile crossed his lips.

"She liked me; I think she liked me quite a lot; but she never would have married me. She knew I had money; she knew all about me—My God, she knew more about me than I think I knew about myself—but in the most important way I was not good enough for her. I'm not sure anyone ever was. She did one thing, just as she started to walk away, something I've never forgotten: She bent down and kissed me on the side of the face and told me she was glad I was the father. Do you know—I must have sat on that bench another hour, all by myself, and I could not stop crying.

"I never saw her again, and I never tried to see her. I did not even know whether she had gone ahead and had the child. Oh, if I had thought about it, I would have guessed that she had.

Mary wasn't the kind of person who would tell you she was going to do something like that and then change her mind. I didn't see her again until the day she walked into the office to tell me that her son—*her* son—had been arrested and almost killed for a murder he did not commit. That was the first time—the only time—she ever asked me for help."

Albert Craven sniffed the air and arched his eyebrows. With a slightly bewildered expression, he shook his head.

"I don't have any feelings about this. I mean, I don't feel any connection, any bond of any sort, with the boy. I'm the biological parent, but I've never met him, and I know, because she told me, that he knows nothing about me. I don't know if I'm supposed to feel something—only that I don't. That troubles me, Joseph; it troubles me a great deal, but I honestly don't know what to do about it. Someone is now on death row, someone to whom I helped give life; but except for the fact I was once in love with his mother, it doesn't seem to mean anything to me. Should it?"

If there was an answer, I did not know what it was. I remembered what my mother had once told me, and I was certain that if it was true, the last person I would ever want to meet was the man who had late one night fathered me. There was no answer, and some questions should never be asked.

We both stood up.

"You did everything she allowed you to do," I suggested as we shook hands across the desk.

I let go of his hand. As I started to turn away, it caught my eye: a large manila envelope with a mailing label in the middle of it.

"Yes," remarked Craven when he saw what I was looking at. "I finally finished it."

"Arkady Bogdonovitch?" I asked, glancing up.

"Andrei's brother. Everything goes to him."

"Bogdonovitch's brother," I repeated, thinking about something Andrei Bogdonovitch had once told me.

"Where is this going?" I asked, glancing quickly at the package again.

Craven was too astonished at the sudden, harsh tone of my voice to speak. I looked again at the package, this time at the address. It was in a place called Bordighera, which I had never heard of, somewhere inside Italy.

I did not try to explain to Albert Craven why I wanted to go, perhaps because I was not sure myself that I believed it; but when I told him that I wanted to deliver the package, not only could he think of no objection, he seemed delighted I wanted to do it. I could not blame him for thinking that a change of scene could only do me good.

Craven made all the arrangements. Bordighera, as he described it, was "very close to Monte Carlo, just the other side of the French border, part of what they call the Italian Riviera." A friend of his, or a rather a friend of a friend of his, knew someone in Milan, who in turn knew someone who spent his summers in a small villa in Bordighera, next to a park that overlooked the Mediterranean. The villa would be available for as long as I needed it. Arkady Bogdonovitch was informed by cable that Joseph Antonelli, described euphemistically by Albert Craven as an associate of his firm, would appear in person to settle the final details of his brother's estate.

On the day of my flight, I came by the office to pick up the package of documents that Craven had kept in his care. Marissa, who had agreed to come with me because she knew I did not want to be alone, waited outside in the car.

"Everything is set," said Albert as he handed me an attaché case inside which he had carefully organized everything I was going to need. "Have a safe trip. I hope the two of you can relax and enjoy yourselves."

I stopped at the door and turned around.

"How did it happen that Andrei Bogdonovitch was there that evening at your house? Was there some particular reason he was invited?"

At first he seemed not to remember. Then, as he thought about it, he began to nod his head.

"Yes, yes, I remember now. It was curious, in a way. I had not seen him in probably the better part of a year. He called me up, just a few days before the dinner, and said he'd like very much to meet you."

I picked up two newspapers just before we boarded the plane and after takeoff started to read. As the plane leveled off at cruising altitude, I pointed to a story on the first page of the second section.

"Look at this," I said to Marissa.

According to the latest poll, Ariella Goldman was running ahead of Augustus Marshall in the race for governor by five percentage points.

"She never could have done it without me," I suggested with a grim smile.

"She hasn't won yet," Marissa reminded me with what I thought was more hope than conviction.

We passed through an orange-streaked sky, scorched by the sun as it fell behind us, and then sped through the abbreviated night. In the morning we shot beyond the barren rock-encrusted coastline and began a long slow turn over the Mediterranean as we made our descent into Nice.

In a rented yellow Fiat we drove out of Nice, heading toward the Italian border, less than twenty miles away.

"If we were going in the other direction," remarked Marissa, a flash of illumination from the depths of her dark penetrating eyes, "we'd go right past where F. Scott Fitzgerald lived for a while, near the beach that was like a 'tan prayer rug.'" She laughed with pleasure at the way Fitzgerald's phrase rolled off her tongue.

"He made it famous, you know," she said, glancing across at me, both her hands on the wheel. "The Riviera, where rich Americans drank too much, and laughed too much, and thought that old age began somewhere just the other side of thirty, and that nothing really had much meaning anyway, except being young and beautiful and rich enough to do whatever you wanted."

"And her voice 'sounded like money.'"

"What?" she asked, laughing.

"That's how he described Daisy's voice in *The Great Gatsby,*" I said. "I just remembered. Her voice sounded like money."

At the border we fumbled for our passports. The guard, bored with formalities, waved us through. We drove a few miles farther on a road high above steep terraced hills, looking out across the shimmering green surface of the sea. It was easy to imagine the coast of North Africa waiting, solemn and mysterious, somewhere just below the line where the sky ran straight up to the sun. Glancing back behind us, you would almost swear you could see the lights of Monte Carlo dancing in the darkness, though the night was still hours away.

The villa, hidden in a cluster of yellow and pink stone buildings, bordered the meticulously tended gardens of a tree-lined park. After we were settled, and with nothing that had to be done until morning, we strolled through the twisted streets of the village under the empty solitude of the blazing sky. Children with the faces of small adults dashed in and out in front of us, chasing one another or dribbling a soccer ball with tiny well-trained feet. We wandered aimlessly until we were finally lost in a labyrinth of jagged cobblestone steps that led through endless gray stone corridors curving between narrow four-storied walls filled with heavy shuttered windows. We followed where it led until it emptied us out into a small square and a modest, crumbling cathedral. On the left side of the square, not far from where we stood, a few cloth-covered tables were scattered outside the doorway to a restaurant.

We sat inside next to a window with a view of the high-crested rocks that, like the stepping-stones of Cyclopes, sloped down toward the sea. Banished below the horizon, the Italian sun left burning behind it an apricot-colored sky.

In a black coat and white shirt buttoned at the throat, an old man with iron-gray hair and a stiff white mustache was bent over a table at the back, a crust of bread in one hand, slowly spooning a mouthful of soup with the other. He was the only other person in the restaurant, and he had not raised his eyes when we entered. He had the unhurried look, seldom seen in America, of someone who had never left the place he had been born.

"Why don't you tell me why we have come here?" asked Marissa after the waiter brought us a bottle of red wine.

"I told you: I have to deliver some papers for Albert Craven."

"No, the real reason."

I watched the old man, wondering how old he was and whether, when you reached that age—whether it was seventy, or eighty, or a hundred—the idea of your own survival was as important as it had been when you were younger and thought you had a lot more life to live.

"The real reason?" persisted Marissa, grinning at me from

behind the thick octagonal glass in which the wine had been served.

"The real reason?" I said, taking my eyes off the old man. "I came here to see someone I used to know, someone who died."

Twenty-seven

Perhaps I had not heard it the way I remembered it; perhaps I had not heard it at all. It seemed suddenly fantastic, now that I was about to find out for sure. I had traveled all this way, halfway around the world, on the strength of nothing more substantial than a chance remark.

I checked my watch and closed the attaché case. Each of the documents was in the order listed in the sheet of instructions Albert Craven had prepared. The sole beneficiary of Andrei Bogdonovitch's will was to affix his signature in each of the designated places; then I was to give him the certified check inside the law firm envelope clipped to the front of the file. If I was wrong, the entire transaction would take less than ten minutes; if I was right . . . well, if I was right, things would become a good deal more complicated.

I got up from the lacquered table in the middle of the room, where, under the indifferent light of a tarnished and decrepit chandelier, I had made a quick review of what Albert Craven had given me. In an alcove, under a pair of shuttered French windows, Marissa lay asleep on a simple unframed bed covered with a light blanket of cream-colored lace. I got to the door and looked back. Her eyes came all the way open, as if, instead of sleeping, she had only closed them a moment before to rest.

"You'll be careful?"

I promised I would. She looked at me to make sure I meant it, then closed her eyes and, that very moment, fell back asleep.

Leaving the village behind, I drove along the hillside until I came to a gravel road that ran along the crest of a spur toward an enormous villa that, like some medieval fortress, dominated everything below it. I stopped the Fiat in front of two black iron gates held together with a heavy rusty chain. I got out of the car, untangled the chain, and pushed them open. Inside the gate, below the gravel drive, was a two-story stone cottage with a dusty tile roof, sheltered from the sun by the gnarled branches of twisted gray olive trees. A diminutive white-haired woman was sitting like a shadow on a faded blue-covered swing on the patio, bent over a book held open on her lap. The morning light filtered through the trees, painting bright the flowers that grew in pots scattered all around.

The long driveway ran out to the very end of the spur, then doubled back to a clearing in front of the tan-colored villa. Stepping out of the car, I walked under a line of thick, luxuriant palm trees to the front entrance, where I climbed a dozen stone steps to a bleached brown double door, taller than I could reach. The circular black metal knocker made a creaking sound when I lifted it up and a dull clanking noise when it struck the rock-hard wood.

The door was too thick to hear anything behind it. I knocked again and waited. With a slight vibration, the huge door started to turn on its ancient metal hinges. It opened slowly, and only just far enough to allow whoever was on the other side to look out.

"So we meet again," said a voice that jarred my senses precisely because it was so unforgettably familiar.

The door swung all the way open and I was face-to-face with the dead. Andrei Bogdonovitch seemed genuinely glad to see me.

"I'm delighted, just delighted," he insisted as he shook my hand like a long-lost friend.

Before I could say a word, he had me by the arm, walking me through a spacious hallway into an enormous living room with marble floors, tapestry-covered stone walls, and, set in deep casements, leaded windows that gave an unobstructed view of the sea.

"I can't tell you how happy I was when I received the cable telling me you were coming," he remarked, an amiable smile on his broad, expansive face. He gestured toward a green silk davenport in the middle of the room.

Bogdonovitch waited until I was seated, as if he wanted to make absolutely certain I was comfortable before he sat down in a matching green silk chair. For a moment he stared at me, like someone who still can't quite believe in this wholly unexpected but completely welcome surprise. He leaned forward, rubbing his large hands together.

"When did you know?" he asked.

Before I could respond, a graceful young woman with discernible hips and a shy, provocative smile appeared with two glasses and a bottle of wine. A faint smile hovered over her mouth as she placed them on the coffee table and then, without a word, left the room.

"My housekeeper," explained Bogdonovitch with a worldly smile. "I lease this place from the owner. She was not included," he added as he began to uncork the bottle. "We have our own arrangement."

Albert Craven would have understood completely.

Bogdonovitch handed me a glass. "I know it's early, but this is such an occasion."

Lifting his glass, he proposed a toast, and I wondered if he intended the irony.

"To long life."

I brought the glass to my lips and then hesitated. When he saw I was waiting for him to go first, he gave me a wounded look and drank from his glass.

"How could you think such a thing?" protested Bog-donovitch, amused, and not the least offended, by my suspicion.

I had been holding the attaché case on my lap. With my thumb, I brushed the cylinders until they moved out of their coded position and the case was again securely locked.

"You've done rather well for a dead man," I remarked, gazing around the room as I set the case on the floor next to my feet.

Bogdonovitch continued to sip on his wine.

"How did you know I was still alive?" he asked when he finished.

I was sitting less than three feet away from him, close enough that if I concentrated in the silence between our words I could hear his breath; and yet, there was a sense in which I still could not quite believe he had not really died in that explosion.

"It never occurred to me that you were anything but dead," I told him truthfully. "I was there; I had just crossed the street at the corner. The whole building blew apart. No one could have survived it. Besides that, a dead body—or what was left of a dead body—was found in the wreckage. We were alone, you and I, and I had only left a few short seconds before. Why would I think you were somehow still alive?"

Bogdonovitch listened avidly, proud of what he had done

and, as I suddenly realized, glad there was someone with whom he could share the story of his adventure. He was particularly glad it was I. Even if he had ever dared tell anyone else, I was the only one who could never doubt that he had not made the whole thing up. Now that he had me as an audience, he could not wait to let me know the full range of his talent for subterfuge and deceit.

"It was done rather well, wasn't it? No," he added quickly, trying to assure me that he had done nothing unnecessarily dishonorable. "I had nothing to do with that stranger's death. Dead bodies—unclaimed dead bodies—are brought into morgues every day. I knew some people," he remarked vaguely, "who could take care of things like that."

"So after I left . . . ?"

"It was not difficult," he said modestly, shrugging his large shoulders. "The body was in the storeroom, just behind the door, next to the gas line where I had already set the mechanism."

"The door was the only thing left standing," I told him. "It was just hanging there, teetering on what was left of a splintered post that was all that was left of the frame."

We exchanged a glance and saw reflected in each other's eyes our own knowledge of the brief uncertainty of existence.

"As soon as you left," he went on, "I set the timer for fifteen seconds and got away up the alley behind the building. It wasn't difficult."

Bogdonovitch reached for the bottle and poured more wine into his glass. It was an excuse to take his eyes away from mine, a way to give himself time to consider what he wanted to say next.

"It was not just that I wanted you there as a witness to my death," he said, slowly raising his eyes. "Everything I told you was true: I was in danger because of what I knew about Fullerton, and so were you. I wanted to warn you. I felt responsible. I had to do what I did. I hope you understand that. After a lifetime of dealing with people like this, I knew the only way I could stay alive was to make them think I was already dead."

Bogdonovitch tossed off the wine, put down the glass, and slapped both knees.

"Now tell me! How did you know?"

Before I could answer, he shouted something in Italian, and, as if she had been standing there the whole time, invisible, the woman immediately appeared. He nodded toward the table. She picked up the half-empty bottle and his empty glass.

"Would you . . . ?" he asked me as she waited noiselessly. I shook my head, and she was gone.

"When we first met, I asked you what it was like living away from your country. You said it was not as difficult as it would have been if you had any family left. You told me that both your parents were dead and that you had been an only child."

He seemed surprised and a little chagrined. He sat back and looked up at the ceiling, his mouth twisted into a smile of self-mockery.

"And so when you learned from my friend Albert Craven that I had left everything in my will to my brother, Arkady Bogdonovitch, you of course remembered what I had said and concluded—quite logically—that if I had invented a brother, I must have invented my death."

He began to laugh, a deep, booming laugh that echoed off the high ceiling and filled the room.

"That's wonderful!" he exclaimed, springing forward until he was sitting on the very edge of the chair, both feet planted firmly on the marble floor. "You're quite an extraordinary man, Mr. Antonelli. I knew it the moment I met you. How many people would have remembered something like that—a single sentence, a passing reference to a biographical fact of no conceivable importance? I mean that—it's really quite extraordinary. And it in no way reduces my admiration that you drew your conclusion from what was, unfortunately, a lie! I do have a brother—Arkady. I haven't seen him in years. He lives in Moscow. I told you what I did because it's always been safer to make people think I had no living relations: No one could threaten them as a way of getting to me."

He looked down at his hands, chuckling to himself. "Well, I suppose in a way it's appropriate that a lie helped you find out the truth," he said, a shrewd look in his eye. "In any event, I'm glad you did."

He flashed a smile and, to underscore the sincerity of what he had said, nodded emphatically. He glanced at the attaché case on the floor.

"But you didn't tell anyone else that you thought I was alive, did you? Albert Craven is far too honest to send along the proceeds of a dead man's estate when the dead man isn't dead," said Bogdonovitch, his eyes narrowed down into a searching look. "You did bring the check with you, didn't you?"

I looked him straight in the eye. "No. I brought the papers that have to be signed before the proceeds can be released, papers that have to be signed by Arkady Bogdonovitch."

I could not tell if he believed me. I think he was not sure. He acknowledged the point about his brother with a smile.

"Yes, Arkady. Fortunately, he also signs his name: 'A. Bogdonovitch.' Well, what do you propose we do?"

"There isn't much we can do, is there? You're not dead, and it's difficult to inherit from someone still alive. Insurance companies frown on that sort of thing; more to the point, courts don't like it at all when a lawyer helps someone commit a crime. They send you to prison for things like that."

The piercing, intelligent eyes of Andrei Bogdonovitch seemed to draw close together. He leaned toward me.

"Perhaps we could come to some kind of arrangement."

I gave him a blank look and said nothing. My silence was all the encouragement he needed. A cryptic smile formed on his mouth.

"It's such a nice day. Why don't we sit outside?"

Bogdonovitch led me out the way I had come. At the top of the front steps, he took my arm, the way he had when he first answered; but as we began to go down them, I became aware that he was leaning on me for balance and support. He stopped at the bottom, slightly out of breath, blinking into the light. A moment later he seemed fine again. His eyes were clear and he moved with a steady, rolling gait. He pointed toward the end of the promontory at what looked like a stone watchtower.

"It was built in the thirteenth century to give warning against the Saracens. It has a more recent fame, however. Monet did one of his best paintings from there, a picture of the old village below. *Bordighera,* he called it. If you know the painting, you can almost feel what he must have been thinking when you see the view. Come, I'll show you."

We crossed over the driveway, the white gravel crunching beneath our feet, and followed a narrow footpath through a small grove of olive trees. With narrow apertures cut along the ascending stairwell that curled up inside and crenellated battlements at the top, the watchtower rose three stories into the air, high enough to see anything that might suddenly appear on the horizon. An oak plank door, with the top hinge missing and the middle one bent and broken, was wide open at the entrance, too heavy to be closed. Inside, rusty shovels and splintered spades littered the ground next to the rotted boards of the wooden staircase. A wheelbarrow lay on its side, encrusted with concrete, two long wooden handles covered in a single spider web. A fly buzzed lazily somewhere overhead.

We sat on a stone bench in the high grass against the side of the tower, looking down on the village Monet had painted and, beyond that, across the sea to the very edge of the visible world. Bogdonovitch removed the thick round glasses he had been wearing and put them into the side pocket of his rumpled brown coat. Leaning back against the tower wall, he folded his arms across his chest and closed his eyes. His head sank down between his shoulders, and for a moment he seemed to crumple up, deflated, as if he had let go of the last breath he was ever going to take. When he opened his eyes again, he did not look at me, but gazed instead into the open distance of the infinite sky.

"I thought there was a chance you would win the trial," he said. "I'm sorry that you didn't. Shall I tell you what really happened? Would you like to know why Jeremy Fullerton was killed?"

Bogdonovitch got to his feet, a little unsteady. When he had his balance, he shoved his hands into his pants pocket and kicked the dirt with the toe of his shoe.

"Come, let's walk a little."

We went back up to the gravel driveway and followed it down toward the black iron gate at the bottom. Through the olive trees, the shoreline stretched into the distance until it gradually disappeared under the gathering haze.

"The last time Fullerton and I talked, he told me things you would only tell someone you trusted completely."

Bogdonovitch paused, a hard shrewd glint in his eye, the look of someone who had spent a lifetime studying his enemies and never quite trusting his friends.

"The kind of things you only tell someone when you want to make sure they trust you."

We reached the gate, closed together by the rusty chain, and turned back, trudging slowly up the curving drive.

"What kind of things did he tell you?" I asked, watching him out of the corner of my eye.

"He told me about the young woman, Ariella. I had met her once." He stopped still. "He brought her here, last spring. This is where we used to meet; never—or almost never—in San Francisco or any other place in the United States. It was too dangerous, too easy for someone to see us together. It was safe here. Everyone comes to Italy, but Americans never come to Bordighera. He brought her, last spring, and introduced me as the owner of this place where he liked to spend a few days once in a while.

"As I say, the last time we talked, he told me about her: how he had used her to get to her father. It was astonishing how sure he was of himself. He knew that once he had Goldman's money behind him, nothing could stop him. He told me everything, things he could never tell anyone else. He was on the verge of getting everything he wanted, and all because of things he could never tell anyone but me. I was the only audience he had; and he knew already that he was not going to have me for too much longer. We had in that last conversation the strange close camaraderie of the victim and his executioner. He knew he had to kill me."

A breeze suddenly kicked up from the south, an African wind that bestowed a restless touch and then, like a brief reminder of mortality, moved on.

Bogdonovitch was standing in front of me, but so lost in the memory of what had happened that he might as well have been alone, talking to himself.

"The woman, Ariella, had told him she was pregnant. He thought it was the most hilarious thing he had ever heard."

Bogdonovitch seemed to remember that I was there. His eyes came back into focus, a puzzled expression on his face.

"It was really quite strange. I didn't know—I still don't know—quite what to make of it. He told me he was not the father, that he was certain of it, but that he had not told her yet. He was stringing her along, making her wait until he had everything he needed and it would be too late for the Goldmans to change their minds."

We reached the top of the drive and lingered by the granite steps in front of the villa.

"Jeremy had nothing but contempt for those people—not just the Goldmans; for almost everybody. In one degree or another, it happens to a lot of ambitious men who start out with none of the advantages. At first they look up to the wealthy, privileged people who seem to have everything and always seem to know what they're doing. Then, when they actually get to know them, when they realize that most of the people they looked up to have few talents and fewer qualities, they are so disgusted they cannot help but look down on them."

Bogdonovitch studied me carefully before he added with a rueful look, "Jeremy reached that conclusion far faster than most other men. I think he knew from the beginning that he was better; if he was surprised at all, it was only by how much better. When you add to this that he believed in nothing, nothing at all, it's not so difficult to understand the reason for his astonishing success. Jeremy knew how to give everyone what they wanted and how to convince them that it was something they had every right to have. He made them think he was doing them a favor while he took away what little dignity—what little independence—they still had left. I've known a great many dangerous men in my life, but I believe that he was the most dangerous of them all. Jeremy Fullerton was the complete nihilist. He was what history left us when history came to a stop."

Abruptly, Bogdonovitch waved his hand in front of him, as if he were trying to rid himself of an unfortunate thought that, no matter how hard he tried to ignore it, kept coming back.

"And despite all that, despite everything I knew about him, I found him irresistible. He had an instinct, the likes of which I have never seen, for knowing just how far anyone would go to get what they wanted. No one better recognizes the moral limitations that, usually without knowing it, we place on our own conduct than someone who has no morality at all. In that sense he was a completely free agent, alone in a world made up of people who one way or the other live their lives under some form of necessity."

A self-conscious smile stole across Bogdonovitch's deeply troubled countenance. "You must forgive the digressions of an old man. I now know what it must have been like for Jeremy when he was talking that last time to me, eager to tell everything to the one person he could trust.

"He told me things about himself that day that, in all the years of our 'special relationship,' he had never told me before—things about the way he grew up, things he did when he first went into politics: the way he had taken advantage of people who thought he believed in the same things they did. It was, if you leave out the complete and utter absence of remorse, like a deathbed confession. Except, as I well understood, it was not his deathbed, it was mine.

"He was going to kill me; or, more likely, have me killed. He had no choice. It is what I told you before—on the day of my death: The files of the KGB were open; it was only a matter of time before someone found something that would point to his involvement. But it would not matter what anyone found if the only KGB agent who had ever had any contact with him, the only agent who could supply the kind of detail—the narrative of dates and places—that would make it impossible to dismiss what was in those files as a crude attempt at political blackmail was already dead. I knew when I first learned that American agents were poring through those records that Fullerton would know what he had to do; and I knew when we had that conversation that I had only a little time left.

"Yes, Mr. Antonelli, I killed Jeremy Fullerton. I waited outside the Goldman apartment, and I followed the two of them to the St. Francis Hotel, and I followed them from there. She pulled up next to his car. I could just see the taillights through the fog. I drove past them and parked around the corner, a half a block above. They sat in her car, talking for a few minutes before he finally got out. You could barely see in that fog, but she drove off fast, squealing her tires as she left. She must have been angry.

"He was standing at the door, reaching for his key, when I called his name. He seemed almost glad to see me. He got inside and opened the other door for me. He was laughing, and he started to tell me what he had just finished telling her, that woman, Ariella Goldman: that not only was he not going to marry her, he knew damn well it wasn't his child and that she knew it, too. He was still laughing when I shot him.

"I think it never occurred to him that anyone, not even I, would be willing to go as far as he would. I won't try to tell you it was self-defense, my friend; but have you never been told that there are times that if you don't strike first, you won't have any chance to strike at all?"

It was an opening, a chance to make things right. I tried to be careful.

"From what you tell me, you could probably plead to manslaughter."

Bogdonovitch knew what I was thinking. He dismissed it out of hand.

"No, Mr. Antonelli, that's not the kind of arrangement I had in mind. I have no interest in spending time—any time—in an American prison. Besides," he added with a cynical glance, "do you think I would be allowed to plead to anything? Do you think I would ever see the inside of a courtroom? It is what I told you before, what I tried to warn you about. The people in power—the president's people—don't want anyone to know what Jeremy Fullerton really was; they want everyone to think he was great man, a patriot, because it makes them look so much better than they are."

It was maddening. Andrei Bogdonovitch had murdered Jeremy Fullerton and seemed perfectly content to let an innocent young man, convicted in his place, languish on death row while he lived out his last few years in the luxury paid for by the proceeds derived from his own fraudulent death. Jeremy Fullerton was a nihilist—what we had been left with at the end of history, according to Bogdonovitch. What was Jamaal Washington—history's last victim?

"You have to come back and confess," I said, quickly becoming angry. "It's the only way I can save an innocent man."

Andrei Bogdonovitch placed his hand on my shoulder. A smile, subtle, crafty, and deep, etched its way over his lips.

"Months ago, just before I died in that terrible explosion, I sent a package to my brother Arkady—here, in Bordighera. I was afraid something might happen to me," he explained, a glint of mischief in his eyes. "I sent it with instructions that it not be opened and that he hand it over to my attorney, Albert Craven, at the time he received the proceeds of my estate."

Pausing, Bogdonovitch gave me a look of assurance. He had thought of everything, though I was fairly certain he had not thought of it at all until he received the cable from Albert Craven telling him I was coming.

"I think you'll find everything you'll need: my confession, a narrative of my dealings with Fullerton, and—oh, yes—a photocopy of the KGB file."

He saw the surprise on my face. As he started up the steps, he slapped me hard on the back and laughed.

"Did you think I would leave the only permanent record of what I did for the KGB in the hands of some degenerate file clerk? I was a communist, Mr. Antonelli; I was never a fool."

At the top of the steps, he turned to me, an ominous look in his experienced eyes.

"Do you know who you're going to give this to? It isn't enough to find someone with the power to do what you want. You have to find someone who wants to destroy Jeremy Fullerton, someone who wants to destroy his reputation once and for all."

I could think of only one person.

Twenty-eight

He'll be in San Francisco Saturday," reported Albert Craven the day after I returned. "He'll see you that evening at six-fifteen. You have ten minutes."

I looked up from the desk in the temporary office that from the moment I had first agreed to become the defense attorney in the murder of Jeremy Fullerton had become my second home. My hands had begun to tighten up, cramped by the monotonous repetitive movement as I sorted through the voluminous documents that had been separated into three bulging black file folders.

"How did you manage to arrange it?" I asked, stretching my fingers.

"I promised a large contribution—a very large contribution," replied Craven dryly. "It always seems to work."

His eye wandered to the parallel stacks. "Is it all in Russian?"

"Along with some English summaries our friend was thoughtful enough to make."

His hands locked together behind his back, Craven leaned forward on his toes. He stared past me, shaking his head in sorrow.

"We live in a strange world," he said, speaking more to himself than to me. Then, as if he had just remembered something that required his immediate attention, he straightened up.

"Six-fifteen. Saturday evening."

He nodded, smiled, and then rapped the knuckles of his left hand on the corner of the desk. "Wish I could be there with you."

Two days later, at ten minutes past six, I entered the lobby of the St. Francis Hotel and, with a passing glance at the dark-paneled bar, walked briskly to the bank of elevators.

It was the same suite as the one I had come to before. This time Augustus Marshall answered the door. Without a jury to persuade, or a roomful of spectators to impress, there was none of that graceful, ingratiating manner that had been on such prominent display when he was a witness at the trial. The wire-rim glasses were in perfect balance with his mouth, which was stretched straight back in a thin, rigid smile of barely controlled impatience. With a quick, cursory handshake, he directed me to the same sofa I had once briefly occupied before. He did not offer me a drink.

Marshall sat on the edge of a chair as if he were already about to get up. "What is it I can do for you, Mr. Antonelli?"

I placed the attaché case I had brought with me onto the glass coffee table and snapped open the two shiny brass locks. I was just about to open it when I changed my mind and laid it down on the table.

"Tell me, Governor, do you think you still have a chance to win?"

Marshall stiffened. "It's the third week in October. There are still two weeks left."

"Yes, two weeks left, and thanks to what happened at the trial you're not only running against a ghost, you're running against the woman he wanted to marry and the child he was going to have. What do you do in the next two weeks to convince people that voting for Ariella Goldman isn't the only way they can honor the memory of a man as great as Jeremy Fullerton?"

Marshall rose from his chair and looked down at me from behind distant half-closed eyes. "I don't believe we have anything more to talk about, Mr. Antonelli. Just because you lost to Ms. Goldman at trial doesn't mean I'm going to lose to her in the election."

"Yes, it does, Governor, and we both know it."

I opened the attaché case and took out the thick folder into which I had organized what I had been given by Andrei Bogdonovitch.

"What's that?" asked Marshall as I dropped the folder heavily on top of the glass table.

"The only chance you've got to win the election."

Marshall searched my eyes, wondering what I was after.

"Read it, and decide for yourself."

His eyes still on me, he sat down and reached inside his jacket for his glasses. He read the first page, then the second, and as he turned to the third, he looked at me in astonishment.

I stayed for almost an hour and then left him alone with the written confession of Andrei Bogdonovitch and the translated summaries of the unexpurgated KGB file on Jeremy Fullerton. I took the elevator down to the lobby and wandered into the bar.

"Haven't seen you in a while," said the bartender.

He put a napkin down on the gleaming mahogany bar and placed on top of it a scotch and soda. I wished my memory were as good as his.

"Tell me something," I said after I took a sip. "Who's going to win the election?"

He had picked up a towel and started to dry a glass.

"Not much question," he replied with a shrug, his eyes on the glass, "especially after tonight."

I took another drink and glanced around the room. A young couple was holding hands at the table where Jeremy Fullerton and Ariella Goldman had sat, drinking, the last night of his life.

"Hard to figure," the bartender was saying. "He's down by seven, eight points, and he walks out of a fundraiser. I just heard about it—just before you came in. He has a crowd of people waiting and he sends someone in his place."

He wiped the glass clean and picked up another one. "Sounds like he's quit to me."

I glanced at my watch, took one last drink, and tossed a tip on the bar. "You play the horses?"

"Once in a while."

"Take the odds. Bet on Marshall to win."

He looked at me like I was crazy.

I left the St. Francis and went to see the one person who more than anyone else deserved an answer. Then I went to Marissa's and slept better than I had slept in a very long time.

The next morning a courier delivered to Albert Craven's office the document Augustus Marshall had promised. At eight o'clock the next evening, I sat next to Marissa on the davenport in her living room and, as the twilight danced red and gold on the bay below, watched Augustus Marshall announce on television that it was his solemn duty to correct a gross miscarriage of justice and to make public a scandal that had threatened the very core of American democracy.

When it was over, I walked to the open glass door that led out to the deck and breathed in the cool autumn air. Beyond the last few sailboats making their way home, the lights of the city flickered in the dusk.

"What's going to happen now?" asked Marissa.

I looked over my shoulder. Sitting on the davenport, her long legs pulled up underneath her, she stared at me with those large open eyes that always somehow managed to dissolve the distance between us.

"Jamaal will be released tomorrow. He should have been released yesterday, but the governor of course wanted to make sure the press would be there. After everything that's happened, I suppose I can't blame him. Jamaal will be a free man, with a full pardon and a trust fund of no insubstantial amount. Thanks to the generosity of the 'late' Andrei Bogdonovitch, he'll be able to go to school without having to work weekends anymore."

I gazed out toward the city beckoning across the bay, promising to make come true all the dreams you had.

"I feel like Jeremy Fullerton," I said without looking around. "I know everyone's secrets, and I tell everyone lies."

The air was getting cooler and the night was getting darker. I shoved my hands down deep into my pockets and thought about the ways in which I had hidden the truth.

"I had to tell Jamaal that Bogdonovitch left him the money in his will as an act of contrition, because I could not tell him it was part of the price I made Bogdonovitch pay to get the rest of the money he was inheriting from himself. I had to tell Albert Craven that Andrei Bogdonovitch's brother gave me his confession, because if I had told him that Bogdonovitch was still alive, I would have made him a party to a fraud. And then, of course, I could not tell Jamaal anything at all about Albert Craven, because . . . well, because I just could not."

From across the room, Marissa's voice seemed to whisper in my ear. "Do you think in his whole life Jeremy Fullerton ever did anything that produced the kind of effect you have? What do you imagine Ariella Goldman is thinking right now?

Lawrence Goldman's grandfather may have put your grandfather in jail, but that isn't anything like what you've now done to him."

I had forgotten all about what had happened to my grandfather and the crooked cop who was chief of police, but Marissa was right about what had now happened to Lawrence Goldman and his daughter. Jeremy Fullerton, the reputed father of Ariella Goldman's child, had in the space of a few minutes gone from an American martyr to an American traitor. More importantly to the limitless ambitions of Lawrence and Ariella Goldman, Jeremy Fullerton had become a major political embarrassment.

"What can they do now?" asked Marissa rhetorically. "Claim she must have been mistaken; that instead of carrying the child of someone who turns out to have been a spy, she must have been made pregnant by some other powerful man with whom she had committed adultery?"

It reminded me of something. I turned around, smiling to myself.

"I once heard someone say something like that about the Borgias; that they had come into the world as 'a declaration of war against morality through incest and adultery.'"

"But, unlike the Borgias, the Goldmans haven't killed anyone," she reminded me with an uneasy laugh.

I could still see the confident face of Augustus Marshall on the television screen, revealing to the world what Jeremy Fullerton had done and the reason he had been killed. He was now so certain he was going to win. First the attorney general had died, and now this. Old Hiram Green had been right: These people all thought they were destined to be president.

"Would you want to be the only person standing in the way of what Ariella Goldman wants?" I wondered aloud.

After we had dinner, after Marissa had gone to sleep, after all the tourists had gone and the narrow streets of Sausalito were deserted, I took a long walk along the bay. I stood for a while at the water's edge, the way his widow had told me Jeremy Fullerton used to do, staring out across the water at the city, shimmering in the night, drawing everything toward it. How close it looked; so close you started to think that all you had to do was lift your hand and it would come closer still, close enough to touch. I kept watching it, thinking about what it must have been like for him, thinking about how far he was going to go and what great things he was going to do. He was in love with what he was going to become and lived so much in the future that the things he had to do to get there were buried in the past, almost before he had done them. I stood there, the only sound in the vast silence the water lapping quietly against the rocks just beneath my feet. I kept looking at the lights of the city, the lights that never grew dim, and I started to see everything the way he must have seen it; and for a brief, fleeting moment I think I felt more of what it must have been like to be him than I've ever known about what it must be like to be me.

Printed in the United States
72066LV00004B/14